EVERYTHING WENT TO SHIT

A HORROR COLLECTION

R.E. SARGENT

EVERYTHING WENT TO SHIT

A HORROR COLLECTION

R.E. SARGENT

Everything Went to Shit
A Horror Collection

By R.E. Sargent

Published by Sinister Smile Press, LLC,
A Division of Crystal Lake Publishing
P.O. Box 637
Newberg, OR 97132

Copyright © 2023 by R.E. Sargent

This is a work of fiction. Names, characters, places, and incidents either are the

Trade Paperback ISBN – 978-1-964398-78-5

www.sinistersmilepress.com

Cover design by François Vaillancourt
Interior design by Steven Pajak

CONTENTS

"Don't look forward to the day you stop suffering, because when it comes, you'll know you're dead."

TENNESSEE WILLIAMS

INTRODUCTION

R.E. SARGENT

Horror. I honestly never thought I would write it, let alone enjoy the hell out of doing so. You see, I started out writing suspense and thrillers, but I couldn't deny the natural progression I saw and watched as some of the elements I wrote about got darker and darker. I wouldn't want it any other way.

Over a couple of years, I ended up writing quite a few horror stories for different anthologies. Then one day it dawned on me that there was no easy way for my readers to read all of my work without buying many different books. That thought led to the book your are holding in your hands. Most of my short stories all in one collection.

As I reread the stories while I was compiling them, I sensed a common theme—not only with the stories, but with life in general. That theme is this: Just when you think things are going just fine, *everything goes to shit*. It happens to all of us. It always will. But not all is lost. Those who persevere—who absolutely dig down deep into their entire being and bring out the beast inside—will come out on top. After all, it beats the alternative.

I hope you enjoy reading these stories as much as I enjoyed writing them.

R.E. Sargent

FOREWORD

DANIEL VOLPE

THE GOLDILOCKS COLLECTION

The world of indie horror is exploding right now. New authors, publishers, and even platforms are popping up left and right. It is a vast sea of blood, guts, sex, and violence, and the readers are gleefully bathing in it. The writing is just as diverse as the writers: gothic horror, quiet horror, extreme horror, body horror, and splatterpunk. Those listed are some of the front runners, but I want to talk about splatterpunk and extreme horror.

These two bastard children of horror are often given a bad name, each being over the top in sex and violence. Yes, other horror elements also have graphic sex and violence, but splatterpunk and extreme bask in the filth. They want to be covered in your muck, tears, vomit, and blood. As a result, a new reader of the indie horror world is often overwhelmed by the options, not knowing where to start. Not only that, but many of these books contain heavy themes that some readers aren't ready for. Sure, they've heard the names like Beauregard, Triana, Lee,

Havok, but one wrong step into any of the work written by those authors could leave a reader belly up.

Why do I mention these pillars of the hardcore community? Great question, thanks for asking. I say them because we, as the horror community, are nice…honestly. We don't want to upset people, just entertain and maybe gross you out a little (okay, maybe gross you out a lot). While the authors mentioned above are amazing, they are the 'deep end' regarding the extreme and splatterpunk sides. But Dan, I'm new to the world of indie horror, and I want to see if I like the extreme stuff. Where should I start? Again, great question, and I'm getting to that. Well, since you're so damn impatient, I'll just tell you.

Everything Went to Shit. Yes, that's the title of the book in your hand. Okay, so let's break it down. You're not a prude, nor are you a horror virgin. Suppose you are and pick up a book with *this* title; more power to you. But let's say you've been around for a while and want to read some stuff that's a little edgier. Let me tell you, you've come to the perfect place. I bet you were wondering why I titled this after Goldilocks, weren't you? It's simple—this collection of short stories has it all. Now, when I say *all* I don't mean the dark and dirty filth of the internet, but there's more than enough blood and guts (and a little sex) to fill the quota. This collection, to me, is Goldilocks and the perfect introduction for a newbie if they want to start to see if extreme horror or splatterpunk is right for them. Not only that, but a gore-hound, like myself, will be more than satisfied with the brutality contained inside of these pages. All in all, this is a great collection, full of well-written, diverse and bloody stories.

Every story in this collection is a hit, but *Reunited* stood out for me. This story has it all and the tension buildup is epic. Let's say you won't look at storage units the same way again.

This collection is a must-read for fans of horror. Whether you like vengeful spirits, hauntings, aliens, serial killers, or dangerous ladies, this book has you covered.

Long Live Indie Horror,

Daniel J. Volpe
9/12/2022
New York

KILLER RADIO

SEPTEMBER 28TH, 1983, COTTONWOOD, ARIZONA

Ricky Jepson yanked the cartridge out of the deck and replaced it with one for the upcoming song. The current song was halfway over, and he grabbed a bottle of water off the counter in the small studio and took a chug, moistening his throat before he had to speak again.

Ricky keyed up his microphone and waited for the last couple seconds of the song before he cut to a live feed.

"That was 'Photograph' by Def Leppard, and *Pyromania* is still tearing up the charts after eight months!" Ricky hit the backlit button under the player, and the opening chords of "Shout at the Devil" by Mötley Crüe cut into the broadcast through his headphones. "Now for the most requested song of the night. Hell, the week! Ever since this song hit the airwaves a couple of days ago, the phones have been lighting up! We got what you want here at 102.9 F.M., K-L-L-R, Killer radio! Rock on, metalheads!"

After cutting the mic, Ricky took off his headphones, pulled out the Def Leppard cartridge—which the DJ's referred to as "carts"—and cued up the reel-to-reel player that was ready to play six songs with a commercial in the middle. He pressed the button that would auto-play the tape on the reels when the previous song ended before he headed back to the dinky bathroom that contained a toilet and a sink. As he relieved himself, he listened to the heavy guitar riffs that were playing through the small station, which could be heard everywhere except the soundproofed booth.

After washing his hands and running his wet fingers through his long brown hair, he stooped down and looked in the mirror. He had not felt this relaxed in years, and even though he worked long hours, he could still see contentment lining his face through the three-day growth that adorned his stubborn chin. He looked at his thin frame in the mirror, knowing he fit the rock-and-roll image, confident he had made the right decision by buying the station. Outside, he propped the back door of the station open with a chair and lit up a Marlboro, taking a deep drag off the cigarette.

Ricky smiled to himself as he listened to the hardcore music wafting through the open door. It was a great time for music, and "hair bands" were coming out of the woodwork. Although he had always been a lover of rock music, it was an exciting decade where the music got heavier and the outfits outrageous. Bands such as KISS and AC/DC had paved the way through the late seventies, and the sounds had morphed from power chords to wailing guitar licks and solos. Ricky loved what he did and was excited for the future.

KLLR radio was born ten months earlier when the previous station—an FM country station—shuttered its windows. Ricky, a thirty-two-year-old DJ at an easy listening station in the nearby town of Flagstaff, Arizona, had heard through the grapevine that the country station had closed. On his next day off, he convinced his wife to jump into their 1975 Toyota

Corolla and trek the sixty-four miles with him to the small town of Cottonwood, Arizona, where the empty shell of the station sat.

He recalled how surprised he was by the size of the building. It was small, like a construction trailer, but was made from brick with an asphalt shingled roof. The single red door was the only opening on the front of the building—there were no windows. The chain-link fence topped with barbed wire surrounded the station, as well as the land around it. The steel-latticed mast that sported the transmitting antenna—which was anchored to the ground and secured by guy-wires— appeared to be over five-hundred feet tall. While his wife, Amy, hadn't quite seen his vision, she eventually gave in to his pleas, and after selling their house, which gave them a nice down payment for the station, they moved into a rental house in Cottonwood and Ricky got to work rebranding the station and taking it live, with the new rock and metal format.

Now, while lighting up his second cigarette, Ricky looked out at the still night air that surrounded the station. As owner of a startup station, advertisers were not quite in abundance yet, and Ricky cut corners whenever he could. He had hired a talented morning DJ for the morning show, which brought in many listeners, as well as an afternoon and evening jockey that were well received; however, he preferred to work the late nights and overnights himself. Not only did it save on salaries, but he could also get away with going for long periods of time without talking in between songs. The later it got, the more he used automation, which allowed him to focus on other station-related tasks. After ten months, the station was doing well, but he still wasn't in a position where he could hire another DJ or two. His long-term plan was to get out of the booth himself and, eventually, add as much automation as he could to mini-mize the need for overnight DJs as well as create efficiencies within the station. He could still hear his dad's advice in his head from when he had been a kid. *Work smarter, not harder.*

Ricky's thoughts shifted to the letter the station had received the week before. It was the third one in the past six months, and he smiled at the hatred that seethed through the words. The anonymous author was apparently sickened by the "music of Satan" that the new station was playing, and the letters demanded the station change their format. The last letter was…well, different. It felt more hostile. More disturbing. Ricky hated people trying to censor what they played, and no one was going to tell him what the people in the area should listen to. When the new Mötley Crüe album came out, he didn't waste any time getting it in rotation, hoping to piss off his oppressors.

As the last song on the reel played, Ricky finished his third cigarette, snuffed it out against the brick wall of the building, threw it in the Folger's can that sat by the back door, and yanked the door shut behind him.

Back in the booth, Ricky added another reel of tape to the other player—this time a longer one—got on the mic to give the station information, and introduced the next song before he moved to a desk in the corner where he started going through the day's mail. As he shuffled through the envelopes, he came to the letter he had received a few days prior, which was hanging out on the bottom of the pile. There was no return address, and the address was written in angry-looking block letters. He smiled again and paused for a few seconds before tossing the entire envelope, letter and all, in the trash can below the desk.

"Eat shit," he mumbled.

Throughout the night, Ricky switched back and forth between the booth and other duties around the station. He cleaned up the mini break room area. He refreshed the paper towels in the bathroom. As owner, he took care of everything that he couldn't afford to hire out and didn't expect the DJs to do. The night rolled into Thursday early morning, and sometime after two a.m., he found some time to get into his tiny office and file away a few papers and organize his desk. "Metal Health" by Quiet Riot pumped through the cramped space, and Ricky couldn't help but scream the lyrics as Kevin Dubrow belted them on the title track of the album. Although he heard nothing over the music, the smell of smoke pulled his attention away from the tasks at hand and alerted him that something was wrong.

Panicked, Ricky ran to the back door and turned the handle, anxious to see what could possibly be on fire outside. The door would not budge. Eyes wide, he took quick, shallow breaths and ran toward the front door of the station. He noticed the smoke more now, and his mind tried to conjure up any plausible explanation for it, knowing that the station was surrounded by a wide-open space. He focused on getting out of the building where the air was fresh and crisp. Once outside, this would all make sense, and knowing what the situation really was, he would know what to do.

"Please, please, please!" he muttered under his breath. There was no reason the back door shouldn't have opened, but he was positive the front one would, yet it was stuck like a Ford truck in a mud-bog.

Turning the handle of the front door, Ricky pushed. It did not move. Trying again, he threw his shoulder at it. Still nothing. Ricky started hacking as he realized he was in deep trouble. The smoke had overcome the top third of the building, and Ricky could hear crackling coming from the roof. A moment later, a shower of sparks and flaming debris fell in on the back side of the station, covering the floor in front of the back door.

Unsure how stuck the back door was, Ricky pulled his t-shirt up over his nose and mouth and ran to the broom closet, grabbing a push broom out of it. He ran to the pile of flaming material and pushed it away from the door and into the open bathroom. Looking up, Ricky saw the flames burning through the roof. It looked like the fire had started from above and was burning its way down into the station.

As his eyes burned, Ricky tried the back door again. When it didn't give, he ran at it and tried to kick it open. The middle of the door dented out, but the door remained unwavering, almost as if it was one with the steel frame that surrounded it.

Wildly looking around, Ricky ran through the station and surveyed every crack and crevice for a vulnerability. He found none. The front and back doors were the only means of escape, each acting as the emergency exit should the other be blocked.

Taking a step back, Ricky blinked rapidly and covered his mouth with his hand. His panic rescinded, and he knew. This would be the end of the road.

Running into the studio, Ricky closed the door and realized there was less smoke hanging in this space. *Maybe if help can get here quickly...* His thoughts trailed off as he picked up the phone and dialed 911.

"Nine-one-one. What's your emergency?"

"This is K-L-L-R, the radio station. The studio is on fire, and I'm stuck inside." Ricky was shocked at how calm he actually sounded.

"We are sending units right now. What's your name?"

"Ricky Jepson."

"Stay on the line with me, Ricky. Units are rolling as we speak."

"They'll never make it in time."

"Just hang tight. We will get to you. Can you get to one of the doors?"

"Yes. Both. Neither will open."

"Have you tried breaking them down?"

"Yes. They are metal and won't budge."

"Either of them?"

"Correct."

"Can you bust out a window?"

Ricky watched through the studio window as more burning debris crashed down on the other side of the wall by the back door. The smoke was getting so thick that he could barely make out the space. The window started to blacken, and he knew it was only a matter of time before it imploded on him.

"There are no outside windows here," Ricky answered solemnly.

"No windows?" the dispatcher repeated.

"None."

"Oh."

If Ricky had not already resolved himself to the fact that he was a dead man, he would have been angered at the helplessness of the single word.

"Hang tight, Mr. Jepson. Try to stay as far away from the flames and smoke as you can. Stay close to the floor and cover your mouth with a wet rag if possible."

Ricky set the phone down on the desk, ripped a sleeve off his T-shirt and poured half his water bottle onto the thin material. He placed it to his mouth and breathed through it, noticing a little improvement. He looked around, watching as flames licked up the interior walls, writhing in angst as they tried to meet up with the flaming roof. His dream was over. He had put everything into the station, and now it was gone—and he would soon follow.

Snapping back to the inferno around him, Ricky noticed the music had stopped. The wires had probably been burned through. He turned to his equipment and was surprised to find the lights still lit. The reel had simply finished playing, and he had not queued up the next one. He was actually broadcasting dead air. Could the listeners still be tuned in? Could they hear him if he turned on the mic?

Knowing this was his final chance to broadcast, Ricky frantically looked through the cartridges that lined the wall, finally found the one he wanted, and loaded it into the player. Keying up the mic, he spoke.

"This is Ricky Jepson, and you are listening to K-L-L-R, 102.9, Killer Radio. Tragically, this will be our final broadcast. Thank you from the bottom of our hearts for the last ten months here at K-L-L-R. You guys kick ass! Oh, and Amy, if you're listening, I love you, babe. Thanks for letting me live the dream!"

Ricky pressed the button on the player, and the sounds of Megadeth's "Countdown to Extinction" filtered through the popping and cracking of the fire. Ricky reached for the dial and turned it up as loud as the speakers would handle without distortion. He glanced over and noticed all the lines for the station had lit up. Evidently, the listeners were still receiving the broadcast. Closing his eyes, he pushed back in his chair and listened to the lyrics, taking them in. When the song ended, radio silence returned, but Ricky was no longer aware as the window imploded, and the flames devoured the studio.

TUESDAY, AUGUST 28TH, 2018, PORTLAND, OREGON

Brittany Stephens honked at the blue Prius in front of her as she tried to navigate around him. She had unknowingly been biting the inside of her cheek for the last few miles as the car repeatedly sped up and slowed down for no apparent reason. Now, she was definitely going to be late for work for the third time this month, and her boss, a narcissistic asshole who thought the world revolved around him, had already warned her about her tardiness.

Finally around the erratic driver, she praised herself for not flipping him off as she got on the I-5 onramp and headed toward Portland. She was thankful that the rain hadn't kicked in yet for the year, which would only have delayed her further. She had fifteen minutes to get to the time clock on the third floor of the office building she worked in, yet she knew it would take her longer than that just to turn into the parking lot.

Pressing down the gas pedal and getting into the left-hand lane, Brittany pulled her long blonde hair out of her face, pressed the power button on the stereo, and her iPhone connected, kicking on the last song she was listening to when getting ready. Five Finger Death Punch filled the small cabin of her Toyota Matrix as she weaved in and out of traffic, trying to gain a few minutes on the drive. Halfway through "When the Seasons Change," the iPhone cut out, and the source changed over to FM radio. The numbers of the stations rapidly counted through the entire spectrum over and over and suddenly stopped on 102.9.

"What the fu—"

Brittany was cut off when background music started broadcasting over the station. A voice—harsh and raspy—cut through the music in the background, and she could make out some static in the broadcast.

"This is 102.9, K-L-L-R, Killer Radio, and I am going to draw one lucky listener's name right now. The winner will receive a tour of our station, after which we will whisk you away by limousine to a private concert by the band Six Feet Below, which will be held at a private eighty-five acre estate in the area. You will join seven other very lucky listeners for an extremely private event. You will also have backstage access to meet the band, check out their tour bus, and party your ass off with them after the show."

Brittany tried to change the source of her stereo back to her iPhone, but the controls did not respond. The voice continued.

"Our winner for today…Brittany Stephens of Portland, Oregon."

Brittany stopped fiddling with the controls, a frown taking over her face as she scratched her cheek. She thought she had heard her name, but she had never listened to this station before, and she certainly hadn't entered her name into any contests. The concert ticket piqued her interest, though, and she turned the radio up. The volume knob responded.

"Brittany Stephens, if you're listening, go to www.102.9K-LLR-Radio.com and claim your prize within the next forty-eight hours. Now for a little taste, here is 'Better Off Dead' by Six Feet Below."

The DJ's voice cut out, and a song started, a guitar riff blasting through her speakers. She turned the radio down a little and tried to get her iPhone to reconnect, but she was unsuccessful. Bewildered, she pushed the gas pedal down again and listened to the song as she drove. Given her taste of music, it was right up her alley, although a little old school, but she had never heard of this band before.

If I have to live tomorrow,
Like I had to live today
It'd bring me too much sorrow,
And I'd have to go away
In the end I can't portray that
Things I've done were ever right
Will it end with sprouting wings,
Or a far more sinister plight
There's no reason to stay,

I'm better off dead, better off dead,
I'm burning borrowed days,
I'm better off dead, better off dead
There's no reason to stay,
I'm better off dead, better off dead,
I'm burning borrowed days,
I'm better off dead, better off dead

Brittany shivered at the lyrics as she pulled into the parking lot, parked, jumped out of her car, and ran toward the entrance. She actually had made up some time and had a minute to clock in. As she ran, she pressed the key fob to lock her car, making a mental note to check out the website after work and see if it was her that had really won.

TUESDAY, AUGUST 28TH, 2018, CHICAGO, ILLINOIS

Seth Peterson got out of his work truck, wiped his dirty hands on his jeans, and went to the front door. When he opened it, the smell of whatever was cooking for dinner assaulted his nostrils in a good way. He tossed his keys on the side table and shut the door behind him.

"Honey, I'm home!" he yelled.

"I'm in the kitchen. Dinner will be ready in twenty minutes."

Seth walked down the hall and entered the dining area while trying to make out what the aroma was.

"What are we having?" he asked his wife Zoey, who was bent over the oven, checking on its contents.

"None of your business!" she warned him, standing up and abruptly shutting the oven door. She turned around to face him and noticed him staring. "Were you just checking out my ass?" she joked.

"Busted!"

"Thanks for noticing," Zoey said, looking down at her breasts before winking at Seth.

"Someone is on ten today," Seth teased.

"And that's different from when?" she bantered. Zoey eyed Seth up and down. "Damn, you're filthy today. Did that boss of yours actually make you work?"

"Can you believe the nerve? I was playing around in the dirt all day."

"Well, you have just enough time to take a shower and get your ass back down here to set the table."

"My thoughts exactly!"

Seth leaned over and gave Zoey a kiss and left the kitchen, heading upstairs to the master bedroom. Their home was a modest three-bedroom, but Seth was proud of what they had achieved, and they were both still under twenty-five. With no children yet, they were both concentrating on building their life together and getting established.

Twenty minutes later, Seth went back to the kitchen wearing a tank top and a pair of basketball shorts. Zoey left the stove and went over to him, ran her fingers through his thick, dirty blonde hair, and kissed him passionately. He wrapped his arms around her thin waist and kissed her back. When they finally separated, Seth took a deep breath.

"What was that for?" Seth asked.

"Well, you clean up so good, I thought I'd have myself a sample," Zoey teased.

"Damn. Can't wait for dessert. What's the occasion?"

"I got my bonus at work today."

"That's awesome. I thought it was going to take another week."

"Me, too. Anyway, set the table, and dinner will be ready in a few."

Seth grabbed the plates and utensils and put them on the table and then grabbed two glasses. A few minutes later, Zoey opened the oven and pulled out a roast, placing it on potholders on the counter. After she served the meat and vegetables, they sat down and started to eat, making small talk about their day. As they were finishing up, Zoey bolted upright in her seat.

"OH! I forgot to tell you. Something weird happened today."

"What's that?" Seth asked, his attention piqued.

"Were you listening to the radio today on the job site?"

"Yeah, we were. Why?"

"Did you hear anything strange?"

Seth thought for a minute. "No, not really."

"Well, we listen to the same station, so I thought…" Her voice trailed off.

"What happened?" Seth prodded.

"A Dire Straits song was playing, and in the middle of it, the broadcast cut to some Megadeth song."

"Oh! Is that what you mean? I remember some metal song came on in the middle, and one of the guys turned it off."

"Then you missed the good part."

"What's good about a Megadeth song?"

"They announced a contest winner. It was you. Or at least someone with your name."

"Wasn't me. I haven't entered any contests. What was the prize?"

"A private VIP concert for a band named Six Feet Below."

"Damn. I've never heard of the band, but a private VIP concert sounds like a blast."

"I wrote down the website where you can claim your prize."

Seth pushed his plate away. "Let's check it out!"

Seth went to the bedroom and grabbed his laptop and

brought it back to the table. Zoey handed him a Post-it note with the website address, and he entered it into the address bar. The site came up. Seth's eyebrows furrowed.

"What's wrong, babe?" Zoey asked.

"It says here that the radio station sponsoring this contest is in a town called Cottonwood, Arizona. The concert is nearby in the same town."

"Must be a different Seth Peterson, then."

"You would think, but it lists Chicago. Should I click the link?"

"How could we possibly have been listening to a radio station from Arizona? It's not like it was satellite."

"Exactly."

"What should I do?"

"Click it! I want to figure out what the hell is going on."

Seth clicked the link as Zoey watched, and the site came up.

Zoey pointed. "Look! That's your name right there…Seth Peterson, Chicago, Illinois."

"So weird."

"Click the button at the bottom to claim your prize," she suggested. "What can it hurt?"

Seth exhaled sharply and followed Zoey's lead; the site prompted for an email address. Seth entered it, and the site instructed him to look for an email and click the verification link. He brought up his account, found the email, and followed the directions. It returned him back to the site.

"Holy shit!" he gasped, his hand covering his mouth.

"They have our address listed!"

"Yup. I don't understand. This has to be some mistake."

"Seems like it. Why don't you claim the tickets and maybe we can go on a mini vacation?"

"To Arizona?"

"It would be nice to get away."

Seth frowned. "It says here it's just one ticket."

Zoey sighed. "What kind of shit is that...one ticket? Figures. Well maybe you could sell it. Or...we could still go, and I'll hang at the hotel."

"So, should I claim it?"

"Do it! What do we have to lose?"

WEDNESDAY, AUGUST 29TH, 2018, DALLAS, TEXAS

"So, you are really doing this?" Jonathan Hunter's mother, Melanie, asked.

"Yeah! The ticket showed up in my email this morning," Jonathan informed her.

"Did you say it's in Arizona?"

Jonathan ran his fingers through his short hair and looked up. "Mom, I'm nineteen."

"I know, but that doesn't mean I just stop worrying about you, you know. Arizona's a long way away."

"It'll be good for me."

"The house will be quiet without you. I'm not ready to live alone."

"It's only four days, Mom."

"Don't you have to work?"

"The boss said I could take those days off."

"Well, can you take a friend with you?"

"I only won one ticket."

"What was the name of the band again?"

"Six Feet Below."

"Sounds morbid. I've never heard of them."

"Me neither. I Googled them but couldn't find anything. Still, they sound bad ass."

"Language, Jonathan."

"Sorry, Mom."

"When was this concert again?"

"September 28th."

"Mark it on the calendar, will you?"

"You got it, Mom. Speaking of work, I gotta go. See you tonight."

Jonathan gave Melanie a hug, went out the front door, and got in his '97 Honda Civic. As he drove off, he cranked up the stereo, looking forward to four days of independence and a wild night of rock and roll.

WEDNESDAY, AUGUST 29TH, 2018, FARGO, MINNESOTA

Calvin Hawkins navigated to a travel website, put in his preferred dates, and brought up the results. It appeared from his research that the nearest major airport was in Phoenix, Arizona, which looked like it would be a couple hour drive once he landed.

He chose to fly a week early since he wasn't currently working, and he would stay at a Phoenix hotel until the day of the concert, then stay at the hotel the radio station had booked for the night after the concert.

Calvin was still confused over the events from the previous day. At fifty-three, Calvin still had a vinyl collection from the days before cassette tapes, then CDs took over. A rocker at heart, Calvin was listening to *Diary of a Madmen* by Ozzy Osbourne when the player had stopped in the middle of the record, followed by the radio turning on. The stereo he had in the living room was old school and had the turntable built into the top of the unit, which also contained eight-track and cassette players. The radio dial was a manual one and required someone to turn a knob to change the station, but as soon as the record had stopped—it hadn't slowed to a halt, it had immediately ceased turning—he could hear the unit flipping through different stations until it landed on a station, which Calvin later noticed was 102.9. He knew there wasn't a local radio station on that frequency, yet the station came through ultra-clear. When he tried to turn off the radio and turn back on the turntable, the controls would not function. It was then he heard the contest winner announcement and his name.

Floored, Calvin immediately went to the website and verified he was a winner of a contest he hadn't even known existed. He was paying so much attention to the website that he didn't even notice when the record had started playing again.

After he had found his name on the website, he tried to find a number for the radio station that was hosting the contest. There was no contact information listed. No matter how many Google searches he did, KLLR did not come up. He hoped to find a phone number for the station as he had so many questions. Finally, as a last-ditch effort, he called information; however, that was another dead end.

After his futile efforts, he decided to click the link and fill out the form. He was surprised to see his name and address on the website. More surprising was the concert ticket that was emailed to him after he registered. Calvin studied the email, hoping it would have contact information. It didn't.

Back at his computer, Calvin finalized his travel plans and paid for the trip. With his airline ticket, rental car, and Phoenix hotel paid for, Calvin went to the kitchen and poured himself a glass of orange juice. As he sat at his small table that overlooked the back yard, he watched as a bird landed on the fence and took off again. He thought about the trip and was excited, not for the concert, because he didn't know if it was real or not, but for the time away. Divorced for the past ten years, he lived alone. The only thing left, his job, had kept him getting out of bed each day with something to look forward to, but when the accident happened, he wasn't able to work for a year, and they couldn't afford to keep him on the payroll. They had paid his medical bills and a very nice severance package, but he missed the human interaction. He hadn't gotten out—really gotten out—in a very long time. He was going to enjoy this vacation and the mild September Phoenix climate, concert or not. A rock-n-roll vacation was just what the doctor ordered.

TUESDAY, SEPTEMBER 11TH, 2018, TOPEKA, KANSAS

Preston Rhodes pulled into the garage and unloaded the suitcase from the trunk. After hitting the button to lower the door, he went into the house, rolling the empty suitcase behind him. He paused when he saw his wife sitting on the couch, watching one of the many crime shows she indulged in throughout the day. Her eyes went from him to the suitcase and back.

"What's with the suitcase?"

"Jesus, Mary, we discussed this."

"Yes, we did, and I said I didn't want you going."

"And I agreed to shut you up, but when I passed the suitcases at Walmart, I decided to buy one. Oh…and I'm going."

"Seriously? You're going to traipse off to some other state to go to some stupid-ass concert for a band you've never heard of? How are we going to afford it?"

"I'll figure it out."

"Like you've figured out how to pay the bills? The water gets shut off in ten days if we don't come up with the seventy-nine dollars."

"I'll pay the damn water bill. I'll come up with the money for the friggin' ticket. I'm tired of never having any fun. I'm going. End of discussion."

"Well, you better have fun, cause I don't know if I'll be here waiting when you get back. I hope it'll be worth it."

"I should be so lucky," Preston mumbled under his breath.

"What did you just say?"

"Nothing."

"I can leave right now if you'd like. Just say the word and I will go back to my mother's house. At least *her* water isn't going to be turned off."

"Do what you want, Mary. I'll do the same. Maybe it's better that way."

Preston tried to stomp off toward the master bedroom; however, the suitcase he pulled behind him hindered his tantrum march, and he stumbled and almost lost his footing, looking like an idiot in the process. Stowing the suitcase in the corner of the room, he went back out to the garage and started puttering with the lawnmower, not wanting to be around his wife. Both in their mid-thirties, they had only been married for a few years, but the romance had definitely been gone for the last half of the short marriage. He wasn't sure why they argued so much, but he knew some of it was financially induced. They were always short of money since she quit her job after six months of marriage, and although she made plenty of promises, she would never get off her ass to go look. To add insult to injury, she gained almost seventy-five pounds because of it and no longer felt like having sex. Their sham of a marriage was a freight train rolling toward a brick wall. He didn't know how much longer he could handle things with her. He needed a break, and he needed this concert.

He thought about how he would feel if she left while he was gone. He was shocked when the first word that came to mind was "relieved." It was then he realized that the marriage had been over for a long time. It wasn't just the loss of income —which Preston desperately tried to make up for; it was also the way she treated him. She was all over his ass about every-thing, and no matter what he did, it didn't seem to be good enough.

Preston thought about life before marriage. He had been single a long time. He attributed it to his looks. At six-foot-two and one hundred twenty pounds, he was a string-bean of a man. He resembled an awkward teenager with stringy brown hair, and he even still had the occasional pimple on his face, but he was far from a teenager and a few years from forty. If Mary left, would he spend the rest of his life being alone? If so, did it matter to him? He was alone before her, and truth be told, he didn't marry her for her looks anyway. He married her because he was lonely and she was willing. The grass had looked greener from the other side, but of course now, he real-ized that wasn't the case.

His mind in torment, Preston wiped a spot of grease off his bird-like leg and counted the days in his head until the concert. Two and a half weeks and he would be gone, whether Mary liked it or not. He hoped she made good on her threat. It would be easier that way.

THURSDAY, SEPTEMBER 20TH, 2018, NORFOLK, VIRGINIA

Around three a.m., Roxanne Lowe finished up with her last lap dance, grabbed her top, and made her way to the ladies' lounge. Earlier, she had finished dancing both the main stage and the secondary stage before she worked the crowd for lap dances. Luckily, she ended the night on a great note, and one of her regulars, who seemed to be a really nice guy, kept her busy for the last hour of her shift, pulling out twenty after twenty to keep her there. Hell, she hadn't even had to perform lap dances for him for half the songs. He just enjoyed her company, and they usually just sat there and talked when he came in. As long as he was paying, she would hang out with him all night, when she wasn't needed on stage, which she had to do on rotation. She didn't mind the shower of dollar bills she received while on the stage, but the lap dances were where the money was.

Back in the lounge, she stripped out of her G-string and got dressed in her street clothes, consisting of a pair of tight jeans, a tighter t-shirt that accented her fake breasts, and a pair of boots. After touching up her makeup in the mirror, she pulled her long blonde hair into a ponytail and pulled it through the back of a baseball cap.

"Are you ready to go, Jasmine?" another dancer asked her. The dancers typically called each other by their stage names, and Roxanne went by Jasmine while at work.

"I am! Let's get out of here."

Roxanne pulled her leather jacket out of her locker and slipped it on, meeting four other girls at the door that led out back. Luckily, the girls didn't have to leave by the front door, where some of the creeps hung out, hoping to catch their favorite stripper after hours where they could hit on them more aggressively.

As they left as a group, not only because there was safety in numbers, but because they typically went out for breakfast every Thursday morning, Roxanne peeled off from the rest and climbed into her red Infinity. She watched and made sure the other girls got into their cars safely before pulling out of the lot.

A mile down the street, Roxanne pulled into the IHOP parking lot, went inside, and grabbed the usual table. The girls filtered in within minutes of each other and slid into the booth. The topic turned to their plans for each girl's next day off.

"What do you got going on, Jasmine?" a brunette that went by the name of Mercy asked.

"I'm actually working straight through until Wednesday, and then I'm taking a few days off."

"You doing anything fun?" Brandy, another brunette, asked.

"I'm actually going to Arizona."

"What are you doing in Arizona?" Mercy asked. "I'd love me a little Arizona weather right about now. It's getting chilly."

Roxanne told them about the concert and the strange event that led up to her getting chosen as a contest winner.

Cherry, a bottled redhead who had been sitting there, quietly joined in. "Trippy! How does that happen? We're pretty much on the other side of the world over here."

Roxanne held up her hands. "I know, right? It doesn't make sense, yet I got the ticket through email, and it promises to be an elite event. I actually have an uncle that lives not too far from there, in Sedona, so I'm hoping to see him while I'm there."

"Does he know you're a stripper?" Cherry asked, laughing.

"Hardly," Roxanne said, smiling. "He thinks I'm a waitress. None of my family lives on this side of the States, so I doubt anyone would ever find out otherwise."

"So why are you all the way out here?" Mercy asked. "So far from home."

"That was the idea," Roxanne answered. "I moved here to get as far away from my train-wreck of a mom as possible."

"Are you going to see her when you go back?" Brandy asked.

"She actually passed a month ago, so no."

"Oh my God, I'm so sorry!" Mercy offered, the other girls offering similar sentiments.

"Don't be. I haven't talked to her in forever, and we didn't really have a relationship. I didn't even go back for the service."

The subject got changed quickly, and the girls finished their breakfast and talked about everything from the strange concert to bikini waxing. By the time the sun peeked up over the horizon, the girls were getting up to leave, exchanging hugs all around.

"Jasmine, make sure you post video of the concert on Facebook. I can't wait to live vicariously through you!" Cherry demanded.

"You got it, Cherry. Just keep the pole warm for me. I'll be back soon."

WEDNESDAY, SEPTEMBER 26TH, 2018, CHARLESTON, WEST VIRGINIA

Reggie Reeves placed his carry-on luggage on the belt and slipped off his cowboy boots. Checking his pockets for the last time, he placed the boots, his belt, and his cap in the gray bin and walked toward the body image scanner. He wasn't used to being without his hat, and he ran his hand through his smooshed-down brown hair, then through his shaggy beard.

In the machine, he held his hands above his head, and when he was cleared to proceed, he gathered his things at the other end of the belt, put everything back on, and proceeded to the gate. He was extremely early, and the gate only had a few other occupants, two of them laying across the hard seats, trying to get some much-needed sleep. Reggie picked a seat that overlooked the tarmac and watched the activity through the floor-to-ceiling windows. Life in West Virginia had been hard on him, and for the past month, he had been couch-surfing, staying at whatever friend's house he was allowed to until he wore out his welcome. Almost out of options, a strange situation with his friend's car radio had him boarding a plane to Arizona. Everything he owned was packed into the one suitcase that would soon rest lazily in the belly of the aircraft. Although he had no idea what he would do after he landed in Phoenix and caught a bus to the city where the concert was, he knew one thing: he would not be coming back to West Virginia.

THURSDAY, SEPTEMBER 27TH, 2018, HOUSTON, TEXAS

Kerry Kelley draped the blanket over her father and made sure he was comfortable, then gave him a kiss on the forehead.

"Great to see you again, Daddy. I'll see you again next week."

"Thanks for coming to see me, baby. I love you. Please be safe."

"I will, Daddy. I'll only be gone five days."

After giving him one last hug, Kerry left the bedroom and found her mother in the kitchen.

"It's hard seeing him like this, Mom."

"I know, honey. The chemo is kicking his ass. He is tired all of the time."

"Please let me know what I can do to help you guys. I'm only a half hour away."

"I know, but Bill and the boys need you. Don't you worry about your father. He's a tough old goat."

"I'm still coming over at least once a week, Mom. Just let me know if you need anything. It's not just him I worry about. I'm sure it's taking its toll on you as well. You look tired."

"Is that your way of telling me I have bags under my eyes?" her mom asked, smiling weakly.

"Those words never left my lips!" Kerry said, smiling back, but she couldn't help notice the dark circles that had become more prominent under her mother's eyes.

At thirty-nine, Kerry had her own responsibilities taking care of her husband, Bill, their two sons, William Jr. and Timothy, as well as working a full-time job as an escrow officer at one of the local title agencies. Her dad getting sick was not supposed to happen, and none of them were ready for it, but cancer had a funny way of doing whatever the hell it wanted.

With all of her responsibilities, Kerry quickly blew off the winning VIP concert ticket that came her way. She didn't understand it, nor did she have time to think about it. She had people that relied on her, and she was needed right where she was.

When she had told Bill about her strange experience while listening to hold music on the phone at her job, both of them had a good laugh about it, but when Kerry had pulled up the website for—as she described—shits and giggles, it all seemed too real. She and Bill fussed over it for the evening, but by the next day, after seeing her dad, working a full shift, and fixing dinner for the family, she had forgotten about it.

Now, it was the day before the concert and her Uber was eight minutes out. Kerry had been raised on rock and roll, and when she and Bill had first started dating—they were high school sweethearts—they started a trend of seeing as many concerts together as they could. Life revolved around music for both of them, which was evident by her ticket collection, which was probably an inch thick. It was the day prior that Bill had presented her with an airline ticket and urged her to go. He had labeled it, using air quotes, as "the chance of a lifetime." After calling her boss and arranging last-minute coverage, she had packed her things and got to bed as early as she could.

Now, at her parents' house, slipping in a quick visit before her flight, she gave her mother a hug and promised to come straight over from the airport when she returned. To make sure she kept her promise, she was leaving her car parked in her parent's driveway.

"Have a great time, honey. That man of yours…he is something else."

"Tell me about it, Mom. He made all the arrangements to make sure he and the kids will be fine without me. I'm trying not to think about the fact that they will probably be eating pizza for dinner every night."

"And if they do? Is that such a bad thing? Stop worrying, Kerry. They'll be fine. You do everything for everyone. It's time you do something for yourself."

"Thanks, Mom. I love you."

Kerry gave her mother a hug and noticed the Uber pull into the driveway.

"I better go. See you soon." Kerry grabbed her suitcase and started toward the front door.

"I love you, baby. Be safe."

FRIDAY, SEPTEMBER 28TH, 2018, CAMP VERDE, ARIZONA

Seth Peterson entered the lobby for Cliff Castle Casino and approached the front desk. The information he had received was to show up, check in, get ready, and be in the lobby at six o'clock p.m. He looked at his Seiko and noticed it was 12:30 in the afternoon. He would have time to get a nap in before the concert.

As he waited in line, he noticed a thin blonde girl at the counter in front of him. She seemed out of place wearing what looked like a sun dress. Another hotel employee came up to the counter and motioned for him to approach.

"Checking in?"

"Yes, sir," Seth answered, handing over his driver's license.

"Ahh, Mr. Peterson. Thanks for coming. It looks like you

are in one of our suites on the top floor. Are you here for the concert?"

Seth felt flushed and noticed out of the corner of his eye that the blonde was looking at him.

"Yes, I'm here for the—"

"Ohmygawd, me too!" Brittany interrupted.

Seth turned toward the girl and looked at her, noticing for the first time that she was attractive. "Awesome. I'm glad to meet someone else going to this thing. I thought maybe I was the only one." He reached out and shook her hand. "I'm Seth."

"I'm Brittany."

"So, Brittany, what can you tell me about this concert? I know nothing about it."

"Then we're in the same boat."

Seth turned toward the person that was coding his room key. "You seem to know about the concert. What can you tell me and my new friend Brittany here?"

"I'm afraid you know everything I know. We have eight rooms reserved for eight winners that won tickets to a very secret concert. We don't know who or where, only that you are all to be well taken care of and that we should remind everyone to meet in the lobby at six."

"I wonder why the big shroud of secrecy?" Brittany asked.

"I don't know, but it's kind of exciting, don't you think?" Seth answered.

"Hell yes. That's why I'm here. That and any excuse to get away from my asshole boss."

"Yeah, those are no fun," Seth sympathized. As the employee handed back his ID, Seth asked, "Has anyone else that's here for the concert checked in yet?"

The man checked the computer. "Not yet. You two are the first."

Seth turned to Brittany. "Want to get a drink?"

"I'm so down," she agreed, smiling.

Seth looked at the employee's name badge. "Doug, is there a bar here?"

"Yes, sir. You'll enjoy our Cliff Dweller's Bar. If you want to drop your bags in your rooms first, you can get there by following this route." Doug pulled out a site map and drew a red line down the path they should take. "Your rooms are on the same floor."

"Thanks, Doug. We appreciate it," Seth told him, taking his room key and the map. "Will you do us a favor? Will you tell anyone else that shows up for the concert that some of us are drinking in the bar?"

"Will do."

"Thanks again, Doug!"

Brittany had already finished checking in, and together, they made their way to the elevator, discussing the concert like they had known each other for years. When they got off the elevator on the top floor, Brittany spotted her room and went to the door and opened it.

"So, Seth, will I see you in the bar?"

"Thirty minutes?"

"Perfect. Gives me time to change and freshen up."

"See you then," he confirmed, and they both made their way to their rooms.

Seth entered the bar and spotted Brittany talking to a guy with a shaggy beard and a ball cap. Guessing that it was some random local trying to pick up on her, Seth made his way to the table to play the hero and protect her.

Brittany spotted him coming, and a smile lit up her face.

"Seth! Glad you're here! I want you to meet Reggie. He's from West Virginia and will be joining us tonight."

Seth was caught off guard for a minute and then remembered they had invited others to join them. "Oh," he said, "you're here for the concert?"

"Yup! Same as you."

"All the way from West Virginia?"

"Yeah…long way. What about you, Seth? Where are you from?"

"Chicago."

Brittany's eyebrows arched. "Holy crap. Oregon here. What are a bunch of random people from all over the United States doing in some small Podunk town for a concert?"

"Hopefully a question that will be answered later," Seth responded. "How did you find out you won?"

"Some radio station cut in when I was listening to my iPhone. It was so freaking weird. Some rock and roll station that is supposedly near here."

"Almost the same thing for me," Seth told them. "What about you, Reggie?"

"Same concept. But how is some local radio station broadcasting all around the United States?" Reggie asked.

Brittany jumped back into the conversation. "You know what's weird? No matter what I did, I was never able to pick up that station again. It says it's 102.9, but I tried that station in Portland, and it's a completely different station. I also tried it in my rental car when I got to the hotel. There is no such station here."

"The mysteries are just piling up," Seth admitted.

A stranger approached. "Sorry to interrupt. Are you guys going to the concert?"

They all turned toward him, and Brittany answered. "We are! I'm Brittany from Oregon. Who are you?"

"Hi, Brittany. I'm Calvin from Minnesota. Nice to meet you."

Seth extended his hand. "I'm Seth."

Reggie did the same. "And I'm Reggie."

"Nice to meet all of you," Calvin told them. "I see I'm the token old guy in the group." He laughed, and the ice being broken, they all followed suit.

"So, Calvin," Seth said, "any idea what this is all about?"

"I'm guessing you guys know as much as I do, which is nothing except we are supposed to be going to a concert tonight."

"That's about where we're at," Brittany said. "I guess we will all find out soon."

The four of them continued to get acquainted and ordered food. As they ate, the last four attendees came into the bar, one at a time, and joined them, each one curious to meet the others and find out any more information. They pulled two tables together, and the newcomers all ordered food and drinks. Because there was no other information available regarding the concert, they all chatted and got to know each other.

"So, Jonathan, I see you ordered a Coke. Do you not drink?" Roxanne asked.

"I do but can't here. I'm only nineteen."

"Ah, that explains it," Roxanne said.

"Well, you win the honor of youngest, and I apparently am the oldest, so we have something in common," Calvin joked.

"You aren't that much older, Calvin," Kerry told him. "I'm almost forty, and Preston over there looks about my age."

"Close," Preston answered. "But it looks so much better on you."

Kerry smiled and turned to Roxanne. "So where are you from?"

"Virginia," Roxanne answered. "You?"

"Texas. Have you ever been here before?"

"Unfortunately, yes. My uncle lives in the next town over, and I used to live in the area before…well…a long time ago. I moved to Norfolk to get away."

"What's in Norfolk?"

"Just my job. I actually found an online ad for a cheap guesthouse and decided that was as good of a place to live as any. I hopped a plane the next day."

"You must have really hated it here."

"I didn't hate *where* I lived…more the people I lived *with*."

"Your uncle?"

"No, I love my uncle. In fact, he's coming by to say hi soon. It was actually my mom I had to get away from. She was evil."

"So sorry you had to deal with that."

"It's all good. I don't let it define me."

The group continued to talk and get to know each other as they ate and drank. Sometime during the get-together, the waitress came to their tables and announced their host was picking up the tab. She wasn't surprised by the barrage of additional food and drink orders she received immediately following her announcement.

Around five o'clock, the group watched as Roxanne jumped up out of her seat and ran to meet a man that had entered the bar. He looked to be pushing sixty. As they embraced each other, Reggie turned toward Calvin.

"Sorry, Calvin. Looks like you're not the oldest any longer."

"It's about damn time," Calvin said, laughing.

Roxanne brought the man to the table and introduced him to her new friends.

"Uncle Joe, I'd like you to meet my new friends. I'll go around the table." She pointed at the group. "You guys correct me if I screw this up, okay? Starting over here on the left, we have Jonathan from Dallas, Texas, then we have Brittany—isn't she pretty Uncle Joe?—she's from Oregon. Reggie over there is from West Virginia, I think. Is that right, Reggie?"

"I was. I'm going to probably stay here now."

"Oh, that's right. Then we have Kerry, and she is also from Texas—I think Houston." Kerry nodded. "In the middle there is Preston from Kansas, who is probably leaving his wife when he gets back, next to him is Seth from Chicago, and next to him, Calvin from Minnesota. I think that covers it. Everyone, this is my uncle Joe, who is my mother's brother. He lives in Sedona, which is close by."

Joe greeted everyone at the table, and they pulled a free chair from a nearby table and offered him a seat.

"So, what do you do, Joe?" Calvin asked.

"I'm semi-retired, but I drive a cab part-time for a privately owned taxi company in Cottonwood."

"How long have you lived here?" Kerry asked.

"Most of my life. My parents moved to this area when I was five. I never left. I like it most days," Joe said, grinning.

"So, do you know anything about this concert?" Seth chimed in. "Any local buzz?"

Joe scratched his head, causing his silver hair to dance around. "I haven't heard a peep. And this is a pretty small community. Can't seem to take a shit around here without someone knowing about it. Fill me in on what you all are doing here. Maybe it might jog something in my memory."

Roxanne explained to him how they had all been contest winners for a private concert in the area. She also explained the strange circumstances around the radio breakthroughs and the fact that not a single one of them had entered any type of contest.

"Any idea who's playing at the concert?" Joe asked.

The group looked at each other, and finally, Jonathan piped up. "I remember. It's Six Feet Below."

Joe squinted. "Never heard of them. Are they new?"

"Not sure," Roxanne told him. "I couldn't find anything out about them. Anyone else know?"

They all looked at each other and shook their heads.

"So, you all know nothing about this concert, how you got entered, why, or who the band even is and yet you all traipsed from all over America to see it? Wow. That's crazy."

Preston spoke. "I think we all have our different reasons for coming. Personally, I needed to get away. The mystery surrounding this was one that I couldn't pass up on."

Others at the table murmured in agreement. Joe turned to Roxanne. "So, knowing how much you hate this place, why did you come back?"

"Cause you're here and it's been years. It was a good excuse to come back, and now with Mom gone, I figured why not?"

"I'm so glad to see you, sweetheart. I missed you."

"Hey, Joe, do you know anything about the radio station that is sponsoring this thing?" Calvin asked.

"I'm sure I would. Nothing gets by me here. Which one is it?"

The conversation at the table ceased as everyone turned to hear Joe's answer to the question.

"K-L-L-R. Some sort of rock/metal station. Have you heard of it?" Calvin asked.

Joe blinked rapidly and glanced around the table. Finally, he spoke.

"I think you must be mistaken. K-L-L-R hasn't been around for a very long time."

Roxanne touched his arm. "Yeah, all the years I lived here, I don't remember it, either."

"That's because you were born in ninety. The station was… er…gone…in 1983," Preston managed to say, clearly shaken.

"What do you mean 'gone?'" Brittany asked. "I have the email right here." She held up her hand with the email and printed ticket in it. "It says 102.9, K-L-L-R. Killer radio. How can it be gone?"

"That doesn't make any sense," Joe said, shaking his head. "I think it's best if I tell you all what happened. This is craziness. I think someone is playing a prank on you. I seriously doubt there is a concert."

"What do you mean?" Jonathan blurted. "I came all this way for nothing? I had to pay for my plane ticket all by myself."

"We all did," Brittany told him. "Chill for a second and let's hear what Joe has to say."

"Thanks, Brittany," Joe continued. "It was the early eighties, and hard rock and heavy metal were starting to take over the music scene. This area had a handful of radio stations, but not really any good rock stations. Some fellow by the name of Ricky…his last name was Jepson…bought an old country station that had shut down, and he rebranded it. When it went live, many of the townsfolk were shocked to find out it was a rock and roll station. Had it been older rock, things might have been different, but the way music was progressing, the station quickly grew a group of protesters that weren't very quiet about their disdain for the station and the music it played. I think they started speaking out in the media about it as 'devil music' or something to that effect. You get the gist.

"The station had a ton of listeners as well, and because of that, it was starting to bring in advertisers. The station had operated for less than a year and was doing well, much to the chagrin of its persecutors."

"Something tells me this story doesn't have a happy ending," Roxanne interrupted.

Joe looked down. "No, hun. No happy ending here. This town has all but forgotten the tragedy that happened on that night in September of 1983. That date will forever be etched into my memory. It was the 28th…your mother's birthday."

"Wait!" Calvin said, jumping into the conversation. "Are you saying that something happened to the station on September 28th, 1983?"

"I am," Joe said, nodding.

"That's today's date!" Calvin stated.

"Maybe they're celebrating a re-grand opening or something," Brittany offered.

Calvin's eyes rolled up in his head as he did the math. "Thirty-five years after whatever this event was—to the frickin' day—we were all invited here to attend a concert. That can't be a coincidence."

"That's some freaky shit," Reggie agreed.

Roxanne held up her hand. "Hold on, everyone. I think we need to hear what Uncle Joe—"

A man in a chauffeur's uniform approached the table as she was talking and interrupted the conversation. "Excuse me, everyone, I believe you are the group I'm picking up. It's time to get going. The agenda for the night, as I am told, is as follows. We are all going to climb in the limo, and I am to take you to the station for a tour and to meet the owner. After that, an hour later, I am to pick you all back up and take you to the concert location, where you will be wined and dined."

Everyone was unsure of what to do and looked at Joe, then Roxanne.

"Where is the concert?" Kerry asked.

"I apologize, but I haven't been given that information yet.

I'm told it will be sent to me right before I pick you all up from the station."

"It can't be," Joe whispered. "The station is gone."

"Maybe they reopened it?" Jonathan suggested. "A thirty-fifth anniversary reopening that is to be kicked off by a kick-ass private concert. I don't know about you guys, but I'm going. I've come all this way, and I'm not chickening out now."

The table erupted in conversation, many of the concert-goers unsure. Finally, Jonathan stood up and joined the chauffeur. "I'm going. Who is joining me?"

The occupants of the table looked at each other. Finally, Brittany stood up. "I'm in."

Seth also stood up. "I'm in, too."

Slowly, the rest of the occupants all stood up, except for Roxanne, who looked at Joe.

"What should I do, Uncle Joe?" she whispered.

"Whatever you want to do, baby girl, but if you go, I'm going with you, as far as I can anyway."

"Deal. Let's go," she said, standing and grabbing his hand. "I can't miss this…I *won't* miss this."

———

THE MOOD IN THE LIMO WAS A MIX OF EXCITEMENT AND nervousness. No one asked anything more about the tragedy that had befallen the radio station, and Joe decided to keep his mouth shut until they got there. He would either be proven right—that the station no longer existed—or be proven wrong, and it would be open and operating. None of these people knew him, so he decided to keep his comments to himself—for now.

More drinks were poured in the limo, and the group chattered idly for the twenty-minute trip into Cottonwood and then the additional ten minutes it took to travel the gravel road that led up the hill to the station. Dusk had approached, and the road was cloaked in shadows as they traveled over it; however, it was light enough to see the road in front of them clearly. As the limo crested the hill and rounded the final bend, Joe inhaled sharply. The station sat in front of them, exterior lights ablaze, looking like it did the day it was built. A lit sign atop the brick building advertised the station as KLLR, 102.9 F.M., Killer Radio. The chauffeur pulled in front of the building, stopped, got out, and came around to open the door closest to the station entrance.

"Okay, all out. I'll be back in an hour. Go on inside. The owner is expecting you."

As soon as all nine passengers were out of the vehicle, the driver shut the door, climbed in the front, and started down the gravel drive. They watched it depart and, when the taillights disappeared, turned toward the building.

"Now what?" Jonathan asked.

"Well," Calvin answered, "you wanted to see the station, so let's go in."

Amazed at the condition of the building, Joe reached over, pulled the front door open, and held it for the group as they all shuffled inside. When he entered the building himself, the door shut behind him, and he joined the rest of the group inside the entryway.

"Hello?" Seth called, looking around and not seeing anyone. Music spilled out of the speakers that were placed throughout the station.

"Is this that band where the girl crawls on the hood of the car in the video?" Preston asked.

"You mean Whitesnake?" Calvin asked. "Yes, and the girl is Tawny Kitaen."

"I love that video," Preston said. "That girl is hot."

"*That girl* is almost sixty now," Calvin said, laughing.

"Gross," Preston said. "Where is everyone anyway?"

"Maybe he's in the can?" Brittany suggested.

"That would be weird, considering he was expecting us," Roxanne said, concern etched into her brow.

The song ended, and the "On Air" light illuminated above the studio booth. A voice bellowed through the speakers.

"That was Whitesnake with 'Here I Go Again.' Thanks for joining us tonight at Killer Radio. 102.9 FM, K-L-L-R. I'm Ricky Jepson, and this is 'The Last in Line' by Dio. Rock on, Cottonwood!"

The sign above the booth went dark, and the song started. Joe went to one of the windows of the booth, placed his face against it, shielded his eyes from the surrounding glare, and looked around.

"It's empty," Joe announced.

"Must have prerecorded this portion," Calvin offered. "Looks like it's on autopilot."

Kerry walked toward the back of the station and found three doors, all of them closed. She knocked on each one. "Hello? Is anyone here?" After a few seconds, there was no response, and she knocked again. There was still no answer.

"Open them," Reggie suggested.

Kerry opened the first door, which turned out to be a small office. It was unoccupied. The second door yielded a storage closet. The third door contained a toilet and a sink, but it was also unoccupied.

"Looks like this is a bust," Jonathan said. "We should get out of here. This place is creepy."

"Says the guy that was so damn gung-ho about coming here?" Roxanne said, her frustration making her come across harsher than she meant to.

"Well, I didn't know. Besides, you guys didn't have to come with me. That's on you."

"No need to argue, you guys," Brittany said. "The limo driver will be back in an hour. We can hang here until the owner gets back, or the limo shows up. Whichever comes first."

"Well, I'm going outside," Jonathan announced. "You guys can stay if you want."

Jonathan went to the door and pushed, but it didn't budge. He tried a second time with the same result. Joe went to the door, panic edging into his face. He tried to open it then rammed his shoulder against it, but it still didn't move.

The song finished, and AC/DC's "Highway to Hell" automatically started playing. Seth and Calvin went to the back door of the station and tried to open it, but it didn't budge.

"Okay, this shit isn't funny," Kerry said. "I have a sick parent I left behind for this. My family is waiting for me. Someone get the door open."

Roxanne looked at Joe, her eyes wide with concern. When she noticed him standing still, staring at the ground, she knew something was extremely wrong.

"Uncle Joe. Uncle Joe! What's going on? What do you know?"

When he didn't respond, Roxanne touched his shoulder. He turned to look at her.

"Uncle Joe, what's going on?" She noticed a small tremor work through his body.

"I…you all…I think you need to hear the rest of my story."

———

EVERYONE GATHERED AROUND JOE TO TRY AND HEAR HIM over the AC/DC tune that was blasting over the speakers.

"On September 28th, 1983, this radio station burned to the

ground. The owner, Ricky Jepson, was trapped in here when it started and couldn't get out. His body was so badly burned, they had to identify him by dental records."

Reggie interrupted. "Isn't that the name of the DJ that announced the Dio song a few minutes ago? Or at least the name used on the recording?"

Calvin nodded. "It was. I remember."

"So how do dead people talk?" Brittany asked.

"They don't," Seth answered, "but remember the voice was recorded."

"What? Thirty-five years ago?" Kerry asked incredulously.

Roxanne held up her hand. "Please!" she shouted. "If you remember, we're stuck in here. I think what Uncle Joe has to say is more important than the name on the recording!"

The other occupants of the room fell silent, and the song ended, then kicked straight into "Fly to the Angels" by Slaughter. The song started off softly, and no one paid attention to the music.

Joe rubbed his right palm across his face and exhaled sharply. "Okay, there's more. Apparently, the owner made a final broadcast saying that K-L-L-R radio would be no more, thanking everybody, and then passing a message on to his wife. He knew he wasn't getting out, and he rode it out until he was gone."

"Why didn't he just leave?" Jonathan asked. "Maybe the doors were stuck. Oh wait, like now! Oh shit! We're all gonna die!"

"Jesus, Jonathan. Calm the hell down. We're not going to die," Brittany chastised him. "Let Joe finish."

"Thanks, Brittany," Joe said, once again resuming his story. "Anyway, there was a big investigation. Turns out that the fire was ruled an arson. Someone set that fire."

The occupants of the small station looked around at each other, shock on their face.

"Who, Uncle Joe? Do they know who set the fire?"

Joe glanced down at the floor, unable to meet Roxanne's eyes.

"Uncle Joe?"

Finally, he looked up and met her stare. His voice was barely a whisper. "No. They never figured out who did it, but I have an idea."

"Who? Who did it, Unc?"

Joe stood straight and took a deep breath. "Remember how I told you it happened on your mother's birthday?"

"Yes."

"She'd been blabbering for weeks about the station and how it was run by devil worshipers. She convinced many people she knew the same. They even got together weekly to discuss it, trying to formulate a plan to get the station shut down."

"No. You're not saying Mom had anything to do with this."

Ignoring her, he continued. "Anyway, the night leading into her birthday, she was celebrating and had a little too much to drink. She made me come pick her up from the bar and take her home. She left her car there. Seems she had no way to get anywhere without her car. That played in her favor later. When the police questioned her, she was at home asleep with no car. The fire happened in the wee hours, the morning of her birthday. Here's the kicker. I had asked her a couple weeks earlier what she wanted for her birthday. She stared me straight in the eyes and said she wanted the station to be gone. It's way too much of a coincidence."

The other occupants of the station watched and listened to the conversation in horror.

"Why didn't you tell the cops, Uncle Joe? She got away with murdering someone and walked away, scot free?"

"I had no proof. Besides, she's my sister. I didn't know what to do, so I did nothing."

"So, on a scale of one to ten, how convinced are you that she did this?"

"Then? Maybe a three. Today? A ten. Absolutely a ten. Comments she has made over the years made me more convinced every day. And I don't think she was alone, either. I think her group of fanatics helped her. They blocked the doors from the outside, set the roof on fire, and let it burn. They murdered Ricky Jepson."

Reggie ran to the front door and tried to open it again and then started kicking it while Seth ran to the back door and tried to get it open again as well. Neither door budged. Defeated, they once again joined the rest of the group in the center.

"We have to get the hell out of here!" Seth yelled. "Something isn't right."

The song ended, and a cover of "Live and Let Die" by Guns and Roses filled the small space. Panic edged in on many of their faces as they realized they were trapped.

The panic ramped up to sheer terror when Calvin spoke. "Um…guys? Um…have you been paying attention to the songs that have been playing since we got here? 'Here I Go Again'…'The Last in Line'…'Highway to Hell'…Now it's 'Live and Let Die.' This is creepy. The station burned down thirty-five years ago today. The doors are locked. The music that is prerecorded is talking about death, and it's happening all over again. Someone needs to call 911 now!"

Those that had brought their phones with them reached for them, trying to call out. One by one, a look of defeat ensconced their faces.

"No signal," Kerry said, her lip quivering.

"Me neither," Brittany agreed.

"Uncle Joe, what is happening?" Roxanne yelled, wiping her clammy palms on her jeans.

"I don't know, honey. I don't know."

"Everyone, spread out and see if you can find another way out," Preston demanded, heading toward the studio and trying the door. It was locked, and he could not get inside, so as the others checked the other rooms, he did a visual inspection of the ceiling to see if there was any access to an attic or anything. He found nothing. The group all rejoined in the main room, and then as suddenly as he was there, Seth ran off into one of the smaller rooms, then came back a minute later.

"What was *that*, Seth?" Brittany asked.

"There was a phone in the office there. I didn't even think about trying it the first time I was in there. I just went back to check it. It's dead."

"Figures," Brittany responded.

The song ended, and the "On air" light lit over the booth. Ricky Jepson's voice boomed over the speakers. The group paused to listen, staring at the speakers.

"That was 'Live and Let Die' by Guns and Roses. This is Ricky Jepson with 102.9, Killer radio, and tonight is indeed a special night. Visiting our lovely little studio are eight contest winners, and we are so happy they are here. Oh, the night we have in store for them!"

Jonathan yelled, pulling everyone's attention to him, but when he tried to speak, the words wouldn't come out. Instead, he covered his mouth and pointed at the back corner of the building. Thick smoke pushed its way down from the roof.

"We want to thank all of our guests for joining us today. We've waited thirty-five years for this! We are 102.9, K-L-L-R…Killer radio and this is Queensryche, 'Take Hold of the

Flame' from their album *The Warning*. Again, this is Ricky Jepson, and I bid you farewell."

The opening bars of the song started playing just as Kerry screamed. Flames started to lick through the ceiling in the back of the building, and the smoke started getting thick. Chaos ensued as everyone from the group started pounding on doors and kicking the walls, but the steel and brick were unrelenting. Flames burst through the roof over the studio portion of the building and started licking down the walls. Panic taking over, some cried, others stared in dumbfounded silence, and those that wouldn't give up hammered at the doors. Over the next few minutes, the entire roof was consumed in flames, and fiery chunks of wood rained down throughout the studio. The smoke was almost impossible to breathe through, and those that were still conscious had their shirts pressed against their mouth and nose.

Calvin and Joe were still trying to get the door open, using a fire extinguisher and an office chair as battering rams, but their strength was fading as the heat and smoke sucked the air out of the room. Joe looked down at the floor next to the door, where his beloved niece was unconscious. A tear slipped down his face, carving a pink line through the soot.

As Joe gave up and slipped to the floor beside his beautiful niece, the song ended, and Metallica's "Fade to Black" started playing. Joe glanced up at Calvin, and they both nodded at each other, knowing that this was the end. The song played on as the fire continued its path of destruction; however, besides the dancing flame and popping chunks of burning materials, there was no other movement.

———

Amy Jepson sat in the chair beside the hospital bed in the ICU, dabbing at her eyes with a tissue. There were tubes and wires everywhere, but the breathing tube that was forced down the throat of the bed's inhabitant was too much for her. Tenderly, she pushed the soiled blonde hair from the patient's face and tried to rub some of the overlooked soot from the patient's forehead.

Startled, Amy looked up as the nurse came into the room. "Hi, there," she greeted the nurse. "I just got here like fifteen minutes ago. Has she…Roxanne…regained consciousness at all since she's been here?"

The nurse set down her clipboard. "We have her in an induced coma. She's tried to wake up a couple times, but we want to keep her down for right now. She is going to be extremely miserable. Her lungs are heavily damaged, and we are worried about infection setting in. It may be another day before we bring her out. Are you family?"

"A friend of the family actually. I heard what happened and rushed down here to see her. I don't know if she has anyone else."

"Her emergency contact is her uncle, but he's admitted, too. Three rooms down, actually, in about the same shape."

Amy looked down at the ground, sniffled, and then turned her attention back to the nurse. "Did…uh…anyone else…you know?"

"Did they what?"

"Make it?"

The nurse walked over and placed her hand on Amy's shoulder. "These two aren't out of the woods yet, hun. It's very touch and go. There was one other victim that came in. He's down the hall. A total of three came in. Not sure how many didn't make it. By the way, does Roxanne have any…um…next of kin besides Joe Grimes?"

"I'm not sure. He's the only one I know of," she lied, having no idea, but not wanting to let on that she actually didn't know Roxanne at all.

"Okay, well, we will keep looking. In the meantime, feel free to stay, but she won't be waking up today. You'd be better off coming back tomorrow."

"Thank you, I'll do that."

Amy got up from the hard chair and tucked her purse under her arm, leaving the nurse to check on the patient. As she left, she glanced at the names on the charts that were beside each door and spotted the one with Joe Grimes' name on it. Peering in the door, she saw a man that was in his late fifties with short gray hair, the same tubes and wires attached. He also appeared to be either asleep or in a coma. Her emotions taking over again, she rubbed her eyes and headed to the elevator, then out to her car.

Inside her Hyundai Santa Fe, she started the engine, pushed aside her shoulder-length brown hair, and put on her seatbelt. She caught the reflection of her eyes in the mirror and gasped. She looked gaunt and lifeless. She rubbed the smeared mascara away from under her eyes and realized that her normally brown eyes looked almost black.

She thought back to that night thirty-five years ago. The night Ricky had died. The horror of the pictures, knowing her soulmate had been inside. One young daughter left without a father. It took her two years for the nightmares to subside… two long, horrifying years racked with dreams of fire, burning, and destruction. When the nightmares finally did stop, she continued to deal with the guilt, knowing if she had just told Ricky that she didn't want to—wouldn't even—leave Flagstaff, if she had never agreed to this crazy idea of opening his own station, he might still be with her now.

It took close to ten years and many sessions of therapy for

her to be able to accept his death and move on in life, letting the guilt drain through the cracks of her broken life. Although no one had ever been arrested or charged for the fire—or his death—she finally was able to let go. That was until the year before.

Putting the car in reverse, Amy backed out of the spot, heading for home. Two minutes later, she broke down and started bawling.

———

THE NEXT DAY, AMY SAT BY THE SIDE OF ROXANNE'S BED, holding her hand. Roxanne was still in the induced coma, but Amy had been informed that they were planning to bring her out a little later in the day.

Running her finger up and down Roxanne's arm, Amy thought about their daughter, Michelle. She would be turning thirty-nine soon, but Amy would not be celebrating the day with Michelle. In fact, Michelle had stopped talking to Amy the day she turned eighteen. Amy had never seen someone pack up and leave so quickly. Michelle had made it extremely apparent that she felt her father's death was Amy's fault. That event had sent Amy into another spiral for several years before she finally joined AA and stopped drinking, cold-turkey. She had been clean for eighteen years.

Roxanne, although younger, reminded Amy of Michelle, and Amy felt a connection with her, even though she had never met Roxanne before. Once again, she tried to hold back her tears as the guilt tore through her body. Life had been cruel to her, but this time, many more had been affected. If she had only known what the dreams had meant, maybe she could have stopped this.

"You're a pretty, young thing, aren't you?" she asked

Roxanne, not expecting an answer. "Probably ten years younger than my Michelle. I'm so sorry. I didn't know. I'm so, so sorry," she repeated, tears slipping out of her eyes before she could stop them.

Grabbing a tissue, she dried the tears again, sniffled, and cleared her throat.

"You didn't deserve this. I promise, I didn't know. I didn't know what it meant."

The lights on the monitors continued to dance across the screen, but Roxanne did not move nor did she open her eyes.

"It was exactly a year ago. September 28th, 2017. I had woken up in the dead of night, drenched in sweat, screaming. It had been thirty-two years since I had nightmares like that. At first, I couldn't remember what it was about, but as I was changing the bed, I remembered. The fire. It was intense. I was there. In the station. I tried to get out but couldn't. That's when I woke up.

"I was confused as to why, after all those years, I would have dreams about the fire again. Brushing it off later that day, I forgot about it. That is until the second night. I had another dream. It was just as bad, but it wasn't about me that night. I saw other faces inside the fire. I didn't know what it meant but again hoped it would be the last one.

"That wasn't the case. For the entire last year, I've dreamed nightly. Always about the station. There was always a fire. Sometimes I was there. Sometimes Michelle. Many times, Ricky was there. He always told me that he would get even with those that had harmed him—killed him. On more than one occasion, I asked him who was to blame, but I never got an answer. The faces were always unfamiliar. Until now. Your face…I've seen it—younger, but familiar.

"It wasn't until the night of the fire—the one you were in— that the dreams clicked. An entire damn year of dreams ramping up to one grand finale—the final event. Ricky brought you all back to the station to make you pay. Thirty-five years after he was killed, he tried to get his revenge.

"I am so sorry I didn't get there sooner. The anniversary of Ricky's death has always been hard for me, but the feeling of dread that I had a couple of days ago was something I had never experienced before. I just knew something was wrong. That evening, I started to have a panic attack, and I felt a driving force. I knew I had to get to the station, even though it had been nothing but a burned-out brick skeleton for thirty-five years. As I got closer, I could see the smoke, and I called 911. They arrived and made me stand way back, but I watched as they cut the door open and started pulling out the bodies closest to the door."

Amy paused, trying to regain her composure again.

"If I had just figured it out sooner. The lady I saw in my dream, I think she may have been your mother. When she died a month or so ago, I think you were destined to take her place. The others? The paper published their names and their pictures. I was up all night researching…trying to make the connection. I made around half of them. I'm going to assume the remainder were there last night for the same reason as you were, and the others I researched.

"Calvin Hawkins is the only other survivor besides your uncle. He had an older brother that lived in Cottonwood for about a year—the same year as the fire. He passed away from heart failure around five years ago. Jonathan Hunter was only a kid, really. Nineteen. Lived in Dallas with his parents. Turns out his grandmother used to live in Cottonwood before moving to Sun City, Arizona. Preston Rhodes was thirty-five. He was born a month after the fire. His parents lived in Cottonwood at the time of the fire and then moved on to New Mexico immediately after, but they died in a freak accident five years later. Kerry Kelley was put up for adoption at birth, but I am thinking maybe her parents or another relative used to live here. I'm going to keep digging, but it all is adding up. Ricky's need for revenge didn't end when his murderers died. Instead, he went after those linked to them. Had I just figured it out sooner, the other six wouldn't have died."

The nurse entered the room. "We are going to cut off the Propofol now and let Roxanne come out of the coma slowly. I'd expect her to become conscious sometime a little later today."

"May I stay? I don't want her to be alone when she wakes up."

"Of course," the nurse answered, changing out the IV bag. "Will you please push the button when she wakes up? We will want to talk to her."

"Absolutely," Amy told her.

"Thank you," the nurse said and left the room.

"Can't wait to meet you," Amy whispered. "I'm here for you. There has been enough loss and tragedy."

ONE MONTH LATER

"How are those tacos?" Amy asked.

Roxanne smiled. "Delicious. Thanks for bringing me to this restaurant. The food is really good here."

"Happy to! How have you been feeling?"

"Better every day. Thanks for giving me a place to stay while I recovered. It was nice to get off of the oxygen, but I'm just now feeling like myself again."

"How does it feel to be back in town?"

"Weird. I've always hated it here, but I'm starting to think that was simply because my mother was here. This place is kinda growing on me now. I suppose I need to get back to

Norfolk soon, though. My apartment is still there, and they're holding my job."

"Remind me why you moved to Norfolk again?"

"Because it was about as far away as I could get from here."

"I get it, but do you really want to go back to that job?" Roxanne had confided in Amy the week prior.

Roxanne sighed. "Well, it paid the bills. Honestly, I don't really want to go back, but I need money, and it's all I have right now."

"Well, why don't you stay here?"

"I appreciate it, Amy. You've been so kind to me. But you don't have to take care of me. This wasn't your fault. You couldn't have known."

"Well, what if I got you a job at one of the bars in Old Town? You certainly have the personality for it, and I bet you'd make the big bucks in tips."

"That actually sounds like fun, but I feel I'm imposing, staying with you. Plus, a girl needs her own space. Not sure slinging drinks will pay the rent."

"What if there is no rent?"

"What are you talking about?"

Amy slid a key across the table toward her. "Your uncle Joe asked me to give this to you. It was for your mother's house. She left it to Joe, but he wants you to have it. It's paid off, by the way."

Roxanne's mouth fell open. "No way."

"I'm serious. He wants you to meet him there after lunch. He has a contractor meeting you guys there as well. He said they can remodel it and make it seem like an entirely different home. You'd have no rent payment. Now what's your excuse?"

Roxanne was silent, trying to process the news. Finally, she spoke. "I'm sorry, Amy, but I have to go back to Norfolk."

"I was hoping you wouldn't say that," Amy said, her eyes tearing up. "We just became friends. I don't want you to go."

"Oh, didn't I tell you?" Roxanne asked.

"Tell me what?"

"I'll be back in a couple weeks! I'm just going to get my stuff and my car."

Amy leaned across the table and hugged her. "I'm so happy. You'll always have a home here."

"Best home I've ever had," Roxanne said, returning the hug and pulling Amy in tight.

EIGHT MONTHS LATER

Roxanne stood up from her seat at the wedding party table and held up her glass, tapping a spoon against it to get the guest's attention. When the room finally quieted down, she recited the speech she had committed to memory.

"Ten months ago, I almost died, along with this strapping man, my uncle Joe. Today, I am so pleased to be able to be here to share this day with him, and his beautiful bride, Amy, who in nine months has been more of a mother to me than I ever had in my entire life. She is a loving, kind, and caring soul and not only saved my life, as well as my uncle's life, but she was the only one that was there for me when I got out of the hospital. I love this lady so much, and although I can't really call her mom since she is marrying my uncle, I can certainly call her Aunt Amy. So, Uncle Joe and Aunt Amy, I wanted you both to know that I think you are perfect together, and I wish you nothing but happiness for the remainder of your days. I can't think of a better place to be than one town over from you guys. Congratulations, you two!"

The guests all clinked their glasses, and Joe and Amy gave

each other a deep, passionate kiss. Roxanne had never felt so complete.

SEPTEMBER 28TH, 2019

Charles Ethan Morgan checked into the hotel and made his way up to the room. Inside, he unpacked his bag, excitement coursing through his veins.

His flight the day before from Vancouver, Canada, was fairly uneventful, but the long layover in Seattle had caused the day to be a long one, and he had spent the night in Phoenix before driving up to the hotel.

At thirty-two, he had lived in Canada most of his life with his mother and his adoptive father, even though his earlier memories were from when they had lived in England. Even though his dad wasn't his real father, he loved him like they were blood. Charlie felt no need to search for his birthfather, Calvin, who had decided he wasn't ready to be a father when he found out his girlfriend—Charlie's mom—was pregnant.

Although Charlie had never been to Arizona, the fact that he won a ticket to a VIP concert experience wasn't something he could pass up, even though he lived a long way away. He wasn't fazed by the fact he had never heard of the radio station, KLLR, before. He was going to have the time of his life.

'TIL DEATH DO US PART

CHAPTER 1

The body collapsed in the alleyway, crimson red flowers blooming through the man's shirt in multiple places, where the bullets had pierced his flesh.

His cell phone rang, yanking Tyler Yates' attention away from the crime show he was watching. Pulling it from the pocket of his basketball shorts, Tyler looked at the display. It said "Hottie."

Tyler smiled and pressed the button to accept the call.

"Hey, sweetie! What're you up to?"

"Not much. Just seeing if you had plans tonight." His girl-friend, Tabitha Reynolds, even sounded hot on the phone. It was definitely not false advertising.

"No plans. Just got home from work an hour ago and was watching TV. Why don't you come over? I'm pretty free this weekend."

"I was hoping we could go out for dinner," Tabitha said.

Tyler looked down at his basketball shorts, thought about his plans for relaxing, and almost told her he didn't want to go out, but then thought better of it. She certainly could get any man she wanted, but he didn't want to give her any reason to *want* to.

"Sounds good, babe. Did you want to come over here, or should I meet you somewhere?"

"I'll come over."

"Perfect. I'll jump in the shower."

"See you in thirty minutes. Bye!"

Tyler ended the call and shut off the TV. He didn't feel like going out, but he knew that a relationship was a balance of give and take. It made it a little easier to say yes knowing he could sleep in tomorrow.

At thirty-two, he felt like he should have more energy. Instead, he was tired all the time, even though he was in great shape physically. He blamed it on his job. It was mentally exhausting. As a software engineer, he exercised his brain way more than he exercised his body. While he hit the gym three times a week, his brain was constantly working through complex problems, even while he was sleeping. Getting a night of peaceful sleep seemed to be a thing of the past for him. He was wondering if that would ever change.

Turning on the water in the shower, Tyler stripped and put the clothes he had been wearing in the closet. He stood under scalding water, not because he got dirty while working at his job, but more so to refresh himself.

Tabitha would want to go someplace nice, so Tyler put on a pair of blue slacks and a button-down oxford shirt. Looking at himself in the mirror, he straightened his collar and brushed his hair before putting a little product in it to keep it in place. He studied his face in the mirror: strong jaw, perfect teeth, just the right amount of maintained stubble. Then he noticed his eyes. The exhaustion he felt was painted clearly in the eyes that stared back at him. He sighed, wondering what he was doing with his life.

As he sat on the edge of the bed putting his shoes on, Tabitha walked in. Tyler had given her a key to his San Francisco Bay Area apartment after they had been dating for a couple months. He had hoped she would move in, but so far, she refused, citing various reasons. Now, after six months of dating, he wondered if they would ever be more than boyfriend and girlfriend.

"Oh good, you're ready," she said.

"Perfect timing!" Tyler ran his eyes down her short, black dress and let out a low whistle.

"Flirt."

"So? That dress looks so good on you."

"Thanks, babe."

"It would look even better on the floor, though," Tyler said, even though he knew what the response would be.

"Keep on dreaming!"

There it was. The response he had been expecting. After six months together, not only hadn't she moved in, but they also hadn't ever had sex. Not even close. Whenever their kissing started getting too hot and heavy, she would put on the brakes, hard. Tyler respected her wishes, and he certainly would wait as long as it took—because he felt she was worth it—but he was dying to take their relationship to the next level.

Pretending her comment didn't bother him—he wanted them both to enjoy the evening, after all—Tyler finished tying his shoes, put on a casual suit jacket, and grabbed the keys to his 2019 BMW i8 Roadster.

"Ready?" he asked.

"Just let me use the restroom."

While Tabitha was in the bathroom, Tyler went over to his nightstand and opened the second drawer down. Under his iPad, he found the item he had placed there three months ago. As he heard the toilet flush, he slipped it into his jacket pocket and closed the drawer.

Tabitha opened the door and came back into the room.

"Let's go!" she said.

"Where do you want to eat?"

"Do you mind traveling a bit?"

"Not at all. It's a nice evening for a drive. Where are we going?"

"Is the Moonraker okay?"

"Heck yes. I love the views there."

"Can we put the top down on the Beemer?"

"Seems like it'd be a crime not to."

CHAPTER TWO

"What are you going to order?" Tabitha asked. Their table overlooked the water and the huge rock formations that jutted out from the surface. They had been there twice before, as a couple, and never tired of the view.

"I'm going with the lobster tail and ribeye. You?"

"I absolutely loved the Dungeness crab legs I had last time we came here. I think I'll have them again. Their seafood is so fresh."

The waiter showed up and took their drink order and then retreated toward the kitchen area.

"So, what's the occasion?" Tyler asked.

"For?"

"Tonight."

"Can't I just want to spend some time with my boyfriend? I've only seen you twice this week."

Tyler smiled. "I know a way we can fix that." He winked.

"I know, I know. I can move in. We've had this conversation more times than I can count."

"Yet you always have a reason why you can't…actually, they sound more like excuses."

Tabitha cocked her head and gave him a look, then started to speak. She was cut off when the waiter arrived with their drinks. After he took their order and disappeared, she started again.

"You know what, fine. Maybe I haven't been as transparent as I should have been with you, but I have my reasons."

"But that's not really fair to me, Tabitha. I like you. In fact, I've refrained from telling you, because I didn't want to scare you off, but I think I'm in love with you."

"Really?" Tabitha's eyes got misty.

"Really."

"Oh shit."

"That wasn't quite the reaction I was hoping for."

Tabitha shook her head. "Sorry. That came out wrong. I'm so flattered…and I love you too. I do."

"If you love me, then why not move in with me?"

"You want the truth?"

"I think I deserve it."

"You're right. The truth is, I'm afraid if I move in, my willpower will diminish. I'd be riding you like a kid rides the horsey carousel at the local Walmart."

"I don't see a problem with that," Tyler said, smiling, the tension from the start of the conversation dissipating.

"But I can't."

"Why not? You're a grown-ass adult."

"Okay, I'll come clean, but you have to promise not to make fun of me."

"I promise."

"I don't want to move in, 'cause I don't want to sleep with

you yet. I don't want to sleep with you yet, because I want to wait until we're married—that is, if we ever take that step. I know we haven't discussed it."

Tyler's eyes widened. "Have you thought about it?"

"Yes. A lot."

"Then maybe the timing is right."

"For?"

"To get married."

"Tyler—"

"Wait!" he interrupted. "Hear me out." He reached into his jacket pocket and pulled out a small pouch. Opening the drawstrings, he dumped something into his hand, then grabbed it between his thumb and first two fingers and held it up.

"Is that what I think it is, Tyler?"

"Yes."

"How long have you had it?"

"A few months. I've just been waiting until the time was right. I figured tonight might be good since we were going out and all."

"Are you asking?"

"I'm asking."

Tabitha covered her face with her hands and let out a low squeal. "Yes. YES!"

The patrons from the nearby tables turned to look, but neither of them cared. Tyler's face lit up at his good fortune, and he slid the engagement ring on Tabitha's finger.

"So, what kind of wedding do you want?"

"The quick and easy kind. I'm not into all of that storybook crap. Let's just make it simple."

Tyler smiled. "Works for me. Now the question is when?"

"How about in three weeks? That will give us time to get our marriage license, and I can give a thirty-day notice on my place. That is, if you still want me to move in." She flashed him a mischievous grin.

"You know I do. I can't wait."

Drinks came and they ordered dinner, the conversation revolving around their upcoming nuptials. Before they realized it, the table was nothing but remnants of a meal that had become a celebration of sorts.

"Dessert?" Tyler asked.

"Tempting, but I'd better pass."

"I can always offer you dessert back at my place, if you like, since we are engaged and all now." He grinned.

"Nice try. Marry me first…then you can have all the dessert you want."

"You mean I have to wait three more weeks?" He pretended to pout.

"I'm worth it."

"I don't doubt that one bit. I'm a lucky man."

CHAPTER THREE

Exhausted, Tyler sank onto the couch. He had worked a little bit every evening over the past week, getting the apartment ready for his fiancée. He took full advantage of the weekend and did the majority of the work, making sure half the drawers were empty in the master bathroom and that half the closet was emptied out. He wanted to make it easy for Tabitha to start moving her things in anytime she wanted.

He turned on the television and started watching a crime show that was in progress. At ten p.m., the news came on, and Tyler watched a story about a man who had been murdered. The police weren't releasing all the details, but they stated the body had been torn apart, some parts missing.

"Sickos."

Tyler watched more of the story and realized the murder had happened in Salem, Oregon, which was a long way away, but definitely not far enough. He shuddered.

With work looming the next morning, he turned off the television and headed to bed. As he peeled back the covers, he thought about how, in three short weeks, he would not be climbing into this bed alone. He had never been married before and, likewise, had never lived with anyone, so this would be a new experience for him. His mind teased him with images of what he thought Tabitha looked like naked, and he imagined her stretched out across the bed, motioning for him to join her. Their wedding night could not come soon enough.

In bed, the cool fabric rubbed over his naked body and that, mixed with the thoughts of his soon-to-be wife lying naked beside him, her smooth skin backed up against him, floated him into a sensual dream, unlike he had ever had before. In the dream, she took him and used him up, until all that was left was a shaking, withered mound of flesh that was unable to move. When he awoke a couple of hours later, he couldn't help but wonder if the dream had been a good sign or an omen.

———

The next week passed by uneventfully. Tyler worked, came home, talked to Tabitha nightly on the phone, watched television, and went to bed. For the first time ever, he realized his life was boring, and he was looking forward to sharing it with somebody. He had no trepidation about giving up his freedom. Since being on his own, he'd been muddling through life, successful and driven in his work, but unfulfilled in his personal life. Though he had never realized what was missing before, it was all too apparent now.

On Friday, when he got home from work, Tabitha was waiting for him.

He had parked his Beemer in the parking garage and rode the elevator up to his floor, tired from the long week at work, but not looking forward to spending another weekend alone. When he slid the key into the deadbolt and tried to turn it, it was unlocked. He cautiously opened the door and peered inside the living room. The lights were on, but the room was empty. He heard noises coming from the kitchen and went to investigate. When he walked around the corner, he froze, in shock.

Her back was to him as she stood over the stove. She was wearing the one apron he kept in the pantry—one that read "Will Cook For Sex"—that he used when he made his famous spaghetti sauce, because no matter what he did, he always seemed to get splatters on his shirt. He couldn't tell what she was making, but he didn't care. She wore six-inch high-heeled shoes. Her long, blond hair cascaded down her back. And underneath that apron, she was bare-assed naked.

Mouth open, Tyler must have stared at her beautiful, curvy bottom for a minute before his dry throat caused him to cough. She whipped her head around, and he caught her ample side-boob.

"Hi, sweetie. Dinner's almost ready."

He tried to speak but couldn't.

"What was that?"

"Um…you're…naked."

She looked down.

"Why yes, yes I am."

"Not that I'm complaining, but why?"

"Preview."

"Of?"

"Of what you are getting by marrying me. Gotta keep you from changing your mind."

"That would never happen."

"Good. Now wash up. It's almost time."

"Do I get naked too?"

"Nope. This isn't about me tonight; it's all about you."

Tyler went into the bedroom and changed as quickly as he could, his mind playing over the firm flesh he had just seen standing in his kitchen. When he re-entered the room, she was sitting at the table, their plates dished and waiting. She no longer wore the apron, but in its place, she wore a red tie. And a smile.

"I didn't realize we were dressing up for dinner. Shall I go put on a tie as well?"

Tabitha smiled. "Nope. Let's eat."

Tyler slid into the chair facing her, never taking his eyes off her body.

"Hey, Mister. My eyes are up here!" She pointed to the emerald-green irises.

"You really can't expect me to focus on your face under these circumstances."

"You act like you've never seen a pair before."

"Oh, I have…just not that particular pair."

"Well, in a few weeks, they will be all yours."

Tyler exhaled deeply. "You know, it's really not nice to tease the animals."

Tabitha laughed. "Maybe not, but it's oh, so much fun!"

After dinner, Tabitha put on Tyler's robe, and they cleaned up the kitchen together. Tabitha put the leftovers away while Tyler cleaned off the dishes and racked them in the dishwasher. Then Tabitha sprayed down the kitchen counters with cleaner and wiped them off.

"It sure is easier to concentrate with you wearing something. What was that about, anyway?"

"Are you complaining?"

"No, Ma'am!"

"Okay then!"

"It just seems so unlike you."

"Just because I want to wait doesn't make me a prude. I have my reasons, but it's not that."

"So, you just wanted to torture me?"

"More like give you a sneak peek of what you are getting yourself into."

"Hopefully over and over."

"If you're good."

After dinner, Tabitha went to get dressed, and Tyler sat on the couch and turned on the TV. The news was on.

…getting reports of another murder, this one in Spring, Texas. Police sources tell us that this murder seems to be connected to the two dozen or so that have been happening all across the United States in the past month. Although police aren't releasing specifics, we are told that each of the victims were missing body parts. The FBI has taken over the investigation. A spokesman…

Tabitha appeared, dressed in a pair of pajamas, and stood between Tyler and the TV.

"Wanna watch a movie?"

"I was just watching this story on the news…people are dying…"

"Depressing stuff…let's watch a comedy."

Tabita grabbed the remote off the couch and brought up Netflix, choosing a newer movie they hadn't seen yet.

"What's with the jammies?"

"Oh, I thought it would be okay with you if I spent the night." She shrugged. "Can I?"

"Of course. But just to be transparent, where will you be sleeping?"

"The bed."

"I see. And where will I be sleeping?"

"The bed."

Tyler's eyebrows shot up.

"No funny business, Mister. You have to wait."

"But this is torture."

"I can leave if you want."

"No. Stay. Please."

"That's what I thought."

CHAPTER FOUR

Tyler opened his eyes and noticed the room was awash with light. He rolled over and looked at the clock. A little after ten a.m. He wasn't used to sleeping so late, but he had needed it.

He then remembered that Tabitha had spent the night, but there was no sign of her in the bedroom, and he could see the adjoining bathroom was empty.

His mind swept back to when they had gone to bed. At first, she had laid on one side of the bed and he on the other. Eventually, he heard her steady, even breathing and he knew she was asleep. Having her right there, but so far away, became too much for him, so he rolled toward her, scooted up against her and held her. He probably would have gotten away with it too, if his body hadn't betrayed him by responding to the feel of her firm buttocks against his groin. He remembered her waking, with a start, and telling him to put it away. Then she compromised and made him roll over, and she played big spoon instead. If he was going to get pokey, she preferred he poke empty air.

He caught her scent on the pillow next to him and

wondered if she had left. Groggily, he got out of bed, opened the bedroom door, and headed into the living room. She wasn't there. A slight breeze caught the white, cotton curtains that covered the sliding door, billowing the bottom out into the room. It was then he heard her voice. She was out on the balcony.

He walked toward the glass door, excited to see his fiancé and hoping she'd let him take her out to breakfast.

"Yes. Less than three weeks. You just need to be patient."

She was on the phone. Tyler stopped in his tracks, wanting to give her some privacy.

"I know we need this one. You've been bitching about it for months. I told you…these things take time."

Tyler cocked his head, wondering what, exactly, Tabitha was talking about. Was she referring to their wedding? Her tone seemed off. Cold. Controlled. It was not the Tabitha he knew.

"I'll give you a status update in a couple of weeks, as we get closer. Yes. Yes, I know. I understand how much is riding on this."

The breeze threw a bigger gust through the open entryway, and the curtains flipped away from the door. He saw Tabitha on the balcony, still dressed in her pajamas, her phone to her ear. The movement of the curtains caught her attention and she turned, spotting Tyler for the first time. A smile spread across her face.

"Anyway, I better go. My honey is awake and I want to spend some time with him. Yes. I understand. Okay, bye."

"Morning, Tabby."

"Morning, sweetie."

"Who was on the phone?"

"Sorry. That was my boss."

"Is everything okay?"

"Yeah. She's just nervous about a deadline."

"Well, do you need to go in?"

"Are you kidding? It's the weekend. She can get lost…I'm not dealing with it until Monday."

Tyler smiled. He had been worried for a second, but her change in tone had most likely been associated with a work call on her day off. He didn't know too much about what her job entailed at the advertising firm she worked at, as she tried to keep work things at work and was reluctant to talk about it when Tyler enquired. Luckily, Tabitha's demeanor seemed to have returned to normal, so he put the conversation he had overheard out of his mind.

"Breakfast?" he asked.

"What are you making me?"

"Nothing. I was hoping you'd let me take you out."

"As long as wherever you take me has strawberry waffles."

"Is there any other kind?"

———

After breakfast, Tabitha left. Tyler shuffled music by his favorite band, Skillet, on his iPhone, and blasted it through his Bugani Bluetooth speaker. He threw a load of laundry in the washing machine and started cleaning the bathroom, knowing he wouldn't have time to do it during the week and wanting to keep a clean place for Tabitha. No way was he going to let her walk into a gross bathroom, or any other part of the apartment.

As he wiped down the mirror, he noticed a smile on his face. He took in his features. Although he had always felt he was average looking, he never felt he was anything special. Certainly, he had lucked out with Tabitha. Never in a million years had he imagined he'd walk into Starbucks to pick up a

Venti Vanilla Latte and get in line behind a Goddess. Even more mind-blowing was when she turned around and started a conversation with him, then, before she left with her Strawberry Acai Refresher with lemonade, she grabbed his phone from his hand, held it to his face to unlock it, went into his contacts, and added her name and number. Then she took it one step further and snapped a picture to add to her contact.

"It's under Tabitha," she had said. "I'll be highly disappointed if you *don't* call."

And with that, she walked out of the store, leaving him staring in disbelief. Things like that never happened to him.

It had taken him three days to get up the nerve to actually call her, for which she had immediately given him a hard time. They had gotten together for a casual dinner that night. Later, they ended up overlooking the bay and somehow, her soft, delicate hand had ended up in his. They'd been a *thing* ever since.

He watched as his smile got even bigger as he recalled the day they met. Maybe she was more than he ever thought he would have, but that didn't mean he didn't deserve her. He did. He was a good guy and he deserved good things. He definitely deserved Tabitha.

When he was done cleaning the bathroom, he moved the laundry over to the dryer and sat down on the couch. Grabbing the remote, he flipped on the TV and flicked through the channels. He stopped on the crime channel he liked and watched the last eighteen minutes of the show that was on, his guts twisting inside. The female victim had been assaulted and kidnapped and then burned alive inside the trunk of her car.

The grisly scene brought his mind back to the murders he had seen on the news…murders and mutilations. Body parts missing. Victims in multiple states. The situation had been nagging at the back of his brain, the thought of a killer traveling the country and committing these heinous acts unfathomable.

Tyler switched off the television and grabbed his laptop off the coffee table. He had to know more. Bringing up a browser, he searched for articles related to the news stories he had seen on TV. It only took a few seconds to find the first one.

When he was done with the first, he read the next, and then another. After six stories, he realized that the details were extremely limited as all of them gave the same information, but nothing more. The authorities were definitely keeping the details close to their chest. The only information available was the number of victims, their locations, and the fact the bodies had been mutilated and were missing body parts. He was unable to find out exactly what body parts were missing.

Looking deeper, Tyler flipped to the second page of results on Google and skimmed the headlines, then the third. A webpage caught his eye and he pulled it up. A murder in Bangkok that, to him, sounded similar. Was it connected? Did the U.S. authorities know about it?

Tyler imagined that a multi-state investigation was difficult, but what if this was actually a worldwide issue? A chill ran up his spine as he rubbed his right temple. Should he call the FBI and tell them about the case in Bangkok? Surely, they would already know about it, right? They were the FBI, after all.

A throbbing in the back of his head mirrored his heartbeat, and his face flushed. Feeling queasy, Tyler pulled off his shoes and laid down on the couch. Before he could make any sense of the situation, he was fast asleep.

CHAPTER FIVE

"Want me to finish packing this cupboard?" Tyler asked.

They were in the kitchen of Tabitha's apartment packing up the last of everything.

"That'd be awesome. Be careful with those glasses, though. They're special to me."

Tyler wrapped each glass in bubble wrap as he placed the contents into the box. They had been working on her apartment for two days and were almost finished packing. Tyler had taken a couple of weeks off work to help her move in and so they could spend some alone time after the wedding. They still hadn't made any plans regarding a honeymoon, but they hoped to slip away for a few days to some beachside vacation rental. Sand, sun, and surf. And sex. Lots of it.

After he had taped the box closed, he wrote what the contents were on the side in black Sharpie.

"Does this one go over to the apartment or in the storage pile?"

"Storage. I figure I'll probably be storing more than I bring over. You only have so much space. One day, if we buy a house, we will have room for both of our things. Your kitchen is pretty well equipped, though, so I really don't need to bring any of this."

"This is so surreal. In a few days, you're going to be my wife. We're going to be living together."

"Yes. That's what most husbands and wives do."

"Ha, ha! Am I the only one who can't wrap my brain around this?"

"Pretty much."

"I never really thought I'd end up married."

"Too late to back out now. I'll get you all trained properly —so you'll be ready for your second wife."

"Yeah, that's a hard pass. I'll stick with one."

"Hopefully you'll still feel that way after we get married."

"Why? Are you keeping secrets from me?" he bantered.

Tabitha smiled. "Oh, you have no idea!"

They finished packing up the kitchen and loaded the last few loose items in a couple spare boxes to take to Tyler's apartment. Tabitha stepped back and took in the piles of boxes stacked around the room.

"I'm going to miss this place a little."

"Hopefully not too much."

"Probably not."

"When are the movers coming?"

"Tomorrow morning. Nine-ish."

"What say we go back to the apartment, take a quick shower, and go grab a bite to eat?"

"That's perfect. I'm starving."

"Me too."

THEY SAT AT A TABLE IN THE BACK CORNER OF THE QUAINT café, both eating BLTs and potato salad. They ate silently, exhausted from the prior few days of packing and cleaning. The silence was interrupted by the waitress, who topped off their glasses of iced tea.

"Okay, so are you crashing at the apartment tonight since your place is pretty much all packed?"

"Yes. No sense in getting a hotel room."

"Works for me."

She gave him a stern look. "No funny business."

"Party pooper. We are getting married the day after tomorrow. Who will know?"

"I'll know."

"I won't tell if you don't."

"Tyler…"

"I know, I know. I'm just being a brat. I've waited this long. I can wait two more days."

"Good. I'm worth it."

"I have no doubt. Anyway, so tomorrow we clear out your apartment and get your stuff over to our place. Then the day after, we are appearing before the Justice of the Peace at what time?"

"Two thirty p.m."

"Okay, so at two thirty, we will tie the knot and then what? Go home? Get a hotel room? Go on a trip?"

"Why don't we go home and then leave the next day? I can book something tonight if you want."

"Perfect. I can't wait to get away and show off my new bride at the same time."

"Oh, there will be no showing me off. Don't even plan on leaving the room."

"Sounds like I better get some rest."

"Not a bad idea. You'll need it."

———

BACK AT THE APARTMENT, THEY TURNED ON THE television and watched a show where crimes were solved through video footage. When it was over, Tabitha grabbed her bag off the floor by the door and headed toward the master bedroom.

"I'm going to get in my jammies, hun."

"Are you coming back out?"

"Of course."

With the show over and Tabitha in the bedroom changing, Tyler turned to the local news channel. He caught the reporter mid-sentence talking about more murders.

...four more bodies were found this morning. Police aren't

releasing the victims' names publicly yet, however, we were able to find out that one of the victims was found in Nampa, Idaho, two in Key West, Florida, and one in San Diego, California. Authorities still believe these and the other victims to all be connected, but they have declined to say how. The FBI is urging anyone with information regarding this string of murders to call their tipline at the number on the bottom of the screen...

Tyler looked up and spotted Tabitha standing at the end of the hallway, in a pair of pink silk pajamas, her eyes glued to the TV.

"You're watching this story again?"

"There were four more murders."

"It's crazy. Thank God we don't have to worry about some killer..."

"Maybe we should be...worried, that is."

"Why? Nothing is happening around here."

"I'm not so sure it matters. Distance doesn't seem to be getting in their way. And did you see? One of the victims was in San Diego. That's pretty close if you ask me."

"It'll all be over soon."

Tyler's eyebrows arched, a puzzled expression on his face.

"What's that supposed to mean?"

"Oh, I just mean that these things happen and then, all of the sudden, they stop...fade into the background, even."

"I don't see this stopping anytime soon. To me, it seems to be ramping up."

"Tyler, I think you are letting the news reports get to you. The media is being irresponsible with this...almost creating panic and chaos."

"I think people need to know this stuff. They need to be ready to protect themselves. Why are you not concerned?"

"I just don't think I'm anybody's intended victim. I lead a pretty boring life."

"But how do you know? What if the victims were chosen at random?"

"We all have to die sometime."

"That's morbid."

"It's reality, Tyler."

"But what about your friends? What about me? What if something happens to one of us?"

"I don't have any close friends. And you know I don't have any family left. All I have is you, and I won't let anything happen to you."

"You're going to protect me?" Tyler gave her a partial smile, trying to hide his amusement.

"You have no idea."

Tyler squinted his eyes at her, unsure how to take her comment.

"Anyway, hun, let's not get all bogged down with that crap. Why don't you go get ready for bed too, and then we can snuggle under a blanket and watch one more movie before we go to sleep?"

"If we watch another movie, we better do it in the bedroom, because I don't think I will make it through another one." He rubbed his right eye as if to back up his claim. "I'm exhausted."

"Works for me."

Tyler got up from the couch, turned off the television, and followed Tabitha into the bedroom. While she propped up her pillows and got in the bed, he went into the bathroom, changed into a pair of basketball shorts, and brushed his teeth.

Back in the bedroom, he slipped into bed beside Tabitha.

"So, I take it that is going to be your side of the bed from now on?" he asked.

"I hadn't really thought about it. This side just felt right."

"Then it's yours."

Tabitha grabbed the remote off the side table and turned on the television.

"What do you want to watch?" she asked.

"There are a few new action movies out."

"Perfect. Any preference?"

"You pick."

Tabitha brought up the guide and searched through the movie channels until she finally found something that looked good.

"How about this one, Ty?"

When he didn't answer, she turned toward him, only to find him already asleep. Smiling, she shut off the TV, slipped her tablet out of her purse, and picked up where she had left off reading *Widow's Point*. Five pages in, the tablet slipped from her fingers and the only noise in the room was the sound of them both breathing.

CHAPTER SIX

Tyler clicked the padlock shut on the storage unit and tugged on it to make sure it was locked.

"Well, that didn't take that long. It's only…"—he looked at his watch—"…two thirty-five. I thought we'd be moving stuff into the evening."

"I don't have *that* much stuff," she said, laughing.

"Still, not bad."

"Then we are pretty much done. I'm not going to unpack the stuff at the apartment until we get back from our mini honeymoon, and I have a cleaning company going in to touch up my old apartment, so we don't have to worry about it. Looks like we have the afternoon off."

"Maybe we can get some rest and pack for our trip. Oh, shit. Did we ever book anything?" Tyler asked.

Tabitha looked sheepish. "I totally forgot to look last night, and I passed out not too long after you did. I'll book something when we get home. Then we can pack. And then we can rest up for tomorrow. It's a pretty big day."

"Yeah, it is. A wedding. OUR wedding. And a trip with you? It doesn't get any better. Plus, I'm so damn glad to be away from that stress pit they label as a job."

"You can forget all about that place, baby. Just you and me now."

BACK AT THE APARTMENT, TABITHA TOOK A QUICK SHOWER and changed into some shorts and a white tank top. She grabbed her laptop, propped some pillows up on the bed, and made herself comfortable.

"I'm going to grab a quick shower as well, Tabby."

"Sounds good. I'll just be here researching places to go for our trip. Do you want to have a say in where we go, or shall I surprise you?"

Tyler's face lit up. "Yes, I'd love to keep it as a surprise."

"Okay, then when you get out of the bathroom, you can go watch TV, or something, in the other room. I don't want you peeking over my shoulder."

"Do you really think I'd do that?"

"Absolutely. Am I wrong?"

Tyler gave a sly smile. "Probably not."

"GO!" Tabitha pointed toward the bathroom.

Tyler started the water, stripped out of his dirty clothes, and climbed in the shower. The jets of water felt good on his back, and as soon as he was used to the temperature, he made it a little hotter. Sticking his head under the stream, he let the heat drain his tiredness away.

His mind ran back through the conversation he and Tabitha had about the murders earlier. She didn't seem concerned at all, which perplexed him. Besides their wedding, it was the only thing on his mind, and even though she wasn't worried, *he* was.

When the water started getting cold, he turned off the valves and grabbed his towel, drying off in the shower before stepping out on the mat.

Multiple victims all over the country.

He ran the towel back over his head to dry his hair a little more.

Each victim was missing at least one body part.

He stepped to the mirror and grabbed a comb off the vanity.

Which body part? Why was it such a secret?

Wearing a fresh set of clothes, Tyler exited the bathroom, kissed Tabitha on the forehead, and headed toward the living room.

"See you a little later, hun."

"Okay. I'll let you know when the trip is booked, in case you want to hang out in here after."

"Deal."

Tyler left the room and turned on the television, but his attention wasn't on the show. Fifteen minutes later, he grabbed his laptop from the side table and booted it up. There had to be more information out there somewhere.

He started with Google and found several articles on the murders. None of them told him any more than he already knew. He looked deeper. One article was more of an opinion piece, which talked about this huge conspiracy against the

American people. The article had a link to a small online blog. He scanned through the paragraphs looking for anything he didn't already know. Then he spotted it.

…and although no one will confirm it, I firmly believe the body parts missing from the victims are their brains. I won't give away my source, but one of the investigation team for the Spring, Texas, murder personally told me the brain had been removed. What kind of sicko kills people and steals their brains? Did I ask if any other body parts were missing? Hell yes, I did, and the answer was a resounding "NO." That tells me only one thing. Every single one of these victims—which law enforcement themselves have labeled as connected—are missing their brains. They have to be. If you weren't creeped the fuck out before, I bet you are now…

Tyler brought his trembling hand to his forehead and then raked it through his hair. If this information was correct, it was worse than he thought. While many serial killers took trophies, brains were not one that commonly hit the list. What was the killer doing with them? Storing them? Eating them? He shuddered.

"All booked."

Tyler looked over to find Tabitha standing in the doorway to the living room.

"Exciting!" he muttered.

"Are you okay, Tyler? You're white as a ghost."

"Yeah, I'm good. Just exhausted," he lied.

"Why don't we go to bed and get some rest? We can pack in the morning or even after we get married. It's only a two-hour drive to our destination, so there is no pressure."

Tyler took a deep breath and closed his laptop. "That sounds like a good idea. We need a little shut-eye."

As Tyler brushed his teeth, Tabitha came into the bathroom. "Are you sure you're okay? You seem…well, for lack of a better way to explain it, *off*."

Tyler paused for a moment, debating whether he should tell Tabitha what he found. He knew she didn't worry about the murders as much as he did, and he didn't want to go through another conversation about it, so he decided to keep it to himself.

"Yeah, babe, I'm good. I think it just hit me all at once."

"Okay, but if you want to talk about it, let me know."

"I will. Promise."

Tabitha bit her bottom lip and looked away. "You still want to marry me tomorrow, don't you?"

This time, there was no hesitation. "More than anything in the world."

"I was hoping that'd be your answer." She smiled and exited the bathroom, returning to the bedroom.

When he climbed into bed, Tabitha was on her side, still wearing her pajamas, the covers pulled up to her waist. He got himself situated, facing away from her, before reaching up and clicking off the bedside lamp. Only a few seconds went by before he felt her roll over and snuggle up against him.

"Tomorrow night, *I* play big spoon," he said.

"Looking forward to it!"

In the dark, he laid awake, listening to the silence, and then, after a few minutes, Tabitha's steady breathing. She was asleep. The murders returned to his thoughts—the brains. Or rather the lack thereof. He couldn't shake the feeling of dread that crept up his spine. Was he in danger? Was Tabitha?

Finally, exhaustion took over, and Tyler could feel himself slipping over the edge into the deep, dark pool of sleep.

———

THE DREAM WAS NOT SOMETHING HE HAD EVER experienced before. At least not that he ever remembered after waking up. He clawed at the bedsheets as she moved her body up and down, riding him, slowly at first, and then faster, faster. Her breath came out in quick, furious exhalations, a low moan escaping the back of her throat. As she neared climax, he felt her speed quicken and her breathing grow ragged. And then it happened. Her body stiffened, and then shuddered, as she came, the sounds emitting from her mouth loud and guttural. A side of Tabitha he had not been aware of. Except this was only a dream. Obviously, a premonition that his mind conjured up in anticipation of what their wedding night would be like. Or at least he hoped. And then it was over. She slid off of him, rolled back onto her side, and immediately fell back asleep. That was when he realized *he* wasn't. He was wide awake.

Reaching down, he touched himself to make sure. He was still erect. And he was covered in remnants of her. Rubbing the back of his neck, he couldn't sort out what had just happened. Tabitha was against sleeping together before marriage. Even the night before. Yet she had just ridden him hard. She had used him for her own pleasure and hadn't even given him a chance to be satisfied. And then she rolled over and went back to sleep. None of it made any sense.

He reached around in the bed and found his pajama bottoms curled up in a ball. He still wore the top. Extending his fingers, he felt her bare back. He lightly ran his fingers up her spine and felt only skin. Tracing the vertebrae down her back, he felt her tailbone, and then his hand brushed her bare buttocks. She was completely naked. And it hadn't been a dream. She had taken him. He didn't even know how to feel about it. And then he realized his hand was still on her butt. He paused for a moment and considered removing it out of respect, but then he remembered what she had just done to him, so he cupped her left cheek in his hand. She stirred.

"Um, Tyler?" she mumbled.

"Yeah, hun?"

"Why is your hand on my ass?"

"The better question is why is your ass bare."

He felt her jolt, and then she patted herself down. Panicked, she asked, "Where are my clothes? Oh my God, what did you do? Please tell me you didn't."

"Oh, I didn't."

"Then why am I…"

"Because *you* did."

"Huh?"

"You don't remember?"

"No."

Tyler grabbed her hand and guided it between her legs.

"OH! Holy shit!"

"Yup."

"Did we?"

"Sort of."

Tabitha sat up straight in the bed. "What do you mean, 'sort of'?"

"I thought I was dreaming, but it turns out I wasn't. I woke up with you riding me. And it was all about you."

"Oh, no. This is terrible."

"Thanks for the ego boost," he replied sarcastically.

Tabitha flicked on the lamp, on her side of the bed, and pulled the covers up over her breasts.

"You don't understand, Tyler. This is worse than you could ever imagine."

"Still hurtful."

"It's not that I don't want to have sex with you. If I could have, I would have, from the day I met you."

"Yeah, yeah, but we weren't married."

"Exactly."

"Yet tonight, that didn't matter to you."

"This wasn't me. I don't know what happened. I'm so sorry!"

"Don't be." Tyler blushed. "It was actually kind of hot."

"That's not helping!"

"I'm not sure what to say besides there's no going back. We might as well do it again, so maybe this time *I* can enjoy it too!"

"Really, Ty? That's your way of dealing with this? Suggesting we do it again?"

Tyler looked at the clock. "It's 1:23 a.m. It's our wedding day."

"Semantics."

"Okay, Tabby. What do you want me to say? It happened. I didn't do it. I'm not sure how to make this better for you. Frankly, I'm not even sure why you're making such a big deal of this."

"You wouldn't understand."

"Then explain—"

Tabitha's cell phone started ringing. She glanced at the display and her shoulders slumped.

"Oh, shit."

"Who is it?"

"My boss."

"Today? Now?"

"It's gotta be urgent or she wouldn't be calling right now. I have to get this."

Tyler just watched, his right hand rubbing the back of his neck.

"Hello?…Hi, Ivy. What can I do for you?…You do know it's the middle of the night, right?…I didn't say you were stupid…Can it wait?…We've got so much going on today, and we're leaving for a trip…It's not what you think…Okay… Yes…I understand…Hopefully we can make it quick…Okay, see you in thirty minutes."

Tabitha clicked off the phone.

"You're going to work now? In the middle of the night?"

"There's a huge issue with one of our accounts, and I need to fix something before we take off. I promise it won't take long."

"Why don't we swing by there in the morning? Before the ceremony?"

"You heard me ask if it could wait, right?"

"Yes. But—"

"But my boss is a hardass. If I don't go in, I'll be in deep shit. Just go back to sleep, Tyler. I'll be back before you know it."

"Doesn't sound like I have a choice."

"Neither do I."

"Fine. Go. Just be safe."

CHAPTER SEVEN

A noise in the other room brought Tyler partially out of his slumber. The front door. Tabby was home. He let himself slip back into the inky murk of sleep, knowing she would join him in a few minutes. Fifteen minutes later, he stirred and reached for her on her side of the bed. It was still empty. Maybe he had imagined her coming home.

"Tabby?" he called, weakly.

"I'm here," she whispered, her voice wavering. She was standing at the foot of the bed.

He was alert now. "You okay?"

"No. Not really."

"What's going on? Come lay down and talk to me."

The room remained silent. He could barely make out her silhouette in the shadows. She remained at the foot of the bed. Tyler reached for the lamp switch, and the room became washed in the soft light. Startled, his breath caught in his throat and an involuntary whimper escaped.

She stood, naked, at the foot of the bed, her right hand behind her back.

"Why are you naked?"

She shook her head.

"Tab? What's going on?"

She stared at him, moisture forming in the corner of her eyes.

"You're scaring me, damnit!"

"Blood," she finally said.

"What about blood?"

"I have to keep it off my clothes."

Tyler's eyes widened, and a shriek tore from his throat when she brought her right hand from behind her back. It no longer resembled a hand. He thought of talons, but there were ten of them, about six inches long, a dark red hue at the bottom, tapering to a bright white at the tips.

Tyler scooted back against the headboard and pulled the covers up to his chin, his eyes wide.

"What the fuck, Tabitha? What is that? What are you?"

"I'm so sorry."

"Sorry? What's going on?" His voice was two octaves too high.

"I told you we had to wait."

"But we didn't."

"No, we didn't, and unfortunately, the bosses didn't like that."

"What the fuck does your boss have to do with this?"

"I'm really sorry," she repeated, moving toward the bed, the talons extended.

"STOP!" Tyler yelled, holding his hand up, as if the motion had the power to keep her at bay. "Are you going to kill me?"

Tabitha hesitated. "I don't want to."

"Then why would you?"

"It's the way things are."

"For my brains?" he asked, throwing caution to the wind.

Tabitha's posture buckled. "Brains?"

Tyler nodded.

"How did you know?"

"I'm a fairly smart guy."

"Which is why we're in this predicament."

"Huh?"

"It's your brains that made you a target."

"What are you?" Tyler asked.

Tabitha shook her head again. "We need people like you."

"Who is we?"

Again, she shook her head.

"What is going on, Tabitha?"

"There's a reason I would not have sex with you. By doing so, I would be sealing your fate."

"How? I don't understand."

"It's what my species does."

"Your species? What are you?"

"Not human."

"Are you kidding me? I was going to marry you. And you aren't even fucking human?"

"No, but I am more loving than most humans."

"But you're going to kill me anyway?"

"I have to."

"Why?"

"It's why we came to earth. To harvest the smartest minds and take them back to our planet, to help repair our environment. Our planet is dying. In our culture, when we sleep with a man, he must die. The collection of brains is a fairly new development."

"So, you were using me this entire time?"

"No. I tried to stop it. I didn't have sex with you, because I love you. I wanted us to be together."

"But it's inevitable that we would have had sex sometime. What then?"

"Anyone we marry is exempt. You would have been spared. That's why we needed to wait."

"Why me?"

"Don't you get it? You are one of the smartest men on the planet. Have you ever checked your IQ? Probably what you call Mensa. We need experts in the fields of medical, engineering, metaphysics, science, and information technology, amongst other areas. I was sent for you. I was supposed to get your brain months ago. I kept stalling, telling them you wouldn't sleep with me. They kept telling me to try harder. They caught wind of our wedding. They controlled me last night while I was sleeping. They made me have sex with you. Then they summoned me to make sure I understood the repercussions if I didn't kill you, get your brain, and get back to the ship."

"Ship? You mean like a boat, right? You can't possibly mean…"

"I said no. They threatened me…told me that if I didn't carry out my mission, they would kill me in front of you and then kill you."

Tyler stared at her, unable to speak. Finally, the words found their way from his lips.

"So, what are you going to do?"

"What I have to."

"I'm going to die?"

"Not if I can help it."

"How can you stop this? If you don't kill me, we'll both be dead."

Her mind made up, Tabitha held out her hand, which was no longer a set of talons.

"Get dressed. There is much to do."

———

WITHIN FIVE MINUTES, THEY WERE IN THE CAR AND exiting the parking structure.

"I hate to ask this, but how do I know you aren't taking me to them?"

Tabitha glanced over at Tyler, who was driving. His face was partially illuminated by the dash lighting.

"If I wanted you dead, you'd already be dead."

"But aren't you putting yourself at risk?"

"Yes."

"While I'm grateful, I don't want anything to happen to you. Although, I'm going to be honest, I don't know what the fuck to think right now or how to feel. Everything I thought I knew was wrong. Everything we had seems like a sham."

"I am so sorry I deceived you, Tyler. It was never my intention. You were strictly a job at first. And then you weren't. Everything changed for me in that instant, and I've been trying to figure out how to deal with it ever since."

He turned and looked at her. "Do you truly love me?"

"I meant everything I said. I still do," she said.

"I'm confused. The you I thought I knew doesn't exist. I don't even know if this is what you look like." The thought immediately registered with him, and he blinked several times, his mouth hanging open. Finally, he spoke again. "Is *this* what you really look like?"

Tabitha looked down at her knees. "No," she whispered.

"Show me your true form."

"It's not that simple."

"I have to know."

"We really don't have a true form."

"I don't understand."

"We've always just adapted to whatever life form we are around, which has been thousands over the years. It's not like you see in the movies where an alien mimics a human but later turns back into their true alien form. We don't have any such form we revert to. I will look like this until we encounter a different species and I adapt my form to be like theirs. Although this isn't what I've always looked like, it's what I look like as a human being."

Tyler drove in silence as he digested everything she said. Finally, he spoke. "So, have you ever been hideous in any of your forms? Like, was I supposed to marry the creature from the black lagoon who is hiding in a gorgeous skin suit?"

"Please," she said, letting out a soft laugh. "I'm not sure of the reference, but I can tell you I'm no creature, and I'm far from hideous. My human form is representative of the being I am, inside and out."

"Good to know." He pointed to the road in front of them. "Do you want to tell me where we are going?"

"Just keep driving. I'm trying to figure that out."

"Why don't we just head to the airport and hop a plane to somewhere far away, where they can't find us?"

"Unfortunately, that's nowhere. You know how the victims have been from all over the globe? The ship can travel to anywhere on this planet within minutes. When they identify a new donor, they travel there, drop off another being like me, and they do what they need to do. Apparently, I'm the only one who can't follow directives."

"I have to say, I'm pretty happy about that. Anyway, what about going into hiding?"

"Also impossible. The mothership can track all Brielle… that's what our species is called. They always know where we are. It's sort of like your GPS."

"Then it sounds like we're screwed," he said numbly.

When Tabitha didn't respond, Tyler looked over at the passenger seat.

"You okay?"

"Yeah. I just had an idea."

"Care to share?"

"No time. Just keep driving around until I can nail down a location." She started entering information into her iPhone.

"Is whatever you're thinking going to work?"

Tabitha looked at him. "God, I hope so."

CHAPTER EIGHT

Tabitha and Tyler walked out of the little bungalow on Bosworth Street in Miraloma Park. They turned around to say goodbye to the man that hung back just inside the doorway, and then Tabitha approached him and wrapped her arms around him, giving him a big hug.

Back at the car, they climbed inside and Tyler started it.

"Where now?"

"I think we need to go into the belly of the beast," she said.

"You mean…"

"Yes. They won't stop looking for us. Maybe we just need to go to them. Maybe we can talk our way out of this."

Tyler glanced at her. "How confident are you that they will listen?"

"Seventeen percent."

"That's it? So you feel there is an eighty-three percent chance that we may die?" he asked, incredulously.

"At least one of us. Maybe both of us."

"And I suppose *I'm* the 'one of us' you're talking about?"

"Sadly, yes, but I wouldn't take you there if I felt there was any other way."

"Even though you're at seventeen percent?"

"Even though."

"Gee, thanks. I'm not feeling good about the odds."

"Unfortunately, they're the best odds we have. If they track us down, they won't even listen to what I have to say."

"You realize I'm putting my life in your hands, right?"

"I do. And I will do everything in my power not to let you down."

Tyler sighed. "Is this what they mean by 'til death do us part?"

"Try to stay positive."

"I'm trying. Anyway, where do I drive to? I can't sit here all night."

"Just move. Anywhere is fine. I will text my boss and let her know I need to see her. She'll tell us where to go. The ship is constantly moving."

"Where do they…park it? Is that the right word? Maybe land it? Does it have an invisibility cloak to keep people from seeing it?"

Tabitha looked up from her phone after sending off the text. "You've seen way too many movies."

"I'm not sure I have anything else to make assumptions off of."

"They don't bring it down into the atmosphere. Basically, they stay out of sight."

"Then how do your people get from the ship to earth?"

"We transport."

"Like in *Star Trek*?"

"Again, you and your movies and television. But I guess it's kind of like that—not with us breaking into particles and rematerializing, but more like we just appear. Obviously, we try to do so in unoccupied areas."

Tabitha's phone chimed. She pulled up the message.

"She's telling me to go back to the parking garage of the apartment and wait in the car."

"Does she know I'm with you?"

"Yeah. She said to bring you too."

"What do you want to do?"

"Follow her instructions."

"We're fucked."

Back at the complex, Tyler opened the automatic gate and pulled into the parking garage, parking in his designated space.

"What am *I* supposed to do?" he asked.

"Just follow my lead."

They sat in silence, craning their necks around, watching for someone to materialize, trying to trace down every stray noise.

Tabitha's car door was yanked open without warning, and when Tyler whipped his head around, he saw another beautiful woman standing there, this one a redhead.

"Get out," the redhead demanded, her tone low and serious.

Tabitha glanced over at Tyler, nodded, and got out of the car. He followed suit.

"You are in some serious shit. We're all going onboard." She glanced over at Tyler. "Him too."

"I can explain…" Tabitha said.

"Save it for now. The others will want to hear what you have to say."

"This wasn't her fault," Tyler piped in.

The redhead turned toward him. "You're the last person who should be talking right now. You're merely an asset."

Tyler tried to say something and found his voice was silent. He could not speak.

The lights in the garage suddenly darkened, and Tyler could barely make out the two women's faces by the glow of the red "exit" lighting. Seconds later, it was replaced by a glowing, purplish hue that seemed to come from everywhere and nowhere at all. The color twisted through the blackness, the light bright enough to cause him to squint. Then he saw the silhouettes of two figures filter through the glow, and the area they were in brightened.

Tyler looked around, not able to ascertain where they were. The walls appeared to be in flux, not really solid, yet they appeared to maintain their flatness. They were blank, no markings, no equipment or fixtures. The room, if you could call it that, was enormous, and he could not make out a ceiling. It was more like a chamber of some sort. The two figures stood before him, human shaped, androgynous, wearing white jumpsuits.

"Is this the one?" Jumpsuit One asked.

"Yes," the redhead, Ivy, said.

Jumpsuit Two remained silent, standing stiff, as if on watch.

"You did not follow your directive. You have proven yourself a liability," Jumpsuit One said. It stared at Tabitha.

Tyler looked from Tabitha, to Ivy, to the jumpsuits, his voice still unable to emit sound. Unsure of what to do, he watched.

"This one is different," Tabitha said.

"Do you really think you are the first one to fall for an

asset?" Jumpsuit One asked. "It has happened before. Those who violated their directives were dealt with swiftly."

"This is on me. Let him go."

"Are you forgetting your mission? He is one of the brightest minds on this planet. We need him to fix our own. Whether or not you followed your directive, he is still an asset we need, and now that he is here, we will take care of what you should have done months ago."

Tyler tried to take a step forward, but his movements were instantly locked, as if an invisible hand held him in place. With no voice and no power to move, he blinked his eyes and watched the scene unravel.

"I'm not forgetting the mission. I'm telling you, this one is better for us alive. Don't you dare lay a hand on him."

Ivy jumped back into the conversation. "We spoke many times during your mission. While the others were carrying out their directives, you had nothing but excuses about how you had to wait…how he would not have sex with you. I mean, look at you. How could you adopt a look like that and not be able to get the asset to fuck you? What happened to you? You used to be one of our best."

"I still am. But things have changed."

"What's changed is you've gone soft," Ivy said. "I should have pulled you off of this detail months ago and took care of it myself." She walked over to Tyler and lifted his chin with her right pointer finger. "I bet you would have tapped this ass," she said, turning her body sideways and smacking herself on the rear. "I would have had you in the sack, and then had your brain in Raptoplasm, before your body turned cold." She looked him in the eyes. "And you would have thanked me for it."

"He wouldn't want you. He's got me."

"Well, congratulations on prolonging his death," Jumpsuit

One said, "but we're out of time. Our planet won't last more than another couple of years at this rate." Turning to Jumpsuit Two, it said, "Strip him and get him ready for Ivy."

Ivy smiled and turned toward Tabitha. "Looks like I get him after all. You lose."

Jumpsuit Two grabbed Tyler and pulled him down on a couch that seemed to materialize out of the floor. Reaching for the button on Tyler's jeans, it unbuttoned them and started pulling them off, Ivy watching in delight as she licked her lips.

Tabitha moved so quickly that Ivy had no time to prepare for the collision. Tabitha smashed into her so hard that the momentum bowled Jumpsuit Two off its feet as well. As Tabitha was getting to her feet to go to Tyler, an arm wrapped around her neck and put her in a chokehold.

"Enough of this little circus," Jumpsuit One said, pulling its arm tighter against Tabitha's throat. "We don't have time to deal with this. We will take his brain, but you must be dealt with as well. I wasn't quite sure what to do with you, but you just sealed your own fate. You're a liability. You must be exterminated."

Still unable to move, Tyler watched in horror as the being's pointer finger turned into a talon-like blade, blood red with a white tip. Just as the tip pierced the flesh of Tabitha's neck, a loud shout reverberated through the chamber.

"STOP!"

All activity in the chamber halted, and all eyes turned toward the figure that floated into the room, seemingly from nowhere. It's hair was pure white, the face wrinkled beyond what any living being's should be. It wore a red robe with gold ropes around its neck that ended in tassels.

"EXPLAIN," the voice bellowed.

"She has not followed her directive. She has turned against us. She must perish," Jumpsuit One said nervously.

"BY WHOSE AUTHORITY?"

"M…mine," Jumpsuit One stuttered.

"YOU FEEL ONE OF OUR OWN MUST DIE?"

"Yes, Jandor."

"VERY WELL."

Jandor outstretched a hand, fingers lifted into the air. Jumpsuit One levitated off the ground and hung suspended from mid-air.

"DO YOU STILL FEEL ONE MUST DIE?"

"No…no, Jandor. Please. No."

"TOO LATE."

Jandor contorted the fingers on its right hand, and Jumpsuit One started to glow. Tyler had to look away as the light was blinding. The body shriveled up into a ball the size of a walnut, dimmed, grew bright again, and then exploded into particles of dust that showered the room. Tyler clamped his eyes and mouth shut and turned his head.

"ANYONE ELSE FEEL SHE SHOULD DIE?" Jandor looked at Tabitha and then glared at Ivy. Ivy rapidly shook her head.

"Come here, my child," Jandor summoned, the rumbling of the voice now gone, replaced by a more subdued whisper.

Tabitha approached Jandor.

"You have broken your covenant."

"Yes, Jandor," Tabitha said meekly.

"You shall not die, but you will no longer be able to work on this mission. You shall return home and work in the labs."

Tabitha nodded. "And him?" She glanced over at Tyler.

"Nothing has changed. We need his brain. He must be sacrificed for the good of our planet."

"Please, Jandor. He is better for us alive."

"It cannot be so, my child. Are you forgetting you slept with him? It is our way."

"Jandor, it is also our way that they will be spared if we marry them."

"But you never married him. You slept with him the night before you were supposed to. I know this, for it is so."

Tabitha lifted her left hand and wiggled her ring finger. "Respectfully, that is incorrect. We got married a couple of hours ago. He is my husband, and you must spare him. I love him."

Jandor was silent, the new information marinating. Then Tabitha heard the words she was dreading. "You were not married at the time you had relations. Therefore, a wedding won't save him." Jandor nodded at Jumpsuit Two, who took Tabitha's arm and held her, the grip like that of a vice. "Ivy, take him to the Fereal chamber. Tell them to move him to the front of production."

Unable to control his body, Tyler watched helplessly as Ivy led him out of the room. He turned toward Tabitha, a tear sliding from his right eye.

"I love you, Tabby. No matter what. Thanks for a great six months."

If Tabitha was capable of crying, she would have as well. "I'm so sorry, Tyler. Please forgive me. I love you too. Thanks for making me your wife." Her voice quavered.

With that, she watched Ivy lead Tyler out of the room, and once he was gone, Jumpsuit Two dragged her from the room.

Back in her quarters, unable to leave, she dry heaved and buried her face in her hands. For a moment, she was human. She had loved and been happy. She had everything she never knew she was missing. And she would spend the next five thousand years regretting the one hundred things she could have done differently.

EPILOGUE

Tabitha entered the most current findings into the massive computer system in the lab. It had been three months since the incident on the ship. It had taken them two weeks, earth time, to get back to their planet. With the harvesting of minds completed, Earth was of no further use to them. In total, they had gathered forty-seven brains, each suspended in Rapto-plasm, and hooked up by nests of intricate wiring to the mainframe.

She thought back to the time she and Tyler had on Earth. It had been perfect. Those memories were something she would cherish for the rest of her life.

A movement from the other side of the lab caught her eye.

"Hey, Tabitha. I was going to grab some lunch. Want to join me?"

"That sounds great, Sasha, but could we do it tomorrow? I'm going home for lunch…maybe take a quick nap."

"Sure thing. Catch you then."

Looking at the clock on the wall, Tabitha took her lab coat off and hung it on the back of the door. She lived five minutes away, and the thought of climbing between the satin sheets and closing her eyes made her feel giddy.

Although homes on her planet were designed very differently from those on earth, she had been able to decorate to make her place resemble Tyler's apartment. It made her feel at home. She smiled as she recalled the memories again. Earth had been more of a home to her than her planet had ever been.

She slid out of her blouse and slacks and left them in a pile on the floor. Her bra and underwear followed, and she slid her smooth body between the equally smooth sheets. She stretched her toes out and propped her head up with her fingers laced behind her hair. Her breathing steadied as she relaxed, thinking about Tyler. Her thoughts were interrupted as the bathroom door opened.

"Been here long?" she asked.

"I just got here a few minutes before you."

"Well? What are you waiting for?"

Tyler eyed the clothes strewn across the bedroom floor and pulled off his robe.

"I love these *lunches* we seem to be having more and more of lately."

"Beats a dry sandwich."

"Seems like a pretty legit diet," he joked. "Skip the food and burn calories instead."

"And to think you made me wait six months! You should have proposed on the first date!"

"Hindsight," he said.

Tyler slipped into bed, and their hands found, and explored, each other. Afterward, wrapped together, they slipped into a sex coma and napped.

Later, the alarm on Tabitha's bedside table went off, and she begrudgingly pulled herself out of bed and slipped into her clothes.

"Wake up, sleepyhead," she teased, playfully kicking him with her foot.

"But I don't wanna go back to work," he grumbled, his voice muffled by the sheets.

"But you have to."

"Give me one good reason why." He blinked a few times and stretched his eyes open.

"Because, if I hadn't broken out of my room, found Jandor, and convinced it that we needed someone with your smarts to run the program, you'd be another brain in a jar. Knowledge is great, but it can only get us so far. If it feels like you weren't the right choice, it might change its mind."

Tyler sat up. "Do you always have to make so much sense? Damn you!"

"It's what I do."

"That, and what you just did…which, by the way, was amazing."

"I figure I have a lot of making up to do. I almost got you killed."

"Why, yes. Yes, you did. You might be making it up to me for the rest of your life."

Tabitha bit her lip and smiled. "I can live with that."

REUNITED

CHAPTER ONE

"One hundred–dollar bid, now one-fifty, now one-fifty, who will give me one-fifty? One-fifty bid, now two. Now two hundred…two hundred, who will give me two hundred…"

"One seventy-five!"

"I have one seventy-five, one seventy-five. Who'll give me two hundred…two hundred…I have one seventy-five going once…twice…and SOLD to the little lady in the purple shirt!"

"YES!" Carly yelled as the other hopefuls gave her varied looks from indignance to daggers. Although only her second time attending storage locker auctions, she had learned from her mistakes her first time and scored three different lockers this round. With the third locker being the last auction of the day, she paid up, placed her own lock on the final unit, and jumped in her truck to grab lunch.

As she parked her rig and went in to order at a nearby fast food restaurant, Carly planned the triage of her three units. It was late afternoon, and she only had forty-eight hours to clean out all three lockers, so she would need to get going. While she could easily come back the next day and pick up where she left off if she ran out of time—or steam—she preferred to get everything cleaned out all at once.

Not one to waste time, Carly ate on the way back and pulled her twenty-eight-foot enclosed cargo trailer up past the first unit.

Taking the lock off, she slid open the door and remembered why she had wanted this unit so badly. While she had no idea what was in the boxes and totes, she noticed how organized and uniform they were. All the boxes were the same size, were all stacked neatly, and were all turned the same direction. Someone gave a shit about the contents of this unit, and for whatever reason, they abandoned it and stopped paying the bill. Now it was hers.

Rather than start opening boxes now, and potentially put herself in a position that she would not get the units all emptied today, she grabbed her utility dolly out of the trailer, slid it under the first stack, and tilted it back, pulling the heavy stack up the ramp of the trailer and depositing it in the front. Methodically, she emptied out the first unit, her willpower beating out her curiosity.

As she worked, she thought about how her life had changed so much two years ago. One single event and her life would never be the same again. One event that started a cataclysmic waterfall of the end of life as she knew it. A ten-year career gone up in flames. Her husband of eight years gone—just walked out the door and never came back.

For over a year, she lived in one of the darkest holes she could never have imagined existed. The grip of depression held her so tight that she didn't know how to escape its grasp. She contemplated doing the unthinkable. Then, one morning, everything changed. When she opened her eyes to the sun filtering through the leaf-patterned curtains, she felt a spark. Like the fight in her had been re-engaged. Like suddenly, the life that had almost taken hers pushed her to fight again. To live again. To be happy again.

Within a week, she had cleaned up the modest three-bedroom home that had turned into a shithole during her depression. She washed the piles of dirty clothes and dishes. She got her hair done and even started wearing makeup again.

A cursory look at her bank account left her surprised that she still had around forty-eight thousand dollars left—more than she thought she would have after more than a year of not bothering to check the balance and not caring what happened to her. The only good news around her husband walking out was that he left everything behind, except a suitcase full of clothes and the five thousand dollars in an envelope they kept hidden in the bottom of the dresser drawer for emergencies.

As she swept out the first unit and slid the door shut, she smiled. She loved what she did, and it allowed her the flexibility to work when she wanted at a pace that worked for her. Although she was trying to get her life back to something that resembled normal, many days, the pain crept back in and she had to spend a day or two fighting to pull herself back up out of the emotional mire that consumed her.

Buying the contents of storage lockers at auction and selling the items for profit wasn't something she had experience in, when her life had been more traditional. It was during her dark days, where she laid in bed all day long with her blackout curtains pulled tight, that she began to binge watch episodes of *Storage Wars*, both old and new. There was something about what the stars of the show did that intrigued her. It was like a treasure hunt to her. It was when she chose to pull herself out of her fog and go on with life that she decided she would try her hand at it rather than go back to a traditional job. She took a huge chunk of the money that was left and bought a cargo trailer to pull behind the Dodge Ram she already owned. It wasn't long before she bought her first two storage lockers and made an agreement with a local secondhand store that would buy the sellable items from her for half of what they felt they could sell them for. Of course, anything of higher value, she would sell herself.

She pulled up to the second and third units, which happened to be almost across from each other. After removing the locks, she rolled up both doors and started the process of loading the items into the trailer. She thought about the measly three hundred dollars she had made for the first two units she had purchased before. She had paid way too much for the units, and she knew it before she even went through the locker's contents, but she had gotten caught up in the excitement. This time, she was more observant and felt confident she would turn a decent profit.

As Carly loaded the last boxes in the trailer, she noticed the sun was sitting low in the sky. She swept both units out, slid down the metal doors, secured the trailer, and slid behind the wheel of her truck. She would just make it home by dusk. Sorting through the contents would have to wait until the next day—something she was anxiously anticipating.

CHAPTER TWO

Carly carried a box of trash to the dumpster that she kept on the side of her house. After the first two units she had purchased, she learned quickly that one man's treasure is another man's—or woman's—trash. She estimated that a quarter of everything she pulled out of those units had not been sellable, so she had ordered the dumpster as a permanent addition to her home and business.

This time was no exception. Carly had unloaded and sorted a quarter of the contents of the trailer, and so far, she had dumped six boxes of crap: a dented toaster, a stained set of bedsheets, a portable commode that was obviously used. All things that exactly no one would be lining up to buy.

Still, for all of the crap she found, the treasures outweighed those items significantly. Her biggest scores, so far, had been an expensive set of golf clubs, seven boxes of old comic books that appeared to be mint and in protective sleeves, and a five-gallon glass water dispenser bottle full of coins that she estimated might be worth the amount she had paid for all three lockers combined. With plenty more items to go through, she knew that she would come out way ahead on these units.

Methodically, Carly brought one box at a time off the trailer, placed it on the sorting tables she had set up in her garage, and worked through them. Clothes were placed in plastic bins with other clothes. Small appliances were placed on shelves over in the corner. Bigger items were staged along the far wall. She brought a bulkier box off the trailer, set it on the table, and opened it. Clothes.

Finding boxes of clothes was the last thing Carly hoped for when she went through her newly acquired items. They really held little to no value, and she would typically sell them to the store for a few dollars per box. Even then, she still had to sort through them and make sure they were sellable. She certainly didn't want to put her arrangement with the secondhand store at risk.

She started pulling out the clothing, one item at a time. Little girl's clothing. Possibly for a five-year-old. Carly froze. Memories came flooding back, and she shoved the items back in the box, closing the flaps as quickly as she could. Tears flooded her face, and she had to walk away and go inside the house. She sat on the couch and bawled, until there were no more tears left in her.

In the kitchen, Carly made a cup of tea and tried to calm down. She thought she was moving on with her life, but there was no way to move on when the pain was still so fresh.

Back in the garage, she tentatively stared at the box. She could dump it in one of the clothes bins without going through it, toss it in the dumpster, or face her demons and open the box. It seemed like an hour before she finally made up her mind. She approached it, opened the flaps, and dumped the contents on the table.

Small pairs of pants in different colors and different patterns. An array of shoes, sandals, and little boots. Carly sniffled and dug through the contents. A patterned dress with flowers and butterflies. Her breath caught in her throat. The dress was exactly like one Gracie used to have. A lump formed in her throat as she remembered her beautiful, bubbly, five-year-old daughter.

CHAPTER THREE

Gracie was everything to Carly and her husband, Brian. After years of being told she would not be able to have children and against all odds, Gracie was conceived. When she was born, she was perfect and healthy in every way.

As a baby, Gracie was happy and rarely fussy. Brian and Carly had multiple conversations about how they had lucked out—how God had been looking out for them and had saved the most special one just for them. As Gracie started crawling, and then walking, the smile never left her face, and Carly could honestly say that she had never known a love as true as the love she held for that little girl.

Now, Carly stared at the dress that reminded her of their

little angel. Tears welled up in her eyes as she tried to hold it together. Gracie would have been seven in a couple of months.

The memories hit Carly like a freight train. Her getting up in the morning to get ready for work. Checking in on their little girl before the nanny arrived. Opening the curtains to allow the morning light to slowly wake Gracie up, so they could get her ready for the nanny. Then the blood. Obscene amounts of it soaked the bedsheets and blankets. Carly frantically yanking the covers back to get to Gracie. Her lifeless form. The pajama top sliced to ribbons, the color unrecognizable.

Carly slumped to the ground, holding the dress. Her mind took her back through the slew of memories. Events that destroyed her life. Her screams. The police showing up. The coroner taking Gracie away, covered by a sheet. The millions of questions. The invitation down to the station, where the interview turned into an interrogation. They had separated Brian and Carly in different rooms and had drilled them about what they had done to their daughter. Eventually, they cleared both of them. No other suspects were identified, but they did find signs of forced entry through Gracie's bedroom window as well as boot prints in the flowerbed below.

At first, Brian tried to console her—to be her rock. But he wasn't prepared for the dark place that she went to hide. After months of trying to help her, and his efforts being rebuked by a torrential tirade of screaming and profanities, Brian couldn't take it anymore. Soon after, he left, and life for Carly was never the same. It was then she sank into an abyss darker than any she had ever experienced before.

Carly snapped back to the dress. Carefully folding it, she carried it into the house and tucked it into the closet of Gracie's old room. She would keep the dress as a reminder of Gracie. All the other possessions belonging to her had been purged from the house by Brian—his way of trying to make it easier for Carly. Instead, he had only made her hysteria worse.

Back out in the garage, Carly numbly started working through the boxes again. She came across several more boxes of clothes, some fairly cheap jewelry, and some other little knickknacks.

The boxes that were all the same size and neatly stacked were all books, and from the way they were all protected and packaged, she had a feeling they were worth some money as well, so she set them aside with the comic books to take to an expert and possibly sell on consignment.

As she was cleaning out the last of the trailer, she noticed a small black duffle bag she had set to the side of the ramp when she was unloading the boxes. She rubbed her temples with her thumbs, then brought the bag over to the table. She was almost done for the day and would wait until tomorrow before she started figuring out what to do with her bounty.

She pulled open the zipper and peeled back the sides of the bag. On top was a piece of clothing. She pulled out a pair of coveralls, dirty and stained. Someone's work bag, evidently. A couple of pairs of gloves followed. In the bottom was a roll of something that looked like black nylon. She scooped it out, noticing its considerable weight. Laying it down on the table, she untied the two strips that were entwined in a bow and unrolled the nylon onto the table. Her breath caught, and an audible gasp left her lips. The roll consisted of ten individual plastic sleeves. Slid into each pouch was a tool: mostly knives, a couple of hand saws, and a sharpener. It reminded her of the summer she had worked at the local grocery store as a teenager, where she had to take out the trash throughout the store as one of her duties. One of the meatcutters—he called himself a floater and worked in different stores daily —had a kit similar to this, but there were a lot less knives. And what were the hand saws about? To her recollection, anything that needed cut with a saw was cut on a big band saw in the back of the prep room.

She knew that knives were expensive and that this kit would be valuable, so she decided she would research it later and try to sell it herself. There was no way it was going to the secondhand store. Rolling the pouch back up, she tied it closed and set the roll on the bottom shelf of the storage racks. She would get to it later, after the books and comic books had been sorted out. And of course, after the big jar of coins—which she needed her utility dolly to move—was carted down to the coin-counting machine that hid out in the lobby of the grocery store a mile away.

Cleaning up the last of the garbage, she slid the black duffle bag, the coveralls, and the gloves into the box and went and dumped the last of it into the dumpster. After a shower and a change of clothes, she decided her night would consist of a stiff drink and a binge watch of a new Netflix series she had her eye on.

CHAPTER FOUR

Over the next several weeks, Carly attended two more auctions and brought home the contents of four more lockers. Her prior lockers had turned a hefty profit, and she had found buyers for the collections.

She had just finished processing the last of the boxes out of the trailer for her most recent run, and turned to place an electric can opener on the shelving units, when she spotted it. The nylon roll of knives tucked into the back of the shelf. She had forgotten it was there. She slid it out and unrolled it on the table again, running her pointer finger over each handle, wondering what material they were made out of. They certainly weren't cheap plastic. Each one had an inlay. Could it be ivory? She had no idea where she could take the set to have it analyzed. Although it wouldn't make her rich, she had a feeling that she could make a few hundred off the kit. She decided she would research it the next morning.

The next day, after she ate a quick breakfast of apple cinnamon oatmeal and toast, she went to the garage to grab the knife set. It wasn't on the table where she thought she had left it. She returned to the shelving unit she had it stored on earlier. It wasn't there either. Methodically, she poked her way through every part of the garage to find it. An hour later, she still could not locate it. She checked the side door to the garage, and it was still locked and showed no signs of forced entry. She had slid the switch the night before to lock out any remotes from opening the large rollup door, so she knew no one got in that way.

I'm losing my damn mind.

Unsure of where she left them, Carly took a break from looking and went inside the house and got on her computer, looking for a place that might buy them from her, or at the very least help her ascertain their value. Only one place looked like it fit the bill, but it was two hours away. Perhaps the next time she was in the area for an auction, she could swing by and get the set checked out. That is if she could figure out what she did with them.

That night, Carly got ready for bed and settled on the couch to watch a show. The television was the only company she had, and it never caused her pain.

A loud noise coming from the television woke her up, and she sat upright. She hadn't even remembered falling asleep. She grabbed her phone from the arm of the couch. Three thirty-two a.m. Definitely time for her to drag her ass to bed.

She turned off the TV and shuffled to her room, her eyes

still half closed. Pulling back the covers, she climbed into bed, pulled the sheet up to her chin, and shifted her body to get comfortable. Her pillow felt lumpy. She tried pushing it down and laid her head back on it, but it still felt off. As she reached under it to scoop it up, her hand knocked against something. Reaching in the dark, she felt something foreign under her pillow. At the edges of her consciousness, she felt like she knew exactly what it was, but she could not identify it for sure in the dark.

Jumping out from under the covers, Carly turned on the overhead light and returned to the side of the bed she slept on. Apprehensively, she moved the pillow, wondering what could be under it as she lifted it. The rolled-up nylon knife case stared back at her.

What the fuck?

Although the mystery of where the case went was solved, she knew damn well that she hadn't put it there, so how did it get there? If someone had been in her house, there'd be other signs of it. Was she losing her mind?

Rubbing the base of her neck, Carly scooped up the set and took it out to the kitchen, laying it on the counter. She was tired and could not process what was happening, but she was sure she would think of a logical answer in the morning when she was more alert. Maybe she had simply been absentminded and moved it there without paying attention. Slipping back into bed, she closed her eyes, and sleep took over almost immediately.

IN THE MORNING, CARLY AWOKE TO THE TRASH TRUCK outside. Rubbing her eyes, she stumbled into the bathroom, turned on the shower, peeled off her pajamas, and climbed inside. As the hot water cascaded over her head, she pumped shampoo into her open hand and started washing her hair. The stinging of her right palm caught her attention, and she rinsed the suds out of her eyes and off her hand to investigate. An angry, two-inch cut adorned the surface. It wasn't deep, nor was it actively bleeding, but it was definitely fresh. She searched her memory for anything that could have caused the wound and once again came up empty.

When she was out of the shower, she dried off and gingerly patted a clean towel against her palm. Pouring peroxide on it, she watched it bubble a bit and when it looked like it was done, she rinsed it again, dried it, and wrapped some gauze around it to keep it clean. Back in the bedroom, a cursory search of the bed provided no clues, however she did note that she bled on the sheets and pillowcase. After pre-treating the blood and throwing the sheets in the washing machine, she went out to the kitchen to make something to eat. She stopped short at the entryway.

Spread out across the kitchen floor were all the knives from the pouch that had been on the counter, the empty holder strewn across the floor nearby. Each of the knives, as well as the saws—*Are those bone saws?*—were haphazardly scattered, a skinny bladed–knife with drops of blood on and around it over by the refrigerator.

Now I know how I got the cut, but was I sleepwalking?

Confusion welled up into Carly's brain and overtook her emotions. She was definitely losing it. She had never sleep-walked before, to her knowledge, but that might explain the strange happenings of the knife set being moved around without her being aware of it.

Carefully, she placed the knives back in the pouch and rolled it up, tying the strings that kept it in place. Placing the kit on the far end of the counter, she opened the refrigerator to grab something for breakfast. Yellow material peeked out at her from the back behind the milk. Carly moved the gallon jug and it hit her. Flowers and butterflies. The dress. The one that was just like Gracie's. What was it doing in the fridge when she had placed it in Gracie's closet?

Carefully, Carly reached for the material and pulled it out. The splotches of blood dotting the fabric immediately caught her eye. Apparently, she had been handling the dress after she cut herself. Despair stemmed through her as she thought about Gracie and all the blood. Then a thought cascaded over her and she fell to her knees, sobbing. What if she had killed Gracie after all? What if she had gotten up during her sleep, grabbed a knife, and stabbed her, going back to bed unknowingly immediately after? Could she really rule that out, knowing what she did now? But…surely, she would have had blood on her hands or her nightgown if that was the case, wouldn't she have? Then there were the boot prints and the evidence of window tampering. No, it couldn't have been her. It wasn't possible, but as she battled with herself, she wasn't so sure.

CHAPTER FIVE

Carly woke up screaming, the dream still vivid in her mind. Every detail of the nightmare was etched into her brain, and being awake brought little relief from the horrors that were conjured up in her head while she slept. Little Gracie. In the dream, Carly had stood over her bed, watching her sleep. The soft light of the moon filtered through the curtains, casting a glow across Gracie's face. She bent down and kissed the little girl's forehead, and then she plunged the knife through her heart. Little Gracie did not even have a chance to scream. Her eyes shot open, she gurgled for a few seconds, and then a vacant look seeped in. Seconds later, she stopped moving.

Carly snapped on the bedside light and sat shivering, the images wreaking havoc with her thoughts. It was all too much…losing Gracie, then her marriage, and then…the weird happenings, possible sleepwalking, and now this. Her thoughts turned to the times that she felt like offing herself…maybe she should have already answered that call loud and clear.

She sat and rocked for about half an hour before finally calming down from the dream. It was all too real. She wondered again if it had any basis on reality.

Switching off the light, finally, she laid her head back on the pillow and burrowed in. A familiar feeling took over, and she reached under her pillow, hoping she was wrong, but her hand latched onto the nylon case anyway. The knives were back under her pillow.

Knowing she needed to get rid of the knives—strange things were happening ever since she acquired them—Carly grabbed her truck keys off of the dresser, ducked outside in her bare feet, and locked them in the backseat of the cab. She would deal with them in the morning.

———

It felt late when Carly finally opened her eyes. She looked at her phone and saw it was after one p.m. A groan escaped her lips, and she thought back to the nightmare from earlier that morning, about the knives. She pulled herself out of bed and climbed in the shower to wake herself up. When she had toweled off, she pulled on a pair of blue jeans and a t-shirt.

In the kitchen, she paused in front of the refrigerator, contemplating making something to eat. Instead, she grabbed her keys and headed out to the truck. The sooner she got rid of those knives, the sooner she hoped life would return to normal. And then it registered with her—what she should have known all along, but was either too ignorant, or too innocent to figure it out…those knives didn't belong to a meat cutter at all. They belonged to a killer. Carly had bought a storage locker that belonged to a fucking murderer and the knives were part of his kill kit. Had the clothing and jewelry belonged to his victims?

The realization caused her to retch, and she tried to hold back, but whatever still remained in her stomach from her last meal found its way out, splattering on the ground by her rear driver's side tire. She wiped her mouth on her arm, took a few deep breaths, steadied herself and opened the door to the truck, peering inside to verify the knife set was still in the back seat. It wasn't. She dug through the contents of the entire truck but could not find it. Shaking, she returned to the house and searched room by room before tearing apart the garage as well. The kill kit wasn't anywhere. It had disappeared, along with another portion of her sanity.

Determined to take her mind off things, Carly tried to process some of the items in the garage, but she couldn't focus. She found herself back in her living room, pulling shut the blackout blinds, pulling her knees up under her chin on the couch, then rocking back and forth. Helpless, Carly felt the darkness creeping back in, deep inside of her—the darkness that she had lived with for so long after losing everything.

Day turned to night and night to day. The world faded out around her, and she stared, blank faced, at the television while the twenty-four-hour programming continued to cater to an inattentive audience. She was unaware of the dishes and trash piling up around her. She had no awareness of eating or using the bathroom. The lights were on, but no one was home.

Carly stood at the foot of the bed. The little girl was dressed in a set of Eeyore pajamas, her blond hair cascading over the pillow. Carly could make out the rise and fall of the girl's chest. She did not recognize the child, but she estimated her to be Gracie's age—at least the age she had been when she was killed.

Not understanding what she was doing in this child's room, she walked closer to the bed. Maybe she would recognize her up close. Carly leaned over and took a better look. The girl was not familiar to her. Still, Carly felt a connection, but in an ominous way. As she watched, it seemed as if the rise and fall of her little chest stopped for a moment, and then the girl's eyes flicked wide open. Before Carly even knew what was happening, she plunged the blade she hadn't even realized she'd been holding directly into the heart of the now-awake child. Just like in her dream, the scream never escaped, and the child's life faded from her eyes quickly.

Carly tried to scream but couldn't. She had no control over her body or her movements. She wondered if she had actually done what she just thought she did. Looking closely in the dim light, she saw the red blooms of blood saturating the pajama top.

Panicked, she looked around the room and spotted the open window. It beckoned to her, telling her to get out of there, and she did. Leaving the scene was a blur, her emotions in a hyper-sensitive state. Before, she had thought she might be going crazy, but this. THIS! How had it happened? How had she even gotten into the child's room and who was she?

Did it really happen? Did I kill her?

Carly found herself back at her house and quickly curled up on the couch, holding her head, deep sobs racking her body. The room was pitch black, and she kept it that way, hiding from the world and herself. Eventually, she cried herself out and fell asleep.

CARLY OPENED HER EYES. LIGHT FILTERED INTO THE room from various places in the house, casting shadows across the floor. The events from the night before immediately entered her brain. She tried to process everything, and then it hit her.

It was a dream, just like the other night.

Breathing a sigh of relief, she sat up on the couch. While she still might be going insane, at least she hadn't killed anybody. She stood up to go to her bathroom to take a shower. The feel of the rubber soles on the bottoms of her shoes stopped her. They felt strange. She looked down. Not shoes at all—boots. But not a pair of the feminine ones she kept in her closet. These were work boots. And they were too big on her—men's boots. Her eyes squinted as she tried to remember where she had seen them before. Then it became clear…the boots were in one of the storage lockers she had purchased, and because they were well worn, she had thrown them in the dumpster. So how had she come to be wearing them? More importantly, why?

Carly fumbled with the laces and pulled the boots off of her feet, opened the front door, and threw them out on the porch. The morning sunlight was bright, and she stopped in her tracks, holding out her hands. *Blood.* She checked her clothes. There was blood on her shirt as well.

Panicked, she rushed back in the house and looked around. The living room appeared to be normal, but it was in the kitchen that she found what she was hoping she wouldn't. In the sink sat a knife, blood coating the blade. She recognized the knife as one from the kill kit. It wasn't a dream. It was real. Someone died at her hand. A child even.

Her thoughts turned to Gracie. The little girl she killed was about the same age. Then she remembered the boot prints outside Gracie's window. Had it been Carly after all? Had she been crazy way back then and hadn't realized it? Was she the fucking monster that took her own daughter's life? A numbness settled over her as she tried to make sense of everything. She picked up the knife and examined it, imagining what it would feel like if she plunged it deep within her own chest.

A thought hit her, and suddenly, she found herself running towards Gracie's bedroom. The dress was in the closet where she had left it. She took it out and held it up. The dress reminded her of Gracie, because Gracie had one just like it, but what if…what if the dress was the actual one Gracie had owned?

Carly turned the dress around and looked at the zipper. The dress had come with a nylon one that had broken. Carly could still remember the tears that slid down Gracie's cheeks when the zipper had come apart. It was her favorite dress. After calming her down, Carly promised to fix it. She remembered that Gracie had made her pinky-promise. And so the next day, Carly had stopped by the fabric store and bought a new zipper. A metal one, in gold. She stayed up late that night, ripping out the stitches holding the old zipper in and then sewing the new one into place. She surprised Gracie the next morning with it, and Gracie had worn it to school that day. Carly was not one to break a pinkie-promise.

Carly ran her pointer finger over the gold metal zipper. This dress wasn't *like* Gracie's. It *was* Gracie's. How did a stranger end up with it when Carly knew for a fact that it was missing when Gracie was killed? She knew, because she looked for it.

She wanted Gracie to be cremated in that dress, but it was nowhere to be found.

The dress. The knives.

Just like a jigsaw puzzle piece that finally fell into place, Carly connected the dots. The owner of the storage locker was the one. The bastard that had killed Gracie. The person that was responsible for destroying her entire life. She had to go to the police. Surely, they could find out who owned the locker, right?

While you are at it, maybe you can explain how one of those knives ended up in the chest of a seven-year-old. That should be fun.

Defeated, she slumped down to the floor of Gracie's closet and cried.

CHAPTER SIX

Carly sat on an old wooden chair in her garage, the knife roll laid out at her feet. She turned the boning knife over and over in her hands. She pressed her right pointer finger against the tip, and a bright red drop of crimson pushed out of her finger and dripped onto the floor.

For the past three weeks, she found herself mired in that place again. The one where she could no longer go on. If she wasn't sleeping, she was plotting, planning. She had concocted thirty-seven different ways to leave the world behind, many of them horrible ways to die. She even came close to trying a couple of them. In the end, she chicken-shitted out. She didn't have the guts to do the only thing that seemed to make sense in a world that had torn her soul to shreds.

Her child was dead. Her husband was gone. And she was just as bad as the fucker that had killed Carly. She had killed a little girl, and two more in the past three weeks. The scenario was always the same. She became aware that she was in each room—most of them adorned with toys, dolls, and a multitude of pink—and then she stabbed. The last two times, when she saw the precious little girls lying in the bed, asleep, she knew. She knew what she was about to do even before she did it. And she tried to stop. Both times, she willed herself to leave, drop the knife, something. Anything that would have saved them—either of them. It's like she was powerless to control her actions. The knives—she knew it was the fucking knives. Somehow, they manipulated her. She wondered how that could even be possible, but she had the blood of three innocent victims on her hands—all little girls—and four, if she was responsible for taking Gracie's life. She couldn't live with herself…was too broken to even try, but too afraid to die.

She screamed, a guttural yell, and threw the knife at the garage door. The handle bounced off, and the knife went skittering across the concrete floor. Unable to go through with what she had planned, she abandoned the knives where they lay and went into the house.

Inside, Carly went to the kitchen and opened the refrigerator door. She hadn't eaten in two days and was starving, but each time she thought about doing so, her stomach churned. She eyed the two plates of food in the sink—her attempts at eating that didn't go as planned. Inhaling sharply, Carly shut the refrigerator door, went into the bedroom, crawled under the covers and closed her eyes.

———

THE GLOW FROM THE LITTLE MERMAID NIGHTLIGHT partially illuminated the room but did not quite reach the dark shadows in the corner. Carly stood, watching, as the little girl, who was laying on her stomach, slept. She didn't have to look

—she knew the knife would be clenched in her right hand. While distraught and frantic on the inside, she was calm and collected on the outside.

She thought about some of the news stories she had recently watched about the murders. The authorities felt the murders were tied back to a string of other child murders years before—murders that had never been solved. Child victims. Including Gracie.

They think I'm him.

Then another thought hit her.

Or maybe he is me.

Could she have been the one this entire time? Was she simply continuing on with what she has started years earlier?

The tools. The dress. They were in someone else's storage locker.

The little girl mumbled and flipped over on her back. The girl was younger than Gracie had been. Carly glanced at the open window, the printed images of Ariel dancing from the slight breeze. She willed herself to walk to the window—to climb through it and just leave. Her feet disobeyed her, and she stood rooted to the floor. She knew what was to happen next. History would repeat itself. She would finally move…and she would stab, exactly once. And the blade would penetrate the precise location it needed to.

Involuntarily, her right foot moved one step forward, and her left followed. She felt her right arm start to rise, and then she saw it, the knife, where she knew it would be.

At the side of the bed, she took in the girl's innocence. An innocence that would be shattered by violence. Carly pulled the knife back over her head, poised, ready to slam it down into the chest of her victim.

Brilliant light flooded the room.

"What the fuck are you doing?" a man standing inside the open door screamed.

Oh shit. Her father.

"Get away from her," he yelled, eyeing the knife. He was frozen in place, unsure of what to do.

Carly tried to speak and couldn't, her body a mere pawn.

"Put the knife down and leave the way you came. You don't want to do this."

She tried to talk again. This time, she almost succeeded. "I —d-d-d…"

"Who are you?" he demanded. "Why are you here?"

She shook her head. "D-don't k-k-know."

He held out his hand. "Give me the knife."

Carly paused, unsure of what to do. She actually felt like she could control her movements for the first time since standing in the room. If she surrendered, then one life would be saved, but her soul would still forever be damned. Then there was the fact she'd rot in jail. She'd rather be dead.

"C'mon. Hand it over. I can't let you hurt Jessie." His tone softened and became luring. Carly hesitated, then held the knife out in front of her, handle first. The man froze, his mouth open, his eyes wide.

"Where did you get that knife?"

"D-does it matter?"

"Yes. It matters. The ivory inlay on the handle is unique. In fact, I have only ever seen that design once before."

The strange circumstances that surrounded the knives—the ones that threw her life into complete chaos ever since she had them in her possession—came crashing down upon her. Before she could react, the man lunged forward and grabbed the knife out of her hand, slicing her fingers in the process.

"Where?" she demanded. "Where have you seen it before?"

The man paused, contemplating his answer. Finally, he spoke.

"I designed this handle and had it custom made."

The past two years' events came ripping through Carly's head like a freight train. Memory after memory flooded her thoughts, like a news highlight reel. Dots started connecting, and she was on the verge of a realization she knew she wasn't ready for, but she had to be sure.

"You designed this knife?"

"Yes."

"Just one?"

"No. An entire set. Where did you get it?" he repeated.

"I think you know," she whispered, menacingly.

"Where is the rest of my stuff? That locker was mine. You had no right to touch my things."

The little girl started stirring in her bed.

"One hundred seventy-five dollars says that the contents are no longer yours. They belong to me now. Including that knife. Give it back."

Carly stared at him, surprised at what she saw. He was thin and small in stature. He wore wire-rimmed glasses on his round face, and his head was balding on top.

The man ignored her request. "Is it you? Are you the one responsible for all the killings on the news?" He looked confused.

"Apparently," she responded.

"How? Why?"

"I was hoping you could answer that question for me."

If she caught him off guard, it was only evident in his expression for a millisecond. He quickly resumed his role as victim.

"Are you a copy-cat killer?"

The little girl mumbled and turned over again.

"Copy-cat? Copying *who*?"

The realization finally smacked her in the head so ferociously that her knees buckled and she sank to the ground. Images of Gracie's dress filled her head. The dress that was missing after Gracie was murdered. The dress that she found in a storage locker she purchased. A storage locker owned by a serial killer.

He didn't answer her. He didn't need to.

"I think it's time we call the police," he said.

Carly paused, contemplating the situation. "You think that's a good idea?"

"You broke into my fucking house. You were about to kill my daughter, for Christ's sake. Yes, I think it's a wonderful idea." He reached into his robe pocket and pulled out his phone.

A dark smile settled on Carly's lips. "What are you going to tell them?"

"The truth."

"All of it?"

"Yes, all of it."

"Are you going to tell them who killed the other girls, before me?"

"What do you mean?"

"I think they will find it interesting that the knives in the set I now own will most likely match up with the stab wounds for all the little girls that died before I got involved."

"As they should. It's your set, so you must have killed them."

"But I can prove when I bought the locker contents."

"I don't recall ever having knives in my storage locker. Prove otherwise."

"I'm sure the company that created the inlays will be able to identify the knives as yours." She glanced at the boots strapped to her feet. "I'm sure these boots have your DNA on them as well."

He frowned. "You're not being very smart about this. You should have left well enough alone."

Flipping the knife around in his hand, he inched toward Carly, ready to strike. As Carly watched, the man brought the knife back, his intentions displayed upon his face.

"Daddy?"

Both their heads whipped around toward the bed. The little girl was sitting up, looking back and forth between them.

"Daddy, what are you doing? Who is that?" She pointed toward Carly.

In a split-second reaction, Carly dove for the knife. The man lost his grip on it, and it bounced on the carpet. Carly dove on it, and the man jumped on her back, trying to get at the weapon before she did. The little girl screamed from her bed, cowering in the corner. The pair tussled on the ground, each one getting a little bit of an advantage and then losing it again. While the man had a slight weight advantage, pure adrenaline was driving Carly's basic will to survive, which—as she scrambled for the knife—surprised her, considering the suicidal state she had resided in for longer than she could care to remember.

As Carly's hand grabbed the handle of the knife, the man slammed his fist down on her wrist. Fireworks exploded in her brain as intense pain shot up her arm. The knife fell from her grasp, and the man picked it up and thrust it toward her heart. The knife blade sunk halfway into Carly's flesh, but it missed its mark as she turned at the last second and caught the cold steel in the shoulder. A howl escaped her lips as the pain flared through her body. She landed a kick to the man's testicles, and he went down, groaning.

"Fucking bitch," he gasped.

Carly looked at the knife that was still sticking out of her shoulder. She knew pulling it out wasn't necessarily a great idea, but she needed it. With a grimace on her face, she grabbed it and yanked. Tears ran down her face as she tried to hold back her screams. The man rolled onto his knees and started to get up. With everything she had, she dropped her entire body weight down as she drove the blade between his shoulder blades and smashed his face into the floor. In the dim light, she watched the blood soak through his pajama top as he moaned into the carpet.

Carly looked over at the little girl who had stopped screaming and had her knees tucked up under her chin, her lips trembling. Carly grabbed the knife with both hands, her right one pulsating with pain, and yanked. With her foot, she flipped the man over, face up. He glared at her, the hatred evident in his face. He didn't move. Carly wondered if she had paralyzed him.

To the little girl, she said, "Close your eyes and cover your ears." When the girl complied, she turned her attention back to the monster before her.

"Do I have your attention now?" she asked. He continued to glare at her. "We all know what you are," she continued. "I just didn't know *who* you were until tonight. And me being here is either one hell of a coincidence or one big twist of fate. Either way, I'll take it. I've waited a long time to meet you."

"Who are you?" he asked again.

"You don't know me. But you were acquainted with my daughter."

"Your daughter?"

"Yes. Cute, blond. She was five when you stabbed her in the heart and ended her life. I think she might have been your last victim."

"Her? You're her…" His voice tapered off.

"I'm her trainwreck of a mother. When you took her life, you took everything from me."

"How…"

Carly shook her head. "I'm asking the questions. And I need to know why. Why did you kill Gracie? And for that matter, the other girls?"

He blinked, his chest rapidly rising and falling. Carly could see resolve starting to kick in. She glanced over at the little girl who still had her face buried against her knees and her ears covered. She made the sound of an injured animal as she rocked.

Carly's tone deepened and she spoke slowly. "Maybe… you…didn't…fucking…hear…me. WHY?"

He looked at her and shook his head. "You wouldn't understand."

"Try me."

"It sounds weird saying it. I'm not a monster. At least I don't think of myself as one. It was simply the one true love I had in my life. I got a taste when I accidentally killed my little sister, who was around the same age. I was so scared…afraid they were going to send me away. But they thought it was some freaky accident, and no one blamed me. I was too innocent in their eyes. I loved her, and I regret what happened, but the surreal power of taking a life and getting away with it was more than I could control. I had the hunger. I fought it for years, but as I became an adult and moved out of my parents' house, I could not keep the beast at bay any longer. It had to feed. It claimed a new victim every time I lost control of it."

"So, my d…daughter. There was no rhyme or reason for it? You just had an urge to quench?"

"It's more than that. It's hard to control. And I never knew when it was going to rear its ugly head."

Carly's face went pale, and she spoke through clenched teeth. "So…why did you stop?"

The man's eyes shifted toward the girl on the bed. "My wife got pregnant and Jessie was born. Suddenly, I had a new love in my life. She grounded me. She made me better. I haven't killed since."

"Touching, but you never paid for your sins."

"Apparently. That time is now, I imagine."

"Apparently. You'll never know how many lives you fucked up. You'll never know how badly you destroyed everything I had. All I've wanted since was a bullet to the brain. Until tonight."

Peace settled across the man's face. "Do what you have to do. Just don't hurt Jessie. She's innocent and shouldn't have to pay for my bullshit."

"You foolish man," Carly sneered. "Do you think I'm going to spare her because you asked me to? After what you did to Gracie, you deserve to watch her die. There's a special place in hell for you. I'll see you there."

Carly grabbed the man by the hair and tilted his head back, gliding the knife across the bare flesh of his neck. His eyes shot open wide as a crimson necklace appeared. His mouth fell open and his lips started to move, but only a gurgle came out.

As the life started to drain out of him, Carly made sure he watched her as she wiped the knife off on the leg of her jeans, repositioned it in her hand, and approached Jessie, the knife raised in the air. That image was the final one burned into his brain when the last of his life leaked out of him.

EPILOGUE

Carly flipped the pancakes over on the griddle, admiring the almost perfect roundness of the fluffy circles. They would be a great start to the day, which already was looking promising based upon the weather forecast that morning. The cotton-candy clouds billowed sparsely across the brilliant blue sky, and she had noticed a slight breeze earlier when she had been outside loading up the truck.

When that batch of pancakes was golden brown on both sides, Carly used the spatula to add them to the plate where the first two batches sat waiting.

Carly looked down at Barley, a Golden Retriever that had won over her heart and whose hair took over the house.

"How many are you good for this morning?" she asked as Barley eyed the pancakes.

"All of them? Don't be greedy. Save some for the humans."

Carly set the plate of food on the table and took the tray of bacon out of the oven that had been warming there. She put the bacon on a plate and added it to the feast before making sure that the three different kinds of syrup were all waiting to drown the flapjacks. Filling a glass with orange juice, she set it on the table and poured a cup of coffee. She was just adding her vanilla creamer when Barley jumped up and ran to the edge of the room.

Carly glanced over at Barley giving kisses and receiving muzzle rubs.

"Good morning, sweetie. How did you sleep?"

"Really good!"

"Did Barley sleep with you again?"

"Yep! But he's a bed hog."

"He just loves his little girl."

"Thank you for getting him for me, Mommy."

"Of course, honey."

Jessie saw the plate of pancakes, and her eyes opened wide. "Are those blueberry?"

"Your favorite!"

"You're a good mommy."

"And you're a good daughter!"

Carly kneeled down and scooped Jessie up in her arms. Jessie was getting so tall. At four years old, she had changed so much in the two years that they had been together.

The first few months had been rough. Jessie had pushed back on everything and constantly asked about her father. It was through many conversations that Carly learned that the mother had died after childbirth. Carly wondered if it had been from natural causes. Eventually, Jessie got to know Carly and grew to like her, and after six months, she confided in Carly. Her father scared her and was not a nice person. As Carly and Jessie grew close, eventually, Jessie stopped talking about her father, and one day, she asked Carly the ultimate question. *Can I call you Mommy?*

The need to kill drained out of her as Jessie's father's blood drained out of him. At that point, Jessie was never in any danger, but it sure made Carly feel better knowing that the last thing he saw as he died was her hovering over his daughter with a knife.

A new house, in a rural town, in a new state, was just what they had needed. It gave both of them the time and space they needed to heal. And although Carly missed every little thing about Gracie, she knew that Gracie would want this. Would want for her mommy to be whole again. And aside from the special place Carly kept in her heart that was reserved only for the memories of a blond little girl who she adored, the rest belonged to Jessie, and Jessie would always know how loved she was.

LUCY

As she wiggled her hips back and forth, Lucy pulled the tight black pair of leather pants up over her ass, buttoned them, and pulled up the zipper. Studying herself in the mirror, she took in her five-foot-six frame, the black leather complimented nicely by the red bra. She turned sideways, checking out her ass to make sure it didn't look too big. The pants had been rather tight, after all, which concerned her.

Pulling her long black hair to the side, she took in her figure from multiple angles. *Not bad.* Satisfied that she would turn heads for the evening, Lucy pulled on a short-sleeved silk top—one that showed a hint of bra—and dug a pair of heels out of the closet. She would not need any makeup, as she was a natural beauty. A Temptress.

Wiping the sweat from her brow, she took one final look at her outfit. It worked well with her golden tan and her large breasts, which weren't necessarily for herself, but for the others. Men. Women. It didn't matter. She liked them all the same. They all served the same purpose.

At the club, she took up a seat at the bar and wondered if a new record would be set for how long it took for some stranger to offer her a drink. Tonight, it was only eighteen seconds. Not quite a record, but damn close.

"Hey, beautiful. Can I get you a drink?"

Lucy turned toward the stranger, eying him once over. He was tall, over six feet, she figured. His jaw square, his eyes steely. She noticed that his right arm was a sleeve of tattoos, but the left one only had a medium-sized Celtic cross on his forearm. *He'll do.*

"I'm going to go with yes. Apple Martini, please."

The man motioned to the bartender. "I'll have a Jack and Coke, and the lady here will have an Apple Martini."

The bartender grabbed the glasses and started mixing the drinks.

"I'm Adam." He stuck out his hand.

"Lucy. Thanks for the drink."

"I've never seen you in here before."

"Is that the line you use on all the hot chicks you hit on?"

"Actually, there aren't that many hot chicks that come in here, especially ones that look like you. I'd say that's a no."

Lucy laughed. "I'm just busting your balls anyway. I've never been in here before."

"Are you here with someone?"

"Just you."

"So, if you've never been here before, what brings you in? There are tons of better places to be on a Thursday night."

"Are you trying to get rid of me, Adam?"

"Oh, hell no. I was just curious."

"Then chill a little. I came out to try and meet people. If you don't piss me off, *you* can be one of those people."

"Sorry. I get a little nervous around women that look like you."

"Yet you still approached me in…what was it, eighteen seconds?"

"You snooze, you lose."

"Looks like that theory worked out for you tonight."

Lucy sipped on her martini, and they made small talk. Four drinks later, the band began to play, kicking off with a rendition of "Round Here" by Counting Crows.

"You know," Adam—who was full of liquid courage—told her, "I really like that red bra, but I'm curious to see what it looks like next to the black pants…on the floor of my apartment." He slurred a little as he spoke.

"What a sweet talker you are, Adam. So, you want to get into my pants, huh?"

"I'm not sure we'll both fit in there, but we can try it," he said, laughing louder than he should have at the played-out joke.

"Adam, Adam, Adam. That was just dreadful. Let's get you out of here."

"Where we going?"

"You said your apartment, right?"

"Oh yeah, let's go to my pa…partment."

"Maybe food first?" Lucy suggested, wanting him to be a little more sober for the night she had planned.

"Food sounds like an idea…a good one."

Outside the bar, Adam directed Lucy to where his truck was parked, and she took the keys from him. The alcohol had no effect on her, and she helped him into the passenger side and got in behind the wheel. The Dodge truck started right up, and Lucy pulled out of the parking lot and turned down the main road. She didn't know the area well, so she decided to keep her eyes open for the first spot that looked good. A mile down the road, she spotted an all-hours diner and pulled into the parking lot.

Inside, they ordered, and the waitress poured them coffee, setting the entire carafe down on the table for their convenience. Twenty minutes later, the meal came out, and Adam dug into his breakfast skillet while Lucy slathered her pancakes with butter and blueberry syrup, cut a big triangle out of the stack, and stuffed it into her mouth.

"How's the food?" she asked.

"Good. Thanks for bringing me here," he said sheepishly. "Sorry I was getting a tad tipsy back there. I feel a little better now."

"There is nothing in this world a good meal can't fix," she said, but then she thought about how tight her pants were and made up her mind that she would start watching what she ate tomorrow. Tonight, she was on a mission.

"So, are we still going to my place? After breakfast, I mean."

"Yes."

"It's my lucky night."

"Depends on how you look at it."

Adam looked at Lucy, unsure of what her cryptic response meant, but when she inhaled and he caught the rise and fall of her chest—his eyes were instantly pulled to her breasts—he immediately didn't care. If she was a train wreck, he would worry about it tomorrow. Tonight, he was going to satisfy his appetite, as it had been three weeks since he had gotten laid. He wasn't just excited about the sex—he knew it would be good—he marveled at how hot she was. In fact, Lucy was probably hotter than any girl he had ever been with and probably would hold that title for years.

After breakfast, Lucy drove them to his apartment as he gave her turn-by-turn directions. At his complex, she pulled the truck into his designated space, and he grabbed her hand and led her to the front door of his downstairs unit. Inside, she took control, pushing him toward the back of the space where she figured the bedroom to be. Inside the room, she pushed him down on the bed and removed her blouse.

"Wow." It was all he could manage to say as his eyes took in the red lace bra and the swollen curves of her breasts.

"Like what you see?"

"I do."

"Then you will probably like this, too." Lucy undid the top button on her pants, pulled down on the zipper, and turned around, her ass facing toward him. She shimmied out of the leather and let the pants drop to her ankles before stepping out of them.

"Damn." Again, just the one word.

"Your turn." It was more of a demand than a statement.

Adam jumped up from the bed and tore his clothes off as quickly as he could. Lucy let her eyes trail down his body, and she stopped when she came to his manhood.

"Someone likes what he sees," she said, nodding toward his erection.

"Oh, he does. Trust me. Now it's back to you. Time to get the rest of your clothes off and get your cute ass over here."

Lucy walked over to him, gave him a soft kiss on the lips, and whispered into his ear. "Not so fast. If I do this for you, I need you to do something for me." Lucy nibbled on his ear, and a shudder went up his spine.

"An…anything," he mumbled, his brain unable to think clearly as the dopamine surged through his system.

"Promise?"

"I promise."

Lucy pushed Adam back on the bed, reached behind her back, and unhooked her bra. She pulled it off and watched Adam's expression. She smirked when his mouth dropped open. He was speechless. When her panties had also landed on the floor, she knew she had him. On the bed, she crawled on top of him, hovering over him.

"Anything?" she asked.

"Anything," he whimpered, and then she took him.

———

ADAM FOUND LUCY SITTING ON HIS COUCH, WEARING ONE of his T-shirts, drinking a cup of coffee, and watching television.

"Morning, sleepyhead. I hope you don't mind. I helped myself to your Keurig and one of your shirts."

"Morning. Of course I don't mind." He plopped on the couch next to her, a deep yawn emitting from his mouth. His eyelids were heavy, and he still looked half asleep.

"So?"

"So, what?" He looked confused.

"How was it?"

"Oh my God. I think you put me in a coma. The BEST ever."

"You're just saying that."

"Um…no. You seriously rocked my world…and I loved how you took control and I didn't have to do anything."

"You'll make it up to me," she teased.

"Oh, I have no doubt," he said, smiling. "Just let me know how."

"I'm about to. You remember your promise?"

"Yes." Adam looked over at her nervously. "What do you have in mind?"

"I need help with my husband."

Adam raised his eyebrows as his mouth fell open. "You're married?"

"Yes."

"Why didn't you tell me?"

"You never asked."

"I didn't see a ring. I always check for rings."

"I don't wear one. He doesn't deserve me."

"Listen, last night was great…and your body is incredible, but I don't want any problems."

"There won't be any."

"You should probably leave."

"But you promised."

"Yes, but I didn't know you had a husband."

Lucy's face fell. "He abuses me. The other night, I told him no, and he raped me. When he's not forcing me, he's getting it from his side-whore." A tear slid out of the corner of her eye.

Adam pulled on his bottom lip. "The miserable asshole. You're right. He *doesn't* deserve you."

"I know, and I want to get away, but I'm scared he will find me and hurt me worse."

"Where is he now?"

"He's a trucker, and he is on the road for a few more days. Please. Will you help me? You promised."

Adam sighed and looked away. Finally, he looked back and nodded, the memory of the night before still fresh in his mind. He was hoping to get more of the same. "Okay. Yes, I'll help you. What do you want me to do?"

"Inject him."

"What the hell! How am I supposed to do that?"

"I'll help you figure it out."

"Inject him with what?"

"Leuprolide acetate. It's a drug that will chemically castrate him. He will never rape me or cheat on me again."

"Wow. That's craziness. Kinda harsh, but I guess he deserves it. Why can't you do it?"

"Because I still have to live with him. It needs to be done by a stranger. It needs to be a surprise."

Adam looked down at the wood flooring. "Damn. I dunno."

"It'll be easy, Adam. I'll give you the syringe. When he gets back, I'll tell you where you can find him. You can wait for him in the parking garage at our complex. Ask him for directions or something. One quick jab and you're done. Drive off and it's over. He won't know what hit him."

"So, what happens when I do this? Can I still see you?"

"Of course," she lied.

"But doesn't that stuff eventually wear off?"

"Not the stuff I'm gonna give you."

Adam sucked in a deep, cleansing breath, his eyes taking in the terrific body in front of him. She even looked good in a T-shirt. "Okay, let's do this."

———

THE PARKING GARAGE WAS LARGER THAN HE HAD expected, but Adam parked where she told him to and waited. If she was accurate with her timing, Lucy's husband should be pulling up any time. Adam supposedly couldn't miss the camo-colored Jeep that he would be driving.

The syringe sat on the passenger seat, and Adam picked it up, holding it to the light. The clear liquid looked harmless, but he knew better. Hopefully, the drug would take away Lucy's husband's urges. If that were the case, there would be more for Adam. And he would take as much of Lucy as she was willing to give.

The movement of the parking garage barrier arm pulled his attention to the entrance, and he observed a late model Volvo enter the garage and park. A mid-thirties blond in yoga pants and a tight top got out and walked to the entrance of the building. Adam couldn't help but check out her ass, and although it was nice, his mind was still on Lucy and her all-over tanned, perfectly shaped body. He still couldn't believe he had landed her. All he had to do was poke her asshole husband with a needle and she would be coming to Adam's bed whenever she wanted it.

More movement at the gate brought him back to the task at hand. This time, it was the Jeep. Making sure the cap was on tightly, Adam slid the syringe into his right pocket and felt inside to confirm it still contained the other item he had placed there earlier. He was all set.

Straining to see past the parked cars, Adam could barely make out the man getting out of the Jeep. He started to walk toward the building and would be walking past Adam soon. Ten car-lengths…then eight…six. Adam got out of his car and opened the back door, pretending to fish around in the back seat. His hand gripped the item in his right pocket. Four cars away. Now two. Adam shut the car door just as the man rounded the corner. Adam spun around and fell in step behind the man, pulling the taser from his pocket. He quickened his steps, taking care to do so quietly, then jammed the taser into the man's back, fumbling with the button to bring the juice.

"What the fu—" The man, startled, started to spin around, and it was then that Adam realized it didn't work. Fifty-thousand volts didn't crackle at the end of the device. No electrical shock was delivered to the stranger. Adam realized in a split second that he had majorly screwed up. He also immediately realized that the man was much bigger than him.

As the man spun, he instinctively noticed something in Adam's hand, and his right arm shot out and knocked Adam's hand away, sending the taser skittering across the parking area and under Adam's car. Adam wasn't sure where he went wrong, but he was hoping he could talk his way out of the situation.

"What's your deal, asswipe?" The man was seething.

"S…sorry, I thought you were someone I knew."

"What the hell was that thing that went under the car?"

"Uh…my phone."

"Do you always sneak up on people like that?"

"No. It was a very bad prank. I thought you were him. Uh…Harry. I thought you were Harry. I was going to scare you and pretend I was going to rob you…er, him."

"That's the kind of shit that is going to end your life if you do it to the wrong person."

"I'm really sorry. I didn't really think it through. You probably broke my phone."

"It would serve you right."

"You're right. I'm an idiot. I'm sorry. I won't make that mistake twice. At any rate, I've learned my lesson. Could you please help me find my phone?"

"Why the hell should I help you after the stunt you pulled?"

"Well, it was you that knocked it out of my hand."

"Do you blame me?"

"No." Adam let his face fall and did his best pathetic impression.

"Oh, Jesus. Fine. Did you see exactly where it went?"

"I think under here." Adam pointed and got down on one knee, trying to look under the car. The stranger got down on both knees next to him and contorted his body to see under the vehicle.

"I think I see it."

"Where?" Adam asked.

"Right behind the rear wheel." He lay down on his stomach and reached for the lost item. "Almost got it."

"Here. Let me help you," Adam offered, removing the syringe from his pocket, pulling off the cap and stabbing it into the man's left butt cheek, depressing the plunger at the same time. The man reacted to the bite of flesh and tried to get up, slamming his head on the underside of the car.

"Son-of-a-bitch! What the hell was that?"

Adam backed away as the larger man scooted out from under the car, springing to his feet faster than Adam thought possible. Nothing was going as planned, and although he had injected the drug—his main goal—he had set himself up for getting his ass kicked. The drug itself would not incapacitate the man. That was what the stun gun was for. Now he wasn't sure what his next move would be, and the man was standing between Adam and his car.

"I'm gonna mess you up, little man. I should have crushed you the first time you came at me."

The man charged at Adam and took a swing. Adam sidestepped his advance and the man missed but quickly recovered and turned toward Adam a second time, his fists at the ready. Before Adam could react, the man's right meat paw landed on Adam's jaw, and it spun him around, slamming him against his car. Adam shook off the pounding in his skull and reached for the door handle. Maybe he could get inside, lock the door, and drive away. His job was done. His promise was fulfilled.

The back of his shirt was immediately pulled tight as he tried to open the door, and he was yanked away from the car, the door flinging open in the process. He felt a knee drive into his back, and pain exploded up his spine a second before he crumpled into a heap on the ground of the parking garage.

"Looks like you didn't learn your lesson after all, dumbass!"

the man snarled, which was followed by a gut-wrenching laugh. "You picked the wrong guy to screw with."

Adam looked up at the man, worried that he would pummel Adam's ass while he lay on the ground, unable to get up. The man approached, and Adam could see his scuffed boots in front of his face.

"Had enough?" the man asked.

Adam remained silent.

"I guess not."

From his point-of-view at ground level, Adam watched as the man took a step back. He started to come forward, and his right boot came up. Adam closed his eyes and braced himself for the impact—one he was sure would crush his skull. It wasn't until he heard the hard thump that he realized he hadn't been kicked. Opening his eyes, he saw the man lying on the ground six feet away from him. The man's eyes stared at him and his mouth was working, but no legible words were coming out. It was more of a high-pitched twitter.

Feeling the need to get the hell out of there, Adam pushed through the pain and pulled himself up off the ground, stumbling to the car.

What the hell was in that hypodermic?

Behind the wheel, Adam grimaced and started the car, throwing it into reverse. He glanced over at the man on the ground, his mouth still slowly moving, his eyes unblinking. Adam pressed the gas and backed out of the spot, and as he shifted into drive, he noticed something on the ground where his car had been.

The stun gun. And it has my prints on it. Shit.

Putting the car in park, Adam forced himself out of the seat and retrieved the stun gun, every inch of his body hurting as he bent down to pick it up. He made his way back to the car and shut the door.

While he had been hell-bent on getting out of there before someone else arrived, his attention quickly turned to the device and why it hadn't worked. The entire scheme had revolved around him shocking the bigger man and temporarily incapacitating him. So much for best-laid plans. As he studied the device, he realized where he had gone wrong. He should have tested it before he approached the man. This model actually had two switches. One had to be turned on before the trigger switch would activate the arc. He slid the switch up and pressed the trigger. The electricity zapped across the two contacts at the end of the device, and a loud crackling filled the car. The smell of ozone, much like what permeated the air after a lightning strike, assaulted his nostrils. Adam wished he had figured out how to use the damn thing before he got himself into this pickle. Maybe he wouldn't feel like he had been run over by a garbage truck. All he would have had to do was press the button—he pressed the trigger button again—and stick the man in the side or neck with it. His body automatically demonstrated what his mind was telling him he should have done, and even though he let go of the button again before he placed the device to his own neck, somehow in the process of acting out the scenario in his painful state, he managed to press the button one more time. The electricity shot through his neck, and Adam dropped the stun gun and fell back against the seat, his scream filling the void that the crackling had left behind when he dropped the device.

Body racked with pain, Adam pushed himself against the seat and groaned, trying to shake off some of the sharp jabs that were still coursing through his flesh and muscles. When the pain dulled to a low roar a few minutes later, he shifted back into drive and pulled to the exit of the garage. Impatiently, with watering eyes, he waited for the gate arm to swing up, and when it did, he pulled out into the sparse traffic.

———

"How did it go? Did you do it?" Lucy eagerly asked.

"It's done."

"Where did you inject him?"

"I did it just like you told me. Right in his ass."

"What did he say to you? Anything?"

"He asked me what I did to him."

"What did you tell him?"

"Nothing. I was too busy getting my ass kicked."

Lucy looked at the bruise on his chin and the burn marks on his neck and winced. "Sorry about that."

"It's all good. He's a big sumbitch, but in the end, I won. Speaking of…you didn't tell me the drug was gonna knock him on his ass. That was the only thing that saved me. He's gonna be all right, right?"

Lucy smiled. "Don't worry. That's normal."

"I suppose when you get home, he'll probably be angry."

"You let me worry about that. For now, since you were such a good boy, you get a prize."

"Nice! What's my prize?"

Lucy licked her lips and grabbed his crotch with her right hand. "Me."

———

Back home, Lucy got undressed and threw on a pair of designer sweats. She had been over at Adam's house every night since the first night they had met in the bar. She was glad to be home and that the job was done. She was looking forward to a night alone. She smiled as she thought about the story that Adam had so easily bought. Abusive husband. Cheater. Neither was true. Corbin Hughes, the man that Adam had left lying in the parking garage, was none of those things, and he certainly wasn't her husband. What he was, though, was a killer. When Corbin's father had passed, he was the sole caregiver for his mother, who was also elderly and ailing. His eyes on his future inheritance, Corbin saw nothing wrong with helping his mother make a faster journey to the other side. Corbin Hughes was a dirtbag and deserved what he got. What Adam didn't know was that the syringe hadn't contained Leuprolide Acetate after all—or that Corbin Hughes never got back up.

———

THE NEXT MORNING, LUCY ARRIVED TO WORK A LITTLE early. She enjoyed her job more than she had a right to. Catching the elevator, she listened to the Musak that piped over the speakers as the car passed floor after floor. She had actually timed it once, and the ride typically took her over four minutes before the doors opened on her floor, which were the executive offices. A couple floors down was where the lower-level employees and worker bees did their thing. She would visit the "grunts," as she called them, from time-to-time, but she spent most of her time either in her office strategizing or out in the field doing a damn thing. No better way to get the results that she wanted—hell, she needed—than to be boots on the ground, leading the charge.

In her office, she went over the weekly production reports and smiled at the positive trend the company was seeing over the past thirty-four weeks, ever since her old man had finally retired—it had seemed like thousands of years that he ran the show—and left the operation to her. She had done nothing but positively increase the numbers since she had taken over. Her ideas were unique. They were fresh. Above all else, they were working.

In need of caffeine, Lucy left her office and headed down one floor, hoping the cafeteria had the coffee ready and maybe something to eat for breakfast. She was a little earlier than normal on this day, but typically she ate her morning meal in her office as she was too lazy to fix something at home, and the food there was actually quite good.

As she stepped out of the elevator and walked by the group of offices she had to pass before getting to the common area, she noticed the door to Stevens' office was slightly ajar, and she could see flashes of color. Laughter erupted from the small gap in the door. Typically, Connor Stevens wouldn't be in for at least another hour. Not only was he in early, it sounded like others were as well. Lucy rapped on the door and pushed it open, as five sets of eyes that were sitting around the office turned toward her. A video played on the big screen TV that took up the end wall of the office.

"You guys having a party and you didn't invite me?" Lucy joked.

"Oh…hey, Boss. We were just watching a video. Didn't know you'd be in yet," Stevens replied.

Connor Stevens was in charge of all the video production and archives for the company. Not only did he work hand-in-hand with marketing when they had an active campaign going, he also was in charge of making sure that all events were recorded and stored. Whenever a video event needed to be viewed or streamed, it was important that it could be recalled within seconds of the request. Stevens had built a system so complex that they had trillions of hours of video archived, and he could bring up any request at any time with instant recall.

It wasn't unusual that Stevens was watching video—it was part of his job—but it was odd that he had invited a group of others to watch. Lucy looked around the room. Swanson, Timmons, Alverez, and the girl Lucy thought Stevens was dating, Mandy Hunt from accounting. This group seemed to hang out quite a bit together after work. She had been invited a couple of times to grab drinks with them.

"So, what are we watching?" Lucy asked, her interest piqued.

Steven's looked a little embarrassed but decided to come clean. "Just about the funniest damn thing you will ever see. Real life stuff."

"You know me. I love a good laugh. What is it?" Lucy's eyebrows shot up.

"You remember that Adam guy you recently brought over to our team?"

"How could I forget? I worked my ass off to get him to do what I wanted."

"Did he tell you about what happened when he injected Corbin Hughes?"

"That he got hit."

"That's it?"

"Did he leave something out?"

"Oh, did he ever!" Stevens' said, while the rest of the people in the room started laughing. "Want me to roll it back to the beginning?"

"I must say that you have my attention. Hell yes, roll it back!"

Steven's took the video back to the part where Adam entered the parking garage. He sped the video up as Adam waited for Hughes and then slowed it down again when the Jeep pulled into the parking structure.

"What is that thing in Adam's hand?" Lucy asked.

"Just wait. It will all become clear."

The group watched the video again with Lucy seeing it for

the first time. As they watched Adam get his ass kicked, they all broke out laughing.

"That's hilarious," Lucy said, laughing. "Adam is a bit of a douchebag. Well deserved."

"It gets better," Stevens told her. "Keep watching."

They continued to watch as Hughes collapsed and as Adam finally pulled himself up and got in the car. As he got back out to retrieve the device that had been under the car, Stevens nudged her and pointed. Just then, they watched Adam put the stun gun to his neck and his entire frame jerked as the electricity coursed through his body. The room erupted again.

"This is good stuff, Connor! Hilarious. How come I am just now seeing this for the first time?" She wasn't mad, but she definitely was giving him a little bit of a hard time.

"Because you never asked?" he said playfully.

"Right…well, make a mental note. Any time you have hilarious shit like this come through, let me know. I can always use a good laugh. In fact, maybe put together a highlights reel for our weekly staff meeting. That will take some of the stuffiness out of the room. Maybe people will actually *want* to come to them."

"You got it, Boss!"

"Okay, I need coffee. Catch you all later." As she left Stevens' office, the image of Adam sticking the stun gun up to his neck and pulling the trigger looped through her mind. "Damn, I love my job," she muttered, a smile taking over every line of her face.

Back in her office, she set her breakfast sandwich, side of bacon, and carafe of coffee on the desk. Wiping the sweat from her brow with the back of her hand, she checked the thermostat and turned it down a few degrees. It seemed that no matter what they did, she was always too hot, which seemed to be a side effect of working in this part of the building. Back at her desk, she took a bite of her sandwich and brought up the local news on the big screen in her office. As she finished her food and was working on her coffee, her attention was pulled to the doorway, where Griffin Fleming from the receiving department stood, a clipboard in his hand.

"I'm sorry, I hope I didn't startle you."

"Not at all, Griffin. Come on in."

"I wanted to let you know that your plan is working, and incomings are up by twenty-eight percent. That's the highest increase we've had in years. Even when your father was running the ship. Pretty impressive."

"I'm pleased. Thank you, Griffin. I believe in being hands-on, and it appears it's helping."

"I never doubted you, but I will say that I wasn't sure you would get the numbers you were looking for. After all, your plan was rather... well...unorthodox."

"I'm sure...especially after all you knew before was my father's way of doing things around here. He was so old fashioned. Never challenged the status quo. Throw a few temptations out into the world and hope you get some action. It's like fishing. Some bite and some don't. My way is so much more effective. And for each one I interact with, it's a two-for-one deal. It doesn't get any better than that."

"Speaking of," Griffin chimed in, "I wanted to let you know, Miss Fehr, that we received the soul last night of one Corbin Hughes. Great job, Boss. There are some sick people up there, but that vile human being murdered his own mother. Glad you could finally get him where he belongs."

"Thanks, Griffin. It's too bad that they have to die in order for us to get their soul. It would be so much easier if we could take it while they are alive. And we can't kill them ourselves. Shit, if that were only the case. It'd make everything so damned easy. It was really nice of Adam to send him to us early, wasn't it?"

"Oh yes. That was indeed nice of Mr. Adam. Too bad for him that he is now a murderer as well, isn't it? Will we see him soon?"

"Oh, you can count on it!" Lucy flashed her most devilish smile. "It's time for me to hit another bar later this week. Gotta keep those numbers up!"

SHADOW OF TORMENT

CHAPTER ONE

Braydon Hunt gasped as he tried to suck the cool, sweet air back into his lungs. The tears streaming down his face gave away the anguish he was in, yet the other kids standing around did nothing to help him; instead, they laughed and called him names.

"Looks like Braydon is a scaredy-cat," one of the other boys at the bus stop yelled.

"Look at Braydon the Bitch!" another called out.

"What you gonna do about it?" Jake Connors challenged. "Do you want another one?"

Braydon was finally able to catch a breath, but as soon as Jake raised his fist again, he cowered, steadying himself for another punch to the gut. Unsure of what he did to provoke him this time—he had been minding his own business—Braydon hoped the bus would show up soon. Surely the bus driver would put an end to this bullshit.

Without warning, Jake rushed Braydon and shoved him so hard, he fell backwards and landed in the gravel on his ass. The pain from the hard landing jarred Braydon and the tears flowed even harder, though he chided himself and told himself not to cry.

The kids began chanting. "Braydon the Bitch! Braydon the Bitch!"

Braydon pulled himself to his feet and reached into the right pocket of his shorts. His palm was abraded from the fall and he was in pain, but more importantly, he wanted the abuse —and the attention on him—to stop. Braydon pulled out the three dollars his mom had left for him on the counter—barely enough for a crappy school lunch.

"If you leave me alone, I'll give you my lunch money." Braydon held the bills out toward Jake.

Jake snatched up the bills. "This only takes care of today, pussy. Tomorrow's another day."

Jake turned around and joined the rest of the kids as quickly as he had focused on Braydon. In an instant, no one was paying any attention to him. Braydon dusted the dirt off his clothes and retrieved his fallen backpack. It was then he heard the deep growl of the school bus as it made its way up the hill toward their stop. He was safe. For now.

On the bus, Braydon took up a seat in the front, which was where the losers got to sit. The cool kids always sat in the back and the one time he had tried to sit back there had ended badly for him. The bus driver, Mrs. Gibson, turned to him after the door was closed, obviously able to tell something was wrong.

"You okay?" she asked.

Braydon turned toward her. He had always liked Mrs. Gibson. She had a kind face and reminded him of his Aunt Betty. As much as he felt he could trust her, he was embarrassed by the situation and he put on a brave face. Being a tattletale would do nothing but get his ass beat again.

"I'm good. Thank you, Mrs. Gibson. I slipped and fell on some loose gravel, but I'm okay."

She gave him that look that moms give their kids when they don't believe them. "You sure?"

"I'm sure," he responded.

"Well, okay then." Mrs. Gibson turned around, flipped off the flashing lights, retracted the "Stop" sign and headed down the street toward the next stop.

Braydon knew they had thirty minutes and six more stops before they got to school. By that time, the bus would be packed to max capacity and he would be extremely anxious. One advantage of sitting up front was he would be the first one off and would be able to make a swift departure to the library —his sanctuary. None of the assholes hung out in the library. He felt safe there.

Braydon had been picked on as long as he could remember. He was small for his age and was hoping that he would grow more before his eleventh birthday. Although he felt he was fairly normal, besides being awkward, he wasn't very coordinated and was terrible at sports. He was also awful at fighting. The one time he decided to grow a set of balls and challenge his tormenter—after watching the first Rocky movie—it had ended badly. He went home that day beat to shit.

It wasn't just the physical bullying that he had to put up with. He was appalled at some of the names the other kids called him. He wasn't even allowed to think about those words. The constant barrage of teasing made him hate his name. "Braydon the Bitch" was tame compared to some days. He hated that his last name, "Hunt," rhymed with one of the more obscene names they called him.

Braydon's lack of coordination and the constant bullying tore at his self-esteem and eventually, he became an introvert, getting lost in the world of books and the anonymity of the internet, instead of doing many of the activities the other kids were doing. While others were hanging out, he was at home shut in his bedroom.

At school, Braydon beelined it to the library and stayed there until the five-minute warning bell, which was his daily ritual. In Mrs. Franklin's room, he settled into his desk and pulled out his homework from the night before. He was good until lunch and if he could make it through that forty-five minutes of torture—he tried to grab his food and disappear— he would be good for another day. That was how Braydon lived his life—day-by-day until he got to the weekend and week-by-week until winter break, spring break and summer break. The in-betweens were the hardest to get through.

Braydon did have a couple of friends that lived in the neighborhood, but unfortunately, one went to a private school and the other boy's parents drove him to school. Braydon once asked if he could ride with them, but he was told no. Something about it being a liability. Braydon had no idea what that meant. Regardless, the circumstances left no one on the bus that had Braydon's back. When he asked his mom if she could drive him to school, she told him no, since she had to leave for work much earlier. She wasn't comfortable dropping him off at the school when no one else was there. He was sure if he told her what was going on, she'd do something to help, but he was embarrassed. He surely didn't want his mom to know he was one of *those* kids—the ones that got picked on all the time. Instead, he never asked her again and he simply dealt with it.

As difficult as life was for Braydon, he was thankful that he didn't have to ride the bus home as well. One benefit of his mom working an early shift was that she was there to pick him up after school most days.

After school, Braydon slipped outside as quickly as possible, staying out of the areas that he knew he would encounter his tormentors. When he spotted the maroon Saturn in the pick-up area, he walked faster and got to the car as quickly as possible. Before he climbed in, he threw his backpack in the back seat.

"Hey Bray! How was school today?"

"It was school."

She brushed his blonde hair out of his eyes. "Care to elaborate?"

"I'm not sure what else there is to say."

Knowing she wasn't going to get more out of him than that, she changed the subject. "Do you have homework?"

"A little."

"Why don't you do it while I make dinner? Then you can do whatever it is you do after dinner."

"I'll probably read."

"What book are you working on?"

"Danny, the Champion of the World."

"OH! Roald Dahl?"

"Yep."

"I used to love his books when I was little."

"Did they even have books when you were little?" Braydon teased.

"Yes, but little kids had to eat bread and drink water for dinner. Which is what we're having tonight."

"Okay, Mom, no need to get all extreme on me."

"But didn't you start it?" she said, winking at him.

"Not sure what you're talking about."

"Thought so. Any big plans this weekend?"

"I was hoping to go spend the night with Adam in his tree fort." Adam was one of only two friends he had. Both friends lived in the same neighborhood.

"Is that safe?"

"Of course. Mr. Henderson built it himself. It even has electricity and a TV!"

"Wow, sounds like quite the place. Maybe I can come, too."

"No way! No moms allowed."

"Well, that's not very nice." Mary, his mother, pretended to pout.

"Can I go?"

"Remind me where this fort is again?"

"In Adam's back yard."

"Will his parents be there?"

"In the house."

"Okay, I suppose that works. Just let me know what night. Oh yeah…you have to text me when you get there, before you go to sleep and, in the morning, when you get up."

"C'mon, Mom. I'm almost eleven."

"Those are the rules. Deal with them or stay home."

"Moooom. Really? It's embarrassing."

"I'm not budging on this one, Bray."

"Fine," Braydon said, crossing his arms.

Sometimes Braydon wished his dad was around. Maybe he would have been more reasonable. Although he had seen him a handful of times in his ten years, he didn't really remember him. His father had another family somewhere that took up all his time.

When they pulled into the driveway and Mary parked the car, Braydon slipped out of the door and went into the house.

"Don't forget to get your homework done first!" she called after him.

"I know!" he called back, disappearing into his room before she could say another word.

CHAPTER TWO

In his room, Braydon sent a text to Adam and when their sleepover had been arranged, he finished his math homework. He actually did well in school and overall got good grades—when he was trying—and he usually worked to keep his grades at an "A" or "B" level to keep his mom off his butt. It worked and she usually left him alone because of it.

After dinner, he jumped online and entered a game of *Sunday, Bloody Sunday*, a multi-player slasher game that revolved around trying to maim or kill the other opponents as grotesquely as possible. His mom didn't allow him to have a gaming system. Little did she know he was gaming anyway, online. He usually played for a couple hours, then read for a bit before bed.

A blip alerted Braydon to an incoming message in a private chat window.

Destroyer_Boy: hey dude, good game

He answered the other player who was one of his online friends.

Braydon_Bites: thx

Destroyer_Boy: how much later u gonna b on

Braydon_Bites: maybe 1 more game. school 2mrw

Destroyer_Boy: yeah...me 2. What u doing this weekend

Braydon_Bites: gonna hang with one of my friends

Destroyer_Boy: Adam?

Braydon_Bites: yup

Destroyer_Boy: whatya gonna do?

Braydon_Bites: he has a kickass treehouse. gonna spend the night there

Destroyer_Boy: fun. i wish i could come

Braydon_Bites: maybe you could if u didn't live in wyoming

Destroyer_Boy: yeah, it sux

Braydon_Bites: well maybe you can come visit sometime

Destroyer_Boy: dude! im 12. not like im driving anytime soon

Braydon_Bites: well maybe one day. aren't u like one state over?

Destroyer_Boy: where do u live again

Braydon_Bites: utah

Destroyer_Boy: hold on…let me google that shit

Braydon_Bites: waiting

Destroyer_Boy: holy balls! Ur right next door. There is a three day weekend coming up soon. Maybe I could talk my dad into driving me there for a couple days

Braydon_Bites: that would be so cool

Destroyer_Boy: will u check with your mom and see if that's ok?

Braydon_Bites: yeah. I'll ask her

Destroyer_Boy: u think yer mom is gonna let u do that? Have me over?

Braydon_Bites: she trusts me

Destroyer_Boy: what about yer dad?

Braydon_Bites: he isn't around

Destroyer_Boy: that sux. I'll let you know what my dad says

Braydon_Bites: I'll let you know what mom says as soon as I get time to ask her

> *Destroyer_Boy: cool! anyway, let's play another game*
>
> *Braydon_Bites: prepare to die!*

Braydon jumped into the game and used his sword to lop off another player's arm. He would occasionally chat with other players, but he had been chatting with Destroyer_Boy—his real name was Damion—for three months now. He was a good friend, but unfortunately lived far away. They would usually chat a little bit each night.

Twenty minutes later, he had used up all his lives—his last one taken when he was sliced in two down the middle—and he shut down the computer. In the living room, he found his mom watching television and he said goodnight and gave her a kiss, before returning to his room to read. He found that since he started seeking her out to tell her goodnight, she stayed away from his room more and more, which eliminated her catching him doing something he shouldn't be.

In bed, he slipped the copy of *Danny, the Champion of the World* out of his backpack and set it in front of him before pulling out the copy of *Pet Sematary* he was reading. He hated lying to his mother, but she was always monitoring what he watched or read. He found it simpler to tell her what she wanted to hear. He could be very convincing, especially when he was smart enough to have a copy of the book he was *supposed* to be reading.

Braydon had only been into the extreme for about a year and a half. He remembered his first taste. His only other friend, Rudy, was lucky, because his parents had all the movie channels one could possibly subscribe to. Rudy also had a television in his bedroom, which led to many occasions where they stayed up all night watching horror-flicks. Enthralled, he started reading any horror book he could get his hands on. Soon, he was enjoying online gaming where he was the one doling out the punishment.

Braydon would never hurt anyone; the games were his escape. Although he had several tormenters, Jake was the worst and the most aggressive. Braydon would often picture Jake's face when he annihilated his opponent. Although it didn't help much, it made each day a little more tolerable.

The next day, Braydon waited until the last minute before he left the safety of his house. Miscalculating, he ran out the door toward the stop as soon as the front of the bus slipped into view. The eight kids piled onto the bus in orderly fashion as Braydon ran as quickly as he could toward the stop, his backpack bouncing against his back and slowing him down.

"Wait!" he yelled as he saw the yellow doors flip shut. He stopped, a good fifty feet from the bus, but Mrs. Gibson didn't notice him. With a hiss of the air brakes, the bus left the stop and continued on. He was too late.

Upset with himself for missing the bus, yet slightly relieved that he didn't have to put up with Jake's crap, he adjusted his backpack and started walking down the hill. It was almost a three-mile walk to school and he would definitely be late. He really didn't want to have to explain this one to his mom. While she usually was pretty chill about things, if he had to explain *why* he missed the bus, she would definitely want to go talk to Jake's parents. If that happened, his ass would be grass and Jake would beat the hell out of him even more.

Jake hadn't always picked on him. Braydon thought back to when they were younger. They used to spend time at each other's houses all the time; in fact, for years, they were inseparable. At some point in time, Jake had moved on, throwing Braydon under his tires as he left. It was easy to feel like it was his fault. No one wanted to be around a goober. Still, Braydon couldn't figure out why Jake had turned on him when they had been so close. He understood Jake not wanting to hang, but torturing him in front of everyone was so uncool. If he felt worthless before, Jake's actions made him feel like the lowest form of life that ever existed.

A little over an hour and fifteen minutes later when Braydon got to school, he headed to his classroom. The walk had been long and he was tired. He was happy it was Friday and he could stop looking over his shoulder for a couple days. At the end of school, he made sure he had everything in his backpack that he needed and he ran out to meet his mom. When he was safely in the car, he let out a sigh, threw his head back against the headrest and closed his eyes.

"Hey Bray. You okay?"

"Yeah, Mom. I'm tired. Can we go home?"

"Isn't that where we normally go when I pick you up?"

"Mom! You know what I mean."

Changing the subject as she pulled away from the curb, Mary steered the conversation toward the weekend. "You never did let me know what night you wanted to stay at Adam's."

"Oh yeah. That's tonight."

"And you were going to tell me when?"

"Now?"

"Fine. You can go, but I need more notice in the future in case I have something planned."

"That would require you to have a life, Mom. Which you don't."

"Ouch, my heart," she told him, holding her hands against her chest in mock pain.

"Well? Do you have any plans this weekend?" he asked.

"Yes. As soon as I get the house cleaned up and our laundry done, the plan is for my butt to be parked on the couch watching TV for the rest of the weekend."

"Living on the edge," he joked.

"Oh, you have no idea," Mary said, smiling.

When they pulled into the driveway, Braydon scooted out of the front seat before she even shut off the car and let himself in the house. Inside, Mary went to his bedroom and knocked on the door.

"Hey! What time are you going to Adam's?"

"Around seven, after he gets home from practice."

"Okay. Just let me know before you leave."

"I will, Mom."

"Do you have homework?" she asked through the closed door.

Braydon whipped the door open. "Yes. Can I do it Sunday?"

"As long as you don't forget."

"Really, Mom. Have you seen my grades?"

"Fair enough. Do me a favor before you get wrapped up with whatever ten-year-old boys get wrapped up in. Please take out the trash."

Braydon rolled his eyes which didn't get past his mother.

"Really, Bray? An eyeroll? In broad daylight?"

Braydon walked past her and into the kitchen to grab the overstuffed bag of trash.

"If you're like this at ten, I can't wait until you hit thirteen," she told him, her voice laden with sarcasm.

"Me neither," he answered, not catching what she was saying.

A knock pulled both of their attentions to the front door. Both Mary and Braydon looked at each other, a puzzled look on their faces. They rarely had visitors and when there was a knock or the doorbell rang, they typically found an Amazon package sitting on the porch, the delivery driver rushing off to deliver the next one. Being the closest, Mary walked over, peeped through the viewfinder and opened the door.

"Oh my! It *is* you! How've you been, Jake? How come we never see you around here anymore?"

"Oh, hey, Mrs. Hunt. How are you? Can I come in?"

"Why, certainly!" Mary stepped back from the door and let him in. Braydon stopped, the overflowing trash bag midair, shocked that his nemesis had just walked into the house. Even worse was that his mother had let him in.

When Braydon said nothing, Mary chided him. "Aren't you going to say hi to your friend, Bray?"

"Um…hey," Braydon said, looking down at the floor.

"What brings you by, Jake?"

"I just wanted to stop by and make sure Braydon was okay."

Oh shit. What is he up to? Braydon thought.

"Of course he is. Why do you ask?" She turned toward Braydon. "Braydon, is something wrong?"

Braydon shook his head.

Jake continued. "Well, it's just that Braydon missed the bus this morning. I'm used to hanging out with him. I thought he might be sick."

Puzzled, Mary turned back to Braydon. "Honey, did you miss the bus? Why didn't you tell me?"

"It's no big deal, Mom."

"Well, what happened?" she asked.

"Yeah, Braydon? What happened? I was waiting for you and you never showed."

"I was just running late. I told you, it's nothing."

"Well, how did you get to school?"

"I walked."

"What? You're ten and it's three miles!"

"I'm aware. On both counts."

"You should have called me."

"You were working."

"Still."

"I handled it."

"Well, if you're going to be missing the bus, maybe you need to get to bed earlier."

"Mooom! Really? It was one time. I'm fine."

"We'll see. Let's discuss this tomorrow."

Jake chimed in again. "Can Braydon come hang out at my house tonight, Mrs. Hunt?"

"Oh, that would be really nice, Jake. You boys haven't hung out in forever." She failed to see the fear in Braydon's eyes.

"Mom, I have plans tonight, remember?"

"I know, but can't you cancel with Adam? You never spend time at Jake's anymore."

"No Mom, I'm not canceling."

"Do you really want to spend the night in some smelly tree fort when you could be inside playing games or whatever it is you boys do?"

Braydon was silent, upset that she had opened her mouth, yet knowing it wasn't her fault since he kept everything from her.

"Oh, that's okay, Mrs. Hunt. I didn't know Braydon was going to spend the night with Adam in the tree fort. I wouldn't want to mess up his plans." Jake shot Braydon a fierce look when Mary wasn't looking. "I'd better get going. I just wanted to make sure Braydon knew I missed him this morning. I hope you both have a great evening."

Jake left and Mary shut the door after him. "It was so good to see him. What a nice boy."

"You have no idea," Braydon mumbled under his breath as he took the trash out the back door and threw it into the trash bin.

CHAPTER THREE

Destroyer_Boy: he did wut?

Braydon_Bites: he showed up here and my mom let him in

Destroyer_Boy: NFW

Braydon_Bites: yes way

Destroyer_Boy: wut did he say

Braydon_Bites: he ratted on me for missing the bus. it was creepy

Destroyer_Boy: did he threaten you?

Braydon_Bites: sorta. i feel like he was trying to scare me

Destroyer_Boy: wut a dick

Braydon_Bites: tell me about it

Destroyer_Boy: so wut r u gonna do?

Braydon_Bites: same as always. try to avoid him

Destroyer_Boy: good luck

Braydon_Bites: thanks. i need it. Why can't he get hit by a truck

Destroyer_Boy: u dont mean that do u

Braydon_Bites: kinda

Destroyer_Boy: he sounds like a little douchebag

Braydon_Bites: a big one

Destroyer_Boy: hey, btw, I forgot to tell you. my dad is cool with going on a trip where u live. u down?

Braydon_Bites: I mean sure. I still haven't asked my mom. if she lets me, sure thing. when is it?

Destroyer_Boy: The 3 day weekend is next

weekend. maybe our rents could drop us off someplace and we can hang out. is there anything fun to do there?

    Braydon_Bites: we have this cool trampoline place

    Destroyer_Boy: that sounds fun. I can show u how it's done

    Braydon_Bites: oh, like u do when I whip your butt on Bloody Sunday?

    Destroyer_Boy: smartass

    Braydon_Bites: I'll talk 2 her today or tomorrow and let u know

    Destroyer_Boy: nice

    Braydon_Bites: ready to play a game or 2 before I have to leave for adams?

    Destroyer_Boy: lets do it!

Braydon entered a new game and he noticed Damion enter the game a few moments later. They teamed up together as they usually did and fought against the other players. Each game would allow ten people to participate and would last until only one player was remaining. Each player was given three lives to use during the game. Once a game was full and it had ten players in it, the next players that logged on would be put into the next game. While one of them would usually die off before the other, there were two different occasions where Braydon and Damion were the last two players. Braydon had won both of those games, although it felt weird to battle against his friend.

Around 6:45, Braydon got killed off and exited the game, sending Damion a message that he was leaving for the night. In his room, he dumped the contents of his backpack out on the bed and stuffed a change of clothes and some sweats into the pockets. In his bathroom, he grabbed his toothbrush and toothpaste and slid them in the side pocket of the pack.

When he was finished gathering his things, he went into the kitchen and grabbed a few snacks just in case, adding them to the other side pocket of the backpack.

"Mom?"

"In the bedroom, honey."

Braydon went to her bedroom doorway and walked in. She looked up from the book she was reading, closing it, her index finger acting as a bookmark. He sat down on the edge of the bed.

"I'm leaving now, Mom."

"Okay. Don't forget to text me when you get there and before you go to bed."

"Sure. Are you going to be okay?" Braydon worried about her being there all by herself, but she certainly could take care of herself and had been doing so since his father had left. Although she had a thin build and was fairly short, she was strong-willed when pushed and knew how to push back when necessary. She reminded him of the actress Mila Kunis, which was a comparison he hated to make, because as a ten-year-old-boy—who was almost eleven—he had a schoolboy crush on Mila. Comparing someone he crushed on with his mother was just gross to him.

"I'll be fine, Bray. I'm going to finish this book and then watch some TV for the rest of the night. When will you be home tomorrow?"

"Probably in the afternoon."

"Okay. Have a great time!"

"I will. Um…before I leave, can I ask you something?"

"Of course. What's up?"

"I have a friend that lives in Wyoming that is going to be in town visiting next weekend. Can I hang out with him?"

"Wyoming? How do you know this kid?"

"I met him online in a chat room."

"A chat room? Braydon, we've talked about this before. Chat rooms are full of creeps and pedophiles."

"Maybe. But they are also full of other kids. I can tell the difference."

"How can you tell?"

"This kid talks just like me."

"That's what they do to make you think they're a kid, Braydon! You haven't given out our address, have you?"

"No, Mom! I know better than that. We've just chatted. Other than our city, he doesn't know where I live."

"How long have you known this guy?"

"A few months."

"What's his name?"

"Damion."

"How old is he?"

"Twelve."

Mary paused. "I don't like this. The answer is no, Braydon. It's my job to keep you safe."

"But Mom…"

"No Braydon. We can't risk it."

"He's going to be with his dad. What if you meet the dad first in a public place? Please? If you meet him and still feel something's off, I won't go. Please?"

Mary sighed, pausing a moment before she answered. Braydon was a good kid and a responsible one. The mom side of her was protective, but she still wanted him to be a kid and have fun. Maybe Braydon's suggestion was a good middle ground.

Finally, she spoke. "Okay, so we all meet in a public place?"

Braydon hopped up and down a little bit with excitement. "Yes! Absolutely!"

"And if my mom sensor goes off that something is wrong, you won't give me crap about leaving?"

"I promise. No crap."

"Why do I feel like I'm going to regret this?"

"You won't. Don't worry."

"Easy for you to say."

"I love you, Mom. Thank you!"

"I love you too, Bray."

Braydon got up and went to her and hugged her before shouldering his backpack and leaving the room. He smiled as he was reminded of how cool she actually was, for an adult. He locked the front door behind him and headed up the hill to Adam's house. Adam's dad opened the door when he rang the bell.

"Oh, hi, Braydon. Good timing. We just got home. Adam is in his room. Go on back."

"Thanks, Mr. Wagner." Braydon walked down the short hallway to Adam's room and tapped on the open door before walking in.

"Hey, Homie. What up?" Adam greeted him.

"Not much. I'm excited you let me come over. It's been a crappy week."

Adam was a year older than him. "Is that prick, Jake, still messing with you?"

"Yeah. Pretty much all the time."

"Maybe I need to start riding the bus again. I bet he wouldn't screw with you if I was there."

"*Or,*" Braydon responded, "he'd just screw with both of us."

"I'm not scared of Jake Connors."

"I seem to recall he used to pick on you."

"That was then."

"Whatever. Anyway, I don't want you to get involved. I'd never live it down."

"So, what are you gonna do?"

"I was thinking of picking up a book on voodoo and trying to make a doll. Do you think it'd work?"

"That sounds fun. I'd stick the pin in his nuts!" Adam said, laughing.

"Why use just one pin?" Braydon responded.

"I like the way you think, dude!" Adam said. "Want to play some X-Box before dinner? My dad's ordering us a pizza."

"Oh, yum! Pepperoni?"

"And sausage."

"I always knew you liked sausage."

"You never complained."

Both boys laughed and Adam handed Braydon a controller.

"Want to play a game of GTA?"

"I love that game! Yes!"

Halfway through the second game, the pizza arrived and the boys went out into the kitchen to eat.

"So, Braydon, how's your mom doing?" Adam's father asked.

"She's doing good, thanks."

"I'm glad she let you come hang out. You don't get over here often enough."

"I know. Thanks for having me over."

"No problem. You guys can hang inside as late as you want and go out to the fort when you feel like it. Adam knows where we keep the flashlights and everything else you might need is up there including sleeping bags."

"Thanks, Mr. Wagner."

"No problem. You kids have fun."

Braydon turned to Adam. "Where's your mom?"

"She's out of town for the week visiting my grandparents."

"Gotcha."

"I wish I could've gone, but you know, school."

"I know, right? School gets in the way of everything."

After they finished eating and putting the leftovers away, they went back to Adam's room and played a few more games. It was sometime after one o'clock in the morning that they decided to shut down the game and head out to the tree fort.

Outside, they both put L.E.D. headlamps on and made their way out to the back yard. The tree was an old oak tree that appeared to be approximately forty-feet tall. The treehouse was about halfway up, and the rope ladder hung down to the ground from the platform that surrounded the inside structure, similar to a wrap-around deck. Adam started up the ladder and as soon as he was on the platform, Braydon shouldered his backpack and started the climb, taking it cautiously as the ladder swung back and forth as he ascended. When he was up on the platform as well, Adam pulled the ladder up and they went inside the fort.

Adam's tree house was no ordinary rustic fort. Because he was in construction, his dad built the most kick-ass tree house for Adam and it lacked nothing. The inside area was almost the size of Braydon's bedroom at home. It had a door that could be closed and locked and wooden shutters that could be closed over the screened window to keep the elements out. Off to one side of the space, he had built in bunkbeds with thin mattresses. The part that Braydon really liked was the small fridge his Dad had hoisted up into the space. Braydon never heard of a tree house with electricity before, but this one had a couple outlets as well as an overhead light. The small TV was mounted to the wall in the corner. One of the other cool features of the fort was 'the funnel.' The funnel was pretty much just that. A large automotive funnel that was inserted into a one-inch PVC pipe and strapped to the two-by-four framed side of the tree house. The PVC was threaded through a hole in the floor of the fort and when it almost reached the ground, it elbowed away from the tree at a forty-five-degree angle and drained off in the bushes. With as many sodas as they drank each time they got together, it certainly was a convenient feature to have when his bladder woke him up in the middle of the night.

In the fort, Adam slipped his comic book collection out from under the bed and they both dug into the familiar stories they had read many times before. It was quiet for about thirty minutes when suddenly, Adam spoke.

"Did you hear about Stan Lee?"

"Yeah," Braydon replied, sullenly.

"It's hard to believe."

"I know. He was like my hero. Marvel will never be the same."

"I'm sure he has people that work there that are as talented as he was."

"I doubt—" Braydon was interrupted by a loud *thunk* on the side of the fort.

"What was that, dude?" Braydon asked, panic edging into his voice.

"I'm not sure. Maybe a branch fell and hit the wall?"

They both sat silently and listened intently when suddenly, another *thunk*, louder than the first one, resounded throughout the fort.

"That's no branch. I'm scared, Adam."

"Yeah, I think I'm about to shit my pants myself."

"Have you ever heard noises up here before?"

"Never. Not anything like this, anyway."

Both boys jumped when an unknown object hit the side of the fort with brutal force, mixed with the sound of splintering wood.

"Shit!" Adam's eyes were wide as he turned toward Braydon. Before Braydon could respond, the sound repeated again and then one more time. Within ten seconds, it started again and multiple objects slammed into the side of the fort.

"LOOK!" Braydon pointed. A sharp piece of metal protruded through the plywood.

"Is that what I think it is?" Adam asked, his voice trembling.

"An arrow tip?" Braydon suggested.

"I think it is."

The attack stopped and the boys sat in the corner of the fort, waiting and listening.

Finally, after a minute, Adam whispered, "I think they're gone."

Braydon's eyes grew wide. "Who do you think it was?"

"No clue."

It was then they heard the gurgling. Both boys looked at each other at the same time, unsure of what the sound was. It grew from a hollow, faint noise to a louder burping, churning, air-gasping crescendo. It wasn't until they realized they were sitting in water that they understood what the noise was. Looking over, they saw water overflowing out of the funnel onto the floor of the fort.

"What the hell?" Adam shouted.

"How can water be coming up the pipe?" Braydon asked, on the edge of panic.

They scooted off the floor and pulled themselves onto the lower bunkbed.

"We have to get out of here, Bray! Let's go!"

"But what if they're still out there?"

"We have to take that chance."

Braydon pointed. "But they have arrows."

Adam's face registered defeat for a moment before an idea

struck him. He pulled out his phone and pushed a few buttons. A few seconds later, the phone was answered on the other end.

"Dad! Help! Someone is attacking the fort. Hurry…I don't know who…please hurry!"

Adam ended the call and turned to Braydon. "He's coming." Braydon nodded quickly, relieved. The water coated the floor of the fort, but was not rising much due to the cracks and crevices that let it drain out almost as fast as it was coming inside. They were in no danger from the water, but the totality of the experience, starting with the arrows, then the incoming water, had them freaked out. Moments later, they heard shouting outside and when they peeked through one of the cracks in the fort, they saw a flashlight beam bouncing around wildly.

"Hey! Stay right there. I want to talk to you!"

Braydon and Adam listened as they heard his father yelling after someone and the sound of scuffling and muffled voices joined in.

"Stop! I have a gun!"

They boys listened for another minute as things got silent when suddenly, the flow of water cut off inside the fort.

"Come on down, boys. Whoever they were, they're gone."

CHAPTER FOUR

Sunday evening, after Braydon was finished with his homework and chores, he headed to his room. He hadn't told his mother about what had happened at Adam's house and he wasn't about to, fearing she would never allow him over there again. A text from Damion pulled his attention to his phone.

```
Damion: u getting online soon?
Braydon: yeah
Damion: cool
```

Braydon: oh hey, I talked to my mom

Damion: wut did she say?

Braydon: we can hang out, but we all have to meet in a public place first

Damion: lame

Braydon: IKR?

Damion: whatever. we'll figure it out. Should I tell my dad we're going then

Braydon: yeah. plan on it and ur dad and my mom can work out the details

Damion: yes!

Damion: btw, how was ur sleepover

Braydon: messed up

Damion: do tell

Braydon: I'll tell you online

Braydon logged on to his computer, brought up *Sunday, Bloody Sunday* and logged in. Damion was already online playing a game when he arrived. Braydon watched the game that was in process, but was unable to join in. Instead, he put himself in a que to join the next game with the same players. As he watched, an instant message window popped up on the right side of the screen. It was Damion.

Destroyer_Boy: give me a few 2 get out of this game

Braydon_Bites: no prob

Braydon watched the game for a few more minutes as Damion went crazy, attacking multiple opponents at the same time. His weapon of choice was a sword and Braydon giggled as Damion lopped off one player's arm, another's leg and a third's head. Within seconds, another player slipped up behind Damion and speared him through the back. With that being Damion's final life, he was out of the game until the next round started. Although new games were starting all the time in other universes, Braydon and Damion preferred to play in Universe 722, because the same players frequented it and they knew most everyone that entered the game. Accordingly, they would wait until the last opponent was standing, and all join in when a new game started. It gave them a chance to get caught up.

Destroyer_Boy: so wut happened?

Braydon_Bites: jake happened

Destroyer_Boy: oh shit

Braydon_Bites: exactly

Destroyer_Boy: wut did he do?

Braydon_Bites: well i can't prove its him

Destroyer_Boy: tell me

Braydon_Bites: he terrorized us in the middle of the night

Destroyer_Boy: how?

Braydon_Bites: he shot the fort

Destroyer_Boy: shot?

Braydon_Bites: with arrows

Destroyer_Boy: WTF

Braydon_Bites: that's an understatement. Adam counted 10 arrows when he went back after it got light

Destroyer_Boy: holy shit

Braydon_Bites: that wasn't all

Destroyer_Boy: ???

Braydon_Bites: he tried to flood us out

Destroyer_Boy: huh? Isn't this fort in a tree?

Braydon_Bites: yup. he pumped water into it. there was no danger of the place filling up, but it was scary. we were freaking out

Destroyer_Boy: wut does this asshole have against u?

Braydon_Bites: I have no idea. we used to be friends. one day he just started picking on me and making my life fricking miserable

Destroyer_Boy: i want to meet this asshole when I come out

Braydon_Bites: leave it alone. It'll only make it worse for me

Destroyer_Boy: too bad he isn't in this game. I'd demolish him

Braydon_Bites: me too

Destroyer_Boy: wut would u do to him?

Braydon_Bites: I'd start by hobbling him. I'd smash his ankles into splinters, so he couldn't walk

Destroyer_Boy: good start. then what?

Braydon_Bites: I'd grab a torch and melt the skin and meat off his hands, leaving just the bones. He wouldn't bleed to death, cause the heat would cauterize the vessels

Destroyer_Boy: your a sicko! me likes! so his ankles are shattered. his hands are melted off. sounds like a great start. wut then?

Braydon_Bites: I'd take pruning shears to his nuts. lop them right off

Destroyer_Boy: ouch

Braydon_Bites: double ouch. but he would still be alive. It would be a great time to peel the skin off his chest and make a hat out of it

Destroyer_Boy: u gonna wear that skin hat?

Braydon_Bites: nope. he is. I wouldn't

want it to fall off though. A few roofing nails will help hold it on his head

Destroyer_Boy: r we still talking video games here? that's pretty specific and last time I checked, this game doesn't have roofing nails in its arsenal

Braydon_Bites: a boy can dream, can't he?

Destroyer_Boy: yeah. the prick deserves that and more. wut would you do to finish him off?

Braydon_Bites: woodchipper

Destroyer_Boy: YES!

Braydon_Bites: I thought you'd like that one

Destroyer_Boy: oh yeah I do. a woodchipper it is

Braydon_Bites: I wish. oh hey, the game is starting. let's kick some ass

Destroyer_Boy: ass kicking commencing

Braydon jumped into the new game and unleashed on one of the other players that he didn't particularly like, taking out his anger on the other opponent. Damion saw what he was doing and started working with Braydon to gang up on the player. Braydon chose a baseball bat as a weapon and smashed the opponent's ankles, bringing him to his knees. It was on.

Later, after a couple of games in which no mercy was shown toward the other opponents—Braydon won one of the games and Damion won the other—the boys jumped back into chat before logging off for the night.

Destroyer_Boy: good games, brutha

Braydon_Bites: u 2. they got what they deserved

Destroyer_Boy: yeah, too bad that prick

jake wasn't there. Wud u really do all that stuff 2 him if you had a chance?

    Braydon_Bites: I'd like to think so. not sure if I'd have the stomach for it though

    Destroyer_Boy: but if it happened to him, you wouldn't be upset?

    Braydon_Bites: I'd throw a party. Jake Connors is a miserable asshole and he deserves to die

    Destroyer_Boy: I don't disagree

    Braydon_Bites: on that note, I'm outtie

    Destroyer_Boy: ok dude. I'll talk 2 u ltr

    Braydon_Bites: cya

Braydon logged out of the game and shut down his computer. In the bathroom, he brushed his teeth and when he was ready for bed, he went and said good night to his mom. He so badly wanted to tell her about the pain and torture Jake put him through, but he felt she would blow it out of proportion and get the entire world involved. He would have to get through it on his own.

In his bedroom, Braydon turned out the lights and crawled under the covers. Dread filled his head as he thought about going to school the next morning. He couldn't be positive that Jake was behind the attack on the tree fort, but it was too coincidental. Not to mention the fact that his mom had told Jake where he'd be. It *had* to be Jake. Would Jake say something the next day? Would he be pissed off, because Adam's dad had chased them off with a gun?

Braydon laid awake in bed for almost an hour before finally falling asleep. His sleep was fitful as he worried over what Monday held in store for him.

In the morning, his alarm went off and he hit snooze a couple of times. Finally, he got up, knowing he couldn't miss the bus again. Showered, dressed and with a stomach full of Froot Loops, Braydon stepped out of the house and pulled the door shut behind him, doing the math in his head for how many weeks were left in the school year. As he approached the bus stop, all eyes turned in his direction and he knew. His day was going to suck.

CHAPTER FIVE

"Well, look who's finally here!" Jake sneered.

Braydon got brave for a minute, his anger from the events of Saturday night fresh in his head.

"Yeah, I just left your mom's house," Braydon retorted.

It took a moment for the insult to register, but when it did, rage filled Jake's face.

Jake grabbed the front of Braydon's shirt with his left hand and slammed his right fist into Braydon's gut, knocking the air out of him again.

"What did you say, you little pussy?"

Braydon gagged for a minute and when he had sucked the air back into his lungs, he gasped out an answer.

"Ask your mom."

This time, Jake's fist landed fiercely on Braydon's jaw, knocking him to the ground. Braydon pulled himself into a sitting position, rubbing his jaw, but he didn't get up.

"I suggest you stay down, or I'll do it again."

Braydon said nothing, knowing that his smarts or quick wit were no match for Jake's fists. The other boys at the bus stop complicated Braydon's situation by egging Jake on, urging him to kick Braydon's ass. Once again, it was the sound of the bus that defused the situation. As Braydon got up off the hard ground, he figured he owed the bus driver more than she would ever know.

As usual, everyone else boarded the bus before Braydon, for which he was thankful, but as Jake boarded, he stopped on the first step, and turning around, he stared straight into Braydon's eyes, a smirk on his face.

"Hope you had a great night in the tree fort. By the way, does that thing have a water bed?"

If he had been unsure before, Braydon knew now. Jake ignored his scathing look, turned back around and climbed on the bus.

———

THAT EVENING, AFTER HOMEWORK, BRAYDON TOLD Damion the story.

Destroyer_Boy: so it was him?

Braydon_Bites: yup

Destroyer_Boy: and he hit you?

Braydon_Bites: twice

Destroyer_Boy: that prick

Braydon_Bites: tell me about it. And I have four more days left in the week

Destroyer_Boy: but then I'll b there

Braydon_Bites: I can't wait!

Destroyer_Boy: too bad I can't go 2 school w/you. how do you put up with this everyday

Braydon_Bites: I'm not sure. My smartass comments didn't help any today

Destroyer_Boy: no kidding. Wut u gonna do

Braydon_Bites: I'm not sure. I can't keep doing this

Destroyer_Boy: well let's play a game and kill sum people

Braydon_Bites: I think I'm gonna skip tonight. I'm pretty depressed

Destroyer_Boy: but u might feel better if you slice and dice

Braydon_Bites: maybe, but I just can't. I'm done

Destroyer_Boy: u ain't gunna do anything stupid r u?

Braydon_Bites: never

Destroyer_Boy: promise

Braydon_Bites: I promise

Destroyer_Boy: k. night bro

Braydon_Bites: night

That night, Braydon read a book that his mother didn't know about. The gore factor was off the charts. As Braydon devoured it, his mind kept drifting to Jake and how he deserved all the horrors inside the pages, and then some.

When his eyes grew heavy, he put the book under his bed and turned off the light, slipping into slumber quickly. His dreams were vivid and gruesome. He had all the power and control over Jake Connors. In his dreams, he did not hesitate to use it.

The remainder of the week was difficult for Braydon. The bus stop was the bane of his existence and he tried to get to it as late as possible each day without missing the bus. Jake Connors took extra care to make Braydon's life miserable each day. Some days were purely verbal abuse, but most involved physical pain. Feeling like he was a glutton for punishment, Braydon still got up every morning and made his way to the stop.

Every evening that week, Braydon put on a brave face with his mother and confided in Damion what was happening. Braydon could tell that Damion was getting angry over the abuse he was suffering. It was nice that someone had his back. He couldn't wait to hang out with Damion over the weekend, before having to go back to school on Tuesday. It would be a nice relief from the daily torture he had to endure.

Friday evening, Mary knocked on Braydon's door.

"Come in, Mom."

Mary entered the room and found Braydon at his desk, doing homework.

"What'cha doing, Bray?"

"Homework."

"On Friday? You have all weekend."

"I just want to get it out of the way, so I don't have to mess with it last minute, what with Damion being in town and all."

"Are you sure you're ten?" Mary asked, a look of amazement on her face.

"Almost eleven," he corrected her.

"Damion's dad said they would be here around noon tomorrow."

"Yeah, that's what Damion said as well. They left after school today and are spending the night along the way."

"So, are you just going to hang in your room all night?"

"Probably. I want to get this done and then I might read or watch TV."

"Okay, well dinner will be ready in forty-five minutes. I'll yell when it comes out of the oven. I'm making your favorite tonight."

"Meatloaf?"

"You betcha!"

"Thanks, Mom! That's the best news I've had all day!"

"I knew that would start your weekend off on a good note. Have fun with that homework." Mary left the room.

"Fun?" he called after her. "As if."

After dinner, Braydon finished his homework and read a

few chapters of the slasher novel he had gotten from a friend. The premise was a familiar one, about a group of campers that were slaughtered as they tried to get away, but Braydon couldn't get enough of that type of book.

He didn't feel much like getting online as he found that Damion was the only one he really talked to in the game. There was no point in playing it without him. Around ten o'clock, he went into his mom's room and told her goodnight and then went back into his room. Bored, he decided to text Damion.

Braydon: how's it going?

There was no response. Braydon tried again.

Braydon: r u guys on the road?

Five minutes later, Damion responded.

Damion: sorry bro. didn't see ur text. Yeah, I'm on the road

Braydon: by yourself? lol

Damion: duh. With my dad

Braydon: when u stopping?

Damion: dunno. whenever we get tired

Braydon: cool. Well I guess I'll c u tomorrow. Can't wait 2 hang out

Damion: me neither. c u then

Braydon: later

Braydon picked his book back up and read eight more chapters, reveling in the extreme ways in which the campers died. The more blood, the better. As he read, he pictured Jake's face on the losing end of a machete. Around one a.m., he closed the book and turned off the light, hoping to get some sleep before the big day.

CHAPTER SIX

"Come on, Bray. We need to go."

"Please. Let me try one more time."

"But we've been waiting here for two hours."

"Maybe they had car trouble. Let me call one more time."

"Fifteen minutes. That's it, Braydon. If they aren't here, we're leaving."

Braydon sent another text to Damion and even though phone calls were a little weird, he pulled up his contact and hit the call button. The call went straight to voicemail.

"Damion, it's me. Where are you? We have to go soon if you aren't here. Call me."

"Voicemail?" his mom asked.

"Duh, Mom."

"Seriously, Braydon? Have you lost your mind? Just because things aren't going the way you want them to doesn't give you the right to be a jerk to me. This is an inconvenience to me as well. I didn't plan on spending half my Saturday in a parking lot."

"I'm sorry. I didn't mean to be. I'm just frustrated. He said he was gonna be here. I texted him last night and he said they were on the road."

"Well, obviously something changed. Let's head home. If they call you later, maybe I can drive you back here. Hopefully there is a good reason for this. It's not like I was comfortable with the idea to start with."

"Can we finish out the fifteen minutes? Please."

"Okay, Bray. And then we're going."

"Deal."

After fifteen minutes, there was no sign of Damion or his father, so Mary drove them home while Braydon continued to text Damion, letting him know that they had left. When they arrived, Braydon shuffled into the house, his head hung low. Mary clicked the lock button on the key fob and followed.

"You okay, Bray?"

"Not really. This sucks."

"It's part of life. Life in general can be disappointing. You have to make the best of it."

"Not helping, Mom."

"Want me to order some pizza? Would that help?"

Braydon produced a weak smile. "Maybe."

"Pizza it is, then. I'll holler when it's here."

"Thanks, Mom."

"Anytime, Sweetie. I have your back."

Braydon gave her a hug and went to his room, occasionally texting or trying to call Damion. None of his texts were returned and every call went straight to voicemail.

The dining room was silent as they ate the pizza. Mary tried to pull Braydon out of his funk, but his one-word responses to Mary's attempts to start a conversation finally got to be too much for her and she decided to let him brood in silence.

Saturday night came and went and there was no word from Damion or his father. Defeated, Braydon went to bed, uninterested in reading or playing online. Sunday was more of the same. The entire day passed without any word from Damion. Braydon even went online to see if Damion was there, but he wasn't.

By Monday, Braydon had given up. His depression grew worse as the day passed, not only because his plans had been ruined, but also because he had wasted an entire three-day weekend waiting on someone that never came. He felt his temper flaring easily and caught himself cussing under his breath at Damion. He hoped he had a good explanation for standing him up. His mother would never give the meeting a second chance. Damion had blown it. On top of having one of the most disappointing weekends he could remember, the next day was a school day and he had to deal with Jake Connor's bullshit again. Monday night, there was still no word and Braydon went to bed as depressed as ever.

When the Tuesday morning alarm went off, Braydon drug himself out of bed, happy that it was a four-day school week but dreading the torture he would have to go through to make it to the weekend. He peeked out the window as the kids accumulated at the bus-stop. He had a pretty good feel for when the bus was about to come, and he always tried to leave the house at the last minute. Knowing he would have to put up with his punishment, Braydon left the house and walked to the stop, scanning the kids' faces looking for Jake. For whatever reason, Jake wasn't there. Was Jake sick? Could this be his lucky day? Did he really get to go one more day without getting his ass kicked?

The other kids glanced at Braydon as he arrived, but without their fearless leader, Jake, they turned away and talked amongst themselves. Shortly after, the bus arrived, and everyone got on. It was going to be an uneventful day. While Braydon was still upset about Damion standing him up, he felt a little lighter knowing Jake wasn't around to foul up his morning.

At school, everyone scurried to their lockers and then their classrooms before the first lessons started. It was around ten o'clock when the principal entered the class. The teacher excused herself and slipped into the hallway with the principal. When she came back a few minutes later, her face was ashen, and her voice trembled as she spoke.

"Class, I have some bad news. It was reported a little bit ago that one of our students is missing. They are working diligently to find him, but they are asking that if any of you knows his whereabouts, please raise your hand. The police want to talk to you. The student is Jake Connors."

A gasp went up across the classroom as students turned toward each other to chatter about the announcement. Braydon sunk down in his desk chair, his stomach churning. Was this some fantasy his imagination had cooked up, or was it really happening?

"Class? CLASS!"

The class turned their attention back to the teacher.

"Has anyone seen Jake Connors yesterday or today?"

The room was silent as each student looked around, waiting to see if anyone else raised their hand. No one did.

"If anyone knows anything, please tell someone. Even if it's anonymous. His parents are worried sick."

The class broke out in chatter again.

"I want everyone to stay put while I go talk to the principal again. I'll be right back. Stay in your seats."

The rest of the day went by as if it was the last day of school before summer. Students gossiped about the conspiracies their minds conjured up. Jake's close friends kept up a macho front. His girlfriend spent the first part of the morning in tears before going home for the remainder of the day. They may as well have sent all the children home, because no learning happened this day.

When the bell rang, Braydon ran to the car as quickly as possible. Mary was parked by the curb as she usually was. As he climbed inside briskly, she could tell something was up.

"You okay, Buddy? What's going on?"

"Mom! Did you hear about Jake?"

"Jake? Jake who?"

"Jake from our neighborhood? The one I used to be friends with?"

"What do you mean, used to be?"

"If you haven't noticed, we don't hang out anymore. He's changed."

"I always thought he was a polite boy. So, what's the big news about Jake?"

"He's missing."

"*What?*"

"They haven't seen him since yesterday. He wasn't in his bed this morning when his parents went to wake him up."

"That's crazy. Have you talked to him?"

"Not at all. I haven't seen him since last week."

"His poor parents. They must be a mess."

"Probably."

"Do you know anything, Bray? Did he say anything to you?"

"No. We aren't close anymore. I have no idea where he is."

"Well I hope they find him. That's the scariest thing a mother can imagine."

"It's totally crazy."

"Are you okay, Bray?"

"Yeah Mom. I'm good. Like I said, we haven't been friends for a while now."

"Well, let me know if you need to talk. OH! I meant to ask you. Did you ever hear back from Damion today?"

"Not a word. He's still a ghost."

"Wow. People are dropping off the face of the earth like flies. Please be extra careful, Bray."

"I will. I promise."

The rest of the week went by quickly and for Braydon, life had changed immensely. He didn't tell a soul, but inside, he was ecstatic. Others would have thought him to be demented —celebrating another person's disappearance, but Braydon didn't see it that way. What comes around goes around. Jake deserved to disappear. Braydon was hopefully rid of his shadow of torment forever. At least he hoped.

Saturday rolled around and Braydon woke up in an uplifted mood. The heaviness that had weighed him down for so long had been lifted. As he made his way out to the kitchen to grab breakfast, he found his mother scribbling a note for him on the back of an envelope.

"Hi Mom!"

"Oh, Bray! You're up. I didn't want to wake you."

Braydon noticed she was dressed. "Are you going somewhere?"

"Yeah, I have to do the shopping and run some errands. I figured with the week you've had, you would want to stay home and relax."

"Thanks. That sounds like a good idea. What chores do you want me to do today?"

"I already did them. When I say I want you to relax, I mean it. You do *you* today. I got everything else!"

Braydon gave her a big hug and held on a little longer than he intended.

"You sure you're okay?"

"Yeah, Mom. Go. Get out of here."

When he had the house to himself, Braydon watched TV for an hour before getting bored. He missed playing *Sunday, Bloody Sunday*. He had tried a couple of times throughout the week, but it just wasn't the same without Damion. It had been a week since Damion dropped off the face of the earth, much like Jake, who still hadn't been found. It was time for him to make a new friend. Braydon loaded the game and went into a different universe, hoping to meet someone he gelled with. As he watched the game that was in action, he entered the player queue for the next game. He watched the players fight each other, analyzing who the best fighters were. Maybe he could befriend one of them. A chime pulled his attention to his private chat window.

Destroyer_Boy: hey dude

Braydon_Bites: Dude! Where u been?

Destroyer_Boy: been busy

Braydon_Bites: seriously? That's all u got? You've been busy?

Destroyer_Boy: wut r u all bent about

Braydon_Bites: for real? I've been trying to get ahold of your ass all week. U stood me up

Destroyer_Boy: it couldn't be helped

Braydon_Bites: what kind of lame shit is that? I think you owe me an explanation

Destroyer_Boy: it's complicated

Braydon_Bites: tell me anyway

Destroyer_Boy: I can't

Braydon_Bites: then we don't have anything to talk about

Destroyer_Boy: please. It wasn't supposed to go down that way

Braydon_Bites: you're talking in riddles

Destroyer_Boy: I did it for you

Braydon_Bites: did what 4 me?

Destroyer_Boy: how is Jake?

Braydon_Bites: Why would u ask about that asshole?

Destroyer_Boy: Check your phone

Braydon's text message chime went off. When he opened his phone, his face went white.

Braydon_Bites: why do u have a photo of Jake?

Destroyer_Boy: he looks scared, doesn't he?

Braydon_Bites: where did u get that?

Destroyer_Boy: I took it

Braydon's heart started beating rapidly as bile rose up in his throat. The message chime went off again. Not wanting to look, but drawn to the next picture like a car crash on the interstate, Braydon viewed the picture.

Destroyer_Boy: u should have heard him scream when I smashed his ankles with the sledgehammer

Fear tore through every cell of Braydon's body as he studied the picture of the feet and ankles, destroyed beyond repair.

Braydon_Bites: tell me u didn't really do something. did u???

Destroyer_Boy: I know what u really want to see. It was a blowtorch that you selected, wasn't it?

Another picture came up on his phone screen. Knowing what he was about to see, but not having the power to look away, Braydon looked at the phone. The picture showed a gloved person holding a blowtorch, the skeletal remains of a hand glowing in the intense flames. Braydon heaved on the floor by the desk, lurching up everything left in his stomach from the night before. Finally, he pulled himself together and responded.

Braydon_Bites: tell me this is some sick joke

Destroyer_Boy: it's sick all right, but no joke. do you remember what's next?

Braydon didn't answer, knowing all too well what the next picture was going to show. The phone chimed. With a tear sliding down his face, Braydon looked at the picture. It was hard to make out, but Braydon knew. There were two oval shaped blood covered objects in the picture. Jake's balls.

Destroyer_Boy: I never knew wut it was like 2 cut someone's nuts off. that shit's crazy! I'm surprised he didn't scream more, but I think he was in shock by that point

Braydon cried harder than he had ever cried before. He didn't actually want Jake dead, even though he said he did. The phone chimed again.

Destroyer_Boy: do u like his new hat? I didn't have roofing nails, so I had to improvise

Braydon let out a moan as he looked at the picture on the phone. Jake looked like he was about to pass out, the gristled bare muscle exposed on his chest. The skin-hat was crudely fashioned and sat at an angle on his head. Braydon could not respond. He was afraid to hear the rest of it, but he knew—as sure the sun would rise the next morning—that Jake was dead.

Destroyer_Boy: are you there, bruh?

Braydon_Bites: what did you do to him?

Destroyer_Boy: do you know how hard it is to get a woodchipper that isn't somehow tied back to you? took me two damn days.

Braydon_Bites: No! Please tell me you didn't

Braydon's typing was interrupted by another chime of the cellphone. He threw the phone down on the bed, willing himself not to look at it. A minute later, he retrieved it, steadying himself while he looked at the photo. The focus of the photo was on an orange woodchipper sitting out in the middle of a field. There was no wood or brush surrounding it. The intake portion of the machine was empty and clean. A single tennis shoe sat on the ground underneath it. It was the other side of the machine that immediately commanded his attention. The entire ground underneath the output and twenty feet beyond was splattered with a mess of blood, bone and gristle. It was then that Braydon knew why Jake had not shown up to school all week.

Braydon_Bites: Why? Why did u do this?

Destroyer_Boy: Isn't this wut you wanted?

Braydon_Bites: Well yes. I mean no. Not really. Not like this

Destroyer_Boy: Well u asked for this. I did what you asked for

Braydon_Bites: I still don't understand. why? u were coming to hang out with me. did you kidnap jake instead? How could you get away with this with your dad in tow? I don't understand

Destroyer_Boy: don't u get it Braydon?

Braydon_Bites: get what? I'm confused.

Destroyer_Boy: I'm not 12

Braydon_Bites: What do u mean? I don't understand.

Destroyer_Boy: I'm a grown-ass man

Braydon_Bites: I don't believe u

A minute went by and suddenly, Braydon's phone chimed again, and he looked at the screen. The picture was of a man, mid-forties, an olive complexion with deep set eyes and wiry hair. He was holding a sign next to his face that read "This is me, Braydon."

Braydon_Bites: Why? why would you become friends with a ten-year-old kid?

Destroyer_Boy: u still don't get it Braydon, do u?

Braydon_Bites: no. I don't. explain it to me

Destroyer_Boy: all along, it was you

Braydon_Bites: what was me?

Destroyer_Boy: I was coming for you

Braydon suddenly couldn't breathe as his heartbeat rapid-fired in his chest. Was he the intended target of the man hiding behind the twelve-year-old facade? If it hadn't been for Jake, would he be dead? He had to ask, but he struggled to type out the message as his fingers kept hitting the wrong keys.

Braydon_Bites: so, what changed your mind?

Destroyer_Boy: as I was driving to meet you—and figure out how to get u away from ur mom—I knew I couldn't do it. False pretenses or not, we became friends. Instead of hurting you, I decided to destroy the one that made your life miserable.

Braydon exhaled sharply, relieved to still be alive and with his mother, but freaked out that he had let a sicko get so close to him. He knew Damion was dangerous. He had to end it now.

Braydon stabbed at the power button on the computer and held it down, shutting down the entire thing, effectively disconnecting himself from the private chat window and the game. He would never go online and play video games again. He knew then that he should have listened to his mother.

His cell phone chimed again. Dread filled his heart as he knew it was another text from Damion. He opened up the text and another picture filled the screen. The woman in the picture was beautiful. The shot was a side view of her as she was getting into a maroon car outside of a house. The house looked just like theirs. The woman looked just like Mila Kunis. It was then

Braydon knew that life as he knew it had changed in an instant.

196

Braydon knew that life as he knew it had changed in an instant.

NO SANCTUARY

There was a chill in the air and Kristen involuntarily shuddered. The dull orange glow from the instrument panel did little to dispel the inky darkness that surrounded the Challenger. The purple exterior—the salesman at the dealership had called it *Helraisin*—disappeared into the shadows as easily as a chameleon blended into the colors of the foliage of its environment. The night was still, quiet, moonless. She could not make out anything beyond the windows of the car.

Kristen turned the temperature a little higher to ward off the cold—she had left the car running, positive that no one would hear the purr of the supercharged 6.2-liter Hemi at normal idle.

Glancing at the clock at the top of the media center screen, she wondered how much longer she would have to wait. It seemed like it had been hours already, but she knew time seemed to drag when she was bored.

She pulled out her phone again, smiled at the picture of her and her pittie on the lock screen, allowed the Face ID to unlock the phone, and started watching TikTok videos, a bad habit she had when she was bored. She didn't detect the danger until it was too late.

The passenger door abruptly opened, and Kristen froze, her breath momentarily stalled as if all the oxygen had been sucked out of the vehicle. The world seemed to stop spinning, the events happening like a video that had been slowed down to a crawl. But then, a large man was sitting in the seat before she even realized what was happening. Then, everything sped up to three times normal speed.

Kristen screamed.

"GO, GO, GO!" the man yelled.

"Who the fuck are you?" Kristen yelled, the passenger not being the person she had been waiting for.

"Just fucking drive!" he yelled.

"Get the fuck out! I'm calling the cops!" She brought up the keypad and dialed a nine before the man swatted the phone from her hand.

"Kristen, what the hell are you doing? Get us out of here before they discover me missing!"

Kristen stopped, her eyes wide, searching the face that was sitting across from her, looking for some familiarity. She turned on the interior light, and the shadows raced from the car, joining the ones outside in the night sky. "Who are you?" she asked cautiously, her eyes blinking at him. "Did Hudson send you?"

"Kris, it's me!"

Kristen looked at him apprehensively. The voice was familiar, but this definitely wasn't Hudson. Although the immediate sense of danger had decreased, she was still on edge.

"Seriously, please drive! We don't have much time."

Kristen stared at him, unable to move. Finally, Hudson reached up and pulled the mask off his face, revealing his true self. He watched as recognition changed her features, some of the fear melting away.

"Drive," he said sternly.

Without another word, Kristen flicked on the headlights, shifted the Challenger into drive, and tore off down the rutty dirt track.

———

"I didn't think you were going to make it." She turned and looked at him, his expression stoic, hard.

"I told you I'd be there."

"You freaked me the fuck out."

"Why? You were expecting me."

"Yeah, you. Not some stranger's face."

"I had to get past the guards somehow."

Kristen turned on the reading lamp and gave him a once-over. "Where is that uniform from?"

Hudson pointed at the road. Swing on the main road here and work your way over to the interstate. We need to head south."

Kristen followed his direction and then turned back to him. "The uniform?"

"I took it off a guard."

"Is he okay?"

"Depends on your definition of 'okay.'"

Kristen studied Hudson's face, frowning. It was then she noticed the smear of blood on his face. "Babe! You're bleeding!" She reached out to touch his face, and Hudson grabbed her wrist and pulled it away.

"It's not mine."

"N…not…then whose is it?"

"The guard's."

"Hudson! You promised me. No one was supposed to get hurt."

"It was the only way I could get out. I had to take his clothes. His keys. His…"

"His what?"

Hudson mumbled something.

"His what?"

"Face, all right? I took off his fucking face and wore it as a mask."

"WHAT THE ACTUAL FUCK, Hudson!! Are you fucking kidding me right now? Get that fucking thing out of my car!! I can't even believe this shit!"

"What do you want me to do with it? Just throw it out the window?"

Kristen pulled off the road onto the dirt shoulder and rolled down the passenger window. "I don't care what you do. Just get it out, now!"

Hudson got out of the car, walked over to the barb-wired fencing that bordered the vast parcel of barren land, and flung the flesh mask as far as he could into the brush, like one might toss a tortilla. Kristen rubbed her forehead and then her temple. When Hudson got back in the car and shut the door, she rolled up his window, turned off the reading light, and pulled back out onto the two-lane blacktop.

"Happy now?" he asked.

"That's an overstatement. Maybe a tad less freaked out. Maybe half a tad if there is such a thing. Did you really have to take off his face?"

"Seemed like the right thing to do at the time."

"Jesus, Hudson. Sometimes I wonder if I should even be helping you. If we get caught, I'm fucked… I'll spend the rest of my pathetic life behind bars too."

"Come on, babe…stop with the righteous act. You were

right there beside me when everything went down. I think you even enjoyed it. The difference between you and me, though, is when I got arrested, I told them you had nothing to do with it. I took full blame, so you weren't locked up too."

"I already thanked you for that. And for the record, I never enjoyed it. I was scared. I tolerated it, because I love you."

"Either way, it's the least you can do, helping me bust out of that place. It's been two years. Two miserable fucking years. I would have been there for the rest of my life and you know it. It'd be bad enough if I was just a prisoner and they left me alone, but no. They have to test me, psychoanalyze me. Fuck with me. I mean I might be a little psycho, but there are guys in there that make me look like a Sunday school teacher."

"Okay, okay. I get it. But I'm never gonna like it. Do you think they know you're gone?"

"I'm hoping not, but you never know. They won't know what vehicle I'm in, though. By the way, damn. This is a sweet ride. When did you get it?"

"Three months ago."

"Things must be good on the outside."

"I've got a huge payment. It's worth it, though."

"You've got to let me drive it."

"Maybe."

"Oh, you WILL be letting me drive it."

"Chill, Hudson. I'm your girlfriend, not your bitch."

Before she could react, Hudson's hand reached out and grabbed the steering wheel and yanked hard, causing the Challenger to fishtail around in the opposite direction, however she threw all of her one hundred and thirty pound body into trying to take control of the wheel to keep them from crashing. Simultaneously, she hit the brakes and the car slid sideways to a stop.

"Are you trying to get us fucking killed, you asshole? Not to mention you could have wrecked my car."

"You've got a little more sass coming out of that mouth than I'm used to. What's that all about? Are you fucking around on me?"

Kristen banged her head on the steering wheel. "Are you serious right now? I stand up for myself for once in my life and suddenly you deduce I am seeing someone else? If that was the case, why would I even be here? Wouldn't I have reported that you were going to escape instead? Jesus! What's your mental?"

"My mental? Is that supposed to be a joke? Just because I was institutionalized doesn't make me crazy."

"That was just an expression, not a jab at you. Stop being so sensitive."

"Then stop disrespecting me."

"I wasn't." Kristen studied his eyes, which burned white hot. She decided to back off before she ignited an explosion she couldn't come back from. Memories of his temper—of his terrifying crazy side—flooded through her mind…memories she tried to suppress, possibly to the point of even fooling herself that he had changed in his two years of lockup.

Kristen looked down. "I'm sorry, babe. I didn't mean anything by it. I love you. Here, you drive."

Kristen shifted the Dodge into park, opened the driver's door, and got out, circling the back of the vehicle on the deserted road. When she got to the passenger side of the car, she opened the door and Hudson got out. She could still see the rage in his eyes. She wrapped her arms around him, but he remained an arm's-length away.

"I'm sorry, baby," she repeated and kissed his lips. She felt some of the tension leave his body and she pulled him in closer. Finally, he relaxed and kissed her back. Then, he pulled away.

"Just be gentle with me, Kris. You have no idea what I've been through."

There was so much she wanted to say to him, but she held back and instead said, "You got it, babe."

Hudson walked around the car and got in the driver's side while Kristen got in the passenger side. He shifted the transmission into drive and whipped the car back around in the right direction, stepping on the gas pedal hard, the tires barking when the transmission shifted to second and then again when it hit third.

"Take it easy," she told him. "This car stands out enough. Don't give them a reason to pull us over."

"I know you're right, but fuck, this car is begging to be *driven*."

"She's a damn beggar, all right," Kristen said, laughing, trying to lighten the mood. "Just don't get us arrested."

"I'm not going back to that shithole."

"Yeah, I can imagine it's not much fun."

"Understatement of the year."

"Where are we going, by the way?"

"I have a friend that lives on eighty-seven acres in the Arizona desert. Things disappear there. I plan to follow suit."

"The desert. Yay." She said this sarcastically, half-heartedly.

"You'll like it okay. He has this bunker. I hear it's amazing. Everything we need, and all underground. Our own little sanctuary. Stays pretty cool down there from what I hear."

"And the car?"

"He has a huge barn. It'll be hidden from prying eyes as well as from the air."

"Arizona it is, then."

"Yeah, but first I need to eat. Taco Bell?"

"You certainly know how to get a girl's attention. Let's go."

———

Kristen made Hudson park in an empty area of a grocery store parking lot that was in the same center as the fast-food restaurant. There was no way she was going to let him spill greasy taco meat on her leather seats.

"Oh my god."

"What?"

"Do you know how long it's been since I have had Taco Bell? It's been forever."

"Sorry."

"It's all good. But damn. I'm so happy right now."

"Glad that's all it takes," she said, smiling at him.

When they were done eating, Hudson changed into some clothes that Kristen had brought with her and they threw their trash and his stolen clothes in the dumpster behind the store. Having already used the bathroom when they ordered their food, they got back on the interstate with Hudson still behind the wheel. A few hours later, Hudson exited the interstate and pulled into a gas station. At the pump, he opened the filler lid and inserted the nozzle, pressing the button on the pump. He pressed the handle, but nothing happened.

"Gotta prepay, babe."

"Hand me your bank card."

"Eh. My account is empty. I pulled out everything I had. Don't want to leave an electronic trail. I'll go inside and prepay cash."

"How much is *everything you had?*"

"A couple hundred bucks. Not nearly enough, but things are tight. The car payment and insurance on this thing are killing me."

"Shit."

"We'll figure something out."

Hudson nodded.

"Do you want me to pick you up a snack while I'm in there?" she asked.

"Nah. I need to take a piss anyway. I'll go in after I pump the gas."

"Kay."

Kristen headed inside and handed the clerk forty dollars, hoping it was enough to fill the tank. At this rate, they wouldn't have enough to get to Arizona, which concerned her.

As the clerk preauthorized the pump, Kristen looked out at Hudson as he began to pump the gas. She remembered the first time she had seen him. She had been walking her pit bull and a car had driven by slowly. She remembered looking at the driver, thinking he was cute. The next day, he coincidentally drove by her again as she walked her fur baby. This time he waved. The third time, she waved him over to the curb and introduced herself, later finding out that his drive-bys weren't coincidental at all. After that first day, he had driven around for hours hoping to cross paths with her again.

There was something about him…rugged good looks with an air of confidence. Kristen could see that person she had fallen quickly for, right on the other side of the glass pumping the fuel, his face expressionless, his eyes staring off into the distance, at everything, at nothing. But what she had quickly come to find after dating him for a hot minute was a man who was troubled—even his demons had demons—but he refused to admit he had a problem, refused to get help. *"I'm not damaged, you are"* seemed to be words he lived by. He was never the problem. Everyone else was.

Despite his issues, they had fun. Kristen chalked some of it up to a rebellious phase she had been going through. The product of strict parents, she had escaped as soon as she had turned eighteen, crashing on friends' couches, sometimes sleeping in her car (back then, she owned a beat up Ford Taurus), and she had even forced her way into vacant houses from time to time just to have shelter. Within six months, she found a little more stability, landing a job that paid enough for her to rent a room and keep food in her belly. Within days, she had gone to her parents' home and kidnapped Sarabie, her pittie—her best friend. And a month after that, she and Hudson were a thing. To Kristen, he was the spark in life that was missing…a wild child. She would never have admitted to herself back then that she was into bad boys, because she didn't even realize it herself. She just wanted to breathe! To live!

"Can I get you anything else?"

Kristen snapped out of her daze and turned her attention back to the lady behind the counter. Reaching over, she grabbed a pack of gum off a display and handed it to the cashier.

"Just this."

"That's two dollars and nineteen cents."

Kristen gave her the cash, took the gum and the change, and joined Hudson outside. He was just hanging up the gas nozzle when she approached.

"Okay if I still drive?" he asked.

Kristen knew it really wasn't a question.

"Of course."

"Cool. I'm going inside to pee. Be back in a bit."

Kristen climbed into the passenger seat of the car, stretched her legs out, and put on her seatbelt. She watched Hudson through the glass again, this time with her on the outside and him inside. He made his way to the back of the store where the restrooms were and disappeared inside one.

Things had been good when they were good. When she was with him, she felt alive. Life was fire. But then she noticed the cracks in his personality. An occasional uncomfortable moment, then some outright red flags. Then the full-blown manic episodes. She had thought about leaving him, but it wasn't something that was easy to do. She loved him…was downright addicted to him, self be damned.

The time of his arrest—their arrests, actually—was one of the lowest times of her life. She knew what he was doing. Had discovered it by accident. Why she hadn't called the cops, she still didn't know. Instead, she had kept quiet. And somehow, he had justified it and convinced her that it wasn't as bad as she was making it out to be, that everything was okay, that what he was doing was perfectly normal.

———

THE HOUSE WAS DARK WHEN SHE ENTERED. SHE CALLED out Hudson's name, but there was no answer. He had promised to be home, yet the house was dark, quiet. She went room-by-room, flipping switches, chasing the shadows away, and replacing them with the brilliance of hundreds of lumen. Unable to locate him, she pulled out a dining room chair and swung it around, straddling it, the back of the chair against her chest. She'd wait for awhile, the plans they had made to go on a long drive in his truck the only thing she could think about. That was when she heard the scratching. Faint. Rhythmic. It came from below.

Rodents, she thought. But no, that seemed wrong. Hudson was too meticulous. Too clean. He would never have vermin. But what was under the house? Was there a basement? Kristen tried a door in the hallway. A coat closet. Another contained towels and linens. No stairs. She slipped out the front door and around the side of the house. She saw no sign of a lower level, but as she rounded the corner at the back of the house, she spotted them. Three low windows at the bottom of the struc-

ture, three single panes of glass in each, all three windows spaced equally apart along the back of the house. They seemed to be frosted, but as she approached them, she saw the brush strokes. They had been painted over…from the inside.

Kristen worked her way around the exterior of the house twice, inspecting every inch, looking for some way to get in the basement. Obviously if there were windows, there was a way in. Convinced the entrance was not hidden outside, she went back in the house.

Inside, she looked everywhere a staircase could be hiding. Originally curious, she soon became obsessed. People don't go to great lengths to conceal something unless there's a good reason, *she thought.* Finally, unsuccessful, she ended up back in the hallway. This passageway felt like the answer, as all the other walls in the house backed to another room, an outside wall, or they had fixtures attached to them, such as in the kitchen and the bathrooms. The house was old. It appeared to never have been remodeled. Paneling covered every wall. She ran her fingers over the seams, putting pressure on the wood. Nothing. Just a solid wall. That was until she got to the fourth panel over. As she was pressing on the wall a few feet from the top, she heard the distinct click of a latch letting loose. A portion of the wall popped a half an inch out. Taking a deep breath and holding it, Kristen popped open the door.

THE CAR DOOR OPENING MADE HER JUMP. SHE HADN'T realized she had zoned out. Hudson got in and started the car without a word before shifting into drive and pulling out of the parking lot. She glanced over at him, his profile slightly illuminated by the dash lighting. He looked serious, almost stern, and his thoughts seemed impenetrable. She decided not to pry.

"Are we going to stop for the night, or keep driving?" she asked.

"I'm not tired. I've been cooped up for way too long. I can drive all night. It will get us there sooner. Plus, we need to save our money."

"Mind if I kick the seat back then and close my eyes for a few? I'm exhausted."

"Go for it."

"Thanks."

Kristen reclined the seat and adjusted her body to get more comfortable. Finally, she pulled a hoodie out of the back seat and balled it up to use as a pillow, settled back into to the seat, and closed her eyes.

———

She felt for a light switch inside the opening and found a metal box mounted to the wall, a single switch attached. She flicked it up, not expecting anything to happen, but the stairway in front of her was washed in bright light. She looked at the single bulb light fixtures that were mounted to the ceiling of the stairwell, three of them in total. Something seemed off, and she couldn't reconcile what it was in her mind, but then it clicked. This was an old house. Everything on the main floor was old and outdated, but the light fixtures, the conduit attaching all of the light boxes together, the clear bulbs that were screwed into the fixture...all of them were shiny and bright, as if they were recently installed. And they were all tucked in behind a hidden door leading to a basement with painted windows.

Her breathing got heavy and she stared at the bottom of the staircase, but she could only see a wall and nothing else as the stairs took a hard turn to the right once they reached the lower landing.

"Hello?" she called, afraid to hear an answer. There was none.

She turned back toward the interior of the house.

"Hudson?"

Still silence.

Knowing there was no way she could not check out what the mystery was at the bottom, she grabbed the handrail and descended the stairs sideways, ready at any given second to swing around and race back up to the main level of the house. The stairs didn't creak, which she thought was odd. The entire situation was odd. She tried to claw through the swirling tornado of her mind to come up with any reasoning that made sense, but it was almost like her thoughts wouldn't let her go there. Nothing good could come from the puzzle pieces falling together in her mind. She would either be conjuring up something that poor Hudson would have no part of in a hundred years, or something so grotesquely fucked up—yet real—that it would be unfathomable.

At the bottom landing, she made the right turn and descended the three additional stairs, finding herself in a big room with concrete floors and workbenches lining the walls. Dozens of tools hung from pegboard or littered the workbench top.

An explosion of air escaped from Kristen's lungs and it was then she realized she had been holding her breath. It was simply a workshop and that was it. Kristen shook her head and chuckled at her stupidity.

Her short-lived relief was broken by the scratching sound she had heard earlier. Curious if there was an animal trapped farther back in the room, she walked toward the sound, the light giving way to shadows as she worked her way back.

At the back of the room, a metal shelving unit sat against the wall, the shelves littered with old paint cans, a couple rolled-up tarps, and some other miscellaneous items. Pulling out her phone, Kristen turned on the flashlight and peered around in the inky shadows. Just walls…nothing sinister. But then, she heard the scratching again, and it seemed close.

Kristen turned toward the metal shelves and removed a paint can and then another. She felt a little like Nancy Drew in the moment, sleuthing a secret passageway. The Secret Staircase was a title that would certainly fit this situation. She turned her flashlight toward the unit and peered between the shelves. She saw wood, where the rest of the basement—so far—was concrete.

Working at a faster pace, Kristen emptied off the rest of the paint and miscellany and slid the shelving unit out of the way. The wood she spotted was actually a door. So why hide a staircase? And a door? She would soon find out. Kristen flicked open the deadbolt lock and yanked the door open, the hinges emitting a loud groan. She placed one foot inside and swung her phone flashlight through the doorway.

———

Kristen awoke to the Challenger slowing and then stopping. She cleared her vision, sat up, and looked around. They were at a gas pump. She looked over at Hudson, who was taking off his seatbelt.

"We need gas already? How long was I asleep?"

"A few hours. We still have half a tank, but I'm hungry. Thought we could top off and drive through that Jack in the Box."

"I could eat."

"Be right back."

Hudson got out of the car and walked toward the convenience store. When he got inside, it dawned on her that he would be right back out since she had the money and he forgot to ask. A minute later, Hudson came back out and walked to the car, opened the gas cap, put the nozzle in the car, lifted the handle, and started pumping. Kristen got out of the car.

"Oh, this one's not prepay?"

"No…it is."

"Um…okay, but I didn't give you any cash." Kristen ran her hand through her hair.

"Don't need it."

"Of course you do."

"Nope…I'm good."

"Okay, what are you not telling me? What the hell am I missing?"

"Just hold on, Kris."

Kristen noticed his forehead was bunched up and he had a scowl across his face, so she decided she would table the conversation…at least until they were back on the road.

When the tank was full and Hudson was back in the car, he pulled over to the drive-thru and pulled up by the menu board.

"What do you want?" he asked.

"A number three, large size, with a Coke. Also could you please ask for ketchup?"

"Yup."

The speaker barked and the employee on the other end asked to take their order. Hudson ordered for both of them and then pulled up to the first window to pay. A sign directed them to proceed to the second window. Kristen reached for her backpack and started to pull her wallet out, but Hudson placed his hand on her arm, then reached into his back pocket and took out a wad of cash, peeling a twenty off and handing it through the window. Kristen's eyes grew wide.

"Not now!" he whispered, giving her a stern look. She gave him a look back, letting him know the conversation was far from over.

When they had their food, they found a place to park.

"Okay, don't think I'm not going to ask again. What the fuck, Hudson? Where did you get the money?"

"You don't need to know."

"The fuck I don't. I'm wrapped up in the middle of this with you. If you did something illegal, I'm going to suffer the consequences as well. We're in *my* fucking car."

"I knew you would get bent about it."

"What did you do?"

"Borrowed a little money."

"Borrowed?" Kristen looked at him incredulously. "Borrowed"—she used air quotes—"from whom?" She had a feeling she already knew the answer, but she needed to hear it from him.

"The last gas station."

Kristen rubbed her hand over her face and took a deep breath.

"Are you just wanting to get caught? The cops have got to be looking for us now. And we stick out like a sore thumb."

"Relax. We aren't going to get caught."

"How can you be so nonchalant about it? I'm sure she already reported it."

"She isn't going to cause us any problems."

Kristen's eyes went wide. "Hudson!! Please tell me you didn't fucking kill her!"

"I didn't."

"Are you lying to me?"

"No."

"Then why do you say she won't cause us problems?"

"Cause she doesn't know who took the money."

"Explain."

"I knocked her the fuck out while she wasn't looking. She literally doesn't know what—or who—hit her."

"HUDSON!! Fucking really?"

"Well, we needed the money."

"Don't you think we could have gotten some another way?"

"Like how, Kris? Are you gonna suck dicks on the corner?"

"You don't have to be an asshole."

"And you don't need to be all over my ass for everything. I'm doing what I need to do."

"And putting me in a bad situation for it. It's not just your ass. I helped you escape. Add all your other crimes to the list and I'm fucked. Sometimes I wonder why I'm even helping you."

"That's a pretty fucked-up thing to say."

"This isn't my life, Hudson. Never was. I mean, I love you and all… Maybe that's the reason I've put up with all your crazy shit…stayed right by your side even when…"

"Even when what?"

———

THE ROOM WAS ESSENTIALLY ONE BIG SPACE WITH concrete block walls. The floor was bare cement as well. A single lightbulb sat at the center of the ceiling, one hundred watts of bright intensity that lit up the center of the room but did little to reach the shadows in the corner of the area.

Kristen's breath caught in her throat, her eyes wide open, disbelieving. Along the far wall were two cells—cages really. They were about five feet high, not tall enough for a person of average height to stand upright in, and each was approximately five feet wide. The cages sat a few feet apart from each other and appeared to be made of steel rods that had been welded together, although definitely not by a professional, as the spacing of the rods was inconsistent and the welds looked like something an amateur would produce.

Each contained a bare mattress…no sheets, no blankets, no pillows. But it was the other contents of each cage that twisted Kristen's stomach in knots.

In the cage on the left, a women was curled up in the fetal position, clearly lethargic and probably in shock. Her blond hair was tangled and ratty, her frame extremely thin, gaunt. She lay naked, her skin splotchy and discolored. Where her feet used to be were merely stumps, the angry, scarred tissue discolored and swollen. Kristen wondered if infection was setting in —the amputations clearly not performed by a medical professional. They had the same crudeness to them as the cage construction—both most likely done by the same person.

Kristen held back the bile that started working its way up her throat, her stomach churning at the horror in front of her. She turned her attention to the cage on the right. The redhead was in a similar condition, but her feet were intact; instead, one entire hand was missing and just the fingers and thumb were missing from her other hand. Her feet hung off the mattress, her toenails scraping across the concrete. That scratching sound I heard.

Kristen covered her mouth and tears leaked from her eyes as she tried to process the scene and figure out what she was going to do next. Neither girl looked at her, like they didn't even notice her there.

Finally, a huge sob burst from her chest and she ran toward the stairs, anxious to get out of this place, to get out of this house. Once she was a safe distance away, she would figure out what to do.

When she got to the top of the stairs and pushed the door open abruptly, stepping into the hallway, she stopped short.

"Kristen."

She stared at him, mouth agape.

"Well, this is unfortunate."

Panic lined her face. "I didn't see anything. Let me be…I'm going home."

"I'm pretty sure I can't let you leave. Besides, I have a great afternoon planned for us. I went to a lot of trouble."

"I'm not going anywhere with you, you sick fuck!"

"It's unfortunate you feel that way, but trust me when I tell you that you'll change your mind."

He moved toward her, and she let out a scream.

———

"Well?" Hudson asked. "You stayed by my side even when…? When what?"

"You know."

"Say it."

"The girls."

"As I said before, don't act all innocent. Once you got past the shock, you were into it just as much as I was."

"No, Hudson, I wasn't."

"Cooked just right, the fingers and toes are better than any hot wings you've ever had. Admit it."

"I don't think that's what they had in mind when someone coined the term 'finger foods.' And for the record, I only ate it because I was scared you'd hurt me if I didn't, but I never swallowed it. I spit it out and slipped it in my pocket and then flushed it when I used the bathroom."

"I don't even know what to say, Kris. After all these years, after everything. Why did you even show up last night?"

She sat there, silent, thinking. Then, shrugging, she said, "You asked. You needed me. I didn't feel like I could say no. I still love you. That's something I've never been able to get out of my system, even when I've tried. You wouldn't believe how many therapy sessions I've attended, hoping to heal from everything: the victims, the shit you got me into, you holding me against my will until I saw things your way. But if I'm being honest, also hoping to figure out how *not* to love you anymore. Obviously, it didn't work, because one message from you and I'm putting *my* life, *my* freedom on the line to help you."

Anxious, not knowing how he was going to react to her admission, she turned to look at him. He was staring at the road, his fingers white-knuckling the steering wheel. Their speed had crept up again, and Kristen noticed he was going about eighty-three miles per hour.

"Hudson?"

He didn't respond.

"Talk to me…I'm sorry if I pissed you off. I'm just trying to be honest with you. I'm not the scared little girl anymore that you knew when you went away two years ago."

"I have nothing to say to you. Obviously, what I thought we had didn't mean shit. I feel like you were playing me the entire time."

"Playing YOU? You were the one who was controlling. You were the one that threatened me. I did what you wanted. I did what I did to survive."

"But I thought you *wanted* to be there."

"You paid attention to me. You wanted to be with me. I mistook bad attention for good attention. But I know better now. These two years you were locked up, I was conflicted, confused. That's why I came. But I finally see it clearly now. I can't be with you anymore. We aren't the same…and I'm not idly going to sit by and watch you hurt people any longer. It's bad enough I never reported the girls in your basement. You may have never gotten caught if they hadn't died and if you hadn't made mistakes when you dumped the bodies."

Hudson was silent again, a deep scowl setting in on his face, his fingers still holding the wheel in a death-grip.

"I care about you, Hudson," she continued. "I really do. And I'm glad I could help you. I'll get you to Arizona…to your friend's place. But I'm not staying once we get there. I'm dropping you off and heading home…to my normal, boring life."

Hudson responded by slamming the accelerator down to the floor, the speed shooting up over a hundred, then one-twenty, then one-forty. Kristen grabbed the "oh shit" handle and held on for dear life, wondering how much of it she actually had left.

———

"Hudson, slow the fuck down!"

"What's the matter, Kristen? Is Crazy Hudson scaring you? Do you not trust me anymore?"

"It's not that," she said, her voice a higher pitch, her words delivered through gritted teeth.

"Maybe we are better off on the other side…you and me, Kris. Burning for eternity together." The car was ripping down the road at a speed faster than she had ever ridden before.

Kristen held on tighter, her muscles tensed up. "If you want to kill yourself, then by all means, do it, but don't take me with you. I'm not ready to die!"

"What? You're too good for me now? Is that it?"

"No, it's just that I'm finally being honest with you. I'm not that scared little girl that is afraid to tell you how I feel. I don't feel good about hurting people, Hudson. I never have."

Hudson was silent for a fifteen seconds, his eyes on the road ahead. Finally he spoke. "You have the power to make this stop, Kris. Just say the word. Say you'll stay with me in Arizona —at our own little sanctuary. We can make it work. I will be better. Just promise me and I'll stop the car."

Kristen looked hesitant…conflicted. "I dunno, Hudson. I can't be a part of all this."

"Please, Kris. I need you by my side."

She gripped the bar tighter and looked down toward the floorboard. "I'm sorry," she whispered.

Hudson immediately reacted by whipping the steering wheel left and right, the car swerving across both lanes of the deserted highway, the tires chirping as they tried to hold tight to the asphalt, the car dangerously cutting a zig-zag pattern across the black surface of the road.

"Damn it, Hudson!!! Fucking knock it off! You're going to kill us!"

"What does it fucking matter, Kris? Huh? You don't care if I live or die!"

"I do! I want you to live, but if you decide to take yourself out, I don't want to go with you. Please stop the fucking car! This ride is over!"

"It's far from over, sweetheart."

The left front tire slipped off the asphalt onto the shoulder and the car began a slide toward the ditch that ran parallel to the road. Hudson yanked the wheel and the car whipped back onto the hard surface, but the aggressive correction forcefully carried the car all the way across both lanes and toward the ditch on the other side. Hudson fought the steering wheel, trying to get control and get the Challenger back on the road.

"HUDSON!!!!!"

Kristen's scream pierced the interior a split second before it happened, but then everything slowed down as the worst imaginable scene played out in front of her. The car completely left the road. They grabbed air as the front end caught in the ditch and then they were flipping, first end-over-end, but then the car felt like it was spiraling before it started rolling. The contents of the car seemed to be void of gravity as the items floated in the air and then pummeled their faces, their bodies. Kristen couldn't count the number of rolls, but it seemed like twenty or more—it was never ending. And then, when she thought they would never stop, the car rolled one last time and slammed into something so hard, it stopped abruptly. Kristen felt like every bone in her body had been turned to powder, then seconds later as she was trying to pull herself out of a surreal haze, the real pain set in and she screamed again.

Yelling through the agony, she tried to get her bearings. She was slumped against the passenger door, her head resting against the cool ground, the window now devoid of glass. She looked around and found Hudson suspended above her, the seat belt being the only thing keeping him from falling on her and crushing her. He was passed out…or dead. Kristen tried to dredge up any type of emotion toward that last thought. She was sad, but not surprised, when she failed.

As she tried to unbuckle her seatbelt, she saw it. The flickering light behind the car. Flames dancing in the night air. They were on fire. They were fucked.

Frantically working at the buckle, Kristen got the seatbelt undone. She stood up and tried to negotiate her way past Hudson, but his body was slumped toward her and in the way. She shook him.

"Hudson. Hudson! HUDSON, wake the fuck up! We're on fire!"

Hudson didn't move, so she tried pushing him to the side and pulled the door handle and tried to push the door up. It didn't budge, a result of the damage it had incurred during the rolling.

The flames grew bigger and Kristin's heart pounded harder,

uncertain if the car could or would explode like in the movies, but not wanting to be around to find out. Out of options for a way out of the car, she laid back on her side in her seat and projected both feet at the windshield. She kicked out—nothing happened. Determined to bust the safety glass out, she kicked again and again, and finally the corner of the windshield tore away from the frame. Six more kicks and the glass on her side of the windshield was flopping in the wind. She started shuffling her body through the opening. The flames grew brighter. The cracking sound became louder. She had to hurry, and just as she was wiggling her shoulders through the opening, she heard him.

"Kri…stennn," he whispered, then a gasp and a wheeze followed. It sounded like something was wrong inside him—in his body this time, not his head.

"Hudson! You're alive."

"Ye…yes. Hurry. Get me…get me out…of here."

Kristen stopped, reached her arm back through the window, and touched his shoulder.

"Oh, Hudson…you don't look so good, sweetie."

"Hu…rry…help me. We have to…to go. Arizona. Safe there."

Kristen grabbed his hand, held it to her face, kissed it.

"Look at you, my love. You don't look so good," she repeated.

He looked at her, the look of an animal that knows it's time, but hoping they are wrong.

"Arizona, Kristen. You…me. Sanctuary. I love…you."

"I love you too, Hudson." She let go of his hand. "Unfortunately, though, there will be no sanctuary. Not now. Not ever. Goodbye, my love."

Kristen pulled herself through the window and rolled away from the car. Every inch of her body screamed at her as she scrambled to her feet, her eyes landing on the Challenger, the body so badly damaged that it was unrecognizable, the flames more consuming than she could have imagined. She turned and ran, her survival mode kicking in, trying to get as far away from the burning car as she could. She made it fifteen steps before the explosion happened, the ass end of the car flinging itself up in the night air before settling back down with an ear-deafening crash.

As she used the pale light from the fire to follow the debris trail back to the highway, hoping someone would eventually come along, she started to concoct a story in her head. He showed up at her house and kidnapped her…made her drive him and then demanded he drive. He must have still been obsessed with her after all these years. She was scared for her life and didn't know what to do. The only way to get away was force him to crash the car. She'd be real convincing. She had to be. She would finally be free. Knowing he would never come back into her life and draw her into his web of sickness, that was *her* sanctuary.

A SHATTERED MIND

CHAPTER ONE

I didn't mean to do it. Yet here I was, sitting on the cold, hardwood floor in what appeared to be a living room in some strange house, my back pressed against the unforgiving jagged edges of the rock fireplace.

When I finally noticed the blood-crusted fire poker in my hands, I knew. Its weight seemed to be ten times what it actually was and it not only felt overwhelming in my hands, but the mere sight of it weighed down my soul as well. The clatter of the poker hitting the oak-slat flooring brought me fully awake and aware of the gravity of the situation.

While the bloodied instrument was my first clue as to the horrors I assumed I would find upon searching the house, I held little hope for a positive outcome based upon the past. This is actually the fifth time that I have woken up in a strange place—under strange circumstances—over the past few months. The other four times, I had killed somebody. Dead. There was no coming back from that. Okay, I am assuming I killed them based upon the dead bodies and the plethora of evidence pointing in that direction. I'm no Sherlock Holmes, but a reasonable person would have to assume that if a stranger wakes up in an unexpected place with a dead body, holding the murder weapon, he is probably guilty. As I looked at the fire-poker in front of me, I came to the realization of what I had done and I had to move quickly to find the bathroom.

As I came upon the kitchen, I realized I was out of time and anything that was left in my stomach from the night before surged up my esophagus and exploded into the sink, coating the few dishes there in a layer of pungent vomit.

I might as well add a little more DNA to the crime scene.

When I was satisfied that my dry heaves were finished, I cautiously explored the house, wondering where the crime had happened this time. The house was on the larger side and I could tell that whoever lived there—or died there—had some money. After exploring a few bedrooms and a study, I came across the master bedroom. It was there that I found what I knew I would locate, yet I had been holding onto that sliver of hope that this time would be different. There was no such luck.

She lay on her side outside the doorway leading from the master bathroom suite. Her white, pasty skin was surprisingly smooth and unblemished. I could tell she took great care of herself as her grooming was impeccable. Her full breasts retained their shape, pointing in my direction, even as she lay on her side. The white, terry bath towel she was holding when she exited the bathroom was lying at her side.

I tried not to look at her head, having caught the trauma out of the corner of my eye. As I summoned all of my willpower to look away—like rubberneckers at a car accident—I was powerless against the pull and I turned my attention to the damage. Her skull had been pierced multiple times with what I assumed was the fire poker—the one I had been hold-ing. Once again, I was nauseated and I ran around her and into the bathroom, trying to puke up something, yet I had nothing to give.

As I went back out to examine the body, for the first time, I noticed the blood splatter that was on the carpet, the towel, and speckled all over the upper portion of her body. I looked carefully at my hands and clothing. They had small amounts of splatter as well. There was no jury in the state of Wisconsin that would not convict me, based upon all the evidence. Hell, I would convict me. It was time to clean up and get out of here.

In the kitchen, I found a dish towel hanging from the oven handle and under the sink, I found some various cleaners. I grabbed the Clorox spray and started with the fire poker. Not only did I clean my prints from it, I also cleaned the blood off of it and the floor, hanging the poker back in the stand it had presumedly been stored in before. I wasn't stupid enough to think they wouldn't find it and identify it as the murder weapon, especially if they used a shitload of luminol in the house, but I certainly didn't want my prints on anything.

I went through the house and wiped down anything I could have touched: faucets, door knobs, the other fireplace tools hanging in the wrought-iron stand. Unfortunately, it was impossible to determine what had happened and why I was waking up to this surprise. To be overly cautious, I cleaned everything I thought I could have touched.

When I was finished, I did one last walk through the house. As I peeked in on the dead body one more time, I held my breath, hoping this was one of those nightmares that you wake up from, only to realize that your life isn't really destroyed. It was wishful thinking. She was just as dead as before. I walked over to the bed, intending to grab a blanket to cover her up. It was the right thing to do, wasn't it? At the last second, I decided against it. I had to refrain from touching more things in the house.

Satisfied that I had covered my tracks, I wiped down the cleaning spray bottle and put it back under the sink, carrying the towel with me as I left. The blood splatter on my clothes was not noticeable unless someone looked closely. As soon as I could get home, shower and change, I would get rid of everything.

Looking out the front window of the house, I noticed the homes that sparsely dotted the neighborhood. There seemed to be no activity this time of morning. I hoped that my luck would hold out as I slipped out the front door, using the bottom of my shirt to pull on the handle. As I started to walk away, I looked up and spotted it. Holy shit. These people—whoever they are—had a security system with cameras.

Instantly, I found myself back inside the house, looking for the guts of the system. If I could not find it—or if it recorded to the cloud—I was toast. My life would be over. Not that it mattered since it seemed to be headed in that direction anyway.

CHAPTER TWO

The Uber dropped me off in my driveway and I went inside, setting the box on the counter. Luckily, nothing seemed to be out of place and there was no evidence inside that anything strange had happened there. The crimes were all being committed elsewhere, randomly. At least that's how it seemed to me.

My house was a modest three-bedroom single level that I used to share with my wife— before she left me for that asshole yoga instructor. That was the start of my life going to shit, but at least we didn't have any children to screw up by putting them in the middle of a nasty divorce. The house was mortgaged to the hilt, because I had to buy out her portion of it and I was now dead broke. It would not be long before the inconvenient letters and phone calls rapidly turned into harassing demands for payment. I haven't been able to pay my bills in five weeks. Luckily, I make small amounts of cash to at least buy food and keep the utilities on. Unfortunately, one can only sell so much blood and semen, and the psychological studies that pay me a hundred dollars a pop are only available to me once per week.

There is something wrong with this world when you work for a company for fourteen years and give them the best, most loyal years of your life, yet they fire you when you don't show up for work three times. Three lousy, frickin' times—out of the more than thirty-five hundred days I was there. It's not exactly like I could tell them I didn't show up for work—or call in—because I killed someone and was busy cleaning up the crime scene. The last thing on my mind when I wake up in close proximity to a dead body is that I have to get to work.

In my bathroom, I peeled off my clothes and shoved them in a plastic trash bag, planning to dispose of them later. I jumped into the shower and the hot water from the shower-head cascading over my naked body never felt better. As I scrubbed my hands, arms and fingernails, any trace of the victim's blood, as well as some of the angst over killing another person, swirled its way down the drain.

When I was done drying off and had put on a fresh pair of clothes, I went out to the kitchen. The box I had set on the counter caught my eye and I went and retrieved it, taking out the DVR that was inside. I was fortunate enough to find it in the study, connected to all of the cameras in the house. It did not appear to have any network connections attached. By taking the DVR, I had effectively removed all of the remaining evidence of the murder.

In the third bedroom, which I used as an office, I plugged the DVR into the outlet and disconnected my monitor, mouse and keyboard from my computer, and connected them to the back of the video recorder. As it went through its boot cycle, I hoped there would be good video. I needed to know what happened before I could figure out how to keep it from happening a sixth time. In the back of my mind, a small voice nagged at me that maybe the video would prove me to be innocent, but I squashed the voice, knowing it was simply foolishness. Still, the more I knew, the better chance I had of figuring out my next move. It's hard to move forward in life when everything around me is in shambles. I feel like my mind is shattered.

As I watched the screen go through its cycle, I started to feel sorry for myself again. A month ago, I was Stan Watson—freshly single, powerhouse accountant at a well-respected firm in Appleton, Wisconsin. Today, I am Stan Watson, a loser who is single, unemployed and months from being homeless. Let's not forget my most endearing quality—murderer extraordinaire. Didn't five victims make me a serial killer? Fantastic. Another label that sums up my life.

Shaking off the pity-party, I went back into my office and checked on the DVR. It appeared to be fully booted, but there were no camera views showing. Unsure of how to control it, I clicked my mouse on the screen and a username/password screen popped up. Lovely. I was shit out of luck.

For the next thirty minutes, I tried entering different username and password combinations, but I'm not a hacker and all of the easy combinations I tried were unfortunately not correct. Frustrated, I walked away from it, knowing I would have to destroy it before I became a suspect and the DVR was found during a home search. The things you have to deal with when you are a killer.

Tired and frustrated, I lay down on the bed and took a nap, hoping I would wake up in the same spot. When I woke up a couple of hours later, some of my angst was gone and I was hungry. I got in my car and headed out to get some food. The traffic was light and I was able to grab something to eat and bring it back to the house in twenty minutes. I had mindlessly turned on the television for background noise, but I wasn't paying attention to the show. I had bigger worries, such as how long I had before I went to jail—or worse yet—was killed. One day, when I show up to attack someone else, the intended victim might get the upper hand and kill me instead. I have no special training or skills when it comes to fighting, so I am completely shocked I haven't been the one to be found dead when the police showed up. At least, then, this madness would be over.

Discouraged, I threw the trash from my meal into the waste can in the kitchen and moved into my office, intending to research the strange events that had screwed up my life. While I had never heard of this type of thing—some type of fugue—happening to someone else, it was a pretty big world and, if it did, the answers might be found on the internet. I could only hope.

CHAPTER THREE

When I switched the light on in my office, I remembered the abandoned DVR that I had tried to hack into. It was time to dismantle it and take the hard drives out. I would hide the DVR itself until I could dump it in Green Lake, but the hard drive would be dismantled into small pieces, the platters would be torched and parts would be left in a dumpster somewhere. There was no way they were tying this murder back to me through the video.

I went out to the garage and pulled a Phillips-head screw-driver from one of the drawers at my workbench and returned to the office. As I disconnected the wires and turned it around to find the screws that held the case on, I did not immediately find them. Perplexed, I turned the unit over. Taped to the bottom was a piece of paper with two words written on it.

packerpower

favre4

No frickin' way. Could this seriously be the username and password? Anxiously, I tore the piece of paper off the bottom, turned the unit back over, plugged all of the wires back into it and turned it back on. The boot cycle seemed to take an hour, but really was only approximately four minutes. I'm pretty impatient though and I paced and yelled at the DVR while it booted. Finally, the screen came up and I touched one of the buttons. The logon screen popped up and I entered the username and password. They worked. Four blank camera views came up.

I found a playback feature and entered in the date and time from when I had left the house that morning. The screens lit up and I saw myself come out of the house for the first time, looking up at the camera that was tucked under the eaves. The three other camera views showed the back of the house, the living room and the kitchen. There was no camera in the bedroom to capture the grisly murder.

I started to watch the video backward, but it was confusing as I watched myself do everything in reverse. Instead, choosing a time two hours earlier, I brought up the video. There I was, passed out with my back against the stone wall. I repeated the process until I was no longer showing in the frame. I was either somewhere else in the house, or I had not arrived yet.

Watching the video forward now, I waited for movement on the screen. I looked at the time in the lower right-hand corner, which was the time of the video recording. It was slightly past midnight in the strange house and the minutes rapidly increased as I fast-forwarded through the stillness. At 12:47 a.m., I caught the first glimpse of movement in the back yard and slowed the video back down to a normal rate. A figure appeared from the shadows and slipped up to the door. I watched intently as the figure tried the door. It appeared to be unlocked as the person simply turned the handle and entered.

As the shape disappeared from the frame of the outside camera, the living room camera picked it up. Goosebumps covered my arms as a shudder ripped up my spine. It was eerie watching the video as the person—presumedly me—walked around, seemingly very alert, looking around the room. Moments later, the person left the room and disappeared from camera view. A few minutes later, I picked him up again on the kitchen camera as he poked around in the drawers. Empty-handed, he left the kitchen in the direction of the master bedroom. It was another ten minutes before the figure came back into camera range, this time picked back up by the living-room camera. What had just happened? I was confused by what was going on.

I jumped when the light was flicked on in the kitchen and my attention was pulled to that camera. The blonde that I had found dead on the floor, now wearing a pair of silk shorts and a silk top to match, went to the refrigerator and pulled some-thing out, stood at the kitchen island and started to eat it. The moment the light switched on, the figure in the living room ducked into the shadows—also surprised by the bright light.

For the next five minutes, the blonde, who I realized was extremely beautiful in life, ate out of the Tupperware container that was on the counter. Satisfied, she snapped the lid back on it and placed it back in the refrigerator. As she left the kitchen, I was surprised when she pulled her top off over her head, her bare back facing the camera. Then it hit me. She must be headed for the shower.

I focused on the living-room camera and after five minutes, I saw movement. The figure slowly retreated from the shadows and slipped towards the edge of the room. When he disappeared from the frame, I held my breath, hoping he would enter the still brightly-lit kitchen. I had to know. Was someone setting me up, or was I the killer? Nothing the video showed sparked any memory for me.

The moment the figure appeared in the kitchen, I knew. It was definitely me. Same six-foot frame, normal build and that was definitely my brown, shaggy hair that was in need of a cut. There was no more wondering. It was real.

I paused the video as my face looked towards the camera, feeling an unease so creepy that I couldn't explain it. While I knew it was me on the screen, something was off. My eyes were distant and glazed, like the lights were on, but no one was home. My features were expressionless, void of any emotion. I looked like a machine.

Pressing play one more time, I watched as I disappeared out of frame, in the same direction the blonde went. Minutes later, I watched in amazement as I went back into the living room, grabbed the fire poker, passed again through the kitchen and back out of camera view. Bile rose in the back of my throat as I imagined the horrors that were happening out of view. This poor, innocent girl had done nothing to deserve this. I was sure of it.

It was another ten minutes before I came back into frame in the kitchen, holding the poker across the palms of both hands, as if presenting a sword. The same expression—or lack of—ensconced my face. I knew what would happen next. I entered the living room, lowered my body to the cold, hard floor and leaned my back against the fireplace, the fire poker still in my hands. Within seconds, there was no other movement. It seemed as if someone shut my switch off.

While most of my questions remained unanswered, I at least now knew one of the most important facts. I was responsible for all the atrocities I woke up to. The big question now was why. Was I mentally ill? Schizophrenic? I had no history of mental illness in my family that I knew of and I certainly hadn't had any problems until recently.

Suddenly, rage surged through me, a response to the injustice that was happening to me. I wasn't perfect, but I certainly didn't deserve this shit. Neither did the victims, of course, but I was more concerned with saving my ass. Ripping the cords out of the back of the unit, I picked it up, held it high over my head and slammed it down on the floor of the room as hard as I could. The padding from the carpet broke some of the fall, but a couple of the screws burst out from the side of the unit and it settled on the floor in a slightly twisted state, the cover half hanging off.

I picked it up, carried it out to the garage and started to dismantle it. As I worked, I never felt more motivated to figure out what was taking over my mind—not to mention my body —at night.

CHAPTER FOUR

The next morning, I woke up, grateful to be in my own bed again. I always worried about waking up in a strange place. Relieved, I got ready and headed to the other side of town, where I had two appointments. The first one was to donate blood, which didn't pay much, but I needed everything I could scrape up. Luckily, the little things I was doing to make money paid for gas, food and utilities as long as I remained frugal.

The second appointment was another psychological study. While there was a myriad of different things they subjected me to, none were invasive. It was easy money to tell someone what

I saw in an ink-blot test, or what I thought of when I watched a video. They always had snacks, so that was a bonus. One-hundred bucks for an hour of my time was well worth it. Too bad I couldn't do that shit full-time. I'd be rich.

After the appointments, I headed back home and got on my computer. On Amazon, I went shopping, found what I was looking for and paid for overnight shipping. Finished, I brought up Google—and then hesitated. I had not been able to bring myself to pull up the information on any of the murders I had committed. I knew I should find out what the papers were saying and maybe learn what the cops knew, but there was something about attaching a name to each murder that made me avoid looking. If I knew their names, it would make them more real. By avoiding the details, I was effectively in denial that I had committed those atrocities. If I didn't remember the murders, there was always doubt I was responsible. It was never real, just a bad dream. Now that I had watched the video, everything was different. I could no longer hide from it. My thoughts were haunted by the visions.

Her name was Sarah Davis, girlfriend of a producer that was on location in Georgia shooting a movie. While the press indicated that the police felt the recent murders were all related, they were unable to determine what the victims had in common. The murders all appeared to be random and they were asking the public for their help by coming forward with any information they had. So far, I wasn't a suspect—that I knew of anyway. As I looked at Sarah's picture, I felt my eyes tear up. I clicked the browser closed, unable to handle the guilt from what I had done to her.

The next day, the doorbell rang and I eagerly opened it, finding a package at the door. I snagged it from the doorstep and took it inside to the kitchen, ripped it open and pulled the contents out. I removed the instructions and read them.

One of the things that I had noticed about the murders was that I always woke up wearing the clothes that I had taken off the night before. I admit that I have a bad habit of getting undressed and throwing my clothes on the floor by the bed. It's a laziness thing, which is silly considering I always pick them up as soon as I wake up in the morning—before I do anything else.

That night, when I got ready for bed, I peeled off my shirt and I attached the body-worn camera to the collar. It held a high-capacity SD card to record the video and only recorded when it sensed movement. If I got up and committed any heinous act in the middle of the night, I was hoping the body cam would record the entire thing, giving me a little more insight as to what triggered the event. As it stood, I didn't know any of the victims. How I was able to commit the acts at the perfect time without getting caught—all without consciously knowing it—was a huge mystery.

With my clothes on the floor, I went to sleep, apprehensive that I might kill someone, but hopeful that if I did, I would gain insight. When I woke up in my bed again the next morning, I was overjoyed that another night had passed without incident.

I repeated the exercise over the next few days and each morning, I was more hopeful than the day before, that the events were a thing of the past. My hopes were dashed the following morning. I knew immediately I had done the unthinkable when I woke up, lying on a strange bed. As I had become accustomed to, I quietly searched the house to ascertain the scope of the situation. The house was extremely clean and overly organized. Everything had been strategically placed and nothing was out of order—until I got to the living room.

The victim this time was male, around forty-five, short, balding, with a pot-belly that was peeking out from beneath his white T-shirt. He wore a pair of boxers as well with an open robe covering him. The scene looked like something out of an action movie. The man lay on his back, his robe open, on a bed of shattered glass, the twisted metal frame of the glass coffee table surrounding him. The side rail of the table had evidently taken the full impact of the victim's head as it was bent in a "U" shape and was lacquered in blood. It was the crimson pool of blood on the carpet below the man's head that told the rest of the story. While the multiple wounds the man had suffered from the jagged glass shards must have been substantial, it was the head wound that was fatal.

My stomach churned as I looked at the scene, but I knew I had to quickly get out of the house. I removed the blanket and pillowcases from the bed and stuck them in the washing machine, added laundry soap and set the cycle to the longest, hottest one I could. I then went back through the entire house and cleaned my prints from everything that could have contained them. As I walked past the man one last time on my way out the back door, I wondered how he had landed with such force. The shattered glass was understandable, but the bent steel frame was mind-boggling.

When I finally got home an hour later, I double-checked my clothes again for blood, but saw none. Regardless, I peeled them off and stuck them in the washing machine, making sure I removed the body cam first. I was anxious to see what secrets its footage revealed.

CHAPTER FIVE

Midnight. The video started as the shirt was being moved from the floor. I slid it over my arms and head. The footage was shaky as I imagined myself getting dressed. A few minutes later, I headed out of the bedroom and out the front door.

I wished I could see my face. I didn't understand how this could be happening without my knowledge or memory of it. I set out on foot, keeping to the shadows and I walked for what seemed like forever. Impatiently, I sped up the video and watched the path of my travel. It was unfamiliar to me. Eventually, I arrived at a house—the house. An hour and thirteen minutes had elapsed. I tried the front door. It was locked. I watched as I went through the gate and around to the back of the house. That door was locked as well. A few minutes later, I found my way in, through a garage service door.

Inside the garage, I waited at the entrance to the house, listening for a few minutes. I must have heard something. I then turned the lever, inching the door open a crack, a sliver of light slipping through. Was the man awake when I showed up? That might explain the robe.

After another five minutes, I entered the house, through a laundry room that was adjacent to the kitchen. The kitchen light was on and I cautiously made my way into that room as well. It was empty. My heart was beating out of my chest as I watched myself inch my way into the living room. That room was also vacant and I walked through it and down the hallway towards what I assumed to be the bedrooms. A doorway at the end of the hall started to open and I retreated back to the living room, hiding around the corner from the hallway. My breath halted in my lungs as I anticipated a confrontation at any moment.

It was then that he came around the corner and it all happened so fast, I paused the video and rewound it, so I could watch it frame-by-frame. The footage was amazing and even though I knew the intruder in the video was me, I could not believe that I was the person behind the motions that occurred. As the frames clicked by, I watched as the man came around the corner, bumping into me. He appeared to scream. My hands immediately reached for his throat and I grabbed him and lifted him into the air by his neck. Even on my best day, I do not possess the upper-body strength to perform such a feat, even with a hundred-pound person. This guy had to be around two-hundred and twenty pounds. It made no sense.

Seconds later, it was over. I picked him up by the neck—while he thrashed and tried to get loose—carried him into the living room, lifted him as high in the air as I could and slammed his body down against the coffee table. It was game over. He did not move again. Minutes later, I nonchalantly headed to the bedroom and stretched out on the bed.

I fast-forwarded through the rest of the video to make sure I didn't miss anything, but I knew the rest already. I slept until the time I woke up on the strange bed, cleaned up after myself and left the house.

Watching the video afforded me few new revelations. I must be as crazy as bat shit, but I certainly didn't feel that way. I felt normal, except for the confusion surrounding my new late-night hobby. My only new takeaways were that I was certainly not in control of my body during the entire situation and that I obviously had some raw power that I was able to tap into when I was in my unaware state. It was scary to think of the damage I could do without even being conscious of it.

As much as I dreaded it, I knew I needed to learn more about the victims. If I could make a connection, maybe I could figure out why they were being killed—rather, why I was killing them. Could it be that they had pissed me off in real life and my subconscious was taking over? None of them looked familiar to me.

I pulled up the internet and started performing searches on each of the murders. On a pad of paper that I had beside my computer, I wrote down their names, date of birth, date of death, occupation, hobbies, marital status and anything else I could gather. I needed some sort of correlation between them to help me figure out a pattern. Why was I killing these people? What made them so special?

The more information I gathered, the more confused I became. Unemployed actor's girlfriend, retail worker, insurance agent, city employee, small business owner and server in a restaurant. There was no rhyme or reason to the list. There seemed to be no connection whatsoever. If I didn't know these people—had zero exposure to them—then why did my subconscious tell me to kill them?

The next few days passed with no more events which gave me a little relief, but it also put me on edge. They seemed to be happening more frequently—almost once a week. If that cadence held true, I was due to wake up who knows where soon, with blood on my hands. My gut twisted as I thought about it. As badly as I wanted to end the cycle, I couldn't figure out how. It would be so much easier if I just killed myself.

Surprised that my thoughts had just turned to suicide, I broke down and cried. Life for me was over. I would either be subject to being an angel of death, spend my life in prison or die. There didn't seem to be any other option. I fought for breath as I ugly-cried for twenty minutes. I'm not a religious man, but I prayed for God to take me right then and there. I was done.

When I had no more tears to shed, I wiped my face on my sleeve and got up. Crying like a baby would get me nowhere. I had to think. I had to make a plan. I had to move.

I took a long shower and got dressed. As I put my wallet in my back pocket, I paused and took out the remaining cash, counting it before putting it back. Twenty-two dollars. It would not last long. Suddenly, I realized it was Thursday and I had my weekly appointments to sell blood and my time. I certainly needed the dough.

The blood-giving was uneventful as always. I was blessed with having good veins, so they never had to poke me more than once. In fifteen minutes, I was out of the clinic, check in hand.

When I got to the testing place, I was anxious to get through with whatever bullshit test or exercise they were going to put me through. Spending an hour there under normal circumstances wasn't a big deal, but right now, I was in an agitated state of mind. I needed to be working on my problem, not playing some bullshit game. Still, a man had to eat.

The waiting area of the suite, which was located inside a medical plaza, was a standard waiting room, much like a doctor's office. The receptionist was very friendly and it hadn't gotten by me that she was a very attractive twenty-something woman as well. While she was way younger than me, there was something about her that made me smile. Her long brown hair touched her shoulders and when she laughed, she flipped her head, her luscious hair swirling back and forth. This was the first time I had seen her.

The wait in the seating area was short and it wasn't long before I was called and taken to a room. The same sixty-something man—clad in a white lab coat—that I was used to seeing each time I visited, came into the room. I believe his name was Henry, but I wasn't positive. After the usual pleasantries, Henry asked me to watch a ten-minute marketing video. I did—I really needed the money—although I was not into it. There were way too many things on my mind to be concentrating on some tribble.

After the video ended, Henry came back into the room and asked me some questions, which I had to answer to get my money. I took a deep breath, having little patience for the process.

"What did you think of the video?"

"It was okay," I answered.

"Could you elaborate a little more?" he asked.

"I'm a little agitated about other stuff to be honest. It was hard to concentrate."

"Are you okay?" he asked, not seeming to be overly concerned.

"I think so. I'm just having a rough time right now."

"Interesting. Are you thirsty?"

I was anything but thirsty. "No, I'm good."

"No, really," he insisted. "You should drink something. It will help hydrate your brain and make you feel better."

I started to protest, but he picked up the phone anyway and asked the voice on the other end of the line to bring in some orange juice. A minute later, the attractive girl from the reception desk brought in a glass of the bright-orange beverage. When he handed it to me, the cold glass and the smell of the juice attacked my senses and I decided I wanted it after all. I drained half the glass on the first chug.

"Are you sleeping at night?" he asked.

I was surprised by the question as he usually stuck to questions around the tests. Even though he wore a lab coat and they were located in a medical plaza, I didn't think he was a doctor. Maybe I was mistaken.

"Some nights. Others are a little rougher."

"What's keeping you up at night?" he inquired.

Without thinking, I answered. "It's not so much staying awake. It's hard to explain. I guess I'm sleepwalking a little." I was relieved to tell someone the big secret I had been keeping. Of course, I couldn't tell him about the murder part. I'd have the cops at my door within hours.

"Sleepwalking. Interesting." His interest piqued. "Do you remember anything when you wake up?"

"No," I lied. Actually, it wasn't really a lie. I didn't

remember shit, but the aftermath spoke for itself. That and the video. There was no disputing that.

"Well I hope everything will be okay," he told me. "Back to the video. Do you remember what it was about?"

I told him what I remembered and we discussed it a little further.

"Perfect. It did its job," he informed me.

My brows raised and my eyes squinted as I processed his last statement. It seemed odd.

"What was its job?"

"Oh, um . . . I just mean that you got out of it what we hope the audiences that it is targeted for will get out of it."

"All right," I answered, dismissing it. I had more important things to worry about.

We finished up our conversation, he brought in my check and I got out of there, anxious to get back home and eat lunch.

As I ate, I thought about my situation and felt sorry for myself once again.

Perfect. It did its job.

The words repeated themselves in my head. The statement was odd to me. Maybe because I was on edge.

I ate faster, anxious to get on the computer. I had some research to do.

CHAPTER SIX

Claxton Research Industries or CRI. Google surprisingly only had a few results for the research clinic. I had a hard time believing that any business would have only a few results. I clicked on each of the links and read through them. There wasn't any information that helped me and I had a feeling deep in my gut that something was off. I couldn't put my finger on it, but I had nothing else to do. I clicked on the link and looked at their website. It looked above board.

I was troubled by the lack of information. The company website had no information about the staff. Any reputable company should have tons of information on the internet about them. This company had next to nothing. Could they be new? I thought back to how I had discovered them. A flyer had been mailed to my home. Did they do a mass mailing, or was it more targeted?

A thought hit me and I pulled up one of the "Whois" sites and entered the website address for the clinic. Unless a website owner paid extra to keep the information private, the registered owner's information would be there. My eyebrows shot up when I realized I got lucky. The owner of the clinic's domain was Henry Walker and his address and phone number were listed as well. He owned the domain which meant he probably was in charge of the website, too. Was it possible that he actually owned the clinic?

As I reread the record, the date the domain was created caught my eye. My stomach churned as the date burned into my brain. It was only ten months ago. Ten months. Before that, this website did not exist. Did that mean the clinic didn't, either? If they were new, was that necessarily a suspicious thing? I didn't know the answer to that.

I spent the rest of the evening trying to work through the details, but I could not concentrate and decided to go to bed. I hoped to have a clearer head in the morning.

———

I awoke, startled. I was wet and, when my head cleared, I realized I was sitting in a jacuzzi, the jets hitting my back full-blast. I looked down and I was fully clothed and when I looked to my left, I saw the body. The guy looked to be about twenty-eight. I assumed he was dead—not only because he wasn't moving, but because the top of a Budweiser beer bottle was protruding from his head, the jagged edges of the broken bottom part of the bottle imbedded deeply into his forehead.

I closed my eyes and took long, deep breaths to control my heart and anxiety. It had happened much sooner this time. Things were ramping up. I had to figure this thing out soon. Time was running out.

As I tried to get out of the jacuzzi, something blocked me from pulling my feet out. There was something in the water. I reached down towards my feet and felt around, feeling a mane of long hair. It was a body. Grabbing onto the hair, I pulled the body above water and away from my feet. Brown hair was attached to the head that I assumed was attractive in life. She had been under the hot water for quite a while and her skin was red and wrinkled. She appeared to be in her mid-twenties. She looked familiar to me, but I could not place her. Perfect, I had killed a young couple.

Anxious to get out of there, I climbed from the tub and left the bodies there, cleaned up and slipped out into the early-morning streets.

Back home, I stripped off my wet clothes and threw them in the washing machine, starting the machine on a hot cycle. In the shower, I warmed up and washed the death from my skin. I had been sitting in a cauldron of dead bodies. Thinking about it weirded me out and I got light-headed, slipping down onto the floor of the shower, the water pummeling the top of my head. I lowered my head and closed my eyes, feeling sorry for myself.

A name popped into my head. Henry Walker. He had to have something to do with this. I could feel it.

I shut off the water, newly motivated, dried off as quickly as possible and pulled on some sweats. In the office, I pulled up a web browser and entered Henry's name. The page lit up with numerous hits, some related to the researcher and some not. As I clicked open the articles, I was unsure of what each article meant in the scope of things. They were like puzzle pieces that were clicking together, waiting for the big reveal of what the picture was.

Henry Walker had been around. He had operated similar businesses in six other states. None of the others were still open. Why was he moving around so much? What secret was he trying to hide? I read on. Finally, after three in the morning, one of the final pieces clicked into place. Henry Walker had made the news thirty years prior when he had conducted groundbreaking research on subliminal messaging. Subliminal advertising and messaging had been extremely controversial since it was first invented in the nineteen-fifties. Could this be what was happening? Could I have been programmed to commit these murders? My mind spun as I started researching subliminal messaging and how it worked. I was blown away by some of the experiments I read. From what I was reading, it was illegal, but I'm not sure Henry Walker cared. Was this man the devil? As my brain churned, I decided I had to find out.

CHAPTER SEVEN

It was a moonless night—for which I was thankful. This time, I actually drove my car, parking it two blocks over, before slipping my way through the residential streets to the address that was listed for the Claxton Research Industries' website owner. This had to be Henry Walker's house.

I walked up to the front door, ready to ring the doorbell and confront him. I changed my mind and found the side gate, slipping into the back yard. From the shadows, I was able to see through the French doors and floor-to-ceiling windows that flanked them. There were no blinds. The television was on in the living room and Henry was sitting on the couch watching it. I knew he could not see me as it was pitch black outside, so I sat and watched, waiting for the right moment. Thirty-minutes later, he got up and left the room. Without hesitation, I slid my small backpack on my back and approached the door. Expecting it to be locked, I tried it, surprised to find it open. I slipped inside and down the hall, in the opposite direction he had gone. Silently, I waited, listening.

The sound of the television reached me, but I could hear nothing else. Uncertain, I waited and finally I heard laughter. He was back in the living room, watching his show. With nothing to lose, I walked into the room and came up behind him on the couch. He caught my reflection in the living room windows and his head and body instinctively snapped around. His eyes grew wide when he saw me.

"What the hell are you doing here?" he asked nervously.

"You know," I answered, not sure if he did, but in my heart, I believed he was responsible for everything.

He paused, fear in his eyes. Finally, he said "I'm not sure what you think you know, but you are wrong."

"Am I, Mr. Walker?"

He flinched when I mentioned his last name.

"What do you want?" he asked.

"Answers."

"About what?" he snapped, becoming bold for a second.

"About why you have me killing people."

His eyes widened and his mouth opened, but no words came out. Finally, he said "You're mistaken."

"I don't think so. I had a realization tonight on my way over."

"And what was that?" he sneered.

"The person you had me kill last night—she was your receptionist, wasn't she?"

His glare answered my question for me. He said nothing.

"How does it work, Walker?"

"You know nothing," he said, anger in his eyes.

"How do the subliminal messages work, huh? Are there hidden messages in the videos you show me that tell me to kill?"

His eyes widened and he jumped off the couch and was out the back door before I could catch him. I hopped the couch and tore out after him. Being younger and in much better shape, I leapt and took him to the ground right before he reached the gate. Two swift blows to the gut knocked the air out of him and I picked up his crumpled body and carried him back in the house.

In the kitchen, I sat him on a chair and used short pieces of rope to tie his legs to the legs of the chairs. I tied his hands behind his back and to the back of the chair. As I was finishing, he got his breath fully back and was able to talk again.

"You'll never get away with this."

"So far, I've gotten away with every murder you had me commit. What's one more?"

"I'll pay you," he offered, desperation seeping into his voice.

"Tempting," I teased him. "But, hell no. You will, however, answer my questions."

"Fuck you," he spat.

"No thanks," I answered. "You aren't my type." With that, I slammed my boot down on the bare toes of his left foot, breaking most of them in the process. He screamed so loud that I worried he would wake the neighbors. I covered his mouth with my hand and applied pressure.

"You yell again and I will gag your ass, do you understand?"

He nodded and I uncovered his mouth.

"Okay, so let's try again. Why are you programming me to kill people?"

"I'm not telling you shit."

"I thought that you were smarter than that," I told him. "I'm disappointed."

I walked to the kitchen and grabbed a dish towel and searched the drawers for plastic wrap, and through his contesting and struggling, wadded the towel up and shoved it into his mouth. I then wrapped the saran wrap around his head, being sure to leave his nose uncovered. I did not want him to die . . . yet.

Satisfied that he would not be able to scream now, I grabbed the thumb on his right hand and twisted it until it snapped. His attempted screams were muffled and he thrashed in his chair, almost falling over on his side. Tears streamed down his cheeks. Frustrated, I pulled up a chair in front of him, sat down and positioned my face within inches from his. His eyes were wide with pain and fear.

"Do I have your attention?" I growled. "Understand that I'm not playing."

I didn't see what was coming and my vision went black as I crumpled to the floor in pain, only to realize he had head-butted me. While the searing pain shot through my skull, he scooted his chair around and slammed it against the center island as hard as possible. After multiple hits, the chair disintegrated and he fell to the floor, struggling to free himself from the fragments of broken chair. Before I could regain my clarity, he was on me, jabbing at my face with both hands. While he certainly didn't have the same power he must have had in his youth, his punches still hurt and compounded the pain from the headbutt. I had to get him off me and I bucked my lower body causing him to fly up in the air a few inches. When he came back down, I had raised my knee and he took it full force, in the groin. His eyes immediately watered and I could hear the muffled scream as he rolled off and grabbed his injured parts. I took the opportunity to slam my elbow back into his gut three times, once again knocking the air out of him. When he stopped moving, I grabbed a knife from the butcher block, grabbed him by the collar and sat him back in another chair, the knife inches from him.

"Enough," I told him, trying to recover from my own injuries. "You decide whether you live or die today. If you don't tell me what I want to know, you die. Are you going to talk to me?"

He nodded his head rapidly, finally understanding that I wasn't messing around.

"Can I take the gag out? Will you be good?"

He nodded again rapidly. Prepared to end it if he betrayed me again, I removed the plastic wrap and the towel. He sucked in as much air as he could, with jagged breaths.

"Why are you programming me to kill people?"

He was silent. I brought the knife up and moved it closer to his face.

"You fit the part."

"What do you mean?"

"I needed someone that was physically capable to pull off what I needed done. You walked into my office at the right time. I started preparing you months before your first kill."

"How did you do it?" I asked.

"What do you mean?" he asked.

I pushed the tip of the blade against his throat. "How were you able to get me to kill people without me remembering it?"

"I imbedded subliminal images and programming in each

video you watched at the lab. Each one specified a particular victim."

"That shit works?" I asked, incredulously.

"To an extent. I do it better than most. I developed a primer for your brain that, when taken, makes your brain completely accept and follow the messages in the video. You seem to love your snacks and orange juice."

Shocked, I asked "Why? Why did these people have to die?"

He hesitated and I put pressure on the knife. He winced as a small trail of blood slid down his neck.

"They were all subjects of mine and knew too much. I've used them for other things . . . to get things I wanted. When I was done with them, they had to go."

"And me?" I asked.

"You were my cleaner. Taking care of the loose ends."

"But am I not also a loose end?" I challenged.

He gulped and said nothing. I pulled the knife away and grabbed him by the throat, applying pressure. Tears fell down his face as his body started shaking.

"Yes, you are a loose end. I've been working on a plan for that."

"To kill me?"

He said nothing.

"This isn't your first clinic," I said, afraid of the answer to the question I was about to ask. "Has the same thing happened in every city you opened up in?"

He squeezed his eyes shut tightly and the tears continued to fall. He nodded.

A chill went up the back of my spine as I shuddered. The totality of his actions finally hit me.

"Let me see if I have this straight. You open a research clinic, use your clients to get things you want or need, have them all killed off by another client and then you get rid of that client, shut down shop, move to another state and start all over again. Does that sum it up?"

Convulsions shook his body as he cried louder and harder than he had before, the reality of the situation washing over him. Again, he nodded.

I couldn't understand why he would do what he had done. He was brilliant and the world could have been his. "Why? Why would you do this? I'm trying to understand."

He wiped his nose on his shoulder and sniffled, trying to control his emotions. Finally, he answered.

"My research was groundbreaking. I knew I had the potential to be filthy rich. I had companies lined up wanting to use subliminal advertising. Unfortunately, all of the backlash and privacy discussions over it killed off any chance I had of making real money from it. I lost my wife. I lost everything. I fell into a deep depression and on a whim, convinced a colleague of mine that she wanted to have sex with me by giving her a video to watch that I had made explicitly for her. When she came on to me, I knew I had power. You know what they say. Power corrupts. Absolute power corrupts absolutely. I started using my power to get what I wanted. Soon enough, I lost control. I tried to stop, but like any addiction, I was too weak. I'm ashamed, but powerless to stop. Maybe you being here is a good thing."

"Maybe," I answered, unsure of what my next move was. Part of me felt sorry for the guy, yet I hated him for destroying my life. Because of him, I lost my job. Because of him, I was a murderer. Because of him, life as I knew it was over. I switched my grip on the handle of the knife and walked behind him, placing the blade to his throat. As I applied pressure, I felt him gulp. He knew it was over.

CHAPTER EIGHT

I greeted Brooke as I entered the clinic. I had hired her a couple of weeks ago to take the place of the girl I had murdered. Brooke was a friendly and eager twenty-one-year-old who I felt brought great energy to the place.

Two weeks prior when I had visited Henry Walker in his home and learned the whole story, I made up my mind to take over the clinic. Although I had no training, I intended to learn and make sure the research that was carried out was ethical. Before I left his property, I had everything I needed to start my new life. No one would be able to stop me.

I went into my office and put on my lab coat, anxious for another day of positivity, the horrors of the previous weeks a thing of the past. The police had never come to visit me—at least so far—and I held high hopes that they never would. I had not killed another person after that night.

As I was getting ready to walk into the testing room and make sure it was ready, the door opened and I looked over, my heart beating rapidly for a second before I realized who it was.

"Morning, Henry."

"Morning, Stan. How are you this fine morning?"

"Great. Anxious to learn more. The past two weeks have been great."

"Honestly, I feel the same. Having you here learning with me has brought back the excitement I used to have before I got mired in a life of corruption. I haven't felt like this in twenty years."

"Glad I could help. Ready to get started?"

"I am. Refresh my memory. We were going to create a production with subliminal messaging in it today for Mrs. Duncan, correct?"

"Yes," I answered. "I can't wait to see the entire process."

"Perfect," he replied. "And just to make sure I remember correctly, the messaging is going to convince her to donate all of her money to our clinic for research purposes, right?"

"You're a funny guy," I told him as I watched him break into a fit of laughter. "I think we agreed to show her subliminal messaging that will boost her self-esteem."

"Oh, that's right. I was close though," he chuckled.

He could tell from my eyeroll that I wasn't nearly as amused as he was, but I was happy to see he was turning his life around. We were using the clinic to benefit our clients. I—for one—was glad I had one less murder on my conscience; however, that burden would not be one I carried much longer. We were also in production on a video that would allow us both to purge the memories of our transgressions. It felt like it would never be ready soon enough. Life was going to be great. I could feel it.

STAYED AWAKE ALL NIGHT

Soaked in sweat, Shane Walsh peeled the damp cotton sheet and the down comforter away from his clammy skin. He grunted, wondering if the heater was not turning off automatically like it should. God knows he shouldn't be sweating when outside looked like pictures he had seen of a frigid Russian winter. Last time he had checked, before bed, there were several inches of wet snow on the ground, and it was only going to get worse.

A chill shook him as a cold draft hit his already glistening body, and he pulled the covers back up. The room wasn't too warm after all.

What the hell?

Rolling onto his left side, Shane slipped one eye open and looked at the clock. Only eleven p.m. He had gone to bed early to get some much needed rest for a job interview in the morning. He had been unemployed for weeks, and the bills weren't paying themselves, so getting this job was paramount for his continued survival.

Falling back into slumber, his mind went back to the dream he had been deeply immersed in when his extreme body temperature had woken him up, only it wasn't a lucid dream and he hadn't remembered it upon waking.

Now, back inside the dream—or what was quickly becoming a nightmare—Shane fidgeted as he was deeply immersed in REM sleep, something that never happened to him so early during his slumber.

He suddenly became aware. Aware that he had just been awake. Aware that he had been profusely sweating and soaking the bed. Aware that something bad—really fucking bad—had pulled him deep down again into a nightmare he had just woken up from. And then he remembered: The hands. The claws.

The atmosphere in the dream was similar to his bedroom. He was lying in bed. The room was eerie, shadows and swirls of black and gray shifting through the air. An orange glow added ambience to the creepiness, but the location of the source was impossible to identify, and although the glow was bright, it did nothing to disperse the shadows.

Shane tried to wake up, sit up, or do anything to pull himself out of this dreamscape he did not want to be a part of, but nothing worked.

A guttural growl and a hiss came from everywhere and nowhere. Shane tried to get out of bed, but his body felt like he was being held down—was this sleep paralysis he had read about? He was confused by the dream, the lighting, the fog and shadows, and the white din that seemed to grow louder as he struggled. Suddenly he was unsure if he was trying to get out of his real bed, or his dream bed. Reality and the world he was now immersed in became one.

He jumped as a hand—at least he thought it was a hand—grabbed his face. Another covered his mouth. He tried to claw them off him, but his arms wouldn't move. More hands grabbed his arms, his torso, his legs, and his feet. He struggled, but his efforts resulted in no more than a body spasm. Pain shot through his side as sharp fingernails pierced his flesh. He tried to scream, but the hand over his mouth clamped down tighter. Suddenly he felt himself being pulled down—into the mattress. As if the mattress was not a solid substance, his body began to press through the material, the springs, the filling. A spring pierced his back and he let out a cry behind the hand—the one clamped down in a death-grip.

Tears leaked out of the corner of his eyes and splotched on the already soaked sheets; dream bed or real bed, or maybe both.

Shane found it hard to breathe as his mouth was covered and his chest was being compressed. He tried to struggle again, to scream again. He continued to be pulled down into the bed, deeper, through the mattress, partially through the box spring. Was the floor next? Would he be yanked into the dark depths of the earth?

The pain in his side increased as the fingernails penetrated deeper. His breath caught in his throat, and he coughed violently. His resolve dissipated as hopelessness took over. He stopped trying to move, hoping to either wake up or never wake up—either option would be better than this.

He coughed again, and his mouth forcefully opened as spittle flew out. A finger pressed inside his mouth. Without thinking, he bit down as hard as he could, severing the digit. A chorus of screams rose up through the room as his throat flooded with the sweet-tasting ichor. As if the hands were all connected to the same being, they all retracted at once, and Shane felt himself spring back up to the top of the mattress, as if he'd been held below the surface of a pool and released only to buoy back to the top.

His sleep paralysis was gone, and in the same instance, the hands were retracted. He tried to get out of bed, got his foot tangled in the covers, and fell headfirst on his face. The breath was knocked from his lungs, and he gasped for air as he tried to get his fill of the sweet oxygen that he had been deprived of.

Minutes later, he started to breathe more freely, and he opened his eyes, not realizing they had been clenched tightly. The room was dark, except for the glow from the red numbers on the alarm clock beside his bed. He was in his room, no longer stuck in the terrifying situation that had seemed all too real. It had only been a nightmare after all.

Hoping to rid himself of the layer of perspiration that had coated his body—not to mention the musky smell—Shane started the shower, stripped out of his shorts, and got in. He would change the bedsheets as soon as he was done and try to get back to sleep. Already, he was anxious about his interview and how this sequence of events was throwing a monkey wrench into his carefully laid-out plans to be properly prepared.

Squirting shampoo into his hand, he washed his newly cut sandy-blond hair and then rinsed it. The nightmare had affected him, and he was still reeling from it, but the magical hot water of the shower was slowly eating away at the negative effects of the experience. Shane always felt that a hot shower had healing powers, and he breathed easier as he stood under the hotter-than-normal stream of the showerhead.

He followed up with a handful of bodywash, then started washing his slightly muscular arms, shoulders, and torso. Already feeling better, he was looking forward to getting back to sleep. A sting of pain stripped away his relief. Grimacing with a slight shake of his head, Shane looked down at his side, where the pain had erupted from. There was an open wound, and blood was dripping onto the bottom of the shower stall, diluting with the water and swirling its way down the drain. Shane touched the wound and winced. It was tender.

"What the fuck?"

This was the exact spot the nails had punctured his flesh in the horrendous nightmare that had paralyzed him. His eyes bulged and his mouth fell open as he leaned his body against the tile walls of the shower and slid down it, his butt landing on the wet shower floor. He watched in disbelief as a small but steady stream of his own blood flowed down the drain.

Shane shook his head, unable to connect all the pieces. "No, no, NOOOO!" His voice boomed in the tiny bathroom as his mind whirled. He was not safe and he knew it.

Frantically, he pulled himself up to a standing position, turned off the water, and got out, grabbing the nearest towel. He patted off some of the water, quickly dried the spot on his side that had been punctured, taped some gauze to it, and grabbed the clothes that he had left on the chair the night before, slipping into them before yanking on his shoes. Grabbing his wallet, phone, and keys, he rushed to the door of his small two-bedroom home before coming to his senses and grabbing a jacket. He pulled it on and grabbed a beanie as well, pulling it over his damp hair. As he was about to exit his room again for the second time, he spotted something on the floor beside the bed. Puzzled, he bent down and picked it up, then screamed and dropped it before running out the front door, slamming it shut behind him.

A finger—it was a fucking finger.

His Toyota RAV4 was covered with at least six inches of snow, but he was grateful that it was all-wheel drive. Unlocking it using his keyfob, he yanked the door open as a cascade of snow slipped off the side above the door and covered his seat and the floorboard. Wiping it off the seat the best he could with the sleeve of his jacket, Shane jumped in, started it, turned the defroster to high, grabbed the snow scraper he had in the back seat, and got back out, scraping the snow off the windows as quickly as he could. He was freaking out about the finger, but he knew he could not drive blind.

When the glass was clear enough to see through, Shane climbed into the driver's seat again, threw the snow scraper behind him into the dark abyss, closed the door, and shifted into reverse. The headlights barely cut through the flurries pelting the windshield, and he had no idea where he was going, but he knew he could not stay home. Something bad had transpired, and he wasn't going to wait around for it to happen again. Next time, he may not be so lucky. Shane hit the gas, and the SUV slid sideways as it rocketed out of the driveway. Shifting into drive, Shane hit the gas and the back of the RAV4 fishtailed as he blasted down the otherwise quiet street, destination unknown.

SHANE DROVE AIMLESSLY FOR A COUPLE OF HOURS. THIS late at night, he didn't really know where to go. He considered pulling into some parking lot, but he was scared he would fall asleep. Sleep was not something he felt comfortable doing at the moment. He thought about restaurants that might be open all night, but none came to mind. With no other options, he decided to wake Becca up. She would know what to do.

His mind drifted and he thought about her short, thin frame, her dark—almost goth—hair. She was really quite beautiful—and sexy. Shane enjoyed spending time with her—in and out of the bedroom—but she was always pushing him to get married and he wasn't ready for that level of commitment. He was still trying to get his own shit together.

Becca had to be up early for work, so he hated to wake her, but desperate times called for desperate measures. He would be happy to see her and have someone to share his experience with. She wouldn't judge him or make him think he was crazy. She wasn't like that. She was a good girl. A much better person than him.

Shane turned right and headed toward her apartment. The streets were empty, and not only had he seen no other vehicles moving about on the road, his seemed to be the only tire tracks. Luckily, the Rav4 handled the snow well, but he drove slowly out of caution. He didn't want to end up sliding into something and messing up his vehicle. The night was already bad enough. A blanket of quiet enveloped him and the streets, the snow creating an effect like he was the only person alive in this little town. He felt like a night wolf, stalking through the streets as if he were looking for prey, but it was quite the opposite. He was trying to *avoid* being the prey.

As if on cue, the wound to his side throbbed, and he winced. He reached under his jacket with his left hand and touched it through his shirt. His hand came away sticky. The blood seeped through the gauze and the material of his T-shirt. He wiped his hand on his pants, reminding himself to ask Becca to look at it.

Her apartment complex was small and no one seemed to be awake. The complex was older and consisted of four buildings with four single-story apartments in each. As he entered the parking lot, he saw the two units on the left and the two on the right. Her apartment was in the building to the right, at the rear of the complex. Apartment number sixteen.

He parked, then approached her door quietly and listened. No sounds wafted to him from the building, and no light leaked out from behind the blinds. He paused a moment longer, then tapped softly on the door. He waited, but she didn't answer. He pulled out his phone and texted her.

Are you up?

He waited a minute with no response. Finally, he knocked.

A minute later, he knocked again, harder this time. Eventually, a light popped on in the apartment. He sensed someone at the peephole, trying to determine what asshat was at her door in the wee hours of the morning. Finally, she must have recognized that the asshat was him and she cracked the door open. Shane could make her out through the slit in the door, glasses on (she normally wore contacts), robe held closed at the neckline with her free hand.

"Shane? Is everything okay?"

"Can I come in?"

"Oh, yeah, sorry." Becca opened the door and let him in, abruptly closing it after him to keep the cold out.

"You okay?" she asked. "What time is it?"

"Late. I…uh, need your help."

Concern crossed Becca's face. "What's going on? It's not like you to come by here in the middle of the night."

Shane took off his jacket.

"Is that blood?"

"Yes. Could you look at it for me?"

"Shane? Are you okay?" she repeated. "What happened? Maybe we should take you to the hospital."

"Not sure what I would tell them."

"The truth? But maybe you can start by telling me."

"Okay. While you clean this up for me?"

"Deal."

Becca took Shane into the bathroom and made him sit on the closed toilet. She gingerly pulled his shirt over his head. The blood-soaked gauze hung partially off his skin.

"Look over there," Becca told him, pointing. When he looked, she ripped the gauze and tape off in one quick motion.

"OW!"

"Would you have preferred the slow tear? Jesus! That looks

terrible. Now tell me how this happened. What's going on with you?"

While Becca cleaned up the wound and rebandaged it, Shane recounted his nightmare and the strange happenings surrounding it.

Becca squinted her eyes and wrinkled her forehead. "Wow. That's a lot to take in. Are you sure it just wasn't *all* a nightmare?"

"Have you seen my side?"

"Yeah, you definitely got hurt, but maybe you did it while you were sleeping."

"That doesn't explain the finger on my floor."

"I forgot about the finger."

"I wish I could."

"Any idea what this is all about?" Becca asked, concern etched across her forehead.

"Not a clue."

"Have you been having other bad dreams recently?"

"No. This was the first."

"So what are you gonna do?"

"No clue. I don't suppose *not* sleeping is an option."

"Probably not. In fact, don't you have that interview this morning?"

"Yeah."

"Are you still going to it?"

"I kinda need to. Getting a job is a necessity."

"So why don't you crash here?"

"Um…"

"I know, but you can't stay awake all night. At least get a little rest. I'll stay up and keep an eye on you. I have some vacation days due me, and I really don't want to go in anyway, so I don't mind staying up."

"I don't know…"

"C'mon, Shane, don't be so stubborn. You're safer here then back at your house."

"I don't disagree with you. It's just—"

"Scary?"

"Yeah."

"I can only imagine. I'm sorry, babe."

"Thanks."

"So really…please. Go lay down on my bed. I got you."

"Will you come with me?"

"Not a chance. Someone has to keep watch."

"Okay, but please leave the door open—and if you hear me fussing in my sleep, come wake my ass up."

"Deal."

Shane went to Becca and pulled her against his chest. She hugged him tight, grabbed his face with her hands, stood on her tippy-toes, and kissed his forehead.

"It'll be okay," she told him. "Go." She pointed toward the bedroom.

Shane slipped into the dark room and turned on the bedside light. He sat down on his side of the bed—the side he slept on when he stayed over. Apprehension crept through him as he pulled off his shoes and laid on the pillowtop mattress, pulling the covers over him as he settled in.

He laid awake and thought about going to sleep. He was exhausted. Then he caught himself *actually* falling asleep, and now he thought it might be better to stay awake. Conflicted, he hoped that the rays of the morning sun would shed some light on the situation. His mind raced as he poured over the events from earlier. He felt himself slipping behind the dark veil of sleep that was overcoming him.

His eyes shot open in the dark room as he was yanked forcefully down into the mattress. A scream tried to leave his throat, but it was stifled as he struggled to free himself. The elements of the mattress started closing in on him as he was forcefully pulled down. He felt sharp claws digging in to both his wrists and ankles.

As Shane tried to pull himself free, he felt himself being pulled down farther, more aggressively. The room glowed, eerie shades of grays, reds, and blacks. He tried to call out to Becca for help, but his voice was a mere whisper. A croak escaped his lips.

Knowing he would not survive this attack if he didn't think of something quickly, he tried to remember how he had gotten free earlier. The finger...of course. He had bit it off. But this *thing* was being more careful, keeping its claws off his face. He had no way to get leverage on it—no way to pull himself free.

A thought penetrated his brain, and as a last-ditch effort, he started throwing his weight to the right, instead of trying to pull himself upward and out of the mattress that was eating him alive. He felt the mattress shift a little off the box spring. Hope flitted through his senses as he flung his weight right again and again. Each time, he felt the mattress shift a little more. The edge started bowing down toward the floor, and he took the opportunity to shift his weight one last time. The mattress finally slipped over the edge, landed on its end, then flipped completely over on top of him as his body thudded on the hard floor.

Shane tried to gulp air into his lungs after the fall knocked the air out of him for the second time that night. The heavy mattress on top of him wasn't helping, either. Finally, he could breathe, and his feet found purchase on the carpet, allowing him to slip out from under the mattress, a half-running, half-crawling maneuver that most likely looked ridiculous had anyone been watching, but he didn't care. His only thought was he had to get the hell out of there.

A bright flash of light filled the room, and it took him a

second to realize Becca had heard the racket and had come in, flipping on the overhead light in the process.

"Shane? What's going on?"

Shane grabbed his shoes off the floor and ran out of the bedroom door, into the living room.

"Shane? What's going on? What happened?"

He slid on his shirt and picked his jacket up off the chair and shrugged it on, making sure his keys and phone were still in the pocket.

"SHANE! Talk to me!"

Shane paused. "I have to go."

"Why?"

"That thing."

"Here? No way."

"Yes. Here. Didn't you hear it?"

"Well…no. I just heard a thump and found you and the mattress on the floor."

"Sorry, Becca, I should have known better. I have to go. I'm not safe here, and you aren't safe with me here, either."

"But where will you go?"

"I have no idea."

With that, he leaned in, gave Becca a peck on the lips, and ran out the door.

"Shane? Come back!" she called after him.

Shane climbed into his SUV, started it, backed out of the parking spot, and exited the parking lot, his tires crunching on the frozen snow. In his rearview mirror, he saw her standing at the door, her hands clutching clumps of her hair. Feeling guilty for leaving her alone, he turned his attention to the road and started driving.

———

SHANE STARED OUT OVER THE FRIGID-LOOKING LAKE, THE instrument panel lights casting a glow across the front seats of the RAV4. He had run out of ideas on where to go. He had considered a motel, but the thought of being near another bed was unthinkable. The cozy air from the heater kept him warm, but he shivered anyway when he thought about the events of the evening. The dashboard proudly displayed that it was two thirty-one a.m. Daylight was several hours away—not that it mattered. He held no expectations that the sun would burn away his problem. He still had to sleep eventually. Daytime or nighttime, he was vulnerable, but at least in the day, it was easier to identify the evil that was coming for him.

Although the vehicle was running, the silence of the winter wonderland was absolute. The hood of the SUV was clear of snow, a result of the heat generated by the engine, but beyond that, nothing was left untouched by the beautiful and serene winter gift. Any other time, the landscape would have had a calming effect on him, but not under the current circumstances.

The snow continued to come down steadily, wiping away any tracks he had created when he had driven to the lake. On this side of the water, there was no sign of people—people typically launched boats or fished from the shore of this side of the lake. It was the other side where the lakeside houses—the "rich fuckers" as him and his friends referred to them—sat, overlooking the water. He could make out some of the lights from behind the foggy glass winking in and out, dancing in between snowflakes.

A pressure in his bladder pulled him from his trance. He didn't remember the last time he had gone.

Time to make yellow snow.

Shane opened the door to the RAV4 and got out, pulling his jacket closed around his neck. There was no wind, but the cold jabbed at his skin, like tiny little needles. Finding a bush nearby, he unzipped his fly and pulled himself free, the stream intense and immediate. He hadn't realized how badly he needed to go. He made a game of trying to melt as much snow off the branches of the bush as possible. He closed his eyes and continued to pee, the relief slow to come, but slowly the burn subsided and he felt liberated—dick hanging in the wind, peeing freely out in the middle of nature during a snowstorm. He opened his eyes when he smelled smoke.

Twirling around toward his vehicle, his mouth fell open, and it took him a minute to realize he was peeing on his shoe. He hurriedly tucked himself back in his pants and zipped up, unable to believe what he was seeing. The SUV was gone. In its place was a huge fire, long lengths of timber burning beneath a large cauldron-like pot. A shape stood nearby—it appeared to be a man, with his hands in the air. Savages surrounded the man, spears at the ready.

"No! Please!" the man sobbed.

The spears were thrust forward and upward, and blood spilled from the wounds, changing the pure-white snow to a crimson mess. The man toppled face-first into the snow, and the savages were on him in seconds. They tore at him, yanking at his limbs. An arm tore free, and the savage held it up in the air in celebration before putting it on a spit over the fire. Within minutes, the body was dismantled, a head simply tilting at an angle from a torso. That was until one of the savages pulled out a machete and severed the head from the torso with one whack. The head rolled a few feet away, leaving a patterned trail of blood across the stark white. Two savages picked up the torso and took it over to the massive fire, the headless, armless, legless hunk of bone, muscle, and flesh, ready to burn. Shane watched in horror as another savage grabbed a sharp stick, impaled the head on it, and walked around the fire, holding the head-on-a-stick high in the air, the other savages cheering, waving their spears in the air.

Shane felt his stomach lurch, and he tried to hold back, but the contents surged up his throat before he could stop them. Any hopes of having a quiet, discreet puke session were immediately squashed as he violently heaved anything that was possibly left over in his stomach. All celebration stopped and all eyes turned toward him—eyes that were penetrating, hungry, rabid.

Petrified, Shane did the only thing he could. He turned and ran as fast as he could over the slippery terrain. As he turned, he heard whoops and the sound of many feet coming after him. He dodged left, then right, anticipating the sharp steel of a spearhead bursting through his body any second.

He ran toward the water, blindly, and he knew he was in trouble, but there was nowhere else to run, nowhere to hide. The screams behind him were still in pursuit, but he felt like he had gained on them as the sound seemed a little farther away. Still, he ran as fast as he could, slipping and occasionally falling but pulling himself back to his feet and scrambling across the rugged landscape. Here, there was no trail. Just a hillside that would eventually lead to the lake.

His foot caught on the base of the brush, and Shane fell on a bush, rolled off it, and slid down an embankment before splashing into the water. The intense cold caused instant pain, and he immediately felt it impossible to breathe. Numb, he scrambled out of the icy water and slipped and slid as he tried to gain traction on the snowy bank. Finally on solid ground, he tried to inhale gulps of air as quickly as he could, his hands on his knees as he tried get his breathing under control.

He shivered, beyond cold, his entire body like a paint shaker, his blood the paint. He needed to get in the RAV4 and crank the heat.

The RAV4. It's gone.

How was that even possible? He remembered when he had turned around from taking a piss and the fire that the savages surrounded was right where his vehicle had been. Had he imagined everything? Shane listened intently and tried to peer through the fat flakes that continued to fall from the sky. He concentrated on *turning up* all his senses—up to ten. He looked, he listened. He saw nothing and heard nothing.

The fire. The smell of the fire caused me to turn around.

Shane inhaled the night air. He could not detect smoke in the air. How could that be with the fire directly up the hill from him? Where was the fire's glow?

Apprehensively, Shane started working his way back up the embankment. If he stayed where he was, he'd get hypothermia —maybe even freeze to death. But if the savages were there, he'd probably be ripped into shreds or burned to death. Either way, his chances were slim.

As he crested the hill, he stopped and reevaluated the situation. All was quiet. He poked his head up to look. No fire. No savages. Only his RAV4, running, and exactly where he had left it.

I'm fucking losing my mind.

Shane apprehensively approached his vehicle and looked around. Everything was as he had left it. There were no savages. There was no dismembered body. There was no head on a stick. Was it all in his mind? What about the incidents at his house and in Becca's apartment? Did they even really happen? He thought about the stress he had recently been under and started to second guess himself.

Teeth chattering, he opened the door to the Toyota and climbed inside, closing the door quickly and turning the heat to the max setting. He reached down and clicked the heated seat to the max setting as well. Although the climate of the interior was much warmer than outside, the conditions out there had been extreme. He peeled off his sopping wet jacket, hoping he would warm up faster.

It was almost twenty minutes before he stopped shivering. Another twenty passed before he felt fairly normal again, even though his clothes were still soaked. He'd have to figure out where to get some dry ones.

Shane shifted the vehicle into reverse and backed away from the edge of the embankment that overlooked the lake. Twenty feet back, his eyes caught something off about the snow. He threw the transmission into park and, grabbing his phone, turned on the flashlight, getting out to investigate.

He approached the area where his truck had been parked, his eyes squinting as he tried to process what he was looking at. He shone his light on the area and bent down to get a closer look. His mouth fell open, and he bolted upright, scrambling backward toward the RAV4. Climbing back inside, he yanked the shifter into reverse and the wheels spun as he backed up enough to turn and tear out of the parking area. The vehicle fishtailed erratically, but Shane did not slow down. All he could think about was getting the hell out of there.

"I'VE BEEN WORRIED ABOUT YOU." BECCA'S VOICE WAS laced with concern.

"I'm worried about me, too."

"Where are you?"

"I'm surprised you are still up. Sorry to call so late."

"It's not like I can sleep after…well…after everything."

"You and me both."

"Where are you?" she repeated.

"Driving."

"You've been driving this entire time? Since you ran out of here?"

"No. I went to the lake."

"The lake? Why?"

"It felt like it would be safe. Peaceful. Becca, am I fucking crazy?"

"Crazy?"

"Yeah, do you think this is all in my mind?"

"I'm not sure what to think."

"Maybe if I tell you what happened at the lake…"

"Something happened?" Her voice raised an octave as she asked.

"Yeah. Something even weirder than before."

"Why don't you start with my apartment. What happened here? Why did you take off?"

Shane recounted the events with the bed, the claws, his escape.

"Damn," was all Becca could say. Then, "Okay, I understand why you took off. Seems like no place is safe. So what happened at the lake?"

"You aren't gonna believe me."

"Try me."

"Fucking headhunters."

"What?"

"Headhunters," Shane repeated.

"Like the people that find employees for their company?"

"No, like the savages that tear people apart, eat them, and keep their heads as souvenirs."

"Okay, I have *got* to hear this story."

Shane recounted his time at the lake, him stepping out of the vehicle to pee, the smell of smoke, his discovery of the savages, the dismembered body, and the fact that they came after him.

"Wait," Becca interrupted. "So these…headhunters… were coming after you?"

"Yes."

"What were their intentions?"

"I think they wanted to invite me to dinner. I was the main course."

"You think they would have eaten you?"

"I have no doubt."

"Don't headhunters only eat the rich? Like that Michael Rockefeller dude?"

"I don't think they discriminate. They definitely didn't ask to see a bank statement."

Becca was silent for a moment, taking it all in.

"How did you get away?"

"I ran. Ended up falling into the lake. Oh my god, it was fucking cold."

"Are you okay?"

"I'm finally warm, but my clothes are still soaked."

"How did you get away from them? Where did you find your car?"

"Me falling into the lake somehow returned things to normal. Another reason I wonder if I'm insane. The RAV4 was where I had left it, still running. But—"

"But?"

"That doesn't explain the blood and the ashes."

"Huh?"

"As I was backing out, I spotted something. I got out of my car to find out what it was. Under where I was parked, there was a puddle of blood in the snow, surrounded by ash and coal. Like you would get from a fire."

The line was quiet.

"Becca? You still there?"

"Sorry. Yeah. I'm just trying to digest all of this."

"It doesn't get any easier."

"Now what?"

"I have no clue. I'm fucked. There's nowhere I can go where I feel safe. I wasn't even asleep this time. I'm beginning to feel like my only two options are a bullet or a padded cell."

"Shane, stop."

"Easy for you to say."

"Come back to the apartment."

"Not a chance."

"Just to get some dry clothes. I washed the ones you left here last week…you could change, I'll pack you some food for the road, make you some coffee, pump you full of NoDoz, and you can be in and out of here in five minutes. I won't leave you alone and whatever forces are coming at you won't come near you."

Shane paused. "I don't know…"

"It's not like I'm asking you to go back to bed. Come in. Change. Grab goodies. Leave. That simple."

Shane sighed. "Fine. I'll be there in about twenty minutes."

"Be safe."

———

THE DOOR TO THE APARTMENT OPENED BEFORE SHANE could even knock on it. Becca grabbed his hand and pulled him inside before quickly shutting the door.

"I really need to make this quick," he told her.

"The clothes you have here are in the bottom drawer of the dresser."

Shane grabbed her face with his hands and kissed her forehead.

"Thanks, babe."

Shane went into Becca's bedroom, flicking on the lights in

the hallway and in the room as he went. He side-eyed the bed, which he assumed Becca had put back together after his hasty departure. There didn't seem to be anything out of place, and if the incident hadn't been burned in his memory, he wouldn't be able to tell that anything had happened here. Still, evidence or not, he knew he wasn't crazy. Everything that had happened in the last several hours was real. He had the throbbing wound in his side—which he had almost forgotten about due to all the other chaos going on—and the finger was real as well. He was certain if he went back to his house, he would find the finger and the associated blood on the carpet of his bedroom.

He rushed over to the dresser, yanked the bottom drawer open, and took out a pair of jeans and a T-shirt, as well as a pair of socks and underwear. He peeled off his wet clothes and dropped them on the floor, grabbed a towel off the bed that Becca had left for him, dried off, and slipped on the clean, dry garments. He looked at his wet shoes, not wanting to put them back on now that his feet were dry. Unfortunately, he did not have an extra pair of shoes at Becca's house.

Scooping his wet clothes up in one hand and picking up the shoes with the other, he left the lights on and joined Becca back in the living room.

"My shoes are soaked."

"Oh, shit. I forgot about those."

"I really want to go, but I need to dry these things a bit first. Can I use your dryer?"

"Yeah. Why don't you dump your wet clothes in the washing machine while you're there? I'll wash them later."

"'Kay."

Shane went into the hallway and opened the folding doors that concealed the washer and dryer. He dumped the wet clothes in the washer and left the lid open. Then he put his shoes in the dryer, closed the door, and turned it to high heat.

The *thump-thump-thump* of the shoes bouncing against the stainless walls was immediate and loud, so he closed the accordion doors to block some of the sound.

Back in the living room, he sat on the couch next to Becca.

"Bec, do you—" He was cut off by the sound of the toilet flushing behind the closed bathroom door. Shane's eyes went wide.

"Who's here?"

"Oh crap, I forgot to tell you. My girl, Amanda, came over a little bit ago. I didn't want to be alone. Not with everything going on."

Shane relaxed a little bit. "I don't blame you. Amanda? I don't remember you having a friend named Amanda."

"It's a fairly new friendship."

"Oh."

Shane heard the bathroom door open from the hallway behind him and sensed a presence out of his peripheral vision.

"Oh, Amanda! Good! I want you to finally meet Shane…"

Shane turned toward the figure that was approaching on his left. His first thought was that she was extremely attractive. His second thought was that she looked familiar.

"Hi, Shane! Nice to meet you!" Amanda held out her hand.

Shane's mouth dropped open, and he was at a loss for words. His third thought was that he was fucked.

Becca touched his shoulder. "Hello? Earth to Shane. Are you going to say hi to my friend?"

Shane turned toward Becca to gage her expression, then turned toward Amanda, reached out, and shook her hand, and tried to return the greeting.

"Uh…hi there…uh…Amanda. I'm…uh…pleased to meet you."

"The pleasure is *all* mine, trust me," Amanda said.

Is she going to keep my secret? Why the FUCK is she here?

Shane brushed his hand through his damp hair, then covered his mouth with his hand. Finally, he spoke, afraid of the answer to his question.

"So where did you guys meet?"

Becca smiled. Shane couldn't help but feel there was something hidden behind the grin.

"We have a friend in common."

"Small world," Shane said.

"Isn't it?" Amanda asked. "Anyway, when Becca told me that she needed me, I came rushing. I don't care what time it is. No one screws with my girl."

Shane let out a nervous laugh.

"Amanda, I thought you were bringing your boyfriend," Becca said.

"I wouldn't really classify him as my boyfriend. Just some guy I'm fucking."

Shane gulped, looking at the carpet.

"I bet he and Shane would get along great," Becca said. "Shane, when all of this is over, you guys should hang out."

"Yeah, Shane. You guys should hang out."

Shane held up his hand. "Just stop, Amanda."

Becca feigned shock. "What's gotten into you, Shane? That was rude. You don't even know Amanda. Do you?"

"No. I don't." Shane gave Amanda a stern look.

Becca looked back and forth between the two of them. "You sure?"

"Positive."

"Not even when you were giving it to her from behind last week?"

Shane's mouth fell open, and he tried to speak, but he only stuttered incoherently.

Amanda smiled. "You sure knew me then, didn't you, Shane? When you were screaming my name over and over?"

"This is bullshit. I'm leaving." Shane got up and headed toward the door.

"I wouldn't do that if I were you, sweetie," Becca said in a saccharine tone.

Shane stopped, looked from Becca to Amanda, grabbed the doorknob, twisted, and opened the door fully, letting a blast of cold air in. It was then that the floor buckled underneath him as his legs were ensnared in the clasp of four brownish-red claws. The claws yanked him down to the ground and tore their way through the flooring to the center of the living room, dragging him through the destruction, the floor repairing itself in the wake of the creature's travels. Wood chunks fell into place and carpet magically repaired itself, leaving no trace of the damage.

Once Shane was yanked back to the center of the living room, in front of the couch where the girls were sitting, the grisly talons held him down to the ground.

Shane's eyes were wide as he struggled to get free.

"What the fuck is this? What's going on?" He looked from his restrained arms to his restrained legs, the claws dug in so deep, five wounds wept crimson from each of his appendages.

"Oh, poor Shane," Becca said, mockingly. "Haven't figured it out yet? Are you that slow?"

"Apparently," Amanda said.

Becca flashed a sinister smile he had never seen before. "You didn't think we would find out about each other, did you?"

"I…I didn't…"

"You didn't what?"

"I didn't want to hurt anybody."

"It's a little too late for that."

"I'm…I'm sor…sorry."

"That you got caught?"

"How did—?"

"Last week when you came over, you smelled like her. I found out later that you had a two-hour marathon fuck-fest with her before coming to my bed. You couldn't even bother to take a shower first. Talk about cocky. Did you know that face recognition passwords on your phone work when your eyes are closed? You really should delete your incriminating texts if you are going to fuck around."

Shane grimaced as the claws dug in deeper. "Becca, you and I weren't exclusive…we never discussed it. For all I know, you were seeing other people, too."

"Uh, no. I'm not a dirtbag, and I would never do anything to hurt you. Wouldn't have before, anyway."

Shane looked defeated, but in a sudden fit, he tried to pull free. The claws ripped deeper into his skin and pulled him back down. He screamed. Between gasping breaths, he said, "What is all of this?" He nodded at his feet.

Amanda spoke finally. "It's anything we want it to be. Mattress monsters, hell creatures, and my favorite, mother-fucking headhunters. I'm quite proud of myself for that one, I must admit."

"Y…You did this?"

"And me," Becca piped in, raising her hand like a timid kid in school. "I have a lot to learn, but Amanda has taught me a few things. You got the better of me, though, when you flipped the mattress off the bed."

Shane's eyes grew wide and his face turned red. "What the hell are you, you bitch?" he yelled at Amanda.

"I prefer witch over bitch, but both work. Did I forget to mention I'm Wiccan?"

In an instant, Shane's expression turned from one of rage to one of fear. Slobber started to drip out of his mouth, and he fumbled over his words. Finally, he mumbled, "Please. I'm sorry. I'm so sorry. Please…get this fucking thing off me and let me up. I'll explain. I was completely wrong, but I'd like to explain. Please?" His eyes pleaded with them both.

Amanda turned to Becca. "Well, Becca? Let's take a vote. Do we want to let him up and listen to his bullshit excuses? Stand and be counted—cast your ballot…if it's a tie, we'll let the creatures decide."

Becca made a show of rubbing her chin as she thought about it.

"Fine. Let the asshole up. Let's hear what he has to say."

Amanda nodded, and the claws disintegrated, a small puff of smoke escaping from each of the disappearing limbs. The floor immediately repaired itself.

Shane sat up, holding one wrist and one ankle. The blood continued to trickle down his limbs and drip onto the carpet.

"So what do you have to say for yourself, asshole?" Becca yelled. "I trusted you. I gave you the best of me. You didn't give two shits about me."

"That's not true. I did."

"Then why did you fuck Amanda?"

Shane shrugged.

"Why?"

"Well…"

"WHY?"

"It's just…"

"YEAH?"

"You're kind of boring in bed. Amanda is like a caged animal. She keeps it interesting."

"You bastard!" Becca yelled as she flew off the couch, her hands wrapping around his throat before she could think about it.

"Becca, STOP!" he grunted, his vocal cords restricted. "I don't care about her…she was just a piece of ass!"

"You piece of shit," Amanda screamed, diving off the couch and going for his eyes. Without even thinking about it, Shane reached for her hair and yanked forcefully, slamming her forehead into Becca's, the sound a loud crack, like that of a baseball being hit out of the park. The girls collapsed into a heap on the floor, and after a couple of twitches, they both fell silent and still.

———

Shane peered down at the two bodies in the cargo area of his RAV4. His breathing was ragged, and he tried massaging his temples, but it did nothing to alleviate the cloudiness that pulsed through his head. He hadn't meant to kill them—actually, he had imagined they would wake the hell up eventually, but they hadn't, and he could not seem to locate a pulse on either of them.

A smart person would probably have called the police and told them about the terrible accident that had transpired, but obviously, Shane wasn't that smart. Plus he was at a loss for what the hell he would have told the police.

You gotta believe me, officer…it was self-defense. These girls are witches, and they summoned demons to snatch me and pull me down into the bowels of hell. I barely escaped.

Yeah, that'd work out well for him.

It seemed like much of his life was one big fucking mistake. Being disowned by his parents. Not having the willpower to ignore her when Amanda had flirted with him in the bar, leaning forward enough to expose plenty of cleavage—a move that was extremely intentional. Screwing up at work and losing his job. But this…THIS! This was the biggest mess he had ever created. If he could just cover it up, maybe he could get his shit together. That's what he needed…a fresh start. Maybe he'd move somewhere and start over, away from this place. Away from the memories. Away from the guilt.

Shane reached in the cargo area and lifted Amanda out, flinging her over his shoulder like a sack of potatoes. He looked around. He could not believe that he had come back *here*, but he didn't know what else to do with the bodies, and with all the snow, it would be several weeks at the minimum before they were found. He would be long gone by then.

The snow crunched under Shane's feet as he carried Amanda's body down to the side of the lake. He laid her down gingerly and brushed the hair out of her eyes. She was definitely a beautiful girl, but Shane had never really had feelings for her—at least feelings of the heart. It was a relationship built on lust alone. She hadn't known about Becca. He was a fool to think he would get away with cheating. But in his mind, he assumed the worst that could happen if he got caught would be for Becca to leave him. What had actually happened seemed surreal. Impossible. Like the bad dream he almost thought it was.

Sadly, this was all his fault—all his doing. He couldn't blame anyone else, and he couldn't rely on anyone else to get him out of this jam. He was on his own.

Shivering, Shane started the trek back up the hillside to the RAV4. All reminders of the previous incident there had vanished—whether entirely, or just hidden underneath a new layer of snow, he did not know.

He approached the cargo area again, glad that the early hour of the day was conducive to him not being seen—the sun was a couple of hours from rising and the snow made visibility poor. Even if someone on the other side of the lake had binoculars, or a telescope, they'd never be able to make out anything transpiring on this wicked side of the lake.

At the hatch door, he reached in and then stopped. His

mouth dropped open, and he froze. Spinning around on his heels, he looked behind him as well as left and right. He was certain that he was mistaken, and so he ran to the driver's door of the SUV and opened it, flooding the interior of the vehicle with light. Back around the back side, he looked once again. The back was not only void of shadows now, but there was no longer a body there. Becca was gone.

"What the actual fuck…"

Shane looked down and saw another set of footprints on the ground. They were smaller, like a woman's. They were headed down toward the lake. Was Becca alive? That would be great news. Maybe he could get her to the hospital and everything would be okay. He could simply say Amanda left town out of embarrassment.

But the footprints were leading toward the lake. How was that possible when she would have had to pass him as he came back up the trail? It didn't make sense, and so he studied the tracks in the snow a little harder. Confused, he pulled out his phone—which he had changed to airplane mode before coming out to the lake—and turned on the flashlight, studying the prints. They followed the same path that he had been on, but how? And then realization smashed into him like a blast of heavy wind, and his stomach lurched.

"Nononononono!"

How could it be possible? The prints weren't leading *down* to the lake after all. The prints were coming *from* the lake.

They'd have to be Amanda's prints then. So where was she? And what the hell happened to Becca? Could they both still be alive?

A whisper reached him through the wind, which had just started blowing, as if on cue.

"Shaaaaaaaane."

He spun around. "Who is it? Stop fucking around."

"Thanks for bringing us to the lake."

It sounded like a chorus of multiple voices—definitely more than two.

"Becca? Amanda? Where are you? Stop fucking around and let's go home and talk this out."

"Shaaaaaaaane…why are we here?"

The voices came from everywhere and nowhere.

Shane edged his way to the fringe of the parking area, looking down the incline to see if they were hiding somewhere among the shrubbery.

"Where are you guys?" he asked.

"Shaaaaaaaaane."

"WHAT?" His nerves caused him to snap back at the voices.

"What were you going to do?"

"Not…nothing!"

It was then that Shane noticed the drums, the volume building like it would have had someone been twisting the volume knob on a radio. Rhythmic. Almost tribal. Shane spun around toward the RAV4, fully intending to get the hell out of there before something really bad happened. He blinked twice, mouth agape. It was too late…something bad was already happening.

The RAV4 was gone once again. In its place was a large fire, a huge black pot cooking over it. The flames were orange and red and danced ten feet in the air. The drums reached a crescendo, and before Shane could take off running, he noticed from his peripheral vision a shadowy figure emerging from the tree line to his right. And then in front of him. And then from the left. The shadowy figures crept closer and then multiplied. Three became six. Six became eighteen. Eighteen became a hundred, and as they crept closer, the light from the fire lit up their faces, their bodies—loincloths, tribal tattoos, bone piercings, and wicked fucking spears held at the ready, waiting to ventilate his body, waiting to create a blood fountain out of his flesh.

Shane froze as they approached, the headhunter directly in front of him clearly in charge, time etching his face in such a way that he looked like a mummy—a mummy that was very much alive. Alive and dangerous.

The savage spoke—a language Shane had never heard before, gibberish. Shane stared at him, shaking, frozen. The headhunter repeated himself, this time more forcefully. Shane gulped, shrugging.

The leader raised his spear in the air, shook it, threw his head back, and yelled another phrase that Shane had never heard. It must have been a command, because savages moved in, surrounding him from all sides. Two of them took Shane by the arms. The touch released him from his frozen state, and his fight-or-flight responses took over. He brought his foot up and kicked the savage to his left right in the kneecap and the man went down screaming. Before the one on this right could react, Shane brought his left knee around and smashed it right into the headhunter's balls, collapsing the man on the spot. Free of the hands holding him in captivity, Shane knew this would be his only chance. He knew he had to take it, or he would never survive. He had stayed awake all night—fought to be aware, fought to be alive. There was no way he was going down like this.

Shane ducked between a gap in the savages and ran toward the tree line. Angry shouts rang out behind him. They would have to be disappointed—he wasn't going to be anyone's dinner.

The distance between him and them multiplied. He was ten feet beyond them. Then twenty. Then forty. The trees were fifteen feet away. Once he got beyond the first of them, he would be able to lose them, hide, escape.

Five feet from the edge of the trees, Shane stopped in his tracks, falling to his knees. He tried to scream, but only a gurgle came out. Pain shot through his body, and he felt blood run from his mouth. Looking down, he saw a foot of metal and wood protruding from his chest.

There's no coming back from that.

Two savages grabbed him by the arms, threw him face down on the ground, and put their feet on his back. His chest didn't touch the ground, the spear holding him a few inches above it. He then felt someone grab the back of the spear, pulling on it, twisting it. The wood snapped, and he was tossed on his back, the head of the spear still protruding. He then found himself being pulled through the snow by his feet, his back being scraped and cut by craggy rocks along the way.

He watched as he was being pulled along, unable to move much, wondering if his spine had been damaged. They drug him back past the fire, back to the leader, who made a motion, causing them to pull Shane back to his feet, supporting his weight for him as he could not.

The leader made hand motions and yelled something to the men surrounding Shane, and before he could understand what was happening, four men grabbed him while another three grabbed his left arm. The pain ripped through Shane's body, and he screamed, as the arm was first dislocated, then yanked free from his torso. The savages held the severed arm in the air while they whooped and hollered, and Shane almost passed out from the pain. He knew he had mere minutes left in this world —or less.

"Help! Becca?" he tried to scream, but it merely came out as a whisper. His eyes grew heavy, and he stopped fighting them, the lure of death becoming more appealing as each miserable second ticked by.

"Shane?"

Shane opened his eyes, trying to focus, wondering if he was hallucinating.

"Becca? Amanda?" His voice was merely a whisper.

"We're here," Amanda said.

"Pl…please…" he whispered.

"Please what, Shane?" Becca said, fire lacing her words.

"H…help me."

"Sadly, no one can help you, Shane."

"I'm…I'm sor…sorry."

"That's the most truthful thing you've ever told us," Amanda said. "You are indeed sorry…a sorry sack of shit. I don't need you. I have someone better."

Shane looked away from Amanda to Becca.

"Becca, pl…please. I'm sorry. You can fix this. You can save me. I need you."

Becca paused, tried to say something, but then stopped. Finally, she spoke. "Sorry, Shane. It's too late for that. Way too fucking late. And I don't need you, either. I also have someone better."

Defeated, Shane let the pain take over…It pulled him down, down toward the edge of consciousness.

In a last moment of lucidity, he watched as Amanda took Becca's face into hers, as their lips touched, as their tongues snaked in and out of each other's mouths.

"Someone so much better!" they said in unison.

That vision seared itself into his brain, so much so that Shane wasn't even aware as the machete took his head clean off, nor was he aware when the head was secured to a stick, a trophy to be treasured by the tribe for eternity.

THE HOUSE ON THE HILL

PROLOGUE

His heart beat loudly as he traversed the hilly terrain. The sound of a twig snapping brought his full attention back to his actions. He slipped behind the closest foliage in case he had attracted unwanted attention. Although the fog had started to settle in, he still had a clear view of the house on the hill. The lights were on and the blinds were wide open. Occasionally, he would see a shape pass behind the glass—obviously someone going about their nightly routine, living their life. Anger rose up through his veins. He felt his muscles tighten and he could almost hear them as they stretched to their limits.

The image of the house on the hill blurred as he reached desperately inside himself, clawing at distant memories, wondering why he was the way he was. The pain in his soul was fresh, raw. He knew he had been through something, but he couldn't discern what. It was as if a fog had penetrated his skull and wrapped around his brain. It wasn't simply that he didn't understand *why* he was this way. It wasn't even because he didn't remember what his name was. His main confusion stemmed from the fact that he didn't know *what* he was.

If I have a name, I must be human. But I don't look human. I don't feel human. But I can think. I can feel.

He reached down and picked up a boulder the size of his meaty fist.

I know this is a stone. How else would I know that?

"Stone," he whispered. "I shall go by Stone."

Stone watched as the lights winked off in the house for the evening—its lone occupant most likely turning in for the night —took one last look at the house and staggered down the makeshift trail toward the bottom of the hill. He then trekked for miles until he happened upon a grove of trees he decided he'd slumber in—the first place he felt safe since he had found himself in this existence hours earlier. He collected a few boughs of branches and handfuls of leaves and put together a sort of bed to rest on. Not that he was tired. He had too many wispy and fleeting thoughts wafting through his brain that conflicted with each other.

The mystery wasn't only who or what he was. He had to find out who lived in the house on the hill. Why had he become so enraged when he gazed upon it?

Stone took a moment to examine himself for the first time. He held his hands out in front of him. He decided they weren't hands after all. More like hand-paws. Was he a dog? Impossible. He had walked upright. He stretched his hand-paws to see how wide the pads would expand. Razor-sharp claws popped out, catching him off guard.

Holy shit! Not paws, claws.

Stone worked the muscles again, and the claws suddenly popped back out of sight. Stunned, he sat there and looked at the details of the meaty mitts. Then it dawned on him. He could see every detail plainly, even though no light from the atmosphere made its way through the copse of trees. He had extraordinary vision.

How he wished he had a mirror.

Mirror. I know what a mirror is. I have intelligence. I must be a man…but how? How did I become…this?

He felt his face and although the pads on his hand-paws gave a completely different sensation than he remembered feeling with fingers—which meant he had to have been in a human's body before—he could feel a full beard. Possibly even an entirely furry face. His ears were sharp and pointy, and it felt like the cartilage had been replaced with stiff cardboard. He felt for his mouth.

Is that a fucking snout?

His teeth were long and felt sharp to his touch. It was then he noticed the thick fur on his arms and legs. He was naked, and he had the uncanny feeling that he should be uncomfortable being so, yet it felt natural. Upon inspection, his genitalia did not appear human to him and he didn't recognize it, but he felt a swell of pride at the sight.

Stone concentrated on the vaporous thoughts and snippets of knowledge as they floated through his mind, trying to latch on to something that might explain what was going on. He was aware that he existed, but he was not aware of existing before this night. His fragmented memory told him that he must have lived in another time as another being, but his mind felt like a puzzle someone dumped back into the box the moment more than two pieces were connected together.

He tried to focus on what little he could retain. He had become aware for the first time earlier tonight at the base of the hill. And he had inexplicably been pulled toward the house. He did not understand it, but he had little control over his mind and body as he traversed the hillside to get a closer look at the outside—at the movement behind the glass.

Before he realized it was happening, Stone's heart started beating at hyper-rate. Thoughts of blood and body parts surged through his brain as images of carnage flashed behind his eyes. He felt aroused and then ashamed, for he did not understand what was happening to him. As he tried to sort through new, overwhelming emotions, new feelings and new thoughts, only one emotion floated to the top when he thought about the house on the hill. Rage. Stone animalistically knew why he was here…even if he didn't *understand* why. The bloodlust.

CHAPTER ONE

Woody McGregor sat near the front deck of his rustic home smoking a Marlboro, watching the sparks pop from the firepit and disappear in the chilly night air. He took a swig off his Miller and pushed back in one of the Adirondack wooden rocking chairs he had purchased when he had bought the place, which was so far out, it was almost off the grid. If it wasn't for satellite wi-fi, he'd have no connection to the world at all.

God knows why I bought two. I've never had company. Ever. He eyed the second chair.

The sky was void of any moon and the house lights were extinguished. The only light came from the thirty-six-inch steel fire pit that sat on the stone sitting area which looked out over the valley and away from the simple 1,080 square foot single-wide mobile home he called his castle ever since his old life ended.

The view of the valley was majestic—during the nighttime with the lights from the small town below and during the day just from the sheer beauty of the landscape—which was one of the reasons he had purchased the place. The other was the lack of people. He had absolutely no other neighbors around him. The rough and rutted dirt road that served his property at the top of the mountain stretched for a couple miles from the main road at the bottom of the hill with no other dwellings along the path. People truly had no reason to be up in his space, and accordingly, he installed a gate at the bottom of the hill and kept it chained shut unless he was driving through it.

Taking another chug of his beer, Woody ran his hand through his thick, graying, beard and thought back on what put him here less than a year ago. The break, which caused him to lose any remaining faith he had left in human beings and the world.

He hardly recognized the man he used to be. The corporate man that wore the suit to work every day. The man that showed up before everyone else and even took calls on the weekend. The man that spent twenty-five years of his life working for the same corporation, moving his way up from an entry-level position to one of the company's highest-ranking managers. With only two people above him, he felt accomplished, like his hard work was finally paying off.

What happened, happened overnight. Woody was well respected, and his professional career was at its peak, even though his direct boss, Ron, was a total prick. What he didn't realize at the time was that the prick—the one he put up with every day, because he knew that in the corporate world, you always had to deal with at least one asshole to make it—felt threatened for his own job by Woody. Woody didn't realize that being smart, achieving the results that he was asked to, and being liked by everyone would be the end of him.

Out of the blue, two hours after arriving to work on a random day, he found himself before a committee and bullshit wild accusations, and within two days, Woody was gone. Unemployed. Stripped of his reputation, his stock options, and his life. Escorted out of the building by security like some criminal.

Downing the rest of his beer, Woody straightened his worn ball cap, scooted himself up off the chair, and went into the house, flicking on the interior light. He heard a movement behind him and turned to watch as Dexter, his ninety-pound German Shepherd, got up off the ground to join him.

"It's okay, Dex…you can stay there. I'm just getting another beer."

Dexter stopped and looked at him, then proceeded to follow Woody into the house and over to his water bowl, where he lapped up the cold liquid, the stray droplets splattering the ground around him.

"What's the matter with your water bowl outside? Did it get dirt in it or something?"

Woody smiled slightly and rolled his eyes, knowing the water bowl outside was fine. Dexter just wanted to be where Woody was, and that was the way it was. Woody used the bathroom and grabbed another beer, heading back out to his favorite chair, which he had added especially comfortable cushions to. Dexter laid down on his dog bed beside Woody with a content "hmmph."

Woody reached down and scratched Dex behind the ears, smiling. Dexter was the only "person" he truly loved any longer.

When Woody had arrived home from work that day, in the middle of the day—to his wife's astonishment—she was the rock he needed. While she tried to push him out of his depression, to keep him moving forward, he had a hard time doing so. The injustice he felt was unreal. He felt betrayed. Tossed away like yesterday's newspaper. He applied for hundreds of jobs. Went on numerous interviews. He knew that if he heard the word "overqualified" one more time, he was going to lose it.

When the money from savings dried up, he desperately

tried to figure out how to make ends meet as his wife's meager minimum-wage job barely paid for food and utilities. Then one March day, his world came to an end. As he left his wife, Marcy, to sleep in while he went out to buy some flowers and pick up some breakfast to celebrate her forty-fourth birthday, he came home to find her still on the bed, deceased. She had never woken up, and the coroner had ruled it as a heart attack.

Woody knew that the stress of their situation had been the end of her. The woman that had been there for him most of his life—and the only actual person remaining in his life since his parents were deceased and his friends and coworkers dropped him like a bad habit—was gone. Just like that.

That was when the break happened. When he slipped into darkness. It wasn't until two days later that he realized he was laying in his own waste beside her, the cold coffee and the stale breakfast laying on her nightstand.

When they had finally taken her, he fell into a deep fog, night turning into day and day into night. He mostly got up to use the bathroom or forage for any remaining food that had been left in the sparse cabinets. It wasn't until the day the electricity went out that he crawled up out of the pit he was living in and assessed his surroundings.

Why hadn't he noticed before that he smelled like shit? When was the last time he had taken a shower? His sweats and t-shirt were stained with things of various colors. He reached down and scraped a dried ramen noodle off his shirt. In the bathroom, he reached for the light switch and flicked it, only to remember the power was off. When was the last time he had paid a bill? Thirty days? Sixty? More?

Reaching for the shower valve, he turned it and was surprised to find water coming out of the showerhead. He decided to take advantage of it while he still had the chance, opened the frosted window enough to shed some light into the room—and stepped into the tile cubicle. He was surprised the water was still hot since they had an electric water heater, but he knew as soon as it cooled off, that was the end of that luxury. As he reached for his soap, he noticed all the stray hair and scum that clung to the surfaces of the entire stall, and he wrinkled up his nose in disgust.

After, he dried off on his mildew-smelling towel, found some clean clothes in the back of the closet and pulled them on, and went and checked the mailbox, which was stuffed full. As he made his way back to the house, he flipped through the envelopes. All bills and junk. And a five-dollar rebate check. Dinner. As he approached the house, it was the two notices taped to the door that caught his attention. They were exactly what he thought they were. Foreclosure notices. He had sixteen days left before his house was gone…the house, and any equity he had in it.

Woody looked back over the twinkle of lights and at his life now. The beer was cold and satisfying. The air danced in his lungs as if it hadn't ever touched another human before. This place was his. A place that the bank didn't have any claim to. Privacy. And the best companion in Dexter he could ever imagine. He would never go back to the corporate world —he got anxious even thinking about it. This was his life now.

When he read that final foreclosure notice, he knew he had to act fast. Calling a real estate investor that had posted a yellow sign at one of the intersections of town claiming to buy homes for cash, he was able to squeak the sale out before the greedy bank grabbed the only thing he had left. Before it closed, he sold all the furniture, packed the things he wanted to keep in twenty-two boxes, and moved everything remaining to storage. With his equity in the bank, which was way more than he thought it would be, he lived in the cheapest motel he could find while he searched. A search that lasted sixty-seven days, and then he found this place.

Although under no obligation to do so, the real estate agent that had listed the property provided the history of the house, taking it to the point of too much information. The house had sat vacant for over a year and a half after the elderly man that lived there was found dead—they estimated for months before they found him. He was found in the yard, his bones picked clean by who-knew-what. While they couldn't find any evidence of foul play, they couldn't attribute his death to natural causes, either, so his death was listed as "unknown." With no heirs and no will, the estate was escheated to the state and finally sold.

That was the start of his new life. An online-only job providing chat support for some random online company. An electric, internet, tax and insurance bill only. An older Chevy 4x4 that was paid off. He adopted Dexter a month after he got the place, and they had been living their life of simplicity ever since.

Although life was simple, for Woody, there was no joy. Not after the curveball life had thrown at him. While Dexter provided some comfort and companionship, it wasn't enough to scrape away at the formation of stone that surrounded Woody's heart. He would be two more beers in before he went inside to get ready for bed, although it was still early by most people's standards. As was his habit, he turned out the lights and slipped into bed, knowing that sleep would overtake him almost instantaneously.

CHAPTER TWO

The pain inside Stone's head was too much to manage, and he curled up in a ball, his paws over his face, his body burrowed into the tree branches. A low whine emitted from his muzzle, which he hoped no other creature of the night could hear.

He tried to understand his predicament. How had he become trapped in a body that wasn't his? He tried to understand his mission. If there was a reason for this—this hellish transformation into some kind of abomination that only movies and folklore supported—what was it? Was he destined to ravage the hillside, desecrating rabbits and any other varmints he could find? Cattle? Horses? Maybe even people?

He concentrated, tried to picture yesterday. What had he done all day? Was he in this body or another? No answers came to him, and images of the house on the hill filled his mind once more.

Is that my purpose? Something to do with that fucking house?

He tried to picture it on the inside. Had he ever been in it? Who lived there? Did he know them?

Feeling his right hind leg bouncing, Stone tore out of his hiding spot, scrambled the miles to the base of the hill and crisscrossed halfway up before slowing down to a crawl, careful not to give away his presence. He felt clumsy in his newfound body. Breathing out through his nose quietly, he concentrated on being stealthier. The scents of the night assaulted his sense of smell—which he had not noticed before. Dampness. Pine. A nearby animal.

Stone stopped and tried to determine the source and direction of the scent. He concentrated on it, trying to channel his anxiety and discourse toward the critter. The animal must become his new focus. The power to focus would be his. The power to choose belonged to him. The animal must die. The draw of the house pulled his attention away from the scent of the unsuspecting meal, and without him even realizing it,

Stone had abandoned the scent of the animal and was creeping closer toward the house on the hill.

He paused at the edge of the yard, sniffed the vehicle beside it, then the grass, and took one step onto the property. The lights in the windows were dark, and although Stone felt like he should be worried that they would all be illuminated at the same time and he would be caught prowling, he chuckled internally.

I think they would be the ones that were scared shitless, not me.

He approached the front window, slinking up underneath it, peering through with eyes that he only imagined looked evil as hell. He could make out the outline of furniture: a couch, a coffee table, a recliner.

Furniture. I know what it is. I've sat in a chair before. On a couch.

There was no movement in the house. Stone made his way to the next window. A dining room. Beyond it, a kitchen. He continued around the side to the back. More windows. All dark. All covered by blinds that were turned down tight. He could not see inside. He turned to his other newfound senses. He listened intently but only heard the whirring of a motor. Maybe a heater? He concentrated on the scent permeating from the home.

A man.

He smelled something else.

There's a dog in there!

Stone felt his hair stand up on his back—a new sensation for him. His lip involuntarily pulled back and his teeth bared. An urge took over him, and he commanded all his control to keep from ripping a hole through the side of the building. He clamped down hard on the avalanche of lust, wanting badly to understand, subconsciously knowing that whoever was in there was just like him—well, like he used to be. He could not lose control. He was not a killer.

Knowing that the smallest noise would send the dog into a frenzy, he crept away from the home, surprised at his new-found stealth. When he was out of earshot, he cut a wide berth around the home and found his way back down the hill.

As he made his way back to his lair, he tried to dissect his fascination with the house and the occupant inside. He tried to understand his urges. He grappled with the strange turn of events that put him in a body built for murder, with no instruction manual.

Back home on his pile of branches, he curled up once again, exhausted. Unable to unravel the threads of his mind, he let the darkness of the shadows overtake him and fell into a deep slumber.

CHAPTER THREE

Woody opened his eyes and sat up in bed. His eyes locked on the digital clock on the nightstand as it clicked over to five thirty a.m.

After all the years of getting up at the same time every day to head into the office, his body had set its own eternal alarm, but unfortunately, it didn't know what weekends were. Woody was up at the same time, seven days a week, whether he needed to be or not.

Dexter raised his head, reluctantly pulled himself up and jumped off the bed. As soon as Woody was done relieving his bladder, Dexter followed him out to the living room and went over and tapped on the back door with his paw.

"Like you think I'm not going to let you out. We do this every morning."

Woody opened the top of the Keurig and pulled out the

empty pod from the last cup of coffee. He replaced it with a fresh one, pressing the brew button.

Dexter tapped on the door again.

"Okay, okay! Geeze!"

Dexter ran out the door and started sniffing around the back yard, taking several minutes to select a spot before he lifted his leg and soaked it.

"Obviously, it was urgent," Woody muttered.

When Dexter had done his business, Woody called him back to the house, dog food bowl in hand. When Dexter didn't come inside, Woody sat the bowl on the counter and went out onto the back deck. Dexter was sniffing below the bedroom window, his nose caught on some scent.

"Come, Dexter. Let's eat."

Dexter stopped sniffing, cocked his head, looked at Woody, and then pawed at the ground under the window.

"Leave it. Come inside now. I don't want you digging up the yard."

Dexter paused again, mid-dig, and looked at Woody. He then looked back at the ground and pawed it again.

"Damn you, Dex!" Woody started down the stairs toward him and Dexter barked once, bounced on his haunches, his two front paws in the air, and then he took off running around the yard. Shaking his head, Woody went back inside and poured cream in his freshly brewed coffee and went to the refrigerator and pulled out the ingredients for breakfast. Dexter waltzed inside and sat in front of the counter, waiting for his food.

"Okay, so now you want it, huh?"

Dexter licked his chops.

Woody set the bowl down on the floor against the wall toward the dining room and prepared his morning omelet and sausage. He had a habit of cooking three eggs into his omelet each morning, but he never ended up eating the entire thing. Dex was a loyal companion, though, and somehow found a way, sacrifice that it was, to fit the remainder into his belly.

After breakfast, Woody cleaned up, took a shower, and changed into clean clothes. Even though he worked from home, he tried to be disciplined, stay clean, and get dressed each day.

By 6:55 a.m., he was sitting at his desk and logging into the company interface where he would promptly be connected to the queue at seven sharp. If there were any customers waiting for assistance, which there typically were, he would automatically be connected to the next one in line.

Woody's work shift was very straightforward and controlled. His breaks and lunches were regimented by the computer. As soon as two hours passed, the computer put him on an automatic fifteen-minute break the moment he finished with the customer he was helping. That usually gave him time to use the bathroom, get another cup of coffee, or smoke a cigarette. After four hours, the system pushed him out of the queue for an hour lunch, and then another two hours after he got back, it made him take his final break. At quarter to four, the system would no longer assign a customer to his queue. Once he finished up with the customer he was currently helping, he was logged off for the day.

Of course, there were overrides built into the system that allowed a support person to alter their automatic schedule if an urgent need arose, but Woody refrained from using it most days as corporate sent you a nasty-gram if you used it more than twice per month. The last thing he wanted to do was be on someone's radar.

Because of this, Woody was shocked when at twelve minutes after ten, he clicked the manual override to start his lunch, before a new customer could be spooled to his chat window.

Confused, he watched as the countdown timer showed he had a little over fifty-eight minutes left before his shift started again. Woody got up from his desk chair and rubbed his right temple. Dex got up as well, wondering if playtime was coming early—Woody usually threw the ball for five minutes during lunch—and traipsed out to the kitchen.

Unsure of why he started his lunch early, Woody followed Dexter out to the kitchen and opened the back door for him when Dex tapped. On the deck, Woody sunk into one of the chairs that overlooked the yard and inhaled the cool air. An unknown worry tugged at the corner of his mind and he tried to reel it in…to grasp it, analyze it. A knot twisted in his stomach as dread kicked in. *You are in danger*, it seemed to say.

Being one that was typically in control of his body, this new turn of events worried Woody. He was a person that had never done drugs throughout his life, simply because he didn't want to ever feel out of control. He even shied away from over-the-counter medications if he knew they would make him feel loopy.

Now, here he was feeling out of control of his body. Simply put, he felt…well…*off*. Like he imagined a bad trip would be —except this trip made him want to simply squeeze his eyes shut tight, curl in a ball, and go to sleep until it passed.

A sound from inside startled him awake—he hadn't realized he dosed off—and he jumped up off the chair and ran inside the house. At his computer, the timer had elapsed for almost two hours and the system was prompting him to click that he was available and back on shift. Because he hadn't been at his desk when his lunch hour finished, the system started sending reminders to confirm that he was back, which then escalated to frequent chimes and flashing messages asking him to acknowledge he was available and ready to take a customer chat.

Woody knew he was going to get an email from his boss once the daily production report hit his boss's desk in the morning, but he didn't care. Woody clicked the override button asking to end his shift. When the system prompted the reason for his request, he checked the radio button labeled "Ill", submitted the request, and then logged off the system. With the sun hitting the bedroom window, Woody pulled off his tennis shoes, wiggled out of his pants, pulled his shirt over his head, and slipped into bed.

Not understanding the break from regiment, Dexter let out a heavy breath, flopped his body down on the floor with a thump, got back up and turned around, then laid back down again. One minute later, Dex stood, jumped up on the bed, turned his back toward Woody, and plopped down next to him, his body stretched out against him. Woody didn't notice as sleep had already consumed him.

CHAPTER FOUR

The power in his legs wasn't something he had noticed the night before. When sleep had overtaken him, Stone had slept most of the night as well as all day. At least it felt like an entire day had passed since he had curled up on his crude bed.

He wondered if he was nocturnal and was supposed to sleep during the day. Still, he didn't remember stirring. He hadn't even been awakened by the need to piss.

Now, his instinct told him to run blindly, and he followed it recklessly. When the landscape turned flat with little obstruction, he found himself sprinting over the flat land at a speed he could not fathom as being possible. Still, possible or not, he had the power. Another thing he noticed was he could run upright, or on all fours. Somewhere along the way, he adopted a hybrid gait—sometimes loping on all fours and sometimes only on the hind legs, depending on the terrain.

The light from the moon fell through a small sliver, leaving shadows alone to wreak havoc among the timid. Stone took advantage of the dimly lit sky and stayed close to the dark, lest he should be seen by an innocent, becoming the fuel that fed their nightmares.

The scent hit his nostrils before he saw it. He slowed his approach, cautious. He wasn't scared of what someone might do to him if they spotted him. He knew his new body could handle itself and he would always be the victor. Instead, he was scared of what he might do to them if they locked eyes. Even now, the thought and anticipation of that warm, sweet flesh brought him once again to that state of arousal. Bloodlust.

He spotted several tents scattered around the area. Farther off in the distance, several campers and trailers were parked. Why had his instincts pulled him to a highly inhabited campground? He was trying so hard to fight the need, yet here he was, a buffet surrounding him, like an alcoholic just hanging out at the bar.

Stone pulled his thoughts away from carnage, trying to focus one more time on what everything meant. He certainly couldn't have been put in this body to ravage and destroy. He had to have a higher purpose. Until he knew it, he would have to control his urges, which would be easier said than done.

Stone spotted the brick buildings then. A duplex of bathroom facilities that many campgrounds had. Curiosity overcame him. Stone scanned the campground, looking for movement. He saw nothing. Listening, he heard nothing but the crackles of a couple almost burnt-out fires.

He estimated it to be in the wee hours of the morning, long after the campers and partiers had slugged their last beer and crawled into their sleeping bags. Cautiously, he stalked toward the restrooms. He had to know.

At the door, he looked around again. Stillness. He wrapped a hand-paw around the pull handle, yanked, and slipped inside.

The room was illuminated by a dimly lit single bulb with a wire cage around it. Along the wall in front of him were two sinks; next to those were two urinals and, in the far corner, a stall.

Stone approached the sinks, looking down. Fear held his eyes to the porcelain. Fear of what he was. Fear that by acknowledging it, he would be destined to stay this way forever.

His eyes shifted to the stranger's in the mirror. The details of his face gave him no indication as to his identity. As he suspected, he wasn't human. He looked at the hair covering his body.

I have fur. I am covered in fucking fur.

His ears appeared to be canine, as were his snout and teeth, but this wasn't ordinary dog. This was dog on steroids and acid and anything else you could think of that took the cute, fuzzy image of a dog and made it terrifying. His jaws were long and powerful, his teeth razor-sharp, as if he could snap a tree trunk in half.

The reflection of his eyes pulled him closer, and he studied them—they were deep red, but semi-covered with patterns of black haze, as if a storm cloud was floating across the surface. The nose was black. He touched it with his hand-paw. It felt dry and cracked.

Catching the sight of his paw in the mirror, he pulled it away and studied it in the dim light. It was bigger than he remembered, almost the size of a catcher's mitt. His paws were connected to beefy forearms, his biceps bulging. The remainder of his body was built and powerful.

What am I?

He stepped back and took in his full seven-foot frame.

Almost like a wolf, but not really.

He thought how he walked upright when he wasn't running at great speeds.

Posture of a man. I think like a man. But what's with the dog suit I'm in?

Stone stared again at his head—his face. A strange creature stared back at him. He felt like he was a passive soul in an alternate life, but the face staring back at him was sinister and foreboding. If it wasn't him inside of the beast, he would have been scared shitless.

A scent caught in his nostrils, and he found himself back outside, scanning the campsite for movement. The scent was strong, sickly sweet and overpowering. He slipped into the shadows on the side of the building, famished, confused, angry, scared.

The click of a latch sounded, and Stone sensed movement from the restroom door—the one on the other side of the building. The scent intensified, and he heard the slapping of flip-flops as they flapped ground to heel, ground to heel.

Before he could react, she was there. Her face mere inches away from his. Her features locked in a portrait of fear, her worst nightmare realized.

The bloodlust took over and, with lightning-quick speed, Stone's claws from his right paw were clamped around the girl's mouth, her body pressed up against the stone wall.

"Don't…scream," he managed to growl, his throaty voice barely a whisper.

Her body trembled and her feet started fighting for purchase on the hard, dirt earth. It was then he realized he had underestimated his strength and he was holding her a foot off the ground.

He caught her heartbeat pulsing through her throat with his peripheral vision.

I must have her.

His face lowered to her neck, and she tried to scream, but he clamped his claw down tighter over her mouth.

"Scream again and die."

Her body relaxed.

The pheromones she gave off ravaged his senses. His mind was rent with conflicting emotions.

Rip her throat out. Her flesh is yours.

He raked one of his fangs across her delicate, white shoulder.

She's an innocent. You're not a killer.

His internal voice caused him to pause, looking into her eyes once again.

Is this what people look like when they know they're going to die?

A tear slid down her right cheek.

What the fuck am I doing? Was I really going to tear her throat out?

He slid her body down the rough surface of the wall until her feet touched the ground.

"Shhh…shhh, please. It's okay. I'm not going to hurt you, but I need you to listen to me."

She nodded the best she could with his hand clamped around her face.

"I'm going to uncover your mouth. Don't yell or it will be your last time. Do you understand?" She blinked rapidly and nodded.

Stone slowly removed his hand from her mouth.

"What's your name?"

Her lip trembled, but she said nothing.

"Please. I'm sorry I scared you. Your name."

"S…Sarah," she whispered.

"You can't tell anyone about me, do you understand, Sarah?"

"Yes." Her head bobbed up and down rapidly. "Yes, I understand."

"If you say anything about me, I'll come back for you."

"I promise."

"You sure? Not a word. Not to your husband. Nobody."

"N…no husband. Here with the girls. Th…they wouldn't believe me anyway. Please. Just let me go." Hope blossomed in her eyes.

"Until next time, Sarah."

She looked at him, unsure.

"Walk back to your camp. Don't turn around. I won't follow you."

"How do I know? I don't want to die!" Fresh tears sprung from her eyes.

"Because, Sarah, if I wanted you dead, you'd already be dead."

She nodded, an understanding sifting to the top of her emotions. After one more glance, she turned, took a few steps, and then stopped. She did not turn around.

"What—?"

"It's better if you don't know," he interrupted. "Please. Go. Before I change my mind."

Before she made it twenty feet, he was gone.

CHAPTER FIVE

Woody sat up in bed, disoriented. The room was dark, and no light filtered through the window blinds. He looked over at the clock. Almost three thirty in the morning. Had he really slept all afternoon and all night? It was unfathomable.

His bladder screamed at him, and he kicked his feet over the edge of the bed. Dexter jumped off the bed and ran out into the living room.

"Oh shit. Sorry, Dex." Knowing Dexter had been locked inside all afternoon and all night and hadn't eaten, either, Woody scurried after Dexter, flipping on lights as he went. He flicked the locks open on the back door, and Dexter tore off to the grassy area, stopping to relieve himself for an exorbitant period of time before he started sniffing in various places while he circled, searching for the right spot to finish his business.

Unable to hold it any longer himself, Woody went to the edge of the cement slab and drained his own bladder on the nearest plant. Dexter cocked his head sideways, looked between Woody and the bush, and then sniffed the bush.

"You aren't the only one that can mark shit around here," Woody said.

Inside, Woody scooped kibble into Dex's bowl and set it down for him and then rummaged around in the freezer for something to eat. Woody's stomach growled loudly, causing Dexter to stop eating and look up from his bowl.

After microwaving an individual frozen pizza, Woody sat down at the table and scarfed it down. He was still hungry after, and in the fridge, he found the leftover salad from two nights before. Only after eating it also did the hunger pains in his gut start to subside.

What is going on with me? I have never slept this long before.

He took inventory of his symptoms: exhaustion, muddled thoughts, lethargy. He knew he didn't have the flu or even a cold—the indicators just weren't there, so what could be causing him to feel the way he did?

Looking at the clock on the kitchen stove, Woody knew it

would be time to wake up in an hour for work. Dare he go back to bed? His mind said no, but his body said yes.

With his decision made, he set his alarm clock just in case, so he wasn't late. He was asleep again within a minute of pulling the covers up to his chin.

CHAPTER SIX

Stone sat and swayed back and forth, having returned to his cluster of trees, to his makeshift bed.

"I almost killed her. I almost shredded her throat."

That's what you do. You're a killer. You were built for this. Embrace it.

"No! I won't embrace it. This isn't me. I don't know what I'm doing here. Let me out. Let me OUT!" he growled.

Don't fight it. It's in your blood.

Stone sprung to his feet and attacked the nearest tree, lashing out at it with his claws, landing thunderous punches against it, bending, twisting, breaking, until it resembled something that had been caught in a hurricane.

"I can't. I won't. She was so innocent. So sweet. This isn't me."

His mind had no response.

"I refuse."

Silence.

"I'll kill myself first."

Stone's mind snapped to his latest concession. He would be too chickenshit to do it normally, but under the circumstances? He had no life. He was stuck in a body that embraced everything he abhorred. Could he really do it? Could this…this beast die? What would happen to him if the body no longer existed? Would his mind—his soul—go back to where they were supposed to be?

The memory of the bloodlust overcame him, looping through his thoughts. He had no choice. When it was time to kill, he would kill. When the grip of the disease steered his thoughts and controlled his actions, his mind was nothing but an unwilling passenger. Or was it? He had been driven to kill Sarah—to tear her throat out—yet he had somehow fought the urge. He fought it, and he won. He was in control then, and he could be in control again. He just had to want it…to fight for it. To hold on to the fact that good would always crush evil.

A scent hit his nostrils.

Not human.

His hunger unsatiated, he knew he must feed.

He silently got up from the ground and waited, listening, watching, smelling. A crackling sounded through the tree line to his left. He made his way to the edge of the pines, slipped into the shadows, and snatched the animal up before it realized he was even there.

His pride turned to panic as he realized he was holding a skunk. He didn't need to have clarity to know how bad things were about to get, and without thinking about it, he ripped the skunk's ass off—tail attached—and hurled it above the trees like a hand grenade with the pin pulled, hearing it land some hundred yards away with a soft plop. The animal was clearly in shock, and Stone immediately removed its head and tossed it to the side before crunching into the furry underbelly of the critter, blood and viscera splattering the front of him and the ground around him. He didn't stop until nothing was left but the fur pelt, the bones strewn about, laying where he had spit them.

Exerted, he slumped to the ground, the adrenaline from the hunt and feast subsiding.

He looked down at his paws, the flesh a crimson color.

Bile rose up in his throat as he tried to calm his emotions.

"Is this what I've become?" His body heaved with sobs as he blubbered into his hand-paws. He loathed himself. He wondered if the talon-like claws on his hands could rend his throat into strips of pulpy fur and flesh. If they could, would he bleed out? Could he die, or was he one of those monsters that was exiled to walk the earth for all eternity, feeding on the bodies and souls of others?

The house on the hill crept into his mind. There was a familiarity about it. He felt drawn there. Yet he knew he should stay away. Just like at the campground, he had been overcome. He was blinded by the need. He couldn't give in. He had to control himself.

But who was that person in the house on the hill? Why was he so drawn to it? Was it the key to all the mystery shrouding his identity? His new-found self?

Suddenly, Stone felt an overwhelming need to know what was behind door number one.

The way to the house was engrained in him, like a map built into a GPS unit. He did not falter as he traveled the distance to the overgrown hillside and started traversing his way up. The air was moist yet crisp. The slight breeze drove away the quiet. The stars were neatly tucked into their cloud blanket. It would still be dark for a couple more hours.

Outside the house, Stone settled down behind a row of shrubs. He waited. Daylight would soon come, and maybe his questions would be answered.

But you've never been out in daylight before.

He hadn't even realized how true the thought was until he had it, and he was overwhelmed by the accuracy. He pondered what that meant. Would the sunlight turn him to dust like a vampire? Would he turn back into the man he was supposed to be? Anxious, he decided to wait it out. One way or another, he would find out what it was he needed in this house. The one on the hill.

Around five thirty a.m., Stone's attention was pulled to the window when a light popped on inside the house.

CHAPTER SEVEN

The scent grew stronger. A door opened. Stone could hear the jingle of a collar as a dog explored the back yard. He slunk back tighter behind the shrub, thankful the breeze was blowing away from the house. The dog went back inside.

Shadows cast against the now-covered windows as the figure inside moved around. Stone tried to imagine who was there and what they were doing inside.

Strange smells of food and fragrance wafted to him, ever so slight, yet they were there. Stone took deep breaths, his chest tightening as he felt that familiar urge.

I have to fight this. I'll never know what this is all about if I give in—if I lose my head.

Sounds permeated the structure as well. Footsteps. A playful bark. The hissing flame of a water heater.

Someone is getting ready to start their day.

A memory flashed.

Why is this so familiar?

He's in the shower himself, yet he had no fur.

Another spark.

Breakfast. Cooking food. Cooking inside on a stove.

Putting on clothes. Not naked. Not furry.

The bloodlust slammed into his senses and took control, and Stone had to physically pull his body back to keep it from ravaging that hole through the side of the house that he had many times fantasized about. The person in there…they're evil. They're responsible. But how? And responsible for what?

He vomited onto the ground, so nauseous at the conflicting thoughts having a boxing match inside his head. He wanted to shred, kill, maim, but he feared that doing so would keep him from ever finding the answers that he was looking for. He pulled himself back, his body shuddering.

He listened, watched. The noises changed from room to room. The first glint of sunlight cracked over the horizon. Some of the shadows were pushed away. His mind snapped and then sprang back, clarity pouring into the void and filling every empty crevice. The bloodlust called for the final time. This time, Stone did not hold back.

The front door came off the hinges with so much force that it shattered the dining room table and sent the shards through the window on the far side of the house. The noise was like an explosion—deafening. As Stone scrambled through the door, he scanned the room. Empty.

A bark immediately started up from the hallway, loud, seemingly ferocious, the dog volunteering to lead the charge against a creature that it had never seen before, a creature that it underestimated.

Stone was surprised to hear a guttural growl come out of his own throat as he rushed toward the hall. Brave to its own detriment, the dog leapt through the air, latched onto Stone's shoulder, and tried to tear a chunk out. Rage overtook Stone, and he reached for the dog's throat, ready to tear it out.

Wait! You have a dog. You love dogs.

This epiphany threw Stone for a loop, and the dog started flinging its body back and forth, trying to use its weight to pull Stone to the ground.

Struggling to keep upright, Stone stumbled over to a door set in the wall by the stove. He flung it open to find a pantry. He stumbled inside, the dog hanging from his shoulder. He reached with his right hand and tried to pull the dog's mouth loose, but its jaw was in a death clamp. Out of options, and not wanting to hurt the dog, Stone grabbed the broom hanging from a hook on the wall and threaded the handle through the empty space at the back of the dog's jaw, the wooden rod pushing through the gap on the left side of its jaw and exiting the right side. Stone applied downward pressure on the broom handle, as if he was jacking a car up off the ground. Finally, the pressure proved to be too much, the dog loosened its grip, and Stone tore his shoulder out from the teeth ripping into it, leaving the dog biting down on the wood handle instead. Giving the broomstick a twist, the dog was thrown onto its back, and Stone took the opportunity to run out of the pantry and slam the door behind him.

The dog went crazy and started tearing at the door with its nails, but luckily the door was solid wood, and the beast wouldn't be loose any time soon.

Stone turned back toward the hallway, a small rivulet of blood running down his shoulder. The brief scuffle with the dog had pulled his attention away from why he was here, but with the dog in time out, his rage returned. The bloodlust returned. He knew his purpose, and it was time to get his.

Obviously, the owner of the house knew Stone was there. He had lost any element of surprise he had when he knocked the door down. Rather than play a game of cat and mouse, he decided to go after what was his. Whatever happened, he could live with it.

Stone stalked down the hallway toward where he knew the bedrooms to be. He paused to look at a painting on the wall—it was one he remembered. He had passed it the night of the last Christmas party here when he had gone to use the restroom. It was cold. Sterile. Like the inhabitant of the house.

At the bedroom door, Stone heard a shotgun slide. He

stepped around into the center of the doorway, the man inside standing beside the bed, the gun pointed in Stone's direction.

"I don't know what the fuck you are, but if you don't get out now, you'll be a dead fuck."

"Hello, Ron." The sound coming out of Stone's throat was cold, calculating.

"How…how do you know my name?" The gun shook in Ron's hands.

"Just like you not to remember. How does it feel to be the most narcissistic asshole on the planet?"

A trickle of familiarity flashed through Ron's eyes.

"I dedicated most of my adult life to that company. I put up with your crap for twenty-five years. And when I couldn't stand by and watch you shit on all the little people anymore, you instead turn on me? Ruin my life?"

"Woody? What happened to you?"

"*You* happened to me."

"I mean…are…are you some fucking animal?"

Woody grabbed the shotgun by the barrel and twisted, both shots firing, sending chunks of splintered doorframe in a shower throughout the room. Smashing the nearby window with the butt of the gun, Woody threw it outside on the back lawn.

"Now, where were we?"

"It wasn't my…my fault, what happened to you. You did it to yourself."

"Because I wouldn't stand by any longer and watch you destroy people? Because I have a conscience? Integrity?"

"Because you messed up. You broke the rules and you had to go. You can't blame that on anyone but yourself. I'm not going to take the fall for that."

"Or at least that's what you told them, right? That I broke the rules? That I was acting inappropriately? Who are they going to listen to? The narcissistic prick who nobody will stand up to, because they are scared of what he might do to them, or the manager that must have lost his mind overnight and done things that were extremely out of character for him?"

Ron glared at Woody, his eyes spewing hatred.

"You know, I never realized just how insecure you really were until right now. I wasn't a bright light on your team to you. I was a threat. You knew I was smarter than you. Better than you."

"Get out of my house, Woody. I'm calling the cops."

"I'm afraid I can't allow you to do that, Ron. Hey, did you know you destroyed my life? Yeah! True story. I pretty much lost everything. Oh yeah, you remember Marcy, don't you? Yeah…funny thing about her. She'd dead. Fucking heart attack, Ron. Her ticker just couldn't handle the stress of what our life had become, thanks to your generosity."

"This is the last time I ask you to leave."

"Or what? What, Ron? What are you going to do about it?"

"I'm go…goo…g—"

"Goo goo, gah gah," Woody mocked. "What's the matter, little baby Ron? You going to shit your pants?"

Ron sprinted toward the open master bathroom door and tried to slam it on Woody, who was already halfway through it before it was even partially closed. Trapped, Ron put the only barrier he could between Woody and himself. He clambered into the shower stall and slammed the glass door between them.

Woody stopped, looking through the glass as if he were selecting a lobster from the tank right before he dropped it into boiling water.

Ron cowered, resolved in the fact he was in no way talking

himself out of this situation. A rancid smell hit Woody's nostrils—urine and feces. The man had soiled himself.

Woody stared through the glass at the man that had ended everything for him. But it wasn't the material things that bothered him the most. It was the fact that he had lost all trust in humanity. This was the true end for him. In a world where he once mattered, he was discarded, tossed away by colleagues and friends. He had become a leper and a loner. He no longer had a purpose in life. He was merely sucking up oxygen in the atmosphere, waiting to die.

Woody's hatred soared, and he felt the raw, overpowering pull to destroy. To rip. To shred. To maul. He finally understood why he was drawn to the house on the hill and what his purpose had become. To live a good life was not going to be enough. It never had been. It never would be.

Woody's fist smashed into the safety glass, shattering it into a million fragmented pieces. Ron threw himself down into the corner of the tile, his arms over his face. Woody's claws shot out from his hands and he pulled back, ready to strike.

This isn't you, remember? You're not a killer.

That nagging voice in the back of his mind was back. It was right. He wasn't a killer. Never had been. He was a kind, compassionate, considerate soul who cared for others and nurtured them, not destroyed them. Who was he to play God? Who was he to decide what was fair? True, this guy was one of the biggest dirtbags he had ever met, but did that mean he deserved to die?

Woody lowered his right arm to his side. The claws retracted. The bloodlust drained from his eyes. Ron must have sensed the change. He lowered his arms, the fear in his eyes turning to wonderment.

The slash across Ron's face caught him off guard, and one

of the claws hooked his left eyeball and pulled it out of the socket. It hung down by the optic nerve, bobbing against his nose.

"See you in hell, Ron, but just so you know, I'm going to be the one in charge this time."

Woody thrust his claws underneath Ron's ribcage and shredded up, pulling out everything he could grab a hold of, like he was removing the engine and transmission from a car. Ron's fluids leaked out of him and his mouth started working, as if he was trying to say something, but only a clicking sound emanated. Finally, his mouth fell open, his face in death mimicking the stupid look he carried on his face during his sordid, pathetic life.

Taking one last look at the carnage he had left behind—he hoped that whoever had to do the cleanup was thankful that he had kept most of the blood in the shower stall—he headed toward the front door. It was then that the barking and growling started up again on the other side of the pantry door, the nails joining in, most assuredly carving deep grooves on the other side of the door.

He must be hungry, Woody thought.

He turned and went back into the bathroom. The corpse looked pale and weak, and it was then Woody realized he should never have let that asshole have so much power over him. He bent down and lifted Ron's chin before grabbing the head in his hands, and with one quick twisting, ripping, movement, he detached the head from the body.

In the kitchen, he held the head in his right hand and grabbed the pantry doorknob with his left.

"Dinnertime!" he yelled, tossing the head inside and slamming the door.

EPILOGUE

"Another rum and coke, please."

"Coming right up."

Woody drained the rest of his glass and waited for the new drink to be served. It wasn't that he had stepped up from beer to hard alcohol. He just liked to mix it up a bit now that he was getting out and socializing a little more.

"Here you go, Woody. Want me to put this on your tab?"

"That'd be great, Bruce. Thank you."

Okay, so he was getting out a lot. Every day, actually.

Woody had a different outlook on life since the morning of the incident that happened in the house on the hill. A house he had been to a couple of times for his company Christmas parties. A house that Ron had owned with his wife before she tired of his bullshit and took half of everything. A house that was on a five-acre lot in a sprawling mountain neighborhood approximately five miles away from Woody's property.

Answering the question of *why* he had changed into something else was a little more difficult. When he found himself back with his own body, in his own house, on his own hill, he was relieved to say the least, but the fear of turning back into that *thing* left him scared shitless. He turned to research—dozens of hours of it—to try and determine how it was all possible. The only random information he was able to turn up was a handful of police reports—all public record—where the old man that owned his home prior reported mysterious happenings on the hill. Some sort of altar he found in a clearing of trees. The sound of chanting carried on the wind. Dead animals. Later, the old man would report a run-in with a stranger and threats of a curse cast upon the property that had him fearing for his life. Woody couldn't help but feel that might explain them finding the dead man's bones months later. The police had thought he was crazy. Maybe he wasn't so crazy after all.

If Woody lived under a curse, there was a chance that he could change again if another huge injustice decimated his life. Rather than move, he decided to be careful—he did not ever want to put himself in a situation again where he woke up to a furry mirror.

Woody took a sip of his drink and pulled a cigarette out of his pack. He grabbed his Bic and lit it, exhaling the smoke up into the air.

"Excuse me."

Woody turned. A pretty girl that was probably in her thirties was standing there. He had noticed her playing pool with three other women earlier.

"Hi there," Woody said, unsure of what else to say, quite rusty at making small talk.

"Could I bum a smoke?"

"Sure thing. You run out?"

"Not exactly."

Woody raised a puzzled eyebrow.

"Um, well, I don't normally smoke, but this seems like a good time to start."

Woody laughed, a light, easy-going chuckle.

"What's the occasion?"

"Not sure. Honestly, I've been sitting over there for the last two games wondering where I know you from. You look so damn familiar."

"I don't believe we've ever met, miss. Although now that you mention it"—he looked into her eyes—"I think I've seen you before, somewhere. Do you come here a lot?"

"First time." She slid up on the barstool next to him.

"Well, we hopefully have time to figure it out." He held out his hand. "Nice to meet you. I'm Woody."

"Nice to meet you, too, Woody. I'm Sarah."

ABOUT THE AUTHOR

R.E. SARGENT is an editor, publisher, and author whose works delve into the sinister depths of horror, suspense, and the supernatural. His story "Lucy," featured in the Splatterpunk Award–nominated anthology *If I Die Before I Wake Volume 3 – Tales of Deadly Women and Retribution*, also resides among the dark tales in his collection, *Everything Went to Shit*. Nestled in the hauntingly beautiful Pacific Northwest, R.E. lives with his wife, their two granddogs, and the unyielding rain—a perfect companion for someone who revels in the eerie. Beneath the perpetual gray skies, he crafts stories that reach beyond the ordinary into realms best left undisturbed. Find out more about R.E. at resargent.com.

MORE FROM R.E. SARGENT

Novels

- *Relative Terror*
- *Fury: The Awakening* (Book one of the *Scorned* series)
- *Fury: Unleashed* (Book two of the *Scorned* series)
- *Fury: Retribution* (Book three of the *Scorned* series) (Coming Fall 2025)

Novelettes

- *One-Star Review* (Book one of the *Karen Carter* series)
- *Becoming Karen Carter* (Book two of the *Karen Carter* series)
- *A Review to Die For* (Book three of the *Karen Carter* series)

Check out **THE HOUSE OF SMARBA** by Mike Duke

From Sinister Smile Press

Debbie and Nathan Loch had the perfect family.

Their little boy Martin and his younger sister Bella were all they could have asked for…until the day Debbie watched helplessly as Bella's life was ripped away in a horrific hit and run accident.

Plagued with grief, and afraid for her sanity, Debbie decides they are moving. However, shortly after transitioning into their new house, Martin begins having vivid dreams of a young boy named Malachi and his toy collection.

Martin has never seen toys like these before, but the descriptions he relates to his parents fill Debbie with concern. Nathan believes she is being overprotective after losing Bella, but Debbie is determined to solve the mystery of the antique toys and find out just who this Malachi kid really is. What Debbie discovers is a rabbit hole that may drag the souls of her entire family kicking and screaming into the abyss of Hell itself.

Join the Crystal Lake community today!

Subscribe to our Newsletter!
(Scan the QR code or click if eBook)

Subscribe to our Patreon!
(Scan the QR code or click if eBook)

**Visit our Linktree for
all social media sites!**
(Scan the QR code or click if eBook)

Download our catalog!
(Scan the QR code or click if eBook)

www.ingramcontent.com/pod-product-compliance
Lightning Source LLC
Chambersburg PA
CBHW030755310726

48969CB00005B/1423